TIZ PHOENIX

AND THE

WITCH'S TREE

BY

K. A. FENWOLFE

COVER ART BY JEROEN VAN VALKENBURG

Tiz Phoenix and the Witch's Tree

k.a.fenwolfe@gmail.com

Cover art by Jeroen van Valkenburg

ISBN-10: 1495487938

ISBN-13: 9781495487934

First Print Edition: May 2014

For Scruffs, my family and all my friends.

CONTENTS

CONTENTS

TIZ PHOENIX

AND THE

WITCH'S TREE

CHAPTER ONE — THE HUNT

RIDING WILD BEARS was more than just an extreme sport to Tiz Phoenix. It was an art form. Although, it was nothing like playing her cello and infinitely more dangerous. But she didn't care. That's why she liked it.

Regardless, her bear-riding days are a tale for another time. In this story, she was on a mission. So that's where we begin...

On a hot evening near the end of summer, Tiz led her friend, Sombra Willow, through the Wailing Woods — an enchanted forest hidden within our modern world, though still vulnerable nonetheless. It was home to both of the thirteen-year-old girls. And they were on a secret mission to keep it safe from harm.

"Come on Sombra, it's up to me and you to save our forest," said Tiz. "No one else is coming to help these trees. Not that fire-prevention bear on TV or his woodsy owl buddy. They just don't seem to give a hoot anymore."

"That's because they're *not* real," huffed Sombra from behind. "They're mascots — silly people in silly suits. That's why they don't give a hoot. They're even sillier than you."

As the two wove a path between old moss-covered trees veiled in part by a thin fog, the forest began darkening around the adventurous girls. Before long, the approaching night would chase away the last rays of sunlight illuminating the Wailing Woods.

"Sombra, please hurry up," urged Tiz. "We're walking so slow that I'm pretty sure I saw a family of turtles pass us a minute ago — even a little baby one. And it looked like he was crawling backwards just to make fun of us."

Sombra sighed in response to her friend's active imagination.

CHAPTER ONE

Sensing a possible mutiny, Tiz blurted, "We're almost there, I swear." Just as quickly, she sniffed the forest air on the fly. "I can smell the buried treasure, it's up ahead." She sniffed again. "Yup, it's definitely up ahead all right, and it smells delicious."

"Sheesh, even if there *is* something there, I doubt it's going to save our forest," said Sombra in her usual gloomy sort of way.

Tiz stopped her friend in her tracks and took hold of her by the shoulders. "Listen to me," she urged. "I know you're having a little trouble believing me about this mysterious treasure. But I'm telling you, it smells delicious. And this trove of underground treats is going to help our woods. So I need you to do me a favor."

"What?" asked Sombra, crossing her arms.

"Pretend like we're pirates hunting for buried treasure," said Tiz. "You're my first mate and we just arrived here. So imagine that this forest is on a deserted island or something. And the rest of our crew? Well, they're back at our ship — the *S. S. Delicious*. I only took you."

Sombra scoffed. "The *S. S.* stands for steamship," she argued. "Pirates on a steamship? That sounds awful fishy to me. Because if my memory serves me right, I sailed here as the captain of another vessel in your imaginary fleet, admiral. But it's *not* called the *Delicious*, it's called the *Suspicious*."

"Sombra, I can't have you captaining the *Suspicious*," said Tiz. "I *need* you aboard the *Delicious*."

"Hmm," contemplated Sombra. "So this buried treasure of yours, does it smell even better than a slice of my mom's freshly baked bread? The one that should be melting in my mouth at dinner right now?" she chided, glancing up at the darkening sky.

"Even better," insisted Tiz as she pulled Sombra by the arm and began leading them on the hunt again. "Sombra, you could slap all the butter in the universe on that bread and it still wouldn't be a contest. Heck, dip that bread in whatever you want. It would still taste like an overcooked noodle compared to our treasure. So after we find it, get ready to be the envy of every other tree nymph that lives in our woods."

Forging ahead, the two aspiring treasure hunters looked no different than any other thirteen-year-old girls. However, they were far from normal in many other ways. Tiz Phoenix and Sombra Willow were in reality members of a secretive race of mystical female beings called tree nymphs; a race that lived deep inside the forests of our world while nearly no one else on our planet knew about them other than their own kind. It was one of the few things that Tiz had previously mentioned that wasn't merely fashioned by her wild imagination.

Though in truth, being tree nymphs made them no taller or shorter, fairer or plainer, funnier or smarter than any other girls, allowing them to blend in with regular people whenever they so desired. In fact, you could never tell a tree nymph apart just by looking at her. Instead, it was the reaction of the forest around her that usually revealed her magical bond with nature. If she permitted it to happen, flowers blossomed at her feet, leaves grew brighter green in her presence and tree branches parted before her path simply out of respect and courtesy for her — especially in this particular instance.

For these two tree nymphs were on a mission to preserve their woods — to save their home.

"Come on," urged Tiz to Sombra once again.

Picking up their pace, the girls began running nimbly through the ancient forest as their flower-covered dresses flapped in the wind. All around them, the woods buzzed with excitement on that warm summer evening, one perfect for a treasure hunt. "We really do have to hurry up," said Tiz. "The longer we wait, the less it's worth — haven't you heard about depreciation?"

Tiz heard Sombra give out a groan that seemed to say, *here we go again*, but even still, Tiz wouldn't have chosen anyone else for this quest.

Though in actuality, the two friends formed a bit of an odd pair in several ways, but especially to the eye. Tiz had a round, jovial face full of freckles with big green eyes as brilliant as emeralds that lit up over a button nose and plump cheeks, making her look like a bit of a tomboy, even in her flowery dress. In the front, her bright red hair was short as a pixy's and as wild as a punk rocker's, spiraling up like a burning torch. But in the back, she kept several strands long, fanning them out like a bird's tail feather so she could revive an old Phoenix family tradition. Her mother called her *Red*, not just for the fire in her daughter's hair, but also for the one in her heart, raging and relentless.

Sombra, on the other hand, was mostly elbows and knees. Her face was long and droopy, reminding some of their less charitable peers of a sad horse that seemed to be a bit lonely. Her long, dark curly hair sagged more than the canopy of a weeping willow tree as she plucked out strands of it to the point where it was a wonder that she had any at all. Her tattered hair and her sticklike frame earned her the nickname *Mop* from other tree nymphs — a nickname neither of them liked.

And while Tiz's outlook on life was as bright as the sun, Sombra's was as gloomy as the growing darkness overtaking the woods around them. Together, their demeanors were not unlike the opposite sides of the half moon rising above them, one side bright, one side night. But that didn't matter to them. And why should it? The two tree nymphs were the best of friends, and like the opposite halves of the moon above, they were different, but also very close to each other.

As they rushed by rows and rows of old moss-covered trees and through an eerie mist that seemed to glow in the fading sunlight, bright flowers mystically burst to life at their feet, blossoming like tiny fireworks displays that didn't fade away.

Tiz suddenly stopped on a dime and Sombra nearly toppled them both. Near a tree, Tiz dropped to all fours, sniffing the ground for the buried treasure like a hungry bloodhound. Slowly, a smile stretched across her face as she got to her feet — she had found the delicious treats. "If a wild pig ate all the truffles around here, it would puff out like a parade balloon," she said.

"What exactly is a truffle anyway?" asked Sombra in her sleepy sort of way.

"It's a super food," replied Tiz. "It's super hard to find, super expensive and super nutritious. Now *that's* a super food."

"Oh yeah? Does it fight crime too?" teased Sombra.

"Not only does it fight crime," said Tiz, "it prevents it."

"That's ridiculous," argued Sombra. "Food doesn't do anything besides grow, it's food. It just lies there."

"Oh really?" questioned Tiz, pulling out a slingshot and arming it with a small truffle that looked like a tiny potato. "See that blue jay up there — the one that's up to no good? I'm gonna scare it away."

Sombra spotted the jay in a treetop without any problem. For all tree nymphs could see like hawks during the day and like owls at night. So despite the fading sunlight, to their eyes, it was as bright as mid-day as they watched the blue jay above them; one that was about to snatch an egg from a robin's nest and have it for dinner.

"I see the jay," said Sombra. "And it *is* up to no good."

Tiz pulled her slingshot back, aiming carefully. "Like I said, I'm just gonna scare it away," she said. "Bye-bye, blue jay."

"Be careful, Tiz," pleaded Sombra, "don't hurt it."

"Sheesh, I would never hurt it," said Tiz, adjusting her aim.

"Not on purpose maybe," argued Sombra. "But if you hit it on accident you'll be no better than the jay — you can't make something right by doing something wrong, that's exactly what your mom tells me, *all the time*."

"Tell that to the egg it's about to eat," replied Tiz. "Or better yet, if my mom was a bird and laid that egg, then what would she say now?"

"Wait," urged Sombra. "Don't you hear a little voice chirping inside your head? One telling you to stop?"

"I hear a little voice chirping all right," said Tiz. "And it's coming from the egg saying, '*Save me, save me.*'"

"Oh boy," worried Sombra, covering her eyes.

Tiz shot the truffle into the tree, scaring the blue jay away. "See?" she said proudly, putting her slingshot away. "Super foods *do* fight crime, especially truffles."

Sombra gave her "the look." "You still haven't answered my question — what is a truffle? Really?" she asked. "Or is it just something you like launching from your slingshot?"

Tiz tapped her chin. "Well...it's sort of an underground mushroom," she said, trying to sound upbeat, "but more of a fungus that you can eat."

"Yuck," said Sombra.

"It's not like it grows between somebody's toes," said Tiz.

"Yeah it does, if that somebody is a tree," replied Sombra. "A tree's roots are like its toes, and that's where it grows, right?"

"I guess you're right," said Tiz. "But I'd rather not think of it that way, especially when I'm having them for dinner."

"Pfff, why do you care about them so much anyway?" sighed Sombra.

"Because if we grow more truffles, it'll save our forest," said Tiz as she stood there surveying the Wailing Woods like a homeowner would a backyard. "I swear, it's a sure thing."

But Tiz wasn't there to argue. She had work to do. She was on a sworn mission to help save the world, one tree at a time, and if need be, leaf-by-leaf and seed-by-seed. So she pointed to an ash tree that usually had enough truffles growing near its roots to fill a small crater on the moon.

Sombra kneeled down by the tree trunk as Tiz handed her a pair of nifty gardening gloves with claws called mole mittens, ones that would help her dig for the underground mushrooms.

"You really should give truffles a try," encouraged Tiz. "They're full of stuff that's good for you — protein, potassium, calcium — they'll make you big and strong. Plus, they'll give you *lots* of energy."

"So basically, they taste terrible," replied Sombra.

"I didn't say that," said Tiz.

"You didn't have to," countered Sombra. "Potassium, calcium, that said it all — it sounds like you're eating rocks. Maybe you should switch it up. Launch rocks from your slingshot, and eat the truffles, or better yet, eat something that tastes good."

"*Ha, ha*," replied Tiz. "I'm sorry, but you don't know what you're talking about, meany. So hop off the *S. S. Malicious* and get on board the *S. S. Nutritious*. That's what I say."

"*Wrong* — you don't know you're talking about," insisted Sombra. "You're the one saying *crazy* things."

"Like what?" asked Tiz.

"Well, for starters, the thing you said about growing more truffles," said Sombra. "How exactly is *that* going to save our forest?"

"Because mankind loves truffles," replied Tiz. "And truffles need trees, just as much as we do."

"What if mankind loves firewood more?" asked Sombra.

"That's where the spotted owls come in," said Tiz. "People protect them like hard-to-find toys at a Christmas sale. Yesterday, I saw a boy standing underneath a nest, he caught a falling egg with his baseball glove, true story. So I built ten more nests today."

"For the owls or the boy?" teased Sombra with a smirk.

Blushing, Tiz tossed a twig at her. "The owls," she insisted.

"Where exactly are you gonna find spotted owls to fill those nests?" asked Sombra, shaking her head.

"I haven't quite figured that part out yet," replied Tiz. "But I know another tree nymph that wants to get rid of a whole flock. Poop everywhere, I mean *everywhere*. Plus she raises squirrels, so I'll get them cheap."

"How much?" asked Sombra. "Some walnuts?"

"Actually, she doesn't want any," said Tiz.

"Really? Then what does she want?" asked Sombra.

"Well, I couldn't understand her very well — her mouth was full of sunflower seeds," replied Tiz. "But she either wants ten chocolate-covered truffles or a French horn."

"Hmm," pondered Sombra as she started digging for the truffles. "Either way, she has pretty good taste."

"The best," said Tiz. "She's French."

"Ew-la-la," laughed Sombra.

"Sacré bleu!" laughed Tiz, sounding like a French chef from a cartoon. "Zeh owls are eating all of my chocolate-covered truffles and tooting my French horn! Haw, haw, haw!"

Sombra laughed as she dug up a brown lump that looked like a truffle and held it up. "Bon appétit."

"Um," said Tiz, considering her friend's feelings. "That's not a truffle. Remember what I said was everywhere?"

"Eww, gross," said Sombra, dropping the poop on the forest floor.

"Be careful," said Tiz, "it's like a giant toilet out here and no one flushes — land mines everywhere."

"That's the least of my worries," said Sombra. "What if someone tries to cut down my life tree? What then? What will happen to me?"

"Well, remember that saying?" asked Tiz. "The one we heard when we were real little — two lives, one soul..."

"If either dies, both must go," they said in unison without the least bit of cheer.

Sombra peeked around nervously. "What about the witch?" she asked. "The one that burned down the Unburnable Forest."

"Her? She's been asleep for like a bazillion years now," said Tiz, joining in on the truffle dig. "At least that's what my mom said. I guess burning things down must be *really* tiring."

"You know what I heard? I heard that she was a tree nymph once, just like us, but *her* life tree never dies," said Sombra. "They call her the Unwithering One. She's been around forever, but never grows old."

"Whaaaat? Never grows old? Then she definitely doesn't have any little sisters," complained Tiz, thinking about her own twin terrors. "Besides, everything grows old and eventually dies, even life trees."

"Not if you know the right kind of magic," whispered Sombra nervously, her smile full of excitement. "Think about it, then we could live as long as *her*. And instead of the Unwithering One, it could be the Unwithering Three."

A sudden gust of cold wind took them by surprise, rattling more than just the leaves. The flowers that had sprouted at their feet withered and died before their widening eyes. Tiz's mood changed as quickly as the weather. She wanted one thing.

She wanted to hide.

CHAPTER TWO — HEART SEEDS

EAGER TO GET OUT OF THE OPEN FOREST and away from the cold, Tiz took her best friend by the hand and led her into a snug tree hollow nearby. As far as Tiz was concerned, she had participated in enough witch talk to last her the rest of her life — a life she was particularly fond of and didn't want cut unexpectedly short. And judging by the look on Sombra's face, she wasn't alone.

"Let's talk about something else," urged Tiz, shivering as they both sat down and rubbed their hands to get warm. "And try not to worry so much, Sombra, we don't even have our life trees yet."

"We will tomorrow," said Sombra, pulling out a necklace made from a tattered string. Dangling from it was a beautiful emerald locket in the shape of a weeping willow tree; it had sapphire eyes that shed magical tears, watering its amber roots. But it was something inside the locket that caught Tiz's attention. Nestled within it was a glowing blue seed in the shape of a heart, pulsing like one too. It lit up the tree hollow like a tiny blue sun, making it feel warm and cozy as the seed's light began pulsing more quickly and in perfect rhythm with Sombra's own accelerating heartbeat, reflecting the tree nymph's excitement.

"Your heart seed!" gushed Tiz, glad to be talking about something that wasn't so grim. "When did you get it?"

"My mom gave it to me this morning," replied Sombra as her seed began beating even more rapidly.

As Tiz eased closer to the glowing seed her big emerald eyes lit up like Christmas trees. Her short red hair, spiraling up like a burning torch, glowed brightly in the magical light as she basked in its warmth, its heat reminding her of sunshine.

Tiz loved to be in the sun as much as possible, climbing

trees as fast as a monkey just to be closer to it, and it showed in her big freckled cheeks, ones so plump that her dearly departed grandmother used to called her the Little Punky Chipmunkey as she pinched them like some kind of giant crab with spectacles until both of her granddaughter's cheeks were bright red. Tiz's smile was just as big and wide, and it always grew brightest when she discovered something she didn't know or invented something new on her own.

But what Tiz wanted more than anything else at that moment, sitting there in the cozy belly of the tree and staring at her friend's seed, was to hold her own heart seed. All tree nymphs were born with one, a heart seed tucked into their belly button at birth. Afterwards, their mother plucked it out for safekeeping. But now, Tiz and Sombra were both thirteen, and in tree nymph tradition, ready to plant. To each of them, their heart seed was as precious as the air they breathed.

"Isn't it weird that something so pretty came from your belly button," said Tiz finally.

"Yeah it is, I thought it'd be more linty, that's for sure," said Sombra.

"So did I," agreed Tiz, entranced by its dazzling beauty. "You're so lucky, Mums is making me wait until tomorrow, until the Great Seed Planting."

"Why?" asked Sombra as her pulsing seed slowed down.

"Because my room is messy," sighed Tiz.

"Just blame it on your little sisters," suggested Sombra.

"I can't," said Tiz, feeling guilty just thinking about it. "They have their own issues, trust me. Besides, they're a couple of neat freaks — Mums would never believe me anyhow. It's just..."

"Just what?" implored Sombra.

"Well, I don't think my messy room is the real reason," said Tiz.

"Okay...then what is?" asked Sombra, admiring her own glowing seed.

"I don't know, but my mom's freaking out like usual — she says I'll use its powers too soon," replied Tiz, tapping her chin while thinking. "She must've found one of my old drawings — probably the electrified fence, the one that could protect the whole forest. It's all lightning rods, five hundred feet tall."

"Five hundred feet tall?" said Sombra. "Is that really necessary?"

"Yeah it is, if you want to see it from space," said Tiz, reaching her arm out of the hollow and up toward a shining star in the night sky. Ever since she fell in love with the phrases *reach for the stars* and *sky's the limit* at the ripe old age of four it became a habit. Quite simply, it gave her hope that she could accomplish anything she focused her mind and hands upon. Maybe even someday, reaching those stars she was stretching her hand toward. After she started doing it, there was no looking back — it was onward and upward. Not to mention the fact that all tree nymphs had a natural affinity for the light and were drawn to the sun, stars and moon alike — Tiz, more so than any other.

"Earth to Tiz," said Sombra, "how's the view of your electrified fence from up there? Over?"

"Roger that," said Tiz, playing along. "But the fence isn't for *me* to look at from space, I wanna give the aliens a light show up there. That way they won't bother to come down and make those boring crop circles, killing half the corn."

"Corn?" asked Sombra, confused. "You're worried about corn?"

"Heck yeah, if I don't, who will?" said Tiz, lowering her arm.

"What about your heart seed?" asked Sombra.

"Well..." said Tiz sadly. "My mom thinks I'll use its magic to clean up my room, and in the end, turn it into a disaster area. She even mumbled something about an emergency search and rescue."

Sombra raised her own magic seed. "Need a maid for the

day?" she asked, swinging her pendant like a hypnotist.

Watching it, Tiz's big green eyes widened even further. "Heck yeah!" she blurted. "I know exactly how to pay you too!" Tiz revealed a diamond necklace hanging around her own neck that would've made a queen turn green with envy.

"Holy smokes!" gawked Sombra. "Where did you get that?"

"Remember that sixty-two pound truffle I found?" asked Tiz as she unclasped the necklace.

"Yeah," said Sombra, "the one you had to roll into town. I thought your mom told you not to sell it."

"She did, she got all weird about it and said, '*Red, just pretend it's your new best friend*'," laughed Tiz as she started putting the sparkling necklace on Sombra.

"Are you sure?" asked Sombra meekly.

"Heck yeah, I'm sure," said Tiz. "The man that sold it to me said, '*Diamonds are a girl's best friend*'," added Tiz with a smile. "But to me, that's just plain silly. Diamonds won't help you clean your room, dig up truffles with you or keep you safe when you're scared. So I'd rather give them to someone that will, through thick and thin, my real best friend."

"*Awww*," squeaked Sombra softly. Slowly, she eased her glowing blue pendant up to the necklace, debating whether or not to clip it on. But when the mystical light from the heart seed made the diamonds sparkle like tiny blue flames there was an audible click that said, "Oh, what the heck."

Tiz patted her friend on the back then finished with the clasp. "There, now it's perfect," she said.

Sombra fidgeted with it, unsure.

But Tiz wanted her to have it — her best friend needed a boost. Lately, Sombra spent so much time worrying about things it looked like she was starting to wilt. Even now the expression on her long face looked conflicted as she plucked out a strand of her hair. The tangled mess atop her head, coupled with her thin frame, were responsible for her nickname — *Mop*. One they badly wanted to change.

"Um, I still don't know," worried Sombra, eyeing the glimmering diamonds, "it's too much, it's not a fair trade."

"That old thing?" dismissed Tiz like the diamond necklace was made out of bottle caps instead of gems. "Those are my digging diamonds. My good ones are at home, somewhere."

"Hmm," pondered Sombra. "Then let's clean up your room and find them."

"Yay!" said Tiz, clapping. "With your magic, cleaning might actually be fun for once. And if we do a good enough job, Mums might even give me my heart seed tonight."

"That would be awesome," said Sombra, getting more and more excited. "I still can't believe we're getting our life trees tomorrow."

"Either can I," said Tiz anxiously. For deep down inside she knew that as great as her heart seed would be, the life tree that grew from it would be a hundred thousand times better; if her heart seed was a scoop of ice cream, then the life tree would be an ice cream factory. It would be the gift that kept on giving, every day for that matter, since all tree nymphs built their homes right inside their tree's canopy. For life trees were much larger and sturdier versions of their normal counterparts. And together over time, the bond between tree and tree nymph would grow to be as strong as the tree itself, bolstering the nymph's power over nature. *That* would help Tiz reach her goal — to nurture all things good and green.

Getting her own life tree was the epitome of what she wanted. "Speaking of trees," said Tiz eagerly. "Wanna open a tree door to zip us home?"

"Do monkeys like magic bananas?" asked Sombra.

"Of course, with all that extra potassium what's not to like?" said Tiz.

"Then let's go," replied Sombra as they left the cozy hollow and stepped into the night, peeking around. "We should find an oak tree. They make the best magic doors."

"There's one right over there," said Tiz, pointing to a gnarled and twisted tree.

"That one?" doubted Sombra. "I don't wanna come out looking like a pretzel."

"Trust me," said Tiz, "we'll be fine, it's a sure thing."

"The last time you said that I ended up with a tail," huffed Sombra. "And not even a cool one, like a mermaid, just a smelly old wolf tail."

"You did, didn't you," laughed Tiz. "I loved that thing. Especially when I came up to say '*hi.*' You'd frown and wag your tail at the same time. I couldn't tell if you were happy or sad."

"Can we just go?" asked Sombra, frowning as she put a hand on the oak tree then offered her other one to Tiz.

"Sorry," said Tiz as she took Sombra's hand. "Let's go."

Yet unbeknownst to them, there was something on the other side of that oak tree that neither girl noticed. It was a robin's egg that had been knocked from its nest. Not by a blue jay, but by a truffle fired from a slingshot. If Tiz had known what she had done then she would have wept with regret. She would have been truly sorry. In a way, it was both a blessing and a curse that she was completely oblivious to her "good intentions gone wrong" as she put her free hand on the tree.

Together, the two friends counted, "One...Two...TREE!" A magical door appeared on the tree bark and swung inward. Hand in hand, they leapt into the mystical doorway and flew through a glowing tunnel, branching off like tree limbs, swerving in every direction.

"This way," yelled Tiz as she yanked Sombra down a passage to the right.

Ahead, they could see a white light at the end of the tunnel, barreling toward them like a freight train in the night.

"Are you sure this is right!" shouted Sombra nervously.

"Right as rain!" yelled Tiz.

"What does that mean!" shouted Sombra.

"I don't know!" screamed Tiz as they vanished into the blinding light.

CHAPTER THREE — KEEP OUT

TIZ FELT DIZZIER than a *Frisbee*. As her eyes reacclimated to the darkness of the woods, she realized she was up in her mother's life tree, hanging on like a monkey in a canopy of green leaves and beautiful purple flowers. Nearby, a spotted owl hooted, its eyes reflecting the moonlight. Past it, Sombra hung upside down by her legs as two robins tweeted at her.

"Home tweet home," said Tiz. But instead of climbing down, both girls climbed up toward a four-story tree house at the top of the majestic tree. Its oval windows glowed orange with candlelight under the starry night sky, making it seem as warm and cozy as the tree hollow they just left behind.

The ancient purple-flowered tree they were climbing was known by several names — the empress tree, the princess tree and the phoenix tree. The last name referred to the magical flaming bird. If it died, then it could rise again from its ashes. Not unlike that bird, if a phoenix tree was cut down or burned down, then it could grow again from its roots, rising back up to its full height.

From above, a motherly voice shouted, "I see you two down there! Sombra, your mother wants you home immediately!"

"Aww, Mums," protested Tiz. "Can't she stay for supper?"

"Not tonight I'm afraid, Red!" yelled Mums, staring down at the top of her daughter's short scarlet hair. "You both have a big day tomorrow! So you better run along now, Sombra! Go to your happy place!"

But Tiz wasn't about to give up her maid so easily. So she started tickling the armpit of a tree limb nearby. Above, Mums started laughing like someone was tickling her own armpit. For tree nymphs always felt what their life trees felt. And for now, Tiz still had to live in her mom's tree home.

"Red, stop that!" laughed Mums. "Or you'll be in bigger trouble!"

"Go to your happy place, Mums!" yelled Tiz with a smile, using her mother's words against her like a verbal boomerang. "Help me, Sombra, please," begged Tiz.

"See you tomorrow," said Sombra as she started climbing down gingerly. "And you better not get grounded. I'll never forgive you if you miss the Planting."

"See you tomorrow," said Tiz, knowing that her friend was right. With a possible grounding looming, Tiz stopped tickling the tree and started climbing up again.

"Phew," sighed Mums, catching her breath. "Such a business, I don't mind a good tickling from time to time, but after a thousand years, my funny bone isn't what it used to be, young lady."

Tiz climbed the rest of the way faster than a squirrel being chased by a bear then swung onto the porch like an acrobat.

Mums might have been a thousand years old but only her salt and pepper hair gave it away. In truth, her face didn't look a day over thirty. Her cheeks were as plump as Tiz's but with a motherly glow. Like all tree nymphs, she would live as long as her life tree.

"Come here, sweetie," said Mums as she held out her arms for a hug.

"Mums, I stopped falling for your hug traps when I was four," said Tiz cautiously. "Besides, my shirt is tickle proof, I invented it when I was six, remember? So don't even try it."

"Try what?" said Mums innocently as her head began glowing with magic, sprouting flower petals as if it were no big deal while her face turned into a giant chrysanthemum, blowing pollen toward Tiz.

Tiz stuffed her nose under her collar. She held back a sneeze but it was like being hit in the face with a dusty pillow. She couldn't fight it. Tiz sneezed like crazy. She watched in disbelief as Mums's fingers turned into giant pussy willows, tickling and spinning toward her like puffy buffers in a car wash.

Tiz ducked past Mums and ran into the large tree home. She dashed up a flight of spiraling stairs and into her messy room then tried to shut the door but a pile of musical instruments was blocking it — an electric guitar, a cello and a set of marching drums.

All around her bedroom, the walls were covered in movie posters. On the far wall, one called *Galactic Warriors* had an imposing looking general on the front of it with the phrase: *This fall! General Invader marches toward a theater near you! Get there, before he gets to you!*

General Invader even had his own evil theme song that he relished making an entrance to, called *Invader's Tyrannical March*. Tiz enjoyed playing the marching beat on her drums, especially when her mother stormed into the room uninvited.

Leaning against the door, Tiz looked up at a poster of her favorite movie on the back of it. As a tree nymph, she loved that it was called *Forest McGee*. But she didn't only like it for the title, she loved how kind the main character was in it. And as strange as it may seem, in some ways, he was like a father figure to her. For Tiz had never met her own father, in fact, no young tree nymph was ever introduced to hers — it had always been that way. It was a rule that Tiz refused to accept, and someday, hoped to change.

But at the moment, Forest McGee's favorite catch phrase at the bottom of the poster, *Don't mess with mums*, seemed to be haunting Tiz as she tried to shut her own mother out of the room, pushing the door against her.

Mums puffed a cloud of pollen spores through a crack between the door and the doorframe that sent Tiz sneezing to the floor.

"Cut it out! You know I'm allergic!" sniffed Tiz.

"And I get hives from dirty rooms," said Mums, entering as a stack of beehives suddenly sprouted from her head, buzzing to life.

"If one of those things stings me, I swear, I'll blow up like a hot air balloon!" shouted Tiz as she watched several bees fly out.

Mums transformed back to normal as the leftover bees flew into her ears.

"Mums, that was amazing," said Tiz as she stood. "You're the best mother ever."

"Tut-tut," said Mums, "I know what you're trying to do. And it rhymes with 'kissing hut', BUT it won't get you out of cleaning your messy room."

Tiz opened her mouth to speak —

"And don't even try to blame it on your little sisters," warned Mums. "It looks like a hurricane hit this room."

"So *that's* why they name hurricanes after little sisters," said Tiz not quite so innocently. "Especially the worst ones."

"Nothing's worse than this," said Mums, pointing to the piles of messy stuff. "Red, one day you just might wake up buried in a pile of trash, you'll see. So why do you keep all this junk anyway?"

"It's not junk, they're my inventions," argued Tiz. "And someday, they're gonna make me famous. You'll see. I'll be on my favorite TV show, the *Piranha Bowl*."

"The *Piranha Bowl*? What in the world?" said Mums as she studied the room.

"Well, the Piranhas are a bunch of kids that have a lot of money," said Tiz. "And if they like your invention, then they help you make more of it."

"What if they don't like it?" asked Mums, worried.

"I'd rather not say," replied Tiz. "But don't worry. I have it all figured out. Even the part where I have to talk underwater."

"Honey, please stop," urged Mums.

"No really," said Tiz. "I'll just show them my mole mittens, the ones I made for digging. I'll use them to cut a hole in the glass bowl and let all the water out. They'll love it, it's a sure thing."

"A sure thing? I don't think so — there are no sure things in life," emphasized Mums, "just ask the chicken that tried to cross the road."

"Huh? I thought he got to the other side," said Tiz.

"He did," said Mums, pointing toward the sky.

"Oh —," realized Tiz. "*That* other side."

Mums nodded as she picked up a pile of messy papers. "And speaking of birds, I want you to stop watching that wacky woodpecker cartoon, whatever his name is — he's a bad influence on you — always laughing like crazy, not to mention the fact that he *is* a woodpecker, you know what they do to trees."

"Mom," sighed Tiz. "It's not like I go around hitting trees with my nose. And he's a woodpecker on TV, *not* a fire-breathing dragon."

"True, but what do a fire-breathing dragon and a TV have in common?" asked Mums.

Tiz sighed. "I know, I know," she replied reluctantly, "both can fry your brain."

"And so can this," said Mums as she held out one of Tiz's drawings. It showed a forest surrounded by a tall electrified fence meant to keep out woodcutters. "Don't even think about it, someone could get hurt," warned Mums as she crumpled it up and tossed it into a recycling bin. "Red, you can't make something right by doing something wrong. A simple 'KEEP OUT' sign should do the trick."

Tiz wished she had one for her bedroom door as she watched Mums hold up another drawing. It showed a forest surrounded by a fog with scary faces in it. "What's this?" asked Mums.

"It's the Fog of Fear, it's super *spooooky*," said Tiz in a haunting voice. "It has ghosts to scare away the woodcutters."

"Hmmm," pondered Mums, considering. "Nope," she

decided as she crumpled it up just the same. "Not gonna happen."

"Stop it," pleaded Tiz. "I can clean up by myself."

"I know you can," said Mums. "But that conversation happened this morning, that was then, this is now."

Mums pointed to a sock puppet of a puppy with its tongue hanging out the side of its mouth and wearing a jester's hat full of bells. It was fully completed with paws and a tail. "And this?" she asked.

"That's Pup Pup," said Tiz. "He's a puppy that's a puppet. I made him myself — sewed him from scratch."

Mums picked up Pup Pup and a dozen slimy hotdogs slid out. "What in the world?" she said.

Tiz started stuffing the hotdogs back inside. "That's his digestive system," she said urgently. "He'll need it when I bring him to life, so he can guard the forest."

"Oh no you don't," said Mums, pulling on one side of the sock puppet. Tiz pulled on the other as Pup Pup stretched into a wiener-dog for their tug of war.

"You'll rip him!" yelled Tiz.

"I hope so!" yelled Mums.

Tiz let go with one hand and started tickling Mums's life tree that ran through the center of her own bedroom.

Mums started giggling. "Stop it!" she yelled as she let go.

Tiz fell backwards onto her bum. "Please Mums, let me do it by myself," she said. "Otherwise I won't have anything left."

Mums studied the room as Tiz slid Pup Pup over her hand and whimpered like a sad puppy left out in the rain.

Mums picked up a tee shirt that said, "Eat a Truffle, Save a Tree."

"Now this one I like," said Mums. "So fold it up neatly." She tossed the shirt to Tiz as she left. "I'll tell your little sisters to help, so be nice to them."

Out of the corner of her eye, Tiz saw a pamphlet tumble

from her mother's dress, drifting to the floor like a falling leaf. Tiz didn't say a word, thinking it was something her mother confiscated. So she quickly snatched it up as she read the title:

Mili-Tree Academy: When Eight Years of Mili-Tree Boot Camp Just Wasn't Enough!

We'll help you get to the root of the problem! Then we'll pluck it like a weed!

Tiz gasped! She felt her skin start to itch as though she was having an allergic reaction simply to the idea.

Mums turned around as Tiz hid the pamphlet inside Pup Pup.

"What's the matter?" asked Mums, looking concerned.

Tiz cleared her throat. "I think something went down the wrong pipe," she replied, clearing it again. "Yeah, something that's definitely hard to swallow, I think it's stuck, but it's probably just a small bug."

"Well, you better get it out," said Mums. "Let me take a look."

"No," said Tiz. "It's okay."

Mums narrowed her eyes and said, "I know what you're doing..."

Tiz swallowed hard. Her words were as stuck in her throat as she would be in Mili-Tree Academy if Mums discovered her ruse. Sensing defeat, she considered sliding the pamphlet back out, until her mother spoke first.

"I think you're trying to get out of singing tomorrow," insisted Mums. "But forget about it. All the planters sing at the Great Seed Planting."

"I—I just don't like the song they chose," whined Tiz. "It's a lament — they're *so* depressing, plus it doesn't even have any words. It'll make me sound like a wailing banshee, one that lost everything — her home, her life, her friends. Yup, a whiny banshee kicked out of her home, that's what I'll sound like."

"You whiny?" said Mums, "I can't imagine you being whiny."

"*Mom*," protested Tiz.

"Red, not everything's about you," said Mums. "It's for the good of the whole family. You'll understand soon enough."

Tiz wasn't sure if Mums meant the singing or the Mili-Tree Academy. That doubt made her heart pound like a drum at a Hawaiian luau. Tiz was afraid, barely able to nod "okay."

Mums patted her shoulder and left, leaving Tiz with one of her oldest enemies — a messy room. It needed to be spotless. She wasn't going to be banished to Mili-Tree Academy in some far corner of the universe without a fight. There, she'd be more than just a fish out of water, she'd be a flounder in space drifting toward a supernova.

CHAPTER FOUR — DEAL OR NO DEAL

TIZ GLANCED AT THE MILI-TREE ACADEMY PAMPHLET one last time before she hid it back inside Pup Pup. Her room was a disaster — clothes piled everywhere, half-finished inventions strewn about, overgrown Cactus Cuties (cacti shaped like cute faces, adorable animals — even skulls) on the windowsill and no less than twenty musical instruments scattered on the floor. The academy was looking more and more like a reality while her chances of getting her heart seed that night were shrinking faster than an ice cube relaxing in a sauna.

But just as she was about to give up hope, in came the cleaning cavalry, her twin little sisters, Verruca and Vervain. The two eight-year-olds were so obsessed with tidying up that pine-scented cleaner was their favorite perfume.

Standing there with their long red hair perfectly brushed, the identical twins looked like a matching set of porcelain dolls, the kind that usually came to life in scary movies.

Their idea of cleaning was to take messy things from Tiz's room and arrange them neatly in their own bedroom. Each twin was like a red-headed vacuum cleaner, but unfortunately for Tiz, more vacuum than cleaner.

Tapping their feet, the twins held out their hands for some make-believe payment they thought was coming. But Tiz wasn't born yesterday. She knew they wanted to clean.

"Spit it out already," insisted Tiz, narrowing her eyes. "What's it going to take?"

"Mums is serving her majestic truffle mousse tonight for dessert," said Verruca. "I want your slice of the pie."

"*And* you'll ask for seconds," insisted Vervain.

Tiz crossed her arms, considering.

"Sharing is caring you know," urged Verruca. "And we're

sharing our precious time."

"Deal," said Tiz.

"And a bedtime story," said Verruca.

"From the story bucket," said Vervain.

"And not a watered-down one either," said Verruca.

"We get to choose," insisted Vervain.

"You little thieves, you've been practicing your haggling..." Then it clicked in Tiz's head like a remote control. "You've been watching the *Piranha Bowl*! That's *my* TV show!"

"You've got three seconds to decide," said Vervain.

"Or we pull the deal," said Verruca.

"One..."

"Two..."

"Fine," agreed Tiz. "But that's it, not a drop more."

The twins looked at each other then nodded. They spit into their hands then shook, stepping right past Tiz like she was a ghost. "Now get out of our way," they said in unison.

"You wish," said Tiz, knowing there'd be nothing left if she did. "I'm gonna watch you two like rats in a cheese factory."

But the twins ignored her, working more like greedy squirrels hoarding for their own nest.

During the cleaning, the twins helped Tiz push most of her belongings into a bottomless pit in the corner of her room. The twins squeaked every time something shiny fell in. "How do you get it out?" they asked.

"That's for me to know," replied Tiz, "and for you to find out. That is, if you don't mind free falling for the rest of your life."

After that, the twins didn't go by the pit anymore.

But the pit was just an illusion Mums had conjured up on Tiz's behalf; a trick that disguised a large magical closet in the floor that organized itself. To Tiz, it was even scarier than her little sisters.

When they were done, Tiz searched the twins like two toddlers passing through airport security. Finished, Tiz had another pile of belongings to shove into the bottomless pit. "If you take anymore of my stuff, you'll both find out if it's really bottomless," said Tiz. "Now go wash up for supper."

"You're welcome," barked Vervain as the twins started storming off.

"Wait," said Tiz, feeling guilty.

The twins stopped, but they didn't turn around, only tapping their feet.

"Thanks," said Tiz, finally.

"You still owe us," said Verruca.

"Yeah, a bedtime story," said Vervain, "*and* your dessert."

"That's right, our just dessert," said Verruca.

"You heard her, our just dessert," agreed Vervain.

Tiz looked at them oddly. "Oh really?" she said, confident that they had butchered the phrase. "And what exactly does that mean? Just dessert?"

Verruca looked down at her feet. "It means..."

"Just give us our dessert, stupid!" shouted Vervain.

The twins started on their way again.

"*So* clueless," grumbled Vervain.

"Sheesh, no wonder she needed our help," added Verruca.

"And don't forget the story!" shouted Vervain.

"She'll probably get it all wrong," complained Verruca.

"You're right," said Vervain.

"Right as rain," said Verruca.

Tiz smiled as she surveyed her room. It was spotless. Despite all the years of agony, there was finally a benefit to having little sisters.

Tiz heard a thump. She turned around and saw a matching pair of throw pillows lying at the edge of the bottomless pit. The pit was a fussy thing, rejecting any sets that weren't complete. But this time, Tiz was sure it had made a mistake. So she marched over and flipped the throw pillows back in.

CHAPTER FOUR

After a few seconds of looking down into the dark pit, she was confident it had realized its mistake. Until a pillow hit her in the face. Then another. Tiz picked up the pillows and squished them together inside one pillowcase then tossed the combination back into the pit. A second later it came flying back out like a ninja throwing star.

After three good karate chops to it, Tiz started putting dumbbells inside both pillowcases when she saw a third pillow gently float out of the pit. A red light was pulsing inside of it, beating in rhythm with her heart.

Tiz grabbed the pillow and tore it apart like a present on Christmas morning, sending feathers everywhere, completely oblivious to all the work she'd undone. In the middle of the pillow she found a small enchanted bubble protecting the most beautiful pendant she'd ever seen. The magical locket was in the shape of a phoenix with illusionary flames rising from its wings.

Inside the locket itself was a red seed in the shape of a heart that beat in rhythm with Tiz's own. As she picked up the bubble it popped, leaving the pendant pulsing rapidly in her palm.

"Need a necklace?" asked Mums from behind, holding up a beautiful one made from bright red rubies.

Tiz nodded, speechless. She clipped the pendant onto the necklace as Mums gently plucked a feather from Tiz's hair. "I'll clean everything up, I promise," said Tiz, worried that her mother might take it back.

"The feathers can wait," said Mums, putting the necklace on Tiz then carefully centering the pendant. "It's beautiful, but it pales in comparison to one thing."

"What?" asked Tiz, unable to think of anything that came close.

"My eldest daughter," said Mums, fixing her oldest daughter's hair.

Tiz felt her eyes well.

"Red," said Mums. "I want you to promise me a few things."

"Anything," said Tiz, admiring her locket and the heart seed within it.

"Promise me that you won't fall asleep with it on," said Mums. "Its power can turn dreams into nightmares."

"I promise," said Tiz.

"Swear that you won't let your little sisters touch it," said Mums. "Otherwise you'll never get it back *and* your dreams will turn into nightmares."

"That's an easy one," said Tiz. "I don't even need to promise."

Mums gave her "the look."

"Never mind," said Tiz. "I swear I won't let them touch it."

"And most importantly," warned Mums. "No monkey business, that means you, Little Punky Chipmunkey, no using its powers at all, especially to scare your little sisters."

"Aww," protested Tiz. "But that's the best part."

Mums flashed a scary look of her own.

"No scaring," said Tiz. "I get it."

"By the way, where are the twins anyhow?" asked Mums. "And don't tell me the bottomless pit."

"Well, it does like matching sets," said Tiz with a smirk.

"WE'RE STARVING!" yelled the twins from downstairs. "WE'RE EATING WITHOUT YOU!"

"Speaking of bottomless pits," said Tiz.

Mums smiled. "Come on," she said. "Let's go eat. While there's still something left."

But Tiz didn't care if the twins ate everything. She now had the one thing she needed to get her very own life tree. And with its power, she hoped to complete her mission — a simple quest to help save the world.

CHAPTER FIVE — A TALE BEST LEFT UNTOLD

TIZ HAD THE BEST SUPPER EVER that night. She wore her pendant over her shirt, talking about it every chance she got. And even though she had to give her dessert and her seconds to her little sisters, she didn't care. Mums just gave her another piece anyhow, so everyone was happy.

When supper was over and they finished clearing the table, Tiz was in such a good mood that she invited the twins to sleep in her room and hear their bedtime story there.

With the twins relaxing in her bed, the last thing Tiz expected was to hear them sniffling like they'd lost their favorite dolls. But Tiz had an idea what it was about. Mums had scared the living daylights out of the twins at dinner, even after she told Tiz not to use her new powers to frighten them. Some of the things Mums said about the Great Seed Planting had the twins shaking like leaves, knowing that one day they'd have to eventually go through it themselves. Even though the chance was small, if something went wrong with the actual planting of the heart seed or something bad happened to it, a young tree nymph could die.

"Don't cry," urged Tiz as she walked around the cozy bedroom in a playful and somewhat mischievous mood, snuffing out two candles at a time to the chagrin of the twins, who eyed the candles as if they were them. "If I don't survive the Planting, you can have all my things," said Tiz.

"We don't want your things," sniffled Verruca next to Vervain. Above their heads the name "TIZ PHOENIX" was engraved on the headboard. The twins looked as snug as kittens in a basket as they thoroughly enjoyed their older sister's comfy bed.

"You're sure? You don't want anything?" said Tiz, smiling.

"Why bother?" moaned Vervain, grabbing one of Tiz's monogrammed handkerchiefs and blowing her nose in it. "We're all doomed."

"Sheesh, you're not going to die," insisted Tiz. "It's just Mums being Mums, she likes planting her little seeds of worry. And right now, I'm watching them grow."

"That sounds just like something grandma once said about Mums's little seeds of worry, *right* before she died," replied Vervain somberly.

"I miss grandma so much," said Verruca sadly.

"So do I," said Tiz, picking up a framed picture of her grandmother who was knitting mittens in a rocking chair. Her long, beautiful hair was scarlet red with two streaks of gray. Her cheeks were nearly as big as Tiz's with a button nose in the middle that made her look as cute as any grandma. "Someday, we'll all get to see again her again though."

"But not *too* soon," worried Vervain.

"I told you we're gonna die," said Verruca.

"Oh brother, you're not going to die," said Tiz.

But the twins didn't look convinced, blowing their noses even harder. So Tiz thought of something else. "Hey, when grandma was still with us, do you remember how I used to overreact whenever she pinched my cheeks?" asked Tiz.

"Uh-huh," said Vervain.

"You screamed like a little baby," sniffled Verruca, "what did you say again?"

Tiz smiled. "Oh nooooooooo! Make it stop!" she whined, pretending like she was going to die.

The twins laughed. "That's so funny, grandma used to latch onto your cheeks like you were hiding her pills in there," said Vervain.

"She used to pinch them kind of hard," said Tiz, "but before she passed away, I figured out a way to change things."

"How?" asked Vervain.

"Well, one day I sucked in my cheeks and told her,

'Grandma, my cheeks are gone, I'm a woman now'," said Tiz confidently.

The twins laughed. "No you didn't," giggled Verruca. "You were her Little Punky Chipmunkey. Your cheeks made her melt like that smelly stuff she rubbed on her chest."

"Vapor rub," said Tiz. "But my point is this, when she pinched my cheeks, it really didn't hurt that much, I just wanted her to know that it could. That's why I overreacted, I planted a tiny seed of worry."

The twins looked at each other and nodded. "We get it now," said Vervain. "The Great Seed Planting might hurt, but the good kind, like a day we used to spend with grandma."

"Well...sort of, but even better," insisted Tiz. "It's going to be the most exciting day of my life. But the two of you won't understand until you get your own seeds."

"Can we see yours again?" asked Verruca. "Please?"

Tiz nodded as she drew her heart seed pendant from her shirt. Its crimson light warmed the room, pulsing in rhythm with her heartbeat.

"Can I hold it?" asked Verruca.

Tiz hesitated, remembering Mums's warnings. She could also hear a little voice inside her head saying, "*Don't*."

"Pleeeeeease," begged Verruca. "Sharing *is* caring."

Tiz sighed. "Okay," she agreed, lifting the necklace over her head, "but just for a second."

"You can't keep it," shot Vervain jealously at her twin.

"I never said I was..."

"It's all right," said Tiz as she handed it to Verruca.

Vervain seemed entranced. "It's so pretty," she said, scooting closer to her twin.

"I wish I could have mine now," said Verruca, swaying the necklace while gazing at her older sister's sparkling seed.

"You're too young" said Vervain, snatching it from her twin.

"Give it back," cried Verruca, reaching for it.

But Vervain held it away from her.

Verruca grabbed at it once more, knocking it to the floor.

"That's enough," warned Tiz as thunder rumbled outside and a gust of wind nearly blew out the two remaining candles. Merely being near her heart seed granted Tiz a great deal of power over nature.

The twins froze, staring at Tiz like she was much older than thirteen.

"If you break it, I can't plant it tomorrow," said Tiz as she picked up the necklace off the floor and dangled the glowing seed near her keen emerald eyes. Tiz felt her heart pound as her seed did the same, betraying her dread. She scrutinized the seed like a jeweler would a ruby, searching for the slightest imperfection.

The twins leaned forward, holding their breath.

Tiz's eyes darted back and forth as her little sisters looked on in complete silence. After what seemed like an eternity, Tiz exhaled in relief. Her heart seed slowed. "It's okay."

Her sisters fell back onto their pillows. "Phew," they said.

"Mums was right," said Vervain. "There's plenty to worry about."

"No kidding," added Verruca. "Mums said that once you plant your heart seed that you grow together with your life tree, inside of it. But how exactly are you supposed to breathe? For five whole minutes, you're part of the tree trunk — wood, bark, leaves — everything."

"You mean like this?" asked Tiz as her short red hair suddenly burst into long green vines, her skin turned to bark and her clothes changed into leaves.

The twins shrieked as Tiz covered their mouths.

"WHAT'S GOING ON UP THERE!" shouted Mums from the floor below as Tiz transformed back.

The twins looked at each other, afraid.

"Nothing!" yelled Tiz.

"Quit showing off," whispered Vervain. "You're not

supposed to be doing that."

"If Mums didn't trust me, she wouldn't have given me my heart seed," replied Tiz.

"She's right," added Verruca. "If Mums trusts her, so do I."

"What?" spat Vervain as she crossed her arms, looking betrayed by her twin.

"It's time for bed," said Tiz, trying to chip away at the iceberg that suddenly formed between the two.

"Not without a story," said Verruca, "one from the story bucket."

"We get to choose," said Vervain. "You promised."

"Yeah," said Verruca, joining her sister's cause.

Together they chanted, "Story, story..."

"All right," sighed Tiz. "Go to my toy chest and grab your favorite plush endangered animal."

The twins bolted from her bed and over to her toy chest, grabbing the stuffed animals they coveted from it. Vervain snagged a baby rhinoceros while Verruca grabbed an exotic green toad with bright red lips. They ran back and dove into bed, ducking under the sheets. "Story, story..."

"All right, all right already," groaned Tiz. "But no screaming, or I'll turn both of you into a pile of leaves. And not the ones that stay evergreen, but the deciduous kind, where you'd turn brown and wilt." Tiz heard the twins gasp as she walked toward the story bucket.

Out of the corner of her eye, Tiz noticed them sticking their tongues out at her.

Verruca turned to her twin. "She wouldn't really turn us into grubby old leaves, would she?" she inquired.

"Don't *even* ask me — you took her side against me earlier," huffed Vervain out of the blue. "So as far as I'm concerned, she's already turned your brain into worms." Vervain licked her finger and wormed it into her twin's ear, exacting her revenge as Verruca squirmed.

"Stop it," protested Verruca, "no wet-willies."

"Vervain," interrupted Tiz, sounding very motherly, "do you want a story or not?"

Vervain stopped her hooliganism immediately.

Tiz brought the story bucket over to them, holding it high enough so they couldn't peek inside. The twins both reached in and fished around as though their heart seeds were hidden within. Together, they pulled out a large drop of story water that looked like a snow globe. Inside of it, a single snow-covered tree stood in the middle of a blizzard as lightning forked wildly across the orb to the spots where the twins held it. Entranced, Verruca and Vervain eased it over to Tiz.

As she took it, a gust of wind rushed in through the windows and blew out the remaining candles.

The twins scooted away from their older sister. "Stop that," insisted Vervain.

"Yeah, cut it out," said Verruca.

But Tiz didn't like the fact that her younger sisters were telling her what to do, especially after they nearly ruined her seed. So she held the snowy orb up to her face, making herself look like a ghost.

Verruca gasped. "I swear, if a worm comes out of your nose I'm going to scream," she said.

"She wants you to scream," said Tiz eerily as she moved closer to the twins, putting on her mole mittens like monster claws, "that's how she'll find you."

"Who?" asked Verruca nervously as thunder rumbled outside.

"*The witch*," said Tiz ominously. "The one that burned down the Unburnable Forest."

Lightning flashed outside, crackling like a fire. "She's coming," gasped Vervain, pulling the blanket over her head.

"Too late," replied Tiz as she leaned against Mums's life tree that ran through the center of the room, "she's already here." Tiz saw a flash of light. Putting her hand on the tree while wearing her magic heart seed was a big mistake, one she realized too late.

The story drop swelled to the size of a hot air balloon. It burst into a tidal wave, swallowing the girls like ants in a flood. Another flash of light blinded Tiz as she heard her sisters screaming. Then darkness...

With her eyes closed and her head throbbing, Tiz could feel a lump on her brow without even touching it. But it was the frigid cold she felt coupled with her wet clothes that bothered her the most. Shivering, she blinked away the blotches from her eyes as she found herself lying in the snow at night underneath an old tree lit eerily by the moonlight. It was as though she traveled through a tree door and into the snowy globe. Worse, her bed was in the treetop above her with her little sisters huddled together in the center, their hair dripping wet. The bed holding them teetered from side-to-side as precariously as a priceless dinner plate balancing on the nose of circus seal. Terrified, both twins clutched their plush endangered animals that were now out of their safe haven and in as much danger as them.

Dizzy, Tiz glanced around — her heart nearly stopped. All of them were at the edge of a slippery cliff overlooking a valley as dark as the bottomless pit.

"Help!" screamed Verruca from up above.

"You opened a tree door!" yelled Vervain, right by her twin.

"She can't understand!" worried Verruca. "Look at her head! She hit it on the bed! She's stupider than ever! We're doomed!"

"Get us back!" pleaded Vervain.

"Grab a branch!" yelled Tiz, anxious to transport them. "We can't take the bed back, it's too dangerous!"

Verruca reached for a branch. The bed started tilting toward the cliff like a lopsided seesaw. Vervain quickly pulled her twin back. They gasped as the tree *creeeeeaked.* But slowly, the bed eased back.

"We can't move!" screamed Vervain. "We'll fall!"

"Then quit moving!" yelled Tiz.

"You told us to!" shouted Verruca.

"Stay still!" yelled Tiz. "I'll get you down!" With her mole mittens that she had put on to scare the twins, Tiz began digging frantically in the snow, trying to reach the ground beneath.

"We're up here!" yelled the twins, looking confused by what their older sister was doing.

Vervain looked at her twin. "I told you!" she said, glancing down at Tiz. "She's clueless! If she tilts her head, her itty-bitty brain will slide out of her ear like a pathetic little sled!"

The bed lurched then teetered like it was Santa's sled hanging over the edge of an icy roof — but the twins' vessel was glaringly devoid of mystical reindeer, and thus, couldn't fly.

The twins screamed!

"You're wasting time!" yelled Verruca. "We're going to die!"

"I don't wanna visit grandma yet!" screamed Vervain.

"We're coming grandma!" yelled Verruca.

"Stop it! I know what I'm doing!" insisted Tiz, scooping out a hole.

"So do I!" yelled Vervain. "You're digging our graves!"

Tiz ignored her, reaching the frozen ground underneath the snow and latching onto it with one hand like a desperate mountain climber. Concentrating, she imagined her free hand was the tree holding the twins as her pendant began glowing brightly, its power traveling through the ground and all the way to the tree's roots. Suddenly, the limbs on the tree began moving like fingers.

Several branches snapped! The bed slipped further toward

the dark abyss beyond the cliff!

Tiz shut her free hand into a fist! With not a moment to spare, the tree limbs caught the bed at the very last second!

Sweat froze on Tiz's face as she summoned all her power. She bent the tree to her will, forcing its limbs to lower her bed with her sisters toward the ground. As the bed plopped down and the tree sprung back into place, Tiz felt faint, falling face first into the snow. Exhausted, everything went white then quickly turned black as she fell into another deep sleep.

Tiz didn't hear her little sisters crunch the snow as they ran toward her. She didn't see them drag her to the bed and tuck her under the blankets. She didn't feel them trying to keep her warm on either side. She didn't hear them pleading for her to wake up.

But more importantly, Tiz didn't see the small crack in her heart seed as its energy seeped out like a ghost, forming a tiny hovering phoenix. Though she was lost in a dream, the life force of the seed knew where to go, floating into Tiz's mouth, drifting through her throat as it flowed all the way to her heart, changing her forever. A change that no one noticed, not even Mums as she suddenly appeared by the snowy tree.

Tiz slept between the twins as Mums slid her bed like a giant sled through the snow and over to the old tree. With a flash of light, all of them disappeared back through a tree door as Tiz's dream slowly twisted and turned into a nightmare.

CHAPTER SIX — RUN GIRL RUN

"OOOOO, YOU'RE IN BIG TROUBLE," said the twins, slamming the door to Tiz's bedroom wide open as they barged in, waking their sister. Groggy, Tiz sat up in her bed, rubbing the lump on her brow as the morning sun melted a clump of snow on her ceiling, causing water to drip down on her like some sort of slow, methodical punishment.

Tiz was glad to be back in her bedroom, though she had no idea how she'd gotten there, nor was she eager to find out, especially since her mother must've had something to do with it. And that was one talk she wasn't looking forward to. So much so, she'd rather use her tongue to clean up her room (even if she had to lick up every last bit of water and snow).

"Pack your things," said Vervain. "When Mums gets through with you I'm going to have my own bedroom."

"Pack this," growled Tiz as she flung a pillow at them.

The twins ducked and it flew into the hall. They yelled, "Nah-nana-nana-nah!"

"Get out! You ungrateful little brats!" yelled Tiz.

The twins slammed the door shut.

Tiz could hear them stomping their way down the stairs like each step was her face, doing their best to get their mother riled up.

One of them yelled, "Mums! She's up!"

"*And* she threw a pillow at my face! I have the evidence!" screamed the second as though she held a smoking gun instead of a pillow. "It's still hot from her big fat cheeks and her stupid hot head!"

"Yeah! She's a hothead! Make her move out!" yelled the first. "Before she does something even stupider! Or else we'll all be living on an iceberg!"

As Tiz listened to their explosive tantrum it conjured up

wicked images of the nightmare she just had. In it, Mums was sending her off to Mili-Tree Academy, but she wasn't taking Tiz to a bus stop, a train station or even opening a magic tree door.

Instead, Mums was stuffing Tiz down the barrel of a circus cannon with a toilet plunger to the rousing applause of an audience, one full of rich kids from the TV show the *Piranha Bowl*, wearing giant fish suits made from bright blue cotton candy. Worse, the twins hopped out of a tiny car dressed as creepy-looking clowns, waving sparklers as they skipped toward the cannon's fuse.

Pup Pup was dancing around all of them on his hind legs, hotdogs falling out of him like a crumbling log cabin. Laughter from the twins echoed down the barrel as they lit the fuse, making it hiss like an angry snake. At the last second, Tiz saw Mums look right at the rich kids and yell, "It's a sure thing!" Just before the BOOM!

The nightmare was so bad that Tiz should have thanked the twins for slamming the door and waking her up. But if she didn't figure out how to explain her "snowy mountain screw-up" to Mums, a more important door would slam shut; one that led to her favorite parks, movie theaters, and carnivals, and more importantly, far away from Mili-Tree Academy.

Chewing her nails, Tiz had totally forgotten about her heart seed. Did Mums steal it back? Tiz patted her shirt down more thoroughly than a rookie cop searching for a stolen donut hole.

"Phew," said Tiz, feeling the pendant underneath. She pulled it out, wondering if her heart seed was thumping as fast as her own heart. But instead, it was flickering like an old light bulb that was about to go out in some dark basement.

"Nooooo..." moaned Tiz on the verge of a panic attack. *Two lives, one soul, if either dies, both must go,* she thought, sensing the steep edge of a slippery slope as dangerous as the snowy cliff near the old tree.

As the light faded from the seed and the color drained from her face, Tiz felt colder than an ice statue. Petrified, she was too afraid to scream. Her hand trembling, she couldn't bear to watch either, so she shut her eyes, expecting to take her last breath. Unbeknownst to her, the seed's remaining bit of crimson energy floated out as she inhaled it. As it tickled her throat, she peeked at the seed. It was as dark and shriveled as a raisin baked in an oven on high.

How? How was she still alive? Why were all these horrible things happening to her? First the snowy cliff, and now this! That's when a light bulb went on. THE TWINS! They dropped the pendant! THEY broke the seed!

Tiz heard her mother shout, "Red, I'm coming upstairs!"

Would Mums believe her? Especially after she warned Tiz not to blame her little sisters for her messy room? "Not gonna happen," Mums would say. Even worse, Tiz wasn't supposed to let the twins play with it in the first place.

From her nightmare, images of the circus cannon flashed in and out of her mind as she heard her mother's footsteps on the stairs. A final count down sounded in Tiz's head as though a rocket ship would be launched into space. And the mission control in her mind knew exactly how many stairs Mums had left. Ten...nine...eight...

"My toy heart seeds," muttered Tiz, hoping one of them would fool Mums until she could figure out what to do. Tiz hopped out of bed and dashed to her dresser, yanking open the drawer. Seven...six...five...

Inside she found a toy heart seed she'd made years ago. She turned it on...nothing...her plan was as dead as the batteries. She found a second toy one — the same thing. Four...three...

Tiz ran over to a giant toy chest where she kept spare batteries. She opened it frantically, grabbing the first thing she saw — an emergency pack. Two...one...strapping it on, she dashed over to her sun-lit window, accidentally knocking an overgrown Cactus Cutie in the shape of a skull to the floor, splitting it open. "Crud!" she blurted, knowing that a cracked skull wasn't exactly the best omen when she was about to climb down a tree to flee her mom.

Tiz heard the doorknob turn. Blast off!

She leapt onto a branch and into the cool morning air faster than a monkey on a sugar rush, tickling her mother instantly. Mums laughed wildly out the window as Tiz climbed down.

"Come back, Tiz!" laughed Mums, unable to control herself. But her mother had her own tricks up her sleeve. The branches on Mums's tree wiggled like the tentacles on a huge octopus that was giggling and jiggling. They reached for Tiz as she dodged left and right, swinging her way down!

Tiz hit the ground, rolling to avoid the last one. Dizzy, she realized how crazy this all was. But before she did something even crazier, like stick out her tongue at her mom, laugh like a certain famous woodpecker or yell, "Go to your happy place, Mums," she sprung to her feet and bolted toward town with her sack of goodies, looking like she was off to sell something her mother wouldn't want her to.

"Red! Come back!" yelled Mums one last time, watching her daughter run through the forest from the window.

Once Tiz was far enough from her mother's tree home, she put on a pair of furry shoes that made bear tracks then doubled back, heading toward where Sombra lived — the Weeping Willow Family Grove.

Tiz ran more quietly through the woods than a ninja wearing bunny slippers. Before long, she was standing underneath the tree home of Gertrude Willow, Sombra's mother, and staring up at the window to Sombra's bedroom. The tattered tree home was nestled deep within a weeping willow, one that unfortunately looked like a dirty mop. Its leaf stems were long and stringy and needed to be climbed like a rope in gym class. But if you pulled too hard and ripped out a strand, Sombra's mom would lose a lock of hair.

So instead, Tiz started cawing like a raven (a deep croaking caw) — her usual signal to Sombra to climb down. But by the second caw, a flock of ravens was circling above. By the third, they were landing on Tiz. By the fourth, she felt like a scarecrow stuffed full of birdseeds. One raven even pecked at the shriveled heart seed inside her pendant.

"Shoo!" shouted Tiz and the ravens took off immediately.

"Holy smokes," said Sombra, sliding down a couple of willow strands. "How'd you do that?" she asked, landing on the ground. "Even with my seed I can only get one to land."

Tiz flicked bird poop of her tickle proof shirt. "Trust me, one is more than enough," she said.

"Yeah, poop everywhere, I mean everywhere," said Sombra.

"That's the least of my worries," said Tiz, her eyes welling. "Look," she said, holding out her phoenix pendant as her hand trembled, rattling her dark and lifeless heart seed inside.

Sombra's eyes ballooned, trying to take it all in. "B-b-but how are you still —"

"Here?" finished Tiz, dreading to even think it. "I don't know."

"Maybe it wasn't the real one," said Sombra. "After all, your mom was worried about giving it to you, you said so yourself."

"I wish," said Tiz sadly. "But it was..."

"You're sure?" said Sombra. "Absolutely positively sure?"

Tiz nodded somberly. "I had it on when I was telling the twins a bedtime story. And since I didn't take it off, I accidentally opened a tree door. It took us to a snowy mountain scare-a-dise. It was almost a one-way trip."

"So *you're* the one they were talking about," blurted Sombra.

"What? What do you mean?" insisted Tiz, more afraid than ever.

"This morning, your mom came over," said Sombra

nervously. "And a bunch of other moms too, from all over. I was listening through the door, they said something really bad happened."

"Greaaaaaaat," moaned Tiz, "now everyone knows."

"Listen, that's not all," said Sombra, glancing around. "Some of the moms kept saying something weird, over and over."

"What?" implored Tiz.

"They said — they said," stammered Sombra nervously. "That you awoke *her*."

"Who?" asked Tiz, growing more nervous herself. "Mums?"

"No," whispered Sombra as she glanced around nervously. "*Herrr*."

Tiz's eyes widened. "The w-w-witch?" she stammered.

"But *maybe* it was a good witch," offered Sombra unconvincingly. "And not the real mean one."

"Yeah right," sighed Tiz, "just like it wasn't my real heart seed."

"So what are you going to do?" asked Sombra glancing at the dead seed.

Tiz didn't know. Desperate, she reached into her emergency pack, feeling around. After a few seconds, she pulled out a rather ominous looking set of cables that people used to bring a car battery back to life called *jumper cables*. The opposite ends of the long cable both split into two separate strands — four strands in total. At the end of each one of those strands was a single clamp that Tiz had specially modified. Each clamp now looked like a hungry little shark with glowing red gems in its eyes, four sharks in total.

"What the heck are those?" asked Sombra.

"My last hope," said Tiz, inspecting the jumper cables. "I was going to use them to bring Pup Pup to life."

"How?" asked Sombra.

"They take energy from one thing and give it to another,"

said Tiz. "But I'll need some help."

Tiz reached into her pack and pulled out another pair of fuzzy shoes that made bear tracks. "You'll need these," she said, showing them to Sombra. "And do you still have those leather football helmets I gave you? The ones that smell like old shoes?"

Sombra gave out a long sigh that seemed to say, *here we go again*, as she started climbing back up toward her room.

CHAPTER SEVEN — HOLY SMOKES

TIZ WATCHED AS STORM CLOUDS DARKENED in the distance. They loomed as ominously as the coming of the Great Seed Planting that afternoon. Time was running out for her to mend her heart seed and she still needed the help of two more tree nymphs that would be planting their seeds that day. In order to "encourage" them, Tiz had Sombra climb back up the weeping willow tree several more times to get additional goodies from her bedroom.

After her best friend slid back down, Tiz led the way to the French tree nymph with all the spotted owls and offered her a French horn if she helped. She agreed, but insisted that Tiz pay her the ten chocolate-covered truffles she owed for the birds as well as a pair of mole mittens. In addition, she made Tiz promise to take the owls off her hands that day. Tiz didn't argue, after all, what was a little more bird poop in an already poopy day?

Luckily, the French girl also had a friend over, Holly Holly, a tree nymph with a lively double name that was so eager to help she nearly broke her own heart seed falling from the French girl's family tree. But Tiz liked her enthusiasm; her spirited nature gave her hope.

Unlike Tiz and Sombra, who were a bit of an odd-looking pair, Frenchy and Holly graduated from the same school of thought when it came to perfection.

Frenchy's face was as thin and sharp as a knife and the words that came from her dainty little mouth often cut like one too. Her perfect little nose was just as pointy and curled up like a great white shark's so it always seemed that she was looking down on you (and in unnerving way too). And since she was taller than everyone her age, her narrow blue eyes usually were. Even when climbing trees, she chose to wear beautiful flowing gowns that moved as gracefully as her and often made a lasting impression on those she deemed worthy of her presence. But it was her long brown hair that usually made the greatest impression. Smooth as silk, it always looked like it had been brushed a thousand times even from the moment she got out of bed.

In fact, her best friend, Holly, had what Frenchy considered "the privilege" of brushing it for her. Although Holly was no slacker either when it came to presenting herself to her peers. Her red dresses were so perfectly pressed and wrinkle-free that they always looked brand new. Like her mother, Joy Holly, she had rosy cheeks and always fashioned her long red hair into braids; ones she then pinned neatly into a circle atop the crown of her head, making it look like a Christmas wreath. Her personality was just as cheerful, which in turn, helped a bit to offset her best friend's aloofness.

With Frenchy, Holly and Sombra in tow, Tiz led them away from all the groves and the prying eyes of little sisters. When they were alone in the woods, Tiz asked Frenchy and Holly to stand next to each other.

"Um," said Tiz nervously. "Can I see your heart seeds?"

"Of course!" blurted Holly, pulling out a brightly decorated holly tree pendant that looked like it was ready for Christmas. Inside, a red heart seed beat with excitement, one that reminded Tiz of her own before her little sisters ruined it.

Meanwhile, Frenchy Yew pulled out a yellow heart seed that was beating just as quickly as Holly's. Its pulsing light illuminated a golden locket shaped like a stylish lily that French royalty often used in jewelry.

"Ewww-la-la," said Sombra. But Frenchy wasn't in the mood. Especially when she saw what Tiz was taking out of her emergency pack.

"Sacré blue!" said Frenchy, staring at the jagged clamps on the modified jumper cables as if they really were small sharks.

"Don't worry," said Tiz, "I know what I'm doing."

Frenchy muttered something in French to Holly.

"What'd she say?" asked Tiz.

"Oh, nothing really," said Holly. "Just something about being fried like an egg, frizzy hair and never seeing her family again. No biggy."

"No biggy?" questioned Sombra. "Maybe to you, but not me. Besides, you're a Holly, you're used to lighting up like a Christmas tree."

"Thanks!" said Holly, striking a cheerleading pose. "You're the B-E-S-T! " she added, forming the letters with her arms.

"That reminds me," said Tiz, "you'll need these." She pulled out four leather football helmets and plopped one on each of their heads.

"Sacré blue," muttered Sombra, adjusting her helmet.

Tiz held out a shark-clamp covered in red to Holly. "Take this one Holly, it's called a positive side, it'll be perfect for you."

Holly took it eagerly. "Wow!" she gushed, petting the clamp like it was the cutest thing she'd ever seen. "You're a little sharky, aren't you? Yes you are, yes you are..."

The red shark clamp was just as eager; its magic pulled her heart seed closer to its jaws like a magnet would a bolt.

Tiz turned to Frenchy and offered a shark-clamp covered in black. Frenchy snatched it then muttered something to Holly.

Before Tiz could ask, Holly said, "You don't want to know."

Tiz gave Sombra a big polite smile as she handed the other shark-clamp covered in black to her best friend. Sombra narrowed her eyes. "Is this a negative side?" she asked.

"It is — b-but it's not what you think," stammered Tiz. "I-I just need you and Frenchy to balance things out, maybe by thinking bad things about me."

"That won't be hard," said Sombra, yanking out her

weeping willow pendant that was clipped to her new diamond necklace.

Holly gasped in awe then clapped happily for Sombra.

"I just thought it would be harder for Holly is all," added Tiz.

"Fine," said Sombra, peeved.

Worried that her best friend might storm off at any moment, Tiz clipped the jaws of a positive clamp onto her heart seed pendant. "Please, if everyone could just do the same thing," she pleaded, holding the cable that would tie them all together.

By the time Tiz looked at Holly she already had hers on, smiling. However, Frenchy and Sombra were still debating as their heart seed pendants gravitated toward the negative clamps they held.

Frenchy watched Sombra, waiting to see if Tiz's best friend would risk it.

Sensing a possible mutiny, Tiz gave Sombra a set of puppy dog eyes that would make an ogre cry.

"All right," said Sombra, attaching her clamp.

Suddenly, they heard a familiar voice calling out. "TIZ PHOENIX! I KNOW YOU'RE OUT THERE!" yelled Mums. "AND IF I CATCH YOU DOING SOMETHING CRAZY, LIKE RIDING ANOTHER BEAR, I SWEAR!"

"Uh-oh," muttered Tiz, looking at Frenchy sadly. "Pleeease."

Frenchy sighed, rolling her eyes. "C'est la vie," she said finally, attaching the negative clamp to her pendant.

"Okay," blurted Tiz. "Holly, think of something positive about me."

"That's easy! We're new best-ies!" said Holly a bit too loudly.

"Put a sock in it," said Sombra. "Or I'll put my clamp on your lips."

"Sombra, that anger right there," said Tiz, "get ready to

direct it at me. You too, Frenchy."

Sombra and Frenchy glared at Tiz with the greatest of ease.

"On the count of tree," said Tiz, her palms sweating. "One......two......TREE!"

Tiz watched the other girls close their eyes as their pulsing pendants glowed brighter.

Shutting her own eyes, Tiz crossed her fingers and toes. She reached her hand toward the sun like she often did, hoping to draw on its power to nurture all things good and green. "Please, please, please," she muttered as she tried to recall something positive about herself. Then it came to her. Tiz thought about how she helped her little sisters using her heart seed, lowering them from the snowy tree and saving them.

POP, POP, POP, POP heard Tiz. She expected to see all four heart seeds popping like popcorn as she opened her eyes slowly. The three other girls were staring at Tiz's seed. Their shock turned to smiles. IT WAS GLOWING AGAIN!

Tiz could barely believe her eyes as the four of them tossed their leather football helmets aside. Tiz smiled down at the glowing heart seed inside her pendant with its illusionary flaming wings. "It's as good as new!" she yelled, no longer caring if Mums found her.

"Is a Phoenix seed supposed to do that?" asked Holly, looking concerned.

Tiz smelled smoke. The pendant felt hot. The seed was glowing because of a fire inside her locket. Smoke poured out like a raging inferno. The seed inside the phoenix pendant was turning into ashes. To Tiz, it was a five-alarm fire.

"Water, water, water," blurted Tiz, looking for some. But there was none. The pendant got so hot Tiz had to throw the necklace off. It landed on dry sticks that roared to life with flames, starting a tree on fire.

Tiz watched helplessly as the fire spread to three more trees. Her face flushed red with anger at herself. Then she let it all out. "*NOOOOOOOO*!" she yelled as a gust of wind bellowed from her mouth so strong it knocked everyone over, blowing out the burning trees like candles.

"Holy smokes," said Sombra, watching the trees smolder as she sat up. Wind usually spread fire to more trees, but this gust was so strong it put them all out.

Nearby, Tiz crawled to what was left of her pendant and heart seed. She picked up the scorched necklace with a stick. The phoenix pendant opened and the ashes fell out into Tiz's trembling hand.

"What's going on over here!" insisted Mums as she rushed over with three other mothers in tow. All four stopped dead in their tracks as they saw what Tiz held.

In the past twenty-four hours, Tiz had nearly gotten her little sisters killed, almost burned down the forest and utterly destroyed her heart seed. She couldn't hold back the tears.

Gertrude Willow, Sombra's mother, had a face like a frog to begin with, but now, it looked like her eyes were about to pop out of her head. "How can this be?" she marveled. "She lives, though her seed does not."

"It's a miracle," said Holly's mother, Joy Holly, her hair shaped like a wreath over her rosy cheeks. "A miracle, yes indeed."

It didn't feel anything like a miracle to Tiz, who feared the looming punishment that lay ahead.

Though instead, Mums put her arm around her daughter, comforting her. "You're alive," she said. "It *is* a miracle."

"But how?" asked Gertrude Willow.

"Zeh question is not *how* she survived," said Frenchy's mother, Marie Yew, in a thick accent. "But rather, *who* survived." Tall and thin as a reed, Marie Yew wore her long gray hair in elegant braids that made her look like royalty as she glided forward. Her yew tree was one of the oldest in the forest and her mind one of the wisest. Marie stepped over to the extinguished trees. "Who saved these trees from the fire?"

"Tiz did," said Holly eagerly. "She blew them out like candles on a big birthday cake, even without her seed."

"Is that true?" asked Mums.

Tiz nodded that it was as she wiped her eyes.

Marie Yew squatted by Tiz and studied her like something strange and unexpected. "Seedless, but not powerless..." she said finally.

"That's enough Marie," insisted Mums. "My daughter's been through enough for one day. I don't want to hear another word from your silly folk tales — it can wait."

"The witch waits for no one," warned Marie, narrowing her eyes at Tiz. "For I am looking at her now. She's come back — awakened within your daughter."

Silence. Not even a bird chirped. Tiz buried her face in her mother's dress. She had suffered enough for one day. She didn't need some huffy French woman accusing her of being a witch and making it even worse.

"What do you mean she's come back?" asked Sombra, coming to her friend's aid. "The witch doesn't grow old and die."

"Zhat is a lie," insisted Marie Yew, "one that the witch herself spread like a wildfire." Marie stood tall over Tiz as the clouds above them darkened. "The Unwithering One is the name of the witch's tree," she said menacingly. "And with a dark spell, near the end of her last days, the witch sacrifices her old and decrepit self. But more importantly, a great portion of her power, everything she's learned for thousands of years. Yet, she never completely fades away, for the same spell allows her spirit to linger — to come back as one of us, to come back as a child. And though her power grows as quickly as she, the witch cannot plant another tree."

Thunder rumbled above.

"When she's reborn, her heart seed is a lie," continued Marie. "But if it is destroyed, she does not die. That is our only clue, as it was written long ago."

Thunder BOOMED!

Marie stalked closer. "Beware of *her*," she added, "for she will return seedless, but not powerless, when she ascends to the top of the Tower of Thorns, at the apex of the Unwithering Tree, she will regain the full power of the enemy, her rage will grow like her fires of old, everything will burn, except for her — the witch of the Unwithering Tree." Marie pointed her long, slender finger at Tiz. "She is *herrrrr*."

Lightning crackled above them. Mums rose to her full height, standing between her daughter and Marie. "*Do not* say that again," she warned. "She is my daughter, nothing less, nothing more."

"Zhat is a lie!" yelled Frenchy Yew, no longer relying on Holly to do the speaking for her. Angry, Frenchy thrust a finger toward Tiz like she was pointing a dagger. "Zhat girl tried to kill us! She's a witch! I've seen it with my own two eyes!"

Tiz tried to ignore her.

"She's not a witch!" shouted Sombra, nervously plucking out a thick strand of her own tangled black hair.

"Quiet, *Mop*!" yelled Frenchy.

"You shut up!" fired back Sombra. "I've known Tiz since I was four! She doesn't even own a toad! I would know!"

But Gertrude Willow didn't seem so sure.

"Good-bye everyone," said Gertrude as she ushered Sombra off despite her daughter's protest. "We'll see you all at the Planting! Drat, sorry! *Some* of you!"

Tiz wished she could curl up like a roly-poly then roll into a hole. Instead, she just stared at the pile of ash in her hand that used to be her heart seed.

"Tiz, we're going," insisted Mums, gathering up Tiz's magical cables while she helped her daughter to her feet. As they left, Mums threw one last glare at Marie Yew.

But Tiz didn't notice, she just kept staring at the ashes in the palm of her hand as she stumbled along behind her mother.

Mums saw her and stopped on a dime, pulling out a small pouch. "Here," she said, opening it. "Put them in."

Tiz tilted her hand to pour the ashes in when a gust of cold wind suddenly blew them into the air. Tiz started chasing the grayish cloud, grabbing at it as though she was trying to stop a ghost. Within the cold wind, Tiz heard the faint cackling of an old woman, and for a second, the ashes seemed to form a laughing witch with a hooked nose, just before they vanished.

"Help!" yelled Tiz. "Help, Mums!" But by then the ashes were gone. Tiz realized no one could help as she fell to her knees, tears stinging her eyes.

Mums ran to her side, comforting her daughter like a warm shawl. She didn't say anything. In a way, Tiz was glad for it. There was nothing Mums could say at that point that would make her feel better. So Tiz continued doing the only thing that did. She cried.

CHAPTER EIGHT — LUMPS AND RAVENS AND MORE LUMPS FOR THE TAKING

BY THE TIME TIZ ARRIVED back home that morning with her mother she had shed enough tears over her lost heart seed to fill a bucket. Her eyes were so swollen from all the crying that they felt as big as her cheeks. Slouching, her body drooped as though it didn't have any bones in it while she plopped down at the kitchen table, elbows on top, hands supporting her chin.

Thunder rumbled, a storm was brewing, both inside and out.

Mums set an empty glass and a carton of milk on the table along with a box of Tiz's favorite fudge brownies with the brand name *Cocoa Lumps* sprawled across the top of it. The mascot was a lump of chocolate named *Lumps* with a crazy look on his face, wearing a straightjacket. Staring at the straightjacket, Tiz wondered how long it would be before she'd be modeling one herself if things didn't improve. Fidgeting with the box of brownies, she flipped it over to another crazy picture of Lumps, this time being chased by a hungry-looking mob, and read the slogan: *Everyone's Loco for Cocoa Lumps.*

Mums watched her daughter read it. "It may be just a rumor, but I think everybody's crazy about that stuff," she said, trying to cheer her up.

Tiz pushed the box away.

Mums patted her on the shoulder and took it from the table.

Tiz heard footsteps on the stairs and looked over.

As the twins came downstairs they froze at the sight of their older sister. With her hair a mess, ashes from her heart seed on her hands and tear-streaked cheeks, Tiz figured she must of looked like a stranger to them, but they didn't need to react like a witch was in their house. For a moment, Tiz actually felt a bit like one. And she didn't care for that feeling at all.

Growing even more upset, Tiz glared at the twins — the two little monsters that broke her heart seed. But before Tiz could say a word, Mums slid two pieces of her majestic truffle mousse in front of her. Tiz stabbed both forks into the slices as she glared at the twins, then stuffed her mouth full to keep herself from yelling at them.

The twins sidestepped to the far end of the table and sat down without so much as a peep. Vervain poured Tiz a glass of milk then slid it toward her. "There you go," she said cautiously.

"S-sharing is c-caring," stammered Verruca.

Mums eyed the twins. "Your sister's been through a lot today," she warned, "so if you're going to talk to her, pretend like you're talking to me after you've broken one of my favorite bird feeders."

Verruca opened her mouth to reply, but before she could, a raven landed on the kitchen windowsill, voicing its croaking caw loudly.

"Shoo," said Vervain, but the raven didn't go away.

Tiz stuffed her mouth with two more pieces as the twins watched.

"Wh-what's the matter," stammered Verruca, looking at a burn mark on Tiz's neck where her necklace and heart seed pendant should have been.

Tiz didn't say a word. She just glared at her little sister.

"Tiz is lucky to be alive," said Mums to the twins while washing some dishes in a sink. "Her heart seed was ruined."

Verruca's mouth shut faster than a bear trap as thunder rumbled.

Mums turned around, looking a bit shocked to hear so much silence from her chatty girls. "Tiz, tell me exactly what happened," she said.

Another raven landed on the windowsill. The two cawed, almost as if they were begging Tiz to say it was all the twins' fault. Mums would probably believe her now, especially after all she'd been through. Besides, Mums seemed to sense something on her own with all the uneasy silence.

Tiz picked up the glass of milk and drank from it slowly, eyeing her sisters. She set it down, watching their lips quiver, unable to say anything. Despite her anger, Tiz couldn't do it. They didn't crack the seed on purpose. "I dropped it," said Tiz finally, looking at her little sisters. "You were right all along Mums, you shouldn't have let me hold onto it."

The twins gulped.

Mums looked at Tiz. "Red, you should have told me that sooner," she said. "Then maybe we could have prevented all this."

"But —," blurted Tiz.

"No buts," interrupted Mums. "You dropped it, then you didn't tell me about it, making it even worse. Didn't I warn you? You can't make something right by doing something wrong. From now on, you need to listen to the tiny little voice inside your head — the one that's telling you 'this doesn't feel right.' Do you understand?"

Silence.

"I guess so," said Tiz sadly as she slid the half-eaten pieces of pie away from her. "May I be excused?"

"You may," said Mums. "Get some rest. The Planting starts in four hours."

"What? I'm not going," insisted Tiz, her voice growing louder. "Why would I?" she argued as two more ravens joined the sill, lining up like shady little undertakers just dying to profit from the tragedy unfolding before their beady lil' eyes.

"Because your friends are going," replied Mums. "And because the Planting is not a sure thing. It could be the last time you see them," she added, looking Tiz right in the eyes. "Out of all the planters, you should understand that."

"But mom, *you* told me to listen to the tiny little voice inside my head," argued Tiz. "And right now it's screaming, '*This doesn't feel right.*'"

"Don't be a lil' smarty-pants, young lady," warned Mums.

"But I don't want to go," whined Tiz, growing angrier. "I feel stupid enough as it is! And all the other kids will be teasing me! I can hear them now, chanting, 'Treeless Tiz! Treeless Tiz!' Everyone will be laughing at me!"

Suddenly, the twins started laughing louder than a pack of hyenas. They covered their mouths, but they couldn't stop.

Tiz flushed red with rage.

Ravens started pouring into the kitchen like some sort of scary movie.

The twins started laughing louder.

Mums tried to shoo the birds away with a broom.

But all Tiz heard was the twins. "It's not funny!" she yelled.

The twins stopped laughing immediately.

"Shoo! Go away you stupid birds!" shouted Tiz as all the ravens flew away, leaving as quickly as they came, but more importantly, doing exactly what she said.

It seemed the madder she got, the stronger her voice became.

Tiz glared at the twins. She decided to test her newly found power on them, and at the same time, teach them a little lesson.

"You two, give each other a wet-willie," ordered Tiz, knowing that the twins hated anything near their face that wasn't cake or candy. Tiz closed her eyes, imagining the twins licking a fingertip then sticking it into each other's ear.

Like puppets, the twins both licked a finger then eased it toward each other's face. But instead of plunging their finger into each other's ear, they thrust them into each other's nostril, digging for gold.

"That's enough!" growled Mums, the anger in her voice dwarfing Tiz's own. Cringing, the twins yanked their fingers out, dashing to the sink to scrub their nails like surgeons preparing for an emergency procedure.

Mums glared at Tiz. "If you don't want to be called a witch, then don't act like one. The ravens aren't helping either."

"I told you so," said Vervain, turning to Verruca. "She's a witch. I win our little bet."

"It *does* explain everything," admitted Verruca reluctantly.

"I win, I win," taunted Vervain, smirking at her twin. "I get to give all your dolls a haircut." Vervain ran off to collect.

"No!" growled Verruca like a mother bear protecting her cubs. She ran after her twin and yelled, "If you touch a single hair on their head you'll wake up looking like a bowling ball!"

With the twins gone and feeling guilty for what she had done Tiz had a million questions for Mums. "What's happening to me?" she asked desperately as thunder rumbled outside. "I feel like there's a storm growing inside of me, but I don't know how to control it."

"Over time, you'll have to learn how," said Mums as she sat next to her daughter, putting a hand on her shoulder.

"But without a tree," said Tiz glumly.

Mums nodded. "Normally," she said, "a life tree sort of acts like an antenna on a TV, gathering and honing our powers, so our abilities don't seem so fuzzy. The tree brings us in tune with nature as well as the forces within it."

"But not me," said Tiz sadly. "I'll be like a TV without an antenna, fuzzy as can be, out of tune with everything."

Mums cleared her throat then sang, "*There's another way to be in tune with things.*"

"Mom," said Tiz, "please, don't tease." The very last thing Tiz wanted to do was sing, even if it usually made her feel better.

"I'm not teasing," insisted Mums. "It's your voice. That's where your power lies now. And you know it — the ravens, the ones you told to get out of the kitchen, and the twins' noses, the ones you made your little sisters browse like aisles in a really gross grocery store."

Tiz sighed. "I guess I did make them put the *gross* in grocery," she admitted somberly. "Sorry."

"*Sorry, my dear*," sang Mums like an angel.

"Whoa," said Tiz. "That was really pretty."

"Why thank you," replied Mums with a small bow. "It was part of a spellsong."

"A spellsong?" asked Tiz.

"A magical song," said Mums, "a kind from long ago, when all nymphs — tree, water, and air — spoke in a musical language. At first there weren't even any words. The tones did the speaking."

"Then how did they understand each other?" asked Tiz.

"They were so in tune with each other, and all living things for that matter, they didn't need to sing any words to say how they felt," said Mums. "It was kind of like the lament you had to learn for the Planting — no words."

"The lament," moaned Tiz. "Now I understand why I had to learn it."

Mums patted her on the shoulder. "If you learn to channel your emotions into song, and likewise, control your voice, you'll find the same harmony in life as if you had a tree." Mums stroked her daughter's hair. "And the best part, creating new songs will be right up your alley," she added with a smile, "just think of them as new inventions — the sky's the limit *and* it's something you don't need a life tree to help you with."

"But I won't live as long without a life tree," worried Tiz, knowing that a tree nymph's bond with their tree allowed them to live as long as it, sometimes for thousands of years. "Without a tree, I'll wilt like a flower left out in the cold. Won't I?"

A chilly gust blew in through the window. There was an uneasy silence. Not even her mother could mask her own concern. "Try not to worry, we'll figure it out," said Mums finally. "I promise."

"Do I still have to go to the Planting?" asked Tiz, hoping to take advantage of Mums's pity.

Mums nodded that she did. "You still have to sing at it too," she said. "For your friends. Now your voice will be more important than ever. I believe it will help them when they merge with their tree."

"How?" wondered Tiz.

"I'm not sure exactly," said Mums as she patted her own life tree that rose up through the middle of the kitchen. "But when I planted mine and merged with this tree some of my own senses were heightened, especially my hearing."

Tiz sighed, too tired to fight anymore, wishing her own ears had lost the ability to hear her mother's decision.

"Get some rest," said Mums. "You'll feel better after you do."

Tiz pushed herself up from the table and shuffled off, doubting she would ever feel better again. If she couldn't save her own heart seed then how could she help save the world? After climbing the stairs, Tiz plopped down into her bed and imagined that she still had her seed as she drifted off into a deep sleep, dreaming of her own tree; one that she now wanted more than ever before.

CHAPTER NINE — A SICK FEELING

WHEN TIZ WOKE UP from her nap, she could hear Mums and several other mothers talking in hushed voices in the kitchen below her room. Tiz could only make out certain words like *ravens, evil, jelly* and *toast*. She was pretty sure the first two words had to do with her being a witch and the last two were involved with making a sandwich.

It made her feel hungry at first then suddenly queasy. But it also gave her an idea. Tiz dashed to her toy chest and threw open the lid. She snatched up Pup Pup and the hoard of lukewarm hotdogs inside the wiener-dog puppet.

If she ate one, then she'd get so sick she wouldn't have to go to the Planting, no lying necessary, it was a sure thing. Tiz plugged her nose then reached inside Pup Pup as his jester's hat jingled merrily. She felt a pamphlet wrapped around a hotdog like a bun. "Ewww," she said, pulling out the weird combo. Separating them, Tiz recognized the pamphlet immediately. She had hidden it there herself.

"Mili-Tree Academy," she uttered, dreading it. She then turned to the first page of the slimy pamphlet and read:

It's Where All the Bad Kids Go...

Instantly, Tiz thought twice about eating the old hotdog. It might get her out of the Planting, but it also could end up being a one-way ticket to Mili-Tree Academy. At that very moment, kids all around the world were punching their very own tickets by throwing rocks through windows, bullying other kids for their lunch money, blowing up dolls with fireworks and starting a whole host of forest fires. That's when it clicked in her head.

"If the real witch is a kid again," said Tiz to herself, "then she'll be there for sure." In a way, it made Tiz want to go even less, something she didn't think was actually possible. Turning to the second page, she read:

It's Where All the Bad Kids Go...to Become *Good*: Good at all these Wonderful Things:

Campfire Responsibility

Archery

Staff Fighting

War Magic

Military Strategy

All to Help Save the Environment!

And don't forget our specialties:

Wrestling your first frost giant

Catching your own dragon egg

Opening portals to new worlds

Governing your own star empire

But that's not all, for those who qualify:

The Ascension — Learn to climb the Witch's Tree

Just Think! Someday Your Precious Little Thing Could Conquer the Universe! All for a Low Monthly Fee!

CHAPTER NINE

Tiz stared at the pamphlet, fearing that the real witch, now reborn, may relearn it all. In her prime, she had reduced a great portion of the Unburnable Forest to ashes. Her magic was her might. And that might was drawn from the most evil of trees.

"The Unwithering One," muttered Tiz, worried.

As if those very words held power, the pamphlet began glowing red. On it, a symbol of a burning tree started forming, its branches, a many-headed dragon called a hydra, growled at Tiz. Spiraling out of its treetop, a twisting tower sprouted sharp thorns. All the letters on the page shuffled around like pieces on an evil board game, spelling out three words as a shrill voice in the air of an old woman whispered, "Learn, grow, *burn...*"

Tiz dropped the pamphlet like it was made of fire. She shut her eyes as cackling laughter filled her ears, reminding her of the witch she'd seen in the blowing ashes of her heart seed. Thankfully, the laughter faded as quickly as it came.

Tiz looked down at the pamphlet, picking it up. It no longer glowed and the pages looked like they had never changed. But the ringing in her ears told her that she had *not* imagined it.

The witch would be at the academy, in fact, she had to go. She had to relearn the tricks that were key to ascending the witch's tree, not only to prove that she was worthy of it, but also to regain all her power. To prevent it, someone would have to stop her before she became a little monster. But who?

Tiz's thoughts were interrupted by a double knock on her bedroom door — a trademark of the twins. "Speaking of little monsters," she muttered, hiding the pamphlet and hotdog back inside Pup Pup.

Afterwards, she went to the door and opened it, letting the twins in. "What do you want?" she said, tapping her foot just like them when they grew impatient.

"Tell her," whispered Vervain to her twin, looking afraid.

Verruca cleared her throat. "Well...we're here to say, we're here to say —"

"Spit it out," insisted Tiz. "Or get out."

"Sorry," said Verruca finally. "We're here to say, 'We're sorry.'"

Those words sounded so strange and foreign coming from her little sister's mouth that Tiz wondered if she'd heard her properly. "Huh?" she said. "Say that again."

"We're really, really sorry," said Vervain, supporting her twin. "Sorry for dropping your seed."

"We'll do anything to make it up to you," added Verruca as Vervain nodded in agreement.

"Fine," said Tiz, "but if you really mean it, then give me one of your heart seeds. You'd still have one left for the two of you to share. After all, sharing *is* caring, just like you said."

"Uhhh...I said that?" asked Verruca nervously.

Tiz stuck out her hand and made the "fork it over" gesture.

"W-would it even work?" stammered Verruca, clearly on the defensive.

"I'm willing to chance it," said Tiz.

"We can't," said Vervain, sounding just as nervous. "Mums has our seeds, and we won't get them any time soon."

"A promise will do," said Tiz, holding out her pinkies. "Both of you, pinkie swear on your heart seeds that you'll do it. Then I'll choose which one I want later."

Vervain staggered back as though she'd been hit by a giant pillow. "Uhhh..."

Verruca whispered something in her twin's ear. Vervain shook her head in disagreement, trying to cover Verruca's mouth, but her sister held her off.

"You can have mine," said Verruca sadly.

Tiz nearly fell over. She never expected either one of them to agree.

Vervain stepped forward, eyes welling. "No, take mine," she said. "Verruca and I will plant her seed and share a tree. Everything will be exactly the way it's supposed to be."

Verruca started crying.

Speechless, Tiz felt sorry for her little sisters and making them cry made her feel rotten inside. She never would have taken one of their seeds. She just wanted them to feel how much the loss meant to her. Now that they knew, Tiz grabbed two of her monogrammed handkerchiefs that the twins liked and offered them. "Here," she said. "Use these."

"Thanks," said the twins, taking them and blowing their noses.

"And just so you know," said Tiz. "I don't want your heart seeds — I know you didn't do it on purpose."

"Phew," sighed the twins, wiping their eyes.

"I just wanted to plant a tiny seed of worry," added Tiz. "Just so you know how it felt. Maybe now, you won't make the same mistake." Tiz paused, not wanting to make the twins feel any worse. "The same mistake as me."

The twins nodded sadly, lowering Tiz's handkerchiefs from their runny noses. "Do you want us to throw out the hankies?" asked Vervain.

"No, it's okay," said Tiz, opening up a laundry hamper for them to toss the matching handkerchiefs in. "I guess I have a soft spot for things that come in pairs."

"Even when they're a little snotty?" asked Vervain.

"Even when they're a little snotty," said Tiz.

The twins smiled as they tossed the hankies in. Then they left without another word as Tiz shut the door, feeling a little better than before.

CHAPTER TEN — COMFORT IN THE FAMILIAR

TIZ PUT ASIDE PUP PUP and his hoard of lukewarm hotdogs along with any remaining thoughts about making herself sick. She realized it was a worse idea than attending the Planting without a heart seed. But Tiz still dreaded going — it would be like six years of Mili-Tree Academy rolled up into one horrible day. However, she figured that if she could get through it, then she could get through anything.

Trying to see the sunny side of things, Tiz dragged herself over to the bottomless pit to call up her outfit for the Planting. But before she even arrived it threw up a putrid green dress and hat as if they had been giving the pit a stomach ache.

The old costume had been patched up and passed down from generation to generation. Its purpose was to make Tiz look like a miniature tree — which was the last thing she wanted. But as if that wasn't bad enough, attached were a set of red and orange phoenix wings that would make her stand out more than a glitter-covered peacock at a petting zoo.

Tiz put on the treetop hat and leafy dress with the thrill of someone that was preparing to go to their own funeral. As she did, she accidentally tore a sleeve. Slouching from defeat, she resembled a wilting flower more than a tree as she shuffled over to a full-length mirror.

Seeing her reflection, Tiz shook her head in dismay. "You look like a weed," she said to herself, "yeah you — you stupid witch weed."

"That's enough of that," said Mums, appearing behind her in the mirror. With a glowing hand, Mums mended the rip in Tiz's sleeve instantly.

In the reflection, Tiz could see that Mums was hiding something behind her back. "Mums, you're not fooling me," sighed Tiz as she faced her mother. "What is it? A broomstick?"

"Not quite," said Mums, pulling out a gnarled wooden staff, the kind an old wizard or druid would use. "Think of it as a portable tree, one that can help you get in tune with your powers. It's an antenna for your me TV." Mums offered the staff to Tiz. "Take it," she said, "you could use something to lean on."

Tiz slowly took the ancient staff as she sat on her bed. Without a life tree, Tiz knew she'd be different from her friends. Their trees would grant them longer lives and powerful abilities. They would also bring them in tune with nature, helping them to hone and control their new skills.

But not Tiz. She knew she had her own powers, but wasn't sure how she had gotten them or how long they would last. Without a tree, she feared her powers might burn brightly for a while, but fizzle out prematurely like a cheap sparkler on the third of July.

"There's one more thing," said Mums, interrupting Tiz's thoughts. Her mother touched the gnarled staff with a glowing hand. Glimmering strings sprouted from the wood, stretching down from the top of the staff to nearly the bottom, turning it into a musical instrument.

Tiz strummed the glowing strings as they *ROARED* like the bass guitar of a heavy metal rock star.

"*Coooooool*," said Tiz in awe. "I needed a new ax."

"An ax?" said Mums with a bit of alarm.

"Jeez mom, that's what rockers call their guitars," said Tiz. "Can I make an ax head for the bottom — can I please?"

"No," said Mums immediately. "For a million reasons, no — I don't want to be the mother that started the trend of tree nymphs running around with axes. Besides, it's called a string-staff, and more importantly, it has another purpose. Can you guess what that is?"

"To rock the palace!" yelled Tiz, strumming the glowing strings once more so they *ROARED*!

Mums stilled her daughter's hand, giving her "the look."

"But you said it's my new antenna," said Tiz. "To help me get in tune with things." Then suddenly it clicked in her head like someone had turned on a microphone and started tapping it to make sure it was working, "to guide my voice."

Mums nodded. "Let's try something," she said. Mums went over to Tiz's bed and picked up Pup Pup as his jester's hat jingled merrily. Without spilling a single hotdog she set the wiener-dog puppet on the edge of the bed, closer to Tiz. "When you and your sisters were younger, I used to sing to you whenever there was a thunderstorm. Do you remember any of the songs?"

Tiz nodded. "*Soggy Puppy Come Hither*, that was my favorite," she said.

"Then close your eyes," said Mums, "and strum your string-staff so it sounds like a grumpy old thundercloud."

"Okay," said Tiz, closing her eyes and playing the cords to produce a low rumbling sound. Outside her bedroom window, darkening clouds joined in on the thundering harmony.

"Now imagine Pup Pup as the puppy in that song," said Mums. "He's afraid, stuck in the rain, soaking in a puddle."

"Eww," said Tiz. "A puddle of what?"

"Concentrate," said Mums.

"Sorry," said Tiz, closing her eyes and imagining the dachshund-like puppet in the rain, soaking in a puddle, his big sad eyes looking up at her from underneath his jester's hat.

"Listen, when we start singing," said Mums, "think of the strings on your staff as your heartstrings, and change the tone accordingly, from sad to happy."

"Sad to happy," said Tiz, "got it."

"On the count of tree," said Mums, "one, two, tree..."

Together they began singing, "*Soggy puppy come hither, get out of that nasty weather...*"

Tiz, like her mother, always had a beautiful voice, but

now, her strange new powers seemed to enhance it. Or was it the string-staff? Tiz didn't know for sure. Regardless, their voices made a choir of angels sound like a flock of geese.

At the sound of the harmony, Tiz grew happier and the chords she played on her string-staff sounded more cheerful. She imagined Pup Pup scampering into her room, tail wagging, thrilled to be out of the rain.

With her eyes still closed, she felt the warmth of the sun's rays shining down on her through her bedroom window. Then she heard a tiny bark.

Tiz opened her eyes, rubbing them in disbelief.

Pup Pup's tail started wagging as the eyes of the wiener-dog puppet grew as wide as silver dollars, looking just as shocked as Tiz. He began glancing over the side of her bed, rattling the bells on his jester's hat, getting ready to leap down. The hotdogs inside him seemed to be making him act like another kind of hotdog, showboating at the edge. But before Tiz could pick him up, the enchanted puppet fell from her bed with a THUMP, all of his hotdogs tumbling out.

Tiz knelt down to pick up the rolling beef franks, but before she could help, Pup Pup started retrieving them himself, gulping them down like a hungry baby alligator.

Tiz laughed as she helped Pup Pup with a hotdog that fell between the floorboards.

"It's not exactly what I had in mind," said Tiz, smiling at Mums. "I wanted to make him a *real* dog, but I guess he seems happy enough, *especially* with the hotdogs." Tiz spotted one underneath her bed that was rolled up in a familiar pamphlet, one that would remind her mother of Mili-Tree Academy. *Yikes*, she thought as she quickly slid under her bed, grabbed it and fed it to him out of her mother's view.

"You don't have to keep retrieving them," said Mums, "we turned him into a magical bag of replenishment — there will always be more and they'll stay fresh too. You can use Pup Pup to multiply any ordinary thing that he can eat — food, rope, clothes — you name it. One day the two of you could even start your own store. But I wouldn't feed him anything magical, it could have strange effects with even stranger consequences. So be careful."

Tiz would have preferred to have heard that warning before she fed Pup Pup a magical pamphlet! She stared anxiously at the puppet as Mums started petting him, expecting a million pamphlets to start flying out of him at any second, covering the room. But instead, Pup Pup just gave Tiz a confused look, tilting his head as he wagged his tail.

Tiz breathed a sigh of relief. As she did, the string-staff tingled in her hand almost as though it was saying, "I'm not a life tree, but I can make you happy." Whether it was from clutching the string-staff too tightly during the recent excitement or from the magical instrument itself, she wasn't sure.

Regardless, Tiz was grateful for the gnarled old staff, but as she studied it, there seemed to be a certain loneliness about it too. She noticed that a small part of it was burnt, making it look even more depressing, while at the same time, fueling her curiosity. She began wondering about its previous owner and where it came from. Was someone missing it? Did someone lose it? In a way, it reminded Tiz of her own problems, and thus, made her a bit sad. But most of all, her new "portable life tree" made her want a real life tree even more. Growing more and more curious about it, she turned to her mother. "Where did this wood come from, it looks like part of it was singed," she said finally.

Mums offered her hand. "Come and see for yourself," she said softly.

Tiz hesitated, glancing once at her mom's hand. She had a pretty good idea what it meant — that Mums would be opening a tree door to take them somewhere dreary. But Tiz was already starting to feel as gloomy as the reforming storm clouds outside, so she wasn't sure she wanted to go. "Is it gonna be *real* sad?" she asked. "Like creepy, scary graveyard sad?"

"I'm afraid so," said Mums in a somber tone. "But it'll help you understand," she added.

"Can Pup Pup come?" asked Tiz.

"Of course," said Mums, stroking her daughter's hair. "I wouldn't have it any other way." Mums picked up Pup Pup, minding his hoard of hotdogs and offered her hand again.

Tiz glanced at her emergency pack. It was her safety blanket plus back up parachute and first aid kit all in one. But her mother's presence had a way of making Tiz feel safer than anything inside of it ever could. So Tiz took her mother's hand then used the string-staff to help herself stand up. "Something to lean on," she said.

"Something to lean on," repeated Mums.

Hand in hand they stepped over to Mums's tree running through the center of Tiz's bedroom. Together, they counted and vanished through a magic tree door. They flew through glowing tunnels on their way to someplace that Tiz was both anxious and afraid to see.

Before long, Mums gently guided them up to a glimmering tree door then she stepped through with Pup Pup in her arms.

Tiz followed closely behind with her string-staff. Upon exiting, she started coughing immediately — there were ashes everywhere. "Whoa," she said in shock as she stood in the middle of a burnt forest. The woods were as still as a painting, one that only used shades of black and gray. But this wasn't just any forest. Underneath a gloomy sky, Tiz saw the remains of tree homes up high in some of the charred treetops. From below, they all looked like giant matchboxes that had caught on fire. Tree nymphs once lived here, but now, they were all gone.

"The Unburnable Forest," uttered Tiz. She'd only seen pictures of it before. But the reality was so much sadder as the smell of ashes made her feel sick. Tiz realized the tree she was standing next to was dying and it was only a matter of time before it would fall over. It was a phoenix tree, and its home up top reminded her of her own home as she felt the weight of that sadness pulling her down like a tar pit.

"The Unwithering One," said Tiz, seeing what could happen to her own forest, and worst of all, to her family and friends.

"The Unwithering One," repeated Mums, as a gust of cold wind blew through the desolate woods. Putting her hood up, her mother turned away, looking grim. "A storm is coming, Tiz," she said sadly. "And its lightning will ignite terrible fires, ones that no amount of rain can put out."

Tiz didn't know how to answer as she heard her mother begin sniffling out of the blue amid the gloom of the sad and strange forest. Stranger still, her mother almost never cried.

Tiz scanned the burnt woods. "So this could happen to our forest," she said. "Our family, our friends."

"Yes," said Mums as Pup Pup whimpered in her arms.

"Do you think the new witch lives in our forest?" asked Tiz.

Silence.

"Yes," said Mums finally.

"Then she should have to go away, far away — she can't stay in the Wailing Woods, just in case, right?" asked Tiz.

"Yes, she must go far away," said Mums, crying. "That is what her mother agreed upon, to save her daughter's life."

"Whose life?" asked Tiz innocently.

Still facing away, Mums didn't answer her, she only wiped her eyes.

Tiz realized what it meant. "M-my life?" she stammered as her own tears stung her eyes. "You think I'm the witch?"

It was the longest bit of silence in Tiz's life.

"Yes," said Mums finally as if the words had to be pried from her mouth. "You are *her*. Only she would do something cruel like this — burn our family trees, then come back as one of its seeds."

Those biting words pierced Tiz's heart like a dagger. "No, no, no," uttered Tiz nervously as Mums put her hand on the dying phoenix tree to open a magic door and leave.

Tiz latched onto her mother's arm. "No, Mums, please," she begged.

"Shhhh," hushed Mums, her tears pouring down on Tiz like raindrops. "You can't come home, if you do, they'll hurt you. You can never go back, promise me, promise me you won't ever go back."

"Don't leave me here, please," begged Tiz. "Not alone."

Mums handed her Pup Pup. "Not alone," she said, drawing closer to her daughter's ear then whispering, "follow him — never lose sight of him." Mums glanced around nervously as if she expected all the other mothers to be eavesdropping.

"No," cried Tiz. "I'm sorry, I'm sorry I broke my heart seed, I'm sorry I started a fire, I'm sorry about everything, I'll do anything you say —"

"Forgive me" said Mums, tears streaming. "I-I had no choice, I'm *so* sorry, my child. The other families would have uprooted my tree, destroying it — *two lives, one soul, if either dies, both must go*." Her tear-filled eyes began to glow green.

Roots burst from the ground and wrapped around Tiz, pulling her off her mother's arm.

Tiz wailed like a banshee.

Her mother covered her own ears. And with a flash, she stepped through a tree door and disappeared.

Tiz broke free of the roots. She ran to the closing door with Pup Pup. But it shut before she could get there. Tiz crumbled under the dark tree, wishing for home and the warmth of her own bedroom. It was the only place that could chase away the growing cold, a place she missed desperately, but a place she could no longer go.

CHAPTER ELEVEN — A SECRET NO ONE CAN KNOW — NO ONE

CRYING ON THE ASH-LADEN GROUND at the base of a burnt tree, Tiz felt like a crushed piece of garbage tossed out by her very own mother, a mother she loved dearly, but also one that could no longer love her back anymore. Pain gripped her chest like a vise. Her heart throbbed worse than a freshly skinned knee with shards of glass stuck in it. It was awful. Not even Pup Pup licking away her tears made her feel any better.

"Why me," she kept repeating as she beat her fist against the ground in front of the charred and dying tree. The Unburnable Forest was full of them, as far as the eye could see, all looking as miserable as her. In the dim, cloud-covered daylight, the forest was now nothing more than a dismal graveyard for trees, each one serving as its own headstone. Tiz still couldn't believe her mother abandoned her in such a grim place. It was the last thing she ever expected to happen. But nevertheless, it did.

She was as oblivious to the possibility as she was to the robin's egg she had knocked from its nest with her slingshot. But now both had been tossed out, shattered and broken — just like her heart seed.

Tiz stopped hitting the ground and looked at her hands. They were covered in ashes. Dark and gloomy, they looked like the hands of someone that had burned down the forest — the hands of *the witch.*

A thought crossed her mind. Had she done so in some previous life she couldn't remember? Angry at her mother, Tiz wondered if she was capable of it, and even worse, would she one day do the same thing to her own grove? She had always dreamed of saving the world, one tree at a time if need be, but from what her mother had said, destiny had the exact opposite in mind.

There are no sure things in life, thought Tiz, just like her mother had warned.

Maybe that's why Mums said it, pondered Tiz. Her mother probably knew all along that she would have to leave her daughter behind. Had she simply been waiting all these years for the right time?

Thunder *boomed*! Tiz looked up. The grim clouds above mirrored her mood. Worse, because of the gathering storm, it was getting darker and darker in an already gloomy forest. And soon, she'd be soaked in more than just tears.

Tiz took off her treetop hat that she had put on for the Planting and tossed it aside. She straightened her leafy dress as she looked sadly at the red and orange phoenix wings attached to her back then plucked them off. She wasn't a Phoenix anymore, not a part of the family. She released the set of wings, watching them drift to the ground like autumn leaves. A change had come, one as cold and bitter as winter.

Tiz eased to her feet then scooped up Pup Pup, hoping to find better shelter from the coming rain than a bunch of leafless and crumbling trees.

In front of her was the dying tree that her mother used to get them there. Carved into the bark by way of magic was a symbol Tiz recognized immediately — a door with an "X" over it. It meant that tree could no longer be used as a tree door. There was no following her mother through there. There was no going home.

Tiz also noticed that the other burnt trees surrounding the one her mother had used were in even worse shape. Even if she could open a tree door, they'd more than likely crumble on top of her before she got the chance to get through it. It was a dangerous thing to use a dead or dying tree for a door. So they were of little use to her. Even still, she felt sorry for them.

Tiz believed that the Unwithering One would look like one of these charred, gnarled and scary looking trees. But instead of a home, the Tower of Thorns would rise from its treetop, just like Marie Yew had said. In her mind, Tiz saw the sinister tower rapidly growing to full height atop the witch's tree, just like it did in the magical pamphlet for the academy. Together, the tree and the tower in her imagination formed a dreadful stronghold; one that an evil witch would relish as a laboratory for her dark experiments. There, roosting in her thorny nest atop the tree, she would spend her days and nights cackling and screaming wildly as she stirred her latest bubbling brew to perfection.

But as scary as it would be, Tiz would very much like to see both the tower and the tree that held it aloft.

As she stood there, staring up at the dying phoenix tree, Tiz realized something important — if she could find the witch's tree, then she could find out the true identity of the witch.

Tiz recalled the last time she tickled Mums's tree and her mother started laughing. As the result of a tree nymph's bond with their life tree, they felt what their tree felt. So if she started tickling the witch's tree, then the witch was sure to come running. Tiz was afraid of what consequences that might have, but even more so, that if she tickled the witch's tree, that she herself would start laughing.

Even though she shuddered at the thought, Tiz had to know. And at the very worst, if she tickled the tree and started giggling, then at least she would have a life tree; something she still wanted very badly, regardless of what kind it was.

And *so what* if the witch's tree looked like one of the burnt trees. She would just use its power to nurse it back to health. Tiz promised herself that she'd be a good witch, for there were such things. "I'd make the witch's tree into what I want it to be," she said to herself, liking the ring to it.

But Tiz also realized that she was getting ahead of herself.

CHAPTER ELEVEN

She needed to either find the witch's tree or find out the witch's true identity by some other means. And she had a pretty good idea where to start. *It's where all the bad kids go*, she recalled the Mili-Tree Academy pamphlet saying. Bad or good, there, they could learn how to climb the witch's tree.

Tiz felt Pup Pup squirming in her arms. Quick as a fox he escaped and leapt to the ground, sniffing around. Before she could corral him, he started following a scent. Pup Pup stopped then barked at her three times and waited for her.

Remembering what her mother had whispered about following him, Tiz picked up her string-staff and did so, putting one foot in front of the other, walking through the ashes — to where, she didn't know. Leaving behind her footprints as well as the barred tree door, Tiz carried the string-staff her mother gave her along with the painful memory she also bestowed.

After Tiz had lost her heart seed, she desperately wanted to avoid the Planting, but never in a million years would she have guessed that it would take place this way. Now, she wanted to be there more than ever before. Even if she didn't have a seed, she wished she could be there with her family and watch her friends plant their own seeds, particularly her best friend, Sombra Willow.

Home had always been a safe place. Now it seemed like the most dangerous place in the world. But everything she owned, including her emergency pack, was there. Longing for her things, especially a change of clothes, she would have gladly traded her new string-staff for some of them.

Lightning flashed and Tiz began counting until she heard thunder. *Boom*! Five seconds had passed. And she knew that for every five seconds, a storm was about a mile away.

The wind in her face started strengthening as she walked into it. The storm was coming her way. With her luck, she'd probably get struck by lightning. Glancing at her string-staff, she wondered what other magic lay hidden inside of it and whether or not it would protect her during a storm.

Lightning crackled and thunder boomed, almost as though nature itself was answering "no." The storm was getting nearer, but Tiz wasn't any closer to finding shelter. And wondering about her staff wasn't going to keep her dry.

Leaning on it, Tiz climbed up a small hill after Pup Pup. She was just about to stop him and seek shelter in a tree hollow that she spotted off to the side. But at the top of the hill she saw something else that made her freeze in her tracks.

Tiz spotted a red parrot walking around the trunk of a burnt tree while inspecting it. The parrot disappeared behind the trunk, but it didn't come back out, instead, a boy in a red-feathered robe shuffled out like some sort of magician finishing a trick. He stopped then stood under the burnt tree, cupping his hands as if he was going to catch something falling from it, right in the middle of the windy and nasty weather.

Tiz recognized the boy instantly. He'd done the same in the Wailing Woods, standing under the nests of the spotted owls there with a baseball glove, in case one of their eggs fell.

Tiz imagined the boy as a parrot again, one trying to fly with a baseball glove then understood why he must have left it at home. But it was now clear to her that this was no ordinary boy with no ordinary hobby.

He had bright blond hair that was almost white and he looked pale for someone that must have spent a lot of time in the sun. His nose was long like a beak, and coupled with his robe of bright red feathers, made him look just like a giant version of the parrot that she first spotted. But it was his eyes that caught Tiz's attention. Whenever she'd seen him before, they were always shut. But now they were wide open. They looked as sleepy as Sombra's eyes, but his were milky white. The boy was blind.

Tiz watched him standing there with his hands cupped, ready to save any egg that the wind might blow out of a nest.

But she couldn't spot a single nest anywhere in the treetop. And any egg hidden inside a small hollow would probably be safe. So she felt as sorry for him as any egg he might accidentally drop.

Tiz wanted to ask the boy what he was doing there, so far away from the Wailing Woods, but she didn't want him to think that she was spying on him. So she stood there, thinking of something else to say as Pup Pup started sniffing him. The boy bent down and pet the enchanted puppet as if it were normal for a wiener-dog made of polyester to be wandering around a burnt forest.

"Phoenix eggs," said the boy out of the blue in such an airy way that it seemed like a part of his mind was someplace up in the stormy clouds. "Have you ever caught one?"

Tiz looked around, shocked. The word *phoenix* alone had startled her. She wondered if her mother had forgotten to give her some kind of secret password. "Who me?" she said instinctively, surprised that he had sensed her presence.

The boy simply nodded.

"N-no," stammered Tiz, confused by the question. "I've never caught one, not a phoenix egg."

"Dragon eggs," said the boy as if he were dreaming, "it's kind of like catching one of those, but a little bit harder. Would you like to try?"

"Um," said Tiz, hesitant. "Should I be skipping over the dragon egg part?"

"Fenris," he said, thinking, "my uncle Fenris caught a dragon egg once. It weighed over a thousand pounds, even so, the egg survived."

"And your uncle?" asked Tiz, so intrigued that she was starting to forget what she wanted to ask him in the first place.

"The dragon egg," he said. "Did I mention that it weighed over a thousand pounds?"

"You did," she said, worried. "And a phoenix egg is harder?"

He nodded.

"Well..." pondered Tiz. "Then why do it?" she asked. "Why help something like that, if it could hurt you?"

The boy turned toward her. There was sadness in his milky eyes, like when Tiz had imagined Pup Pup fully soaked in a rainstorm. "Loneliness," he said finally. "Because if it were me and I were falling, I'd want someone to catch me."

Tiz felt a rush of warmth from those words. She smiled at him. "I think I get it," she said, now almost sure that her mother had arranged this. "And by any chance, did a little birdie tell you to meet me here?" she asked.

He nodded once then put his finger to his lips, urging her to stay quiet.

Tiz glanced around nervously. "Um..." she mumbled, trying to think of what secret agents would do, then decided to continue their conversation, just in case it was code for something. "The phoenix egg," she said finally, "I think I should watch you catch one first."

"Mole mittens," he said. "Any chance you have a pair?"

Tiz nearly fell over, wondering if her mother had told him about them too. "How did you hear about them?" she asked, glancing around.

"The *Piranha Bowl*," he said. "It's my favorite TV show. Just the other day I heard a girl selling them. She had the loveliest French accent."

"Frenchy," grumbled Tiz. "She stole my idea. I've traded her several pairs in the past — one just recently for some spotted owls. But now she puts the *traitor* in *trader*."

"Sorry," said the boy, "I didn't mean to upset you." He offered his hand. "I'm Dargen Darkshir, Warlock, tenth class."

"Tiz Phoenix," she replied as she shook his hand.

"Phoenix?" he said. "As in the bird?"

Tiz looked at him curiously, wondering if he was embellishing his lack of knowledge on purpose. If so, his little ruse was pretty convincing. "No, as in the tree," she replied finally.

"Which?" asked Dargen. "I know several kinds of trees that are nicknamed 'phoenix tree' — the Chinese parasol tree, the empress tree —"

"That's the one," said Tiz. "The empress tree. It has the prettiest purple flowers you'll ever see." *Then* she remembered he was blind. "Sorry," she said, blushing.

"It's all right," he said.

"A phoenix egg," blurted Tiz, eager to change the subject. "You're going to catch one?" she asked. "Even though it's more dangerous than the dragon egg that crushed your uncle?"

He nodded. "Don't worry," he added. "I'll have my eyes open the whole time."

Tiz laughed, quickly smothering it with a hand, feeling terrible. "I'm sorry," she said again, knocking herself in the forehead.

"It's okay," he replied. "It was supposed to be funny."

"Yeah, but I still feel like a goof," she said, still mad at herself.

Crackle! *Boom*! Lightning struck the tree next to them. Tiz and Dargen went flying.

Tiz sat up, her hair fluffed, singed and smoking, her eyes searching for Dargen — he wasn't moving. Tiz ran to his side. His eyes were closed. Tiz started slapping his cheeks. "Wake up, wake up," she begged. "Please, please, please."

Dargen sniffed the air with his eyes still closed. "A barbecue," he said calmly, "I smell roasted hotdogs."

Tiz spotted a charred hotdog rolling past her. "Ugh," she groaned, worried that Pup Pup had been blown to bits. Turning around, she saw that it wasn't the case. The spell that brought him to life also seemed to protect him. He was fire-proof, like a mystical oven mitt with big floppy ears and a jester's hat. Tiz smiled as she picked up Pup Pup and inspected him, making sure that he was okay.

Pup Pup promptly squirmed from her hands and bolted after a charred hotdog rolling by.

Tiz laughed as she helped him with one that had fallen halfway down a rabbit hole.

"He looks as happy as you," said Dargen from behind them.

Tiz froze — Dargen shouldn't be *looking* at anything. Tiz turned around and studied his face. His eyes were no longer a milky gray. They were sky blue, fixated on Pup Pup. He could see again.

Staring at him in awe, Tiz wondered if it was because of the lightning.

"Blindness," he said before she could ask. "It was only a spell. I don't like wearing a blindfold all the time, it gets too itchy. So I put an enchantment on myself so I couldn't see what I was catching."

"Why?" asked Tiz. "Why make catching the phoenix egg even harder?"

"Mountains," he replied as if it was a perfectly good answer.

"Mountains?" asked Tiz.

"Mountains," he repeated. "Why do people climb them?"

"I don't know," said Tiz. "To see if they can get to the top?"

"Maybe," he pondered. "But I think it's to see farther. To see what they couldn't see before, about the world, but more importantly, about themselves."

Tiz wasn't exactly sure what he meant. But in a strange way, it did make sense when it came to her predicament. She had a lot of questions that needed answering, a mountain of her own to climb so to speak. Smelling the burnt tree, she turned her thoughts to the lightning bolt that nearly fried them. Did she have something to do with it? She *was* angry with herself right at the moment it hit the phoenix tree. *That poor tree*, thought Tiz, looking over to what remained. It was starting to occur to her that maybe she indeed might be a danger to her family. Like her mother said, her powers seemed the strongest when her emotions ran high, happy or sad, glad or mad. And she didn't like that at all, considering that her anger at herself almost put an end to her and Dargen.

As she picked up her string-staff, a device that could help her get in tune with her new abilities, she felt a growing sense of urgency to learn how to control her powers better. And from what she read about Mili-Tree Academy, power and discipline were sort of their specialty.

Tiz went to the tree that the lightning destroyed and gently ran her hand over it. She crouched near its base then looked up. "The phoenix eggs," she lamented. "I must have ruined them."

"No," said Dargen as if he was completely sure. "It's a tough bird, when it dies, it burns up — quick as lightning, then it rises again from its own ashes."

"Even the eggs?" asked Tiz.

"Even the youngest phoenix," he said, looking at the charred tree. "They're sort of like a phoenix tree — if it's burned down or cut down, it rises again from its roots, or feet if you prefer."

Tiz picked up Pup Pup then rose from the ash-laden ground, dusting off the flakes from her own clothes. As she did she heard the roar of fire like a flamethrower — two newborn phoenixes flew from the remains of the tree, chirping loudly. Before Tiz could even blink they were nearly gone.

"Amazing," she said, reaching her own hand toward the tiny bright dots in the distance like they were stars. "Sky's the limit," she added. "Reach for the stars." Tiz gazed at their trail of smoke, wishing that she and Dargen could be the birds, flying all the way to the Wailing Woods. Standing there and watching them soar out of view gave her an idea.

Lightning crackled, lighting up the dark sky, closely followed by thunder.

"We have to get somewhere safe," she said. "A place that takes all kinds of kids — witches, nymphs, warlocks." Then, she lifted Pup Pup into the air and said, "Show him, boy."

Pup Pup shook his head as though he was shaking his favorite chew toy and when he stopped, he was holding a pamphlet in his mouth like it was a morning newspaper.

Tiz plucked it out and showed Dargen. "We have to get to here," she said.

"Mili-Tree Academy," read Dargen. "Safe from the other mothers." He glanced around. "A place where a certain mother bird wants her fledgling to go."

Tiz nodded. "Exactly how much magic do you know?" she asked.

"Straight A's," he said proudly.

"Good," she whispered. "At least one of us knows what they're doing. And it couldn't come at a better time. I need some stuff from my bedroom, but no one can know we're there. No one."

CHAPTER TWELVE — QUITE A COLORFUL PLAN

A STEADY RAINFALL TURNED the ash-laden ground of the Unburnable Forest into a messy paste. Tiz poked her string-staff into a burnt tree hollow to make sure no creature was living in it then motioned for Dargen and Pup Pup to join her inside. It reminded Tiz of all the times she'd huddled in a tree hollow with Sombra — how she missed her best friend, how she missed her family. Reuniting with them was now as important to her as having her own life tree.

She missed home and everything that came with it — the smell of cinnamon rolls on Sunday morning, hot cocoa in the evening, and even the twins. She missed it so much, she planned on going back home and no one was going to tell her otherwise. She didn't plan on staying, but if she was going to try to clear her name, it would have to start there. The Planting would be taking place shortly and she had to see it firsthand; it was an important piece of the puzzle.

Tiz told Dargen what Frenchy's mom had said after she accused Tiz of being a witch. In her best menacing French accent, Tiz said, "Zeh Unwithering One is the name of the witch's tree. And though her power grows as quickly as she, the witch cannot plant another tree."

Thunder rumbled outside.

"I have to go back," stressed Tiz. "I have to see which one of the planters can't grow a life tree."

A flash of light. Electricity forked across the stormy sky.

"Lightning," said Dargen. "It's just as dangerous as you going back. Is it worth it? Just to see who can grow a life tree?"

"It is," insisted Tiz. "It's as important as rain is to a tree. After a planter plants her heart seed then her life tree grows immediately, all the way to full size. At the same time, she merges with the tree trunk. After a few minutes, she separates, going back to her family and friends. The real witch won't be able to do that."

"Seedless," he said, "her heart seed is a fake, another life tree she cannot make, because she has one already, somewhere."

Tiz nodded. "We have to get back to the Wailing Woods," she said. "And the sooner the better, the Planting will be starting soon."

"But —," started Dargen.

"But nothing," said Tiz. "Plus, there's a million things I need from my room, clothes for starters, my emergency pack, and some money, from what I read, Mili-Tree Academy isn't free."

"Wait," said Dargen. "That reminds me." He stretched his robe pocket out like it was a dresser drawer. Reaching in, he pulled out a baseball glove, a football helmet with a fishing pole attached to it, and a crystal statue of a hawk. His pocket was a magical bag of holding. It was like a miniature bottomless pit.

"Whoa," said Tiz, watching all the cool things come out.

The last thing Dargen pulled out was a familiar ruby necklace and locket in the shape of a phoenix with illusionary flames rising from its wings. It was the one Mums had given Tiz to hold her heart seed. And if he didn't know that already, he might have been able to surmise it by the surprise in her widening eyes. "The mother bird," he whispered, "she left this with me, for her fledgling, to buy things at her new nest."

"The mother bird should have taken the fledgling there herself," replied Tiz.

"Impossible," said Dargen, "she couldn't. No, no, no — the other mother birds are like hawks, they wouldn't allow it. At the new nest, the fledgling would learn how to soar. Something they fear more than anything else. So the little bird will have to get there through another route." He offered the necklace again, closing his magical pocket. "Take it, please."

"Hold onto it," said Tiz sadly, wishing he could pull a life tree out of his pocket. Then a thought occurred to her. "Do you think you can fit my string-staff in there?" she asked.

"A zipper," he said, pulling one out of his pocket. "May I put it on your dress?"

"Um, I guess," she said, easing forward the end of her leafy skirt.

Dargen applied the zipper like a sticker and then unzipped it. "A bag of holding," he replied. "Squirrel away." He then dropped the necklace and pendant right in.

Tiz did the same with her string-staff, sliding it in. But the greatest thing about it, it didn't weigh her down at all.

"How about Pup Pup?" asked Tiz.

"Paws," said Dargen," he might rip the pocket."

"Hmm," pondered Tiz out loud. "Then he'll have to come with us."

"A tree door," said Dargen, "not a good idea. The other mothers might sense it in their bones like a coming storm."

"I wasn't going to use a tree door," she said, "unless there's an emergency of course, and we need to get out of there. So we better make sure I can open one, just in case. In fact, maybe I'll open a tree door to take us near my forest, but not too close."

"Risky," said Dargen, "like holding a lightning rod during a storm."

Tiz took Dargen by the hand then led him out of the hollow and into the rain. She pointed up at the crumbling tree homes in the charred treetops. "Do you see them?" she asked, squinting from the raindrops.

He nodded.

"Good," she said. "That's what my home will look like if you don't help me — and for me to have a chance, I need to see what's going on at the Planting. I also need my things."

His expression saddened as he looked down at his feet.

Tiz put a hand on his shoulder. "I need to find the real witch," she said. "And the Planting might be my best clue. Now do you understand why I have to go back?"

"The other mother birds," said Dargen, "they'll be angry with me if we get caught."

"Imagine what they'll do to me," said Tiz. "So we'll need disguises — good ones. Can you conjure some up? For Pup Pup too?"

"Eavesdropping," he said grimly. "What kind of disguises?"

Tiz smiled as she already had something in mind. Her grin was so mischievous that Dargen's eyes widened with worry.

Not long afterwards, Tiz opened her first tree door, risking it on a dying tree, but succeeding. She was so overjoyed that she gave Dargen a huge hug. She then promptly picked up Pup Pup with one hand and took Dargen by the other, leading them all through the glowing threshold.

She was glad to be leaving the dark and dreary forest behind as she transported them to Mr. Everly's farm across the road from the Wailing Woods, about twenty miles from her grove.

Tiz led Dargen and Pup Pup into a rickety old barn to explain the rest of the plan. As she passed by a garbage can, she glanced inside, stopped on a dime then back-tracked to it. Tiz unzipped her new pocket and pulled out her string-staff.

Reaching into the garbage can, she lifted out an ax head that was missing its handle. She took the ax head and slid it onto the bottom of her string-staff until it was nice and tight. "I'll add some resin later," she said, remembering that she had some in her emergency pack at home.

"Question," said Dargen, "what are you doing?"

"I have an ax to grind," said Tiz, plucking a string on her ominous-looking guitar.

CHAPTER TWELVE

"Violence," said Dargen. "It's not —"

"Not the answer," interrupted Tiz. "I know, but if we get caught, I'm going to give them a show. One they'll never forget." With that, Tiz opened her magical pocket and slid her new and improved "ax" back inside. Tiz decided it was best not to tell him what else she had in mind for the ax. For if she found the witch's tree and it wasn't what she'd hoped it would be, then she would indeed need a plan B (which in her mind stood for Battle-ax). But for now, she had another situation to deal with, one more pressing.

As Tiz laid out the rest of her original plan to Dargen there turned out to be a little hitch (at least it was minor in her mind). She'd been playing things by ear, making decisions as she went along, riding "the wave" so to speak. But the more that they discussed the plan, the more and more potentially dangerous the "little" hitch grew to be. Like say, getting your long scarf caught in a wood chipper kind of dangerous — if it unravels then you have some time to get away, but if you don't escape, oh boy.

Tiz explained to Dargen that she had been hoping he could turn the three of them into birds so they could watch the Planting up in a tree while quietly chirping to each other. That way, none of the other mothers could hear what they were saying. Tiz had even decided on a species of robin that was common to her forest to makes sure no one would suspect a thing.

It all sounded great coming out of her mouth, she had it all figured out, but there was just one tiny problem; the only bird Dargen could turn them into was a parrot.

"Red, orange or yellow," he said. "Which would you prefer?"

"You might as well turn us into flying elephants, ones with neon signs that have our names on them," replied Tiz.

Dargen looked at her with an expression that made it seem like he was tempted to try.

"The parrots will do," she said quickly. "Since you're already wearing red, I'll take orange, I just wish it wasn't the same color as a prison jump suit."

Tiz picked up Pup Pup and looked him in the eyes. "When you're a parrot," she said to him seriously, "no eating heart seeds, even if you're starving. Do you understand?"

Pup Pup licked her nose like it was a vanilla ice cream cone.

"That better not be a maybe," said Tiz. "Now let's do this."

The sensation of turning into a bird was just as weird as the look on Farmer Everly's face when he saw an orange parrot fly out of his barn, followed by a red one and then a yellow one, the last one, struggling to fly with what looked like bird seed pouring wildly out of its hind quarters underneath a late afternoon sun. The yellow one calmly circled, catching a mouthful of seeds as though it was perfectly normal, then resumed flying after the other two.

Flapping her wings as an orange parrot, Tiz saw Farmer Everly lean his rake against the barn wall. He adjusted his eye patch to make sure it was on right then he pulled out a silver flask from his overalls. He took a swig, a second, then a third. After a fourth, he resumed his raking, ending his takes from the flask. Living next to the Wailing Woods, he was probably used to seeing strange things, but this one was what he called a "quadruple take."

Flying over the forest, Tiz turned her keen eyes toward her family's grove, searching for her bedroom. She wanted her things, but secretly, she wanted to see her family even more, even the twins. She wasn't sure what she would say to her mother if she worked up the courage to confront her, but after abandoning her, Tiz had a few choice words in mind. Yet deep down, she hoped her mother would ask for her forgiveness then take her back. And if she did, then Tiz would gladly forget about her plan to head to Mili-Tree Academy.

CHAPTER TWELVE

As Tiz flew over the forest, she heard the rustle of leaves and the calls of birds. But it was what she didn't hear that worried her.

By now, she should have heard the chirps of flutes, the groans of violins, and the plinks of harps blending with the sounds of the forest. To Farmer Everly's ears they would have sounded like birds chirping, the wind rustling through the trees, and a running stream flowing through the forest. But not to Tiz. She would have recognized them as the music of the Great Seed Planting — sounds that weren't playing for some reason.

Spotting her family's grove, Tiz swooped down toward the phoenix tree that had been her home for the last thirteen years and circled around her bedroom, glimpsing in through an open window. It looked empty — a good sign. Excited, her little bird heart pounded so hard that she thought it was going to burst as she dove toward her room, one she was forbidden to return to by her mother.

Her room was once her safe haven, but now, it seemed like the most dangerous place in the world to her.

CHAPTER THIRTEEN — WHICH WITCH IS WHICH

FLAPPING HER WINGS, the orange parrot that was Tiz flew into her bedroom through a window, gliding carefully over three Cactus Cuties sitting on her sill — the lucky ones she hadn't destroyed while trying to flee from her mother with her broken heart seed during her misguided plan to fix it.

Skimming a cactus with her claws, nearly knocking it over, she landed on her toy chest, right by her emergency pack. She had managed to avoid one prickly situation so far. It was a good sign.

Behind her, the red and yellow parrots landed next to each other in an empty spot on the windowsill. Within seconds, the red parrot's eyes were glowing and Tiz felt her feathered skin begin to stretch like plastic wrap as she molted like crazy, transforming back to her normal self.

"Phew," whispered Tiz, plucking a feather from her mouth. She looked at the red parrot that was Dargen. "No wonder you have enough feathers to make a robe," she added, staring at what was now the second feathery mess she had made after cleaning her room with her little sisters. It brought back the fond memory of the pillow she tore apart in order to get to her heart seed and her pendant.

Tiz glanced around, wishing she could find a way to stay.

The red parrot looked at her and squawked, "You're a bird, I'm a boy."

"Shush," hushed Tiz. "You're a boy *and* a bird — a boy bird."

The red parrot flew toward her bed. "Squawk, you're a bird," it repeated as it landed on her headboard with the name "TIZ PHOENIX" engraved in big letters.

The red parrot even reminded her of a phoenix. "Okay, so

you're right," she admitted.

The red parrot flew back to the windowsill, squawking proudly.

"Shhh," shushed Tiz as she grabbed her emergency pack and tiptoed around the room, just in case. She gathered the things she wanted to bring with her — mole mittens, her bear-track slippers, money — shoving them all inside her pack.

"Squawk, hurry up, hurry up," said the red parrot.

"All right already," said Tiz.

Suddenly, the door to her room flew open and her twin sisters backed in with boxes, as if one of them was moving in.

When the twins turned and saw Tiz they dropped their cargo, squealing like they'd seen a ghost.

Tiz covered their mouths, but not in time.

"GIRLS! IS EVERYTHING ALL RIGHT UP THERE?" yelled Mums from the kitchen below.

Tiz put a finger to her lips, urging her little sisters to stay quiet.

The twins stared past Tiz toward the red parrot as his skin started to stretch, his feathers turned into a robe and his beak shrunk into a broad nose. The look in their eyes seemed to say, "AND she brought a BOY into her room too."

Pup Pup, still a yellow parrot squawked, "He's a boy, not a bird."

It was almost too much for the twins to handle. Their faces scrunched like they were holding back a sneeze. Tiz knew they were fighting the urge to tattle. It was like asking guard dogs not to bark at intruders. It was what made the twins the twins.

Finally, Verruca glanced at the box she dropped and yelled, "We're fine Mums! Something just dropped by the windowsill!"

"Yeah, dropped by the windowsill!" added Vervain, less enthused, as if getting her own room was now slipping through her fingers as quickly as the boxes she had dropped.

"IF IT'S NO GOOD ANYMORE, MAKE SURE YOU THROW IT OUT, BE CAREFUL!" added Mums.

"We know!" yelled the twins in unison.

Dargen *squawked* loudly. "After effects," he said. "*Squawk*, of the spell." He covered his mouth. "It should go away soon — *squawk*!"

"*You* should go away soon," grumbled Vervain in a hushed voice. "You're gonna get us in a lot of trouble."

"You're the ones in trouble," whispered Tiz. "It hasn't even been a day, and you're already moving into my room?"

"It's not what it looks like," insisted Vervain, "we're trying to help you. We're setting up base here."

"WHO ARE YOU TALKING TO UP THERE?" yelled Mums.

Vervain looked at Dargen. "A bird!" she yelled. "It won't go away!"

"He's a boy, not a bird," squawked the yellow parrot.

Tiz shushed Tweety Pup as she picked up a book that had spilled from one of the boxes the twins had been carrying. She read the title: *Which Witch is Which.*

"Where did you find this?" asked Tiz.

"Mums's library," said Verruca, "please don't tell her we borrowed it."

"I haven't told her that you broke my heart seed," said Tiz, "have I?" Then a thought hit Tiz like a truck. "Wait a minute, what other stuff are you hiding?" she asked.

But Tiz didn't wait for an answer. With her emergency pack on her back, she tucked the book under her arm and bolted up the stairs, heading for the twins' bedroom.

The little monsters were right behind her, followed by Dargen and Tweety Pup.

Tiz threw open the twins' bedroom door. "What the heck?" she exclaimed. The walls were covered with mass-produced versions of her mole mittens, bear-track slippers and worst of all, cheap imitations of Pup Pup — poodle versions with bright pink bows. Tweety Pup landed on her shoulder and whistled at them like they were a bunch of pretty girls. They all woke up, barking like a pack of startled Chihuahuas!

"QUIET!" yelled Vervain as the twins shoved their way into their bedroom, spreading their arms so their older sister couldn't get past.

Tiz glared at them. "Are you two crazy?" she whispered. "You're mass-producing your own Pup Pup? Did Mums enchant these?"

"Uh-huh, but please don't be mad," said Verruca meekly.

"And we're not mass-producing anything," argued Vervain. "We're artisans, we hand craft each one from start to finish."

Tiz pushed her way past her little sisters and walked over to an enchanted poodle puppet then read its label. "Made in Guristonia? Where the heck is that?" she demanded, watching the ear fall off the puppet as it yelped. "Forget it, I don't even want to know. You can keep your poodle puppets."

"They're called Pupp Pupps, with two *p's*," added Verruca. "Correct me if I'm wrong, but your version only has one."

"Oh I'll give you a *P*," said Tiz, making a fist to punch her little sister. "And I'll plant it right on your nose where you can see it."

The poodles started barking.

"You better muzzle those things," warned Tiz as Tweety Pup flew from her shoulder to seek the safety of Dargen's.

"The muzzle's sold separately," replied Vervain, making their older sister even angrier.

"Wait!" begged Verruca. "You wouldn't hit an artisan, would you?"

"Stop!" insisted Vervain. "We're selling them to help you!"

"For your 'Innocence Fund'," added Verruca. "We need money to help you — it's called a war chest — you can keep all of it if you want."

Tiz stopped. She took a deep breath as she stepped back.

Vervain eased forward. "Listen sis, we really *are* trying to help you, that's why we borrowed the book," she insisted, pointing at the one under Tiz's arm. "I swear, just like we promised we would, but we were afraid that Mums might search our room and find the book here. But if she found it in your room, then it wouldn't be such a big — never mind."

Tiz gave them the stink eye as she opened the book. But she had no time to read it. "What's it about?" she asked, handing the book to Verruca.

"It has a chapter about *her*," whispered Verruca.

"Tell me," insisted Tiz. "Tell me everything you know."

"Well," said Verruca nervously. "It says the witch dies, but her tree never does. The tree sounds meaner than the witch."

"I know," said Tiz. "What else does it say?"

"When the young witch returns, she has to win her tree back," said Verruca. "She has to train and get stronger. To reclaim the tree she has to prove herself worthy. She has to reestablish her full link to her tree to complete the bond."

Verruca flipped to the chapter about the witch. At the top of it there was a symbol Tiz recognized immediately — a burning tree. Some of its branches ended in dragon heads, making it looked like a mythical beast called a hydra. Within the treetop sat a twisting tower encased in thorns.

"The mark of the witch," said Verruca uneasily as she lowered her finger to a sentence below and read, "Reach the top of the tower and claim the living key, unlock its power to gain the witch's tree."

"Then that settles it," said Tiz. "Whoever the real witch is, I have to stop her."

"There's more," said Verruca. "It says, 'Should you so desire, you can change your destiny, bathe the recipient of the living key in fire, and unmake the Unwithering Tree.'"

"Whoa," said Tiz, "so it *can* be destroyed."

Dargen nodded as Tweety Pup squawked, reminding Tiz

of something.

"Why can't I just fly to the top," asked Tiz, imagining herself again as a parrot. "Like with a magic broom or something?"

Dargen shook his head "no." "A dark cave," he said. "The tree is inside of one. A tight one. And its twisted tower rises between the stone. Besides, if you didn't climb the tree, it would know and the door to the tower wouldn't open."

"*Great*," sighed Tiz.

"Tell her about the *Nine*," said Vervain.

Verruca began reading again. "Once the witch has returned," she said, trying not to look at Tiz. "Eight more candidates, all tree nymphs who haven't planted yet, are chosen to challenge the witch for her tree. After the choices are made, the witch and the eight candidates together are collectively known as the *Nine Climbers*. If a candidate reaches the top and figures out the living key before the witch — proving herself worthy, then she can claim the tree for herself, or destroy it."

"It's a competition?" asked Tiz.

"Training," said Dargen, "one of the darker purposes of Mili-Tree Academy. Throughout history, it's where the Nine have always gone. The counselors there help them find the tree. Without the academy, no one would ever reach the top."

"Nine climbers?" asked Tiz. "Why nine?"

"I know why," said Vervain. "The witch and the eight candidates always come from the nine oldest families of tree nymphs," she explained. "The Oaks, the Blackthorns, the Yews, the Hollies, the Alders, the Rowans, the Phoenixes, the Elms and the Willows."

Sombra! thought Tiz, remembering the biggest day of her best friend's life. "The Planting," she said, "why aren't you there?"

"It's over," said Vervain as if Tiz should have known.

"Most of the planters didn't plant," said Verruca.

Tiz bit her nail, thinking. "I bet I know why too," she said as her eyes widened with realization. "So the witch could hide her fake seed."

"Maybe," said Dargen. "But that's not all. The tree nymphs that have a real heart seed, but didn't plant on purpose, now have a chance to claim the witch's tree. They wouldn't be able to do it if they already had their own life tree."

"Well, that's not the reason some mothers gave," said Verruca.

"Then what?" insisted Tiz.

Verruca scrunched her face as though the words she was about to say were as sour as a lemon. She tried to say something but nothing came out, so she just pointed at Tiz.

"Me?" said Tiz.

"They were afraid you'd come back," said Vervain, fidgeting. "Crazy right? Since we *definitely* didn't see you here."

Tiz grew silent as she sat down on one of her sister's beds.

Dargen sat next to her. "The witch's tree," he said, "a chance to claim it only comes around once in a life time, even for your kind."

Tiz looked even sadder. "I'm one of the best climbers in the forest," she said. "So I bet they always wanted me out of the way. But why would you want the witch's tree in the first place?"

"Power," said Dargen. "Some believe they could use it to save the world."

"Can they?" asked Tiz anxiously.

"A tiger," said Dargen, "can it change its stripes?"

Tiz imagined herself petting a sleeping tiger as she gently painted one of its stripes green. The tiger woke and snapped at her. Could she change the tree? Maybe. But what would her family and friends think of her if she tried to claim it?

Tiz looked at the twins. "What about Sombra?" she asked.

"She's the only one that planted," said Verruca.

"Her mom didn't want her to," said Vervain, "she was furious."

"But Sombra insisted you were her best friend," said Verruca, "and that she had nothing to be afraid of."

"But she was afraid," argued Vervain, "afraid of being a candidate for the witch's tree."

Tiz recalled her conversation with Sombra the day before, when they were hunting for truffles. Sombra had talked about using the "right kind of magic" so her and Tiz could live forever, joining the witch and becoming "the Unwithering Three." But when a cold wind rushed in at those very words, wilting the flowers at their feet, Sombra didn't look too keen on that idea anymore.

Vervain cleared her throat, gaining Tiz's attention. "She didn't want to be *her*," insisted Vervain. "That's why she planted."

"And in a hurry too," said Verruca. "Before the storm clouds could ruin the ceremony."

"What about her tree?" asked Tiz anxiously, "did it turn out okay?"

"Well, one part did," said Verruca sadly, "her tree did."

"Don't joke about it," said Tiz sternly. "What do you mean just her tree?"

"She's still stuck inside of it," said Vervain nervously, "and they're blaming you."

CHAPTER FOURTEEN — VENTING AND LAMENTING

TIZ REMEMBERED HEARING her little sister say that Sombra was still stuck inside her life tree, but after that it was a blur. She could not have cared less about what was said afterwards either. In fact, she wanted to get to where her friend was trapped in her new tree so badly, she risked something she would have never done with a clear mind. She used her mother's life tree to open a tree door near Sombra's tree.

To Mums, it was the equivalent of setting off a burglar alarm. *It fits in a way*, thought Tiz, as she darted through the magical door with her emergency pack stuffed full of goodies, including a certain book from her mother's library. She was in a hurry to see her best friend, not caring who knew or who followed.

Tiz leapt out of a tree door that glowed in the night on the side of a willow tree. She turned around and saw Sombra's new life tree. Tiz gasped as she dropped her emergency pack. Sombra was frozen in the trunk of her tree like a wooden statue. Her mouth was on the verge of screaming as if she'd seen a monster that could petrify her.

The leaves around Tiz spiraled up in a sudden wind. They formed an image she'd seen once before that was comprised by the blowing ashes of her heart seed — an old crone with a hooked nose. Cackling laughter filled Tiz's ears as the spirit of the witch taunted her once again, pointing to a spot on Sombra's tree. The leaves fell and the wind faded as quickly as it came. Trembling, Tiz saw something on the tree bark that she hadn't noticed before.

She inched closer, afraid, her hands shaking. She looked at the spot. There, emblazoned into the bark of Sombra's tree, her prison, was a symbol she'd just seen in her mother's book — the burning tree, the Unwithering One.

"No," said Tiz, growing angry. "It can't be." *That's why they're blaming me*, she thought.

It was personal now — her heart seed was gone, her mother disowned her, and now the real witch was trying to take her best friend.

As if that wasn't bad enough, things had been piled under Sombra's life tree as if she'd been hit by a car near the edge of a road and died on the spot. There were funeral wreathes, little purple teddy bears and giant cards telling her how much they missed her. Well, if they missed her so much, why weren't they doing something about it? Were some of them getting her out of the way too? Maybe they *all* were.

Tiz flushed red with rage. She started kicking over the wreathes and ripping up the giant cards. She punted a plush purple teddy bear so far it landed in Sombra's mother's treetop, startling the woman inside.

"What's going on out there!" yelled Gertrude Willow.

It snapped Tiz out of her tantrum.

She had been so mad that she hadn't even noticed the twins and Dargen, with Tweety Pup on his shoulder, watching her.

A tidal wave of emotion suddenly swept over her, flooding her eyes with tears.

Tiz fell to her knees, sobbing underneath the weeping willow tree imprisoning Sombra. She gazed up at the terrified wooden statue of her as though it stood at death's door. That was her best friend in there. How can you just leave your best friend at their greatest time of need? The answer is you don't. You roll up your sleeves and get to work. But even though Tiz now had an ax, she couldn't just cut her out. No, instead, she needed time, time to figure it out.

Tiz grasped the frail hand of the girl she'd gone truffle hunting with just the other day. A friend who risked her own heart seed to try and save another's. The only girl who stood by her side when Marie Yew accused her of being a witch. "Please, don't leave me," pleaded Tiz, her emerald eyes welling, "please, don't leave me too."

But nothing happened. It was the lowest Tiz had ever felt. Her words had no effect. But she remembered what Mums had told her. Her voice had been quivering, shaking like a leaf. She had to gain control of it. She had to channel all her emotion into it, focusing her sorrow.

Slowly, Tiz began singing the lament she learned for the Planting. There were no words, only tones, ancient in nature, low and woeful, but just as beautiful as they were sorrowful.

As she sang, she didn't notice the other tree nymph families coming down from their tree homes. She didn't care. Focusing on her lament, she kept holding the hand of her friend, knowing this might be the last time she ever did.

Throughout the Wailing Woods her mournful tones filled the air, carrying a message to Sombra.

"*Come back*," they pleaded. "*Follow my voice*," they begged, "*Come back.*"

Behind Tiz, Mums arrived nearby, leaping out of a tree door. She stood and watched her daughter in amazement, as though entranced by her child's song.

Sombra's mother dropped down from the lowest branch of her willow tree, looking worried. She stared at Tiz as if she meant to pull her away. But before she could Mums held Gertrude Willow back.

By now, tree nymphs from every family began forming a wide circle around the tree, listening. Any fear they had of Tiz seemed to dissipate for the time being like a fog in the morning sunlight. And to their surprise, they saw something radiating from Tiz; a red glow pulsated from her heart. It was as if her heart seed had never been broken, only traveled somewhere else.

A host of tree nymphs now stood in a circle around Tiz, Dargen, Pup Pup and the twins, watching in awe, but more importantly, listening to an angel.

But it was Mums who was the first to join in the singing. She took Gertrude Willow's hand and Joy Holly's on her other side. They too joined in. And one by one, so did the remaining tree nymphs, Dargen too, even Pup Pup sung as a bird. No words, just tones that were not only heard, but also felt deep down inside as if a loved one had been lost.

The beauty emanating from the Wailing Woods traveled miles away. In his farmhouse, Mr. Everly sat in front of his TV, tears pouring down his cheeks as he took a sad and lonely swig from his flask. Watching him from across the room, two pet ravens on a perch cawed at him. They flew to his shoulders as he pulled out a handkerchief. Farmer Everly wiped his cheeks and dried his eye patch while listening to the lament. Outside his window, his corn crop was growing unnaturally fast, as though he had planted magical seeds.

Tiz, completely unaware of anything else around her, squeezed Sombra's cold and lifeless hand. Nothing. Tiz lost hope. As she was about to let go, the most amazing thing she'd ever felt happened — Sombra squeezed back.

The chorus rose, becoming so loud and powerful that the leaves began to shake.

Tiz looked up.

Cracks rippled through Sombra's bark-like skin faster than fissures in an earthquake.

Tiz sung louder as she saw a blue heart begin to glow and beat in the chest of her friend, not unlike the red one pulsing in her own. Tiz grabbed Sombra's arm with both hands as tears of joy now rained down her face. And as if the sky sensed it, it rumbled, crying as well.

Tiz stared at her friend. "Come back!" she yelled, pulling with all her might. "Come back!"

Sombra's body creaked and groaned inside her willow tree as Tiz anchored her feet against the trunk, doubling her effort.

Crack! Tiz pulled Sombra free! Both of them fell to the

ground — Sombra on top of Tiz.

Tiz wiped sap from her friend's face.

"Y-you found me..." stammered Sombra weakly.

Tiz smiled. "I found you," she said, hugging her friend. Together they lay there in the night, their hearts glowing like two halves of the same moon.

Tiz glanced to the side. Her reunion with Sombra looked like it was going to be a short one as she helped her best friend to her feet. They stood in the middle of the circle of mothers near Sombra's life tree in the dark of night as it drizzled. Nearby, Dargen fidgeted nervously with Tweety Pup's feathers as the twins slowly backed up and blended with the rest of the tree nymph families.

But Tiz wasn't afraid. Helping her friend overcome adversity gave her courage. She picked up one of the remaining "funeral" teddy bears and threw it at Gertrude Willow.

"You should be ashamed of yourself," she said then scanned the rest of the mothers. "All of you, abandoning her like that." Tiz narrowed her eyes at Mums. "Especially you."

Mums tried to say something, but a weird noise came out instead.

Tiz shook her head, disappointed, then turned to Sombra. "I'm going now," she said. "And I'm never coming back."

"Take me with you," begged Sombra, steadying herself. "I never want to see another tree as long as I live. A city, let's go to a city."

"You need to stay here, with your family," said Tiz, "with your tree."

"No," begged Sombra. "Please, don't leave me here, alone."

That plea had more meaning to Tiz than Sombra would ever realize. How could she just leave her there? Especially after what Mums had done to her.

"Okay then," said Tiz. "Let's go."

"Excuse me," squealed Gertrude Willow. "Where exactly do you think you're going?"

"Indeed!" barked Marie Yew in her thick French accent as she pushed her way through the crowd. "Zeh Willow girl stays here!"

"Stay back!" shouted Sombra, picking up one of the plush toys around her — a pink unicorn broomstick horse. She pointed its stuffed horn toward Marie Yew and the other mothers, holding them back like she held a sword, oblivious to how ridiculous it looked.

Unbeknownst to Sombra, from behind, Tiz pulled out her ax to support her friend.

All the other tree nymphs gasped.

But to Sombra, it looked like they were afraid of her toy unicorn, pink riding bridal and all.

"That's right," said Sombra, jabbing it at them. "You mess with me and my unicorn — you get the horn." She jabbed it in their direction a few more times, just for good measure.

Tiz picked up her emergency pack then eased Sombra over to her life tree. Dargen joined them with Tweety Pup. All three quickly put their hands on the tree. But as Sombra did, she seemed more afraid of her own willow tree than anything Marie Yew had to say.

"I SAID ZEH WILLOW GIRL STAYS HERE!" yelled Marie Yew as if shouting it would make them stop.

"LET THEM GO!" yelled Mums, finding her voice as she looked at her daughter. "I'm sorry, Tiz. I'm sorry for everything."

Tiz couldn't look at her mom. She took Dargen's hand and Dargen took Sombra's, who looked at him strangely, like someone trying to remember where they'd seen a certain person before. But before Sombra could say a word, Tiz counted to *tree* and pulled her friends into a magic door, trying to escape from the only home she'd ever known, fleeing those she loved but now also feared.

CHAPTER FIFTEEN — IGGY CITY

AMID THE DARK OF NIGHT, Tiz led Sombra, Dargen and Tweety Pup out of a glowing tree door and into the Unburnable Forest. Once there, Tiz didn't waste any time, she used her ax to carve a picture of a door into the bark of the tree they emerged from then slashed an "X" through it to seal it off.

"Just in case they change their mind," said Tiz to her friends.

Holding the pink unicorn broomstick horse, Sombra stared at Tiz's new ax — its blade and its glowing strings. "Whoa, that thing you're holding, it sure has a lot going on with it," she said.

Tiz glanced at Sombra's pink unicorn hobby horse. With an ornate horn atop its head, its mane sparkled with glitter and its snout was adorned with a bright pink bridle. "So says the girl with the sparkling unicorn," she replied, squeezing its plush neck where a sticker said, "Press Here." Out came a loud galloping sound, reminding her of their escape. After what seemed like forever, the galloping stopped and was followed by three long, high-pitched whinnies from the toy, finishing with a short, exasperated exhale that sounded like vibrating lips.

Silence. They all looked at each other and started laughing.

"I thought it was never gonna end," said Sombra.

"The toy? Or you being stuck in your tree?" asked Tiz.

"Both," laughed Sombra. "But I'd rather listen to Pink Unicorn all day, if you know what I mean."

Tiz hugged her friend, glad to have her back and out of her life tree. No longer requiring the services of her new ax, Tiz unzipped her magic pocket and slid it inside.

CHAPTER FIFTEEN

Sombra watched in amazement, still a bit wobbly on her feet. "Do you think you can fit Pink Unicorn in there?" she asked.

Tiz nodded as she stretched the pocket out, allowing Sombra to slide the broomstick horse right in.

After that, they all leaned against the tree as Tiz took the time to fill Sombra in on everything that happened.

"A city," mentioned Sombra afterwards, shivering like she was sick. "One with no trees. That's where we should go."

Sombra was suffering from tree separation illness. It happened to all planters that traveled too far away from their new life tree too quickly — whether they liked their new tree or not.

"Um, cities have trees," said Tiz finally, putting an arm around her friend.

"Then a city with lots of lights," said Sombra. "So I can see them coming."

Tiz pulled out the pamphlet for Mili-Tree Academy and held it out in front of Sombra. "Sorry," she said, "more trees, and one that I need to find badly."

"The witch's tree," answered Dargen.

At the sound of those words, the pamphlet Tiz held glowed red for a second. But only she seemed to see it. Sombra was busy staring at Dargen as though she had just noticed him for the first time, probably because of the illness.

"Who's he?" asked Sombra, seeming a bit more aware of her surroundings.

Dargen extended his hand. "Dargen Darkshir, Warlock, tenth class," he said. "Nice to meet you."

Sombra ignored his outstretched hand.

"He's helping me," said Tiz. "My mom asked him to."

Sombra squinted at Dargen then her eyes widened with realization. "You're that boy — the one that stands under trees and catches falling eggs."

Dargen bowed deep.

Sombra said nothing.

He looked right at her. "Egg number two," he said, "I guess that's you."

"I'm not falling from a tree," insisted Sombra. "Well, at least not right now. And you didn't catch me either, it was Tiz."

"A gold star," said Dargen. "Tiz gets one for catching you. I must have taught her well."

Sombra frowned at him as Tiz slid between them, holding the pamphlet up to her best friend again.

"Mili-Tree Academy, I know," sighed Sombra. "In some ways, it's kind of a city, but more like a prison. No...scratch that, going to prison would be a lot better than having to —"

"Untrue," interrupted Dargen. "Don't listen to —"

"Don't interrupt me," interrupted Sombra. "*And* don't tell my best friend what to do, that's *my* job," she added, sticking her tongue out at him.

"Please," said Tiz. "Can you both try to be nice to each other. I know you're both just watching out for me, but please."

Sombra crossed her arms. "*Anyhow*, " she said. "What I was trying to say, *before* I was rudely interrupted, is that my mom threatens to enroll me there every year. And whenever I get in real big trouble, she takes me on a tour of the academy. She calls it a 3-D warning. But guess what?"

"She never follows through..." said Tiz.

"Shocking, right?" said Sombra. "Until now that is. She's probably filling out the paperwork as we speak — Dear Sir or Madam, please accept one runaway daughter. Yuck, what a waste of paper," she added, scratching her head. "Oh yeah, but that reminds me, can I see the pamphlet?"

Tiz hesitated, moving the pamphlet out of Sombra's reach. "You're not gonna rip it up, are you?" she asked.

Sombra gave her "the look" so Tiz lent it to her best friend. Then Sombra promptly tore it into three pieces.

Tiz smacked herself in the forehead.

Sombra offered two of the three pieces in her outstretched hand as they started glowing an eerie green in the darkness. "The pamphlet has a built in trick," she said. "Any brat that rips it up gets sent there automatically. For me, it's better than having to listen to my mother lecture me, *blah, blah, blah,* all the way there. Here, take a piece, hurry."

Dargen took one. But Tiz looked at the last glowing piece like a ticket to a loop-de-loop roller coaster with no seat belts.

It was her last chance to change her mind, to forget her plan and go somewhere else. She didn't really want to go to Mili-Tree Academy. That hadn't changed. But deep down inside, she knew that any other path would lead to nowhere good in the end. Even if she found the witch's tree on her own, she wouldn't know how to climb it. And what if the other mothers found her first?

No way, she couldn't risk that again. Mili-Tree Academy would at least protect her from Marie Yew and the other moms.

But above all, Tiz wanted her life back. Climbing the witch's tree was more than just about finding out what was at the top of its tower and trying to satisfy her insatiable curiosity. It was about saving her friends and family. But to Tiz, even that was just the tip of the iceberg. It was also about regaining a normal life and maybe even winning her own life tree. She knew the last two were both selfish things, but she wanted them nonetheless. And if she helped save the world in the process, well, what an immense bonus.

With that in mind, Tiz grabbed the last glowing piece, hoping she could fulfill her new quest to conquer the witch's tree.

Tweety Pup squawked in approval as he flew to her shoulder. "Here we go, here we go," he repeated, flapping his wings.

Tiz took a deep breath then grabbed Sombra and Dargen

by the hand. They would be her handlebars for the scary ride ahead — a daunting journey into the unknown — her mountain to climb, so to speak.

A light flashed below their feet. Cosmic stardust flew up all around them, encasing them in a thick transparent tree root similar to the magic tunnels beyond the tree doors, but bigger, and growing up toward the clouds like a magical beanstalk.

A sucking sound came from the top of the tunnel like an invisible cloud giant was drinking from an enormous straw, making their hair and feathers stand straight up.

With a flash, the four of them glowed like beams of light and shot toward the sky through the glowing tunnel. They passed through the highest clouds in less than a millionth of a second, rushing into the blackness of outer space — their cheeks rippling from the force as they yelled, "AAAAAAAH!"

Tiz soon realized they were rocketing through the roots of the Great Cosmic Tree, the one the ancient Vikings called Yggdrasil (ig-dr*uh*-sil) and whom the tree nymphs called Iggy Stardust, for short. That's right, they thought of it as a person, for every tree nymph viewed a tree as they would their brother or sister. To them, Iggy was a rock star. Likewise, where they were headed to was considered the rock star of Mili-Tree Academies by every single mother with a bratty child.

Flying through space faster than the speed of light, Tiz tried to focus on the dizzying journey. When she had fallen in love with the phrase *reach for the stars* at the age of four, she never imagined she'd experience them in such a spectacular way. It was like seeing a million firework displays to the music of Mozart, but even so, nothing could truly describe what she was witnessing.

The universe seemed to have a voice, singing softly at first, then rising as they left the solar system and streaked past one last icy sphere — the demoted dwarf planet called Pluto.

Flying through the Milky Way Galaxy she realized that the

singer and orchestra weren't merely in her mind as she watched Dargen bobbing his head to the beat. The music emanated from the stardust tunnel, playing louder and louder as it erupted into a roar along with a symphony of explosions. As though inspired by the bangs and booms, the angelic voice began singing one word over and over — *Lacrimosa.*

Tiz turned to Dargen. "What does that mean?" she asked.

"Weeping," he said, wiping his eyes. "From the beauty."

As the four of them gained speed, they streaked through stellar nurseries called molecular clouds, glimmering like rainbows, nurturing their young suns. The growing star clusters were like families, and watching them made Tiz miss her own even more.

In a nanosecond they passed out the other end. Here, there was a bleakness to outer space, a chilly and dark side. The music became somber and foreboding, reflecting the gloominess.

To her left, Tiz spotted a cloud of gas and cosmic dust glowing an eerie blue from the light of a distant star of the same color. The cloud looked like a witch's face from the side — long nose, big chin and a pointy cap you couldn't miss. Unbeknownst to Tiz, some astronomers called it the Witch Head Nebula. But based on how it looked, the *Evil* Witch Head Nebula would have been more accurate.

For a moment, it appeared as though the eye on the side of its face was following her, its pupil watching her every move. But after she blinked, the eye was nothing more than a cloud again. Staring at it, Tiz realized that the witch and her tree would be much more than just deadly adversaries. Like the eerie nebula, together, they would be a force of nature on a cosmic scale, their power reaching farther than her own eyes could ever see.

"Look," said Dargen, pointing ahead as the four of them slowed, gliding through the stardust tree instead of rocketing.

In the distance was a huge transparent bubble that

reminded Tiz of a gigantic snow globe. Its centerpiece looked like the stardust tree they were flying through, but inside the bubble, the roots, trunk and branches of the tree solidified into an ebony bark nearly as dark as the black of space around it.

It would have been almost impossible to see if it wasn't for the stardust peppering the ebony celestial tree, making it seem like they were flying into a huge city at night in the shape of a giant ash tree that was pruned like a bonsai tree.

As they drew closer, Tiz realized that some of the stardust spots were actually windows with all manner of beings and creatures moving past them inside the tree, ones of vastly different shapes and sizes, some even crawling on all fours.

"Behold!" said Dargen quite dramatically, gazing proudly at the sparkling Mili-Tree Academy. "The splendor that lies before your eyes is the one and only Yggdrasil Citadel!"

"It's called Iggy City for short," insisted Sombra like she'd spent her entire life there rather than just getting a few tours.

Gawking, Tiz barely heard. She was staring at nine huge magical spheres orbiting Iggy City. All were attached to the tree by mystical vines, allowing them to swivel around the roots and branches like some sort of magical model of a solar system that a wizard would love to have in his laboratory.

The three orbiting spheres at the top of Iggy City were bright and filled with light — one gold, one green and one light blue. The three in the middle each consisted of a separate primal element — one flaming with fire, one frozen in ice, and right in the middle, one that resembled the planet Earth. The three on the bottom, near the roots, were varying shades of black. The lowest and darkest one swirled with a white mist that formed a skull so grim that Tiz got queasy just looking at it.

"What's with the spheres?" asked Tiz.

"Portals," said Dargen. "To the nine realms of existence. See the very middle one that looks like Earth? Well, here it's called Midgard, but never mind, it leads to our world. The other ones lead to realms in different universes."

"Cool," said Tiz, "I wonder if there's a Miss Universe Pageant in each one — I could probably sell them some jewelry at a good price or do some fancy truffle catering, wow, now I can't wait to go."

"Unlikely," said Dargen, "they're off limits to new cadets, so pretend like you didn't see them."

Tiz wasn't exactly sure how she was going to put nine giant spheres out of her mind, especially ones orbiting the place she would be living in. But as they drew closer to the tree-city, she turned her attention toward twenty-six large objects spread out all over the tree while hanging from its branches like fruits. In fact, that's what they resembled.

The outside of each giant fruit had a working clock face with visible moving gears, giving the fruit an antique look, like an old pocket watch. Each clock had twenty-four numbers instead of twelve, one for each hour of a normal Earth day. It was called military time and a "00" at the top of each clock instead of a "12" marked the start of morning. Tiz realized it would come in handy since there were a billion tiny suns outside but no typical sunrise. And without there being any night or day, it would be better to have a clock face with twenty-four hours instead of twelve.

As they flew closer, Tiz saw that the clock-like fruit farthest to her left was an enormous apple, ten times the size of her mother's tree home, but just like it, had cozy little windows. Next to it was a banana home that looked just as welcoming. As her eyes kept drifting to the next one, she realized the antique fruit-like dwellings were in alphabetical order, ending on the far right with a Zucchini (heck yeah it's a fruit).

"Mili-Tree Barracks," said Dargen. "Alphabetically, 'A' through 'Z', one for each company of cadets, just like the units in the military. Each of us gets assigned to one."

"Which one are you in?" asked Tiz, assuming that he

would be in D Company because his name was Dargen Darkshir.

But instead of pointing to the Dragonfruit which she assumed stood for "D", he steered her eyes to a rather ominous looking fruit at the far end, one that looked like a fang and was blood red. Tiz recognized it immediately. "Wolfberry," she said.

"W Company," he added. "And that's our barracks."

"*Our* barracks?" she questioned.

"Alphabetically," he said. "Warlocks and witches — that's us — and they both go in W Company. Boys and girls, separate barracks of course, especially for the werewolves."

Tiz didn't like the sound of that at all as she stared at W Company's dormitory. As she did, she noticed a small hatch open at the bottom and something eject out of it like an escape pod, floating toward them in zero gravity. It looked like an emergency raft made out of wood, but with two levels instead of one. As it got closer, Tiz realized that it was a bunk bed with two girls that were using broomsticks like boat paddles, stroking frantically to escape.

"What in the world?" said Tiz.

But before Dargen could answer, something ticking and clicking crawled out of a window of Iggy City, a mechanical creature just as big as the drifting bunk bed. It resembled a giant flying squirrel made out of what looked like left over pieces that they used to make the clocks. It glared at the escaping witches as its eyes rang like the bells atop an old-fashion alarm clock and while a little wind-up bird popped out of its nose screaming, "Cuckoo, cuckoo..."

Tiz would find out later that the clockwork squirrel was called a *boarder hoarder* because it scooped up any nuts trying to escape the academy. The ticking beast leapt into the zero gravity inside the bubble, flying after the escapees, who had a good head start.

The fleeing witches started paddling twice as fast. Their

bunk bed hit the bubble surrounding Iggy City, stretching it.

Tiz gasped. She feared that if it popped then the kids would suffocate and freeze in outer space. Could it be that bad at the academy?

The bunk bed kept stretching the bubble until it formed a smaller sphere around them, allowing them to enter space.

But by then, the hoarder had caught up, snagging their bubble like a giant acorn and pulling them back inside the larger one protecting Iggy City. The hoarder then burst the witches' bubble, and in more ways than one by the look on their faces.

Tiz looked at Dargen. "Is it that bad there?" she asked.

"Discipline," he replied. "Follow every rule, and you won't look like a fool. That's the motto."

But following rules wasn't Tiz's strength and she knew it better than anyone.

"Cuckoo!" bellowed the boarder hoarder as it shoved the bunk bed with the girls back inside the wolfberry-shaped barracks.

"Don't say that I didn't warn you," said Sombra. "Prison would be better."

"Cuckoo," muttered Tiz miserably as they flew through the huge outer bubble and toward Iggy City — a crazy choice, but in the end, her own choice. One she was now regretting as the stardust tunnel they were traveling through steered them toward two large and immovable-looking doors in the tree trunk, just above the roots of the glimmering tree fortress. To her, the academy looked nearly impossible to enter, let alone, escape from. But what if things went terribly wrong there and she had to try to get away? What if there was a dire emergency? Especially, if she got on the wrong side of someone, like *the witch*? What then?

CHAPTER SIXTEEN — STRANGE COMPANY

TIZ LANDED IN FRONT OF THE ACADEMY DOORS with Tweety Pup still on her shoulder, right by Dargen and Sombra. The red-robed warlock raised a fist to knock, but before he got the chance, a peephole blinked to life in the form of an eyeball.

"You're late," said an old man with a squeaky voice from behind the doors. The eyeball shut then disappeared as the doors slowly creaked open like a casket in a haunted house.

Standing in the doorway was the oddest old man Tiz had ever seen. His right arm was like a magical gadget knife, with a screwdriver, a bottle opener and scissors, just to name a few. He wore a monocle over his right eye while a tangled mess of white hair covered his left, not unlike a mad scientist that loved to play with electricity. His black uniform was as dark as the cosmic tree with a vast array of medals that glistened like stardust. "Very late indeed," he stressed.

"Very late, very late," squawked Tweety Pup.

The old man trained his monocle upon the yellow parrot. "Well, well, what do we have here..." he said, studying Tweety Pup as his monocle began to glow. "Ah yes, make like a tree and *bark*."

Tweety Pup gave out a bark as he changed back into Pup Pup, tumbling from Tiz's shoulder with a bloodcurdling yelp as his jester's hat jingled merrily.

Luckily, she caught him before all his hotdogs fell out, catching two of them between her fingers and quickly stuffing them in her magical pocket. Call her crazy, but it didn't seem like the best time to be retrieving hotdogs, especially if they rolled into the zero gravity behind her and started drifting away.

The colonel gave Dargen a look that seemed to say, "So,

we're changing puppets full of hotdogs into birds, are we?"

Dargen turned redder than his feathered robe, saluting the old man. "Colonel Monocle," he said. "I can explain."

"Come on," said the colonel, flipping open a pocket watch that summoned a miniature sun and sundial that combined to cast a shadow on the landing, showing the time of day, "we don't have a moment to spare. Double-time it, all of you."

Tiz felt a rush of nervous excitement, exactly the kind you get on the first day of school — new friends, new teachers, new things to do, but also, new bullies, new challenges — no scratch that, two really bad bullies — the witch and her tree.

Tiz stashed Pup Pup in her pack as she and her friends followed the colonel into the fortress. Behind her, the doors slammed shut with a loud thud, echoing her heartbeat. If they walked any faster, then her poor heart was going to fire out of her chest like a cannon ball and hurt someone — so much for first impressions.

Before long, they entered a colossal foyer resembling a museum. Artifacts and trophies that looked like they'd been captured by an environmentalist army adorned the walls. There was a whaling harpoon snapped in two, a giant bear trap with its teeth filed down and a fur coat with red paint all over it.

Rising from the center of the foyer, twenty-six different spiraling staircases, each matching a color of the fruits outside, twisted together for two stories then split up in different directions to lead the cadets to their barracks. From below, it reminded Tiz of a spiraling rainbow lollipop.

All around them, the foyer rang with the chatter of children and offspring of every living being and creature that Tiz had ever read about at Grovington Elementary School, a full compendium of youngsters, A through Z, from abominable snow men (boys and girls) to zombies, ranging from first graders to super-duper seniors in the fourteenth grade. Most were already organized into rows and standing in Companies

A through Z, except for certain latecomers that preferred not to be mentioned of course.

Though for Tiz, trying to be discreet in her leafy dress was sort of "out the door" along with trying not to gawk at everyone as she noticed that most of the students were already wearing uniforms matching the color of their company's fruit. How could you not stare at an eight-year-old hobgoblin in a honeydew-colored uniform? Pure and simple, it was candy for the eyes, and in addition, some of the cadets even had glimmering medals that shot out tiny sparks, indicating that it wasn't their first year.

Colonel Monocle cleared his throat in manner that said *stare less* as he led the four of them past Apple Company. As if on cue, abominable snow boys and girls began beating their chests as they passed by, some of them wearing bright green uniforms that made them look like giant granny may apples. Their chest beatings seemed to be a greeting so Tiz waved back then saluted just like Dargen was doing.

Tiz began walking on the tips of her toes to see over the abominable snow boys and girls and spotted other kids that looked like giant ant-men with big pincers near their mouth. A tall ant-boy clacked his mandibles at Tiz as she turned away, reminding herself that it wasn't polite to stare at someone, especially when that someone could remove your personal observatory with one bite.

Being rather fond of her own, Tiz turned her attention to Banana Company and their bright yellow uniforms. An electrified fence had to be erected to protect them from the ape-like abominable snow-kids in A Company, who still tried to climb it anyhow, howling and grunting that they'd be back. Tiz elbowed Sombra and pointed to the electrified fence with a smile.

"I know, I know," said Sombra, "but look at that." She pointed to the first platoon of B Company and the motley group of young creatures and kids holding musical instruments, comprising the school band.

However, this band would have made a pack of screeching alley cats sound like a symphony. Tiz never saw anything like it before. There was a boy dragon holding an oboe, a vampire girl with a flute and a young male troll with a harp. It was the biggest disaster waiting to happen that she'd ever seen. Even worse, the second platoon of B Company had a group of banshees. Every time the troll plucked a string one of the banshees would scream.

"Banana Company," said Tiz, elbowing Sombra. "How do you *peel* about it?"

"Ha, ha," feigned Sombra. "How do I feel? Well, I'm not exactly *bananas* about it, that's for sure. In fact, I'm pretty happy I'm not in there."

But before they moved away, Tiz gave it a second glance, thinking about the string-staff in her new magical pocket.

Continuing on, they followed Colonel Monocle past Coconut Company, which seemed almost as cuckoo as Banana Company. Its first platoon held centaurs with the lower bodies of horses and the upper bodies of teenage boys and girls, rearing up on their hindquarters and kicking at each other. Second platoon was packed with three-headed chimera children, each with the head of a lion, a goat and a snake, whispering to each other in a strange language.

As they stepped in front of Dragonfruit Company, the colonel stopped. "Dryads," he said, looking at Sombra. "It's another word for tree nymph. That's you. Second platoon to last, right after the druids and before the dwarves."

"Dryad," groaned Sombra, "I hate that word."

"So do I," agreed Tiz. "For some reason it makes me want to put lotion on my skin."

"You must be reading my mind, child," said the colonel, producing a bottle of lotion that smelled like a tiny skunk lived in it.

"It'll help keep the boys away, especially the druids," he

said to Sombra. "Otherwise, they'll fall for you like leaves, but the kind that pile up, then eventually smother you. So you might want to put some on before you go back there."

The cap was already off the bottle. Sombra held her nose, slathering it on thick.

"What about me?" asked Tiz, growing worried.

"You're not a dryad," he said. "No tree." But after noticing the frown on her face he pulled out another jar and handed it to her. "Maybe you better put some on anyway, just in case you two eat lunch together."

Tiz uncorked it and gagged, capping it quickly. No tree, just a stinky bottle of skin grease was all she got.

Sombra must have seen Tiz's expression because she gave her a hug. "Don't worry," she said. "I'll see you soon enough. Besides, with this lotion, if there's any swimming, we'll probably get out of it."

"It's waterproof," said the colonel. "But nice try. Now run along Sombra."

Waving to each other, the two friends parted again. A platoon of drooling dragonlings watched Sombra approaching as she quickly rubbed some more of the lotion on. "It's not barbecue sauce!" she shouted at one of them.

"Come along," said the colonel. "She'll be fine. Besides, we still need to find a spot for you."

Dreading where that might be, Tiz slathered some lotion onto her arm (wishing it was vanishing cream) then followed the colonel and Dargen.

They passed by Elderberry Company, full of tall and elegant elves that pinched their noses shut as she passed. Tiz blushed and she kept blushing all the way over to a company full of kids and creatures wearing blood-colored uniforms just as red as her face. Werewolves, pointy-hatted witches and warlocks with high-collared capes packed Wolfberry Company.

Tiz heard footsteps from behind — a small group was

coming her way. She turned around and saw seven of the *Nine Climbers* from the Wailing Woods that would challenge her for the Unwithering Tree. Tiz was number eight, and Sombra would have been number nine, but lucky for her, she already had a tree. Frenchy Yew led the seven, followed by Holly Holly, Jenna Oak, Bethany Rowan, Gomorrah Blackthorn, Cindy Elm and Alice Alder — all now suddenly aspiring witches.

How convenient, thought Tiz, watching their heart seeds pulse around their necks, ones that they purposely didn't plant. And even as much as Tiz wanted a tree (even the witch's tree) standing there next to Dargen and the colonel in front of Wolfberry Company was the last place she wanted to be.

Frenchy stopped in front of Tiz and plucked a withered leaf from Tiz's tattered dress for the Planting. "I cannot believe zhis garbage bag that you're wearing is your dress for the Planting," she said in her thick accent. "But I see zhat you cared for it as well as you cared for your seed."

Most of the other girls snickered, relishing the moment.

"Never mind them," said Frenchy to Tiz. "My apologies, I forgot, you don't have a seed anymore. *Le poof — au revoir*."

Some of the other climbers snickered again.

"Quiet!" barked Frenchy.

Her lap dogs obeyed.

Frenchy glared at Tiz, examining the leafy dress that was supposed to make her opponent look like a phoenix tree. "*Tsk, Tsk*," she chastised, walking around Tiz as if she was circling prey. "If fashion was an eye, then this dress would surely blind it," she hissed, flicking a leaf on its top. "Even still, you should keep this disaster of a tree dress in better shape. For you will never have a *real* tree." She stopped right in front of Tiz's face. "Especially, zeh witch's tree."

Tiz balled her hands into fists, standing her ground. "We'll see about that Frenchy — you better hope you have a strong grip on the tree, because you sure don't have one on reality," she growled.

Frenchy's heart seed began beating rapidly, betraying her embarrassment right through her poker face.

The other climbers snickered as Frenchy blushed. Embarrassed, she shut her cronies up with a glare as she hid her heart seed underneath her jacket.

The colonel seized the opportunity to step between them.

Tiz glared at him. "What are they doing here anyhow?" she grumbled. "Shouldn't they be in D Company with the dryads?"

"Not technically," he replied. "Their future trees are currently around their necks as seeds, so they could also join Wolfberry as witches. But in this case, all candidates for the witch's tree are considered witches until proven otherwise," he said as politely as he could. "But don't worry, there might just be a tree for you too."

Before the colonel could say another word Tiz blurted. "I want to be in the band — any instrument, I'll play any."

"*Bwack, bwack, bwack, bwack...*" clucked several of the other climbers like chickens.

The sooner Tiz could get out of there, the better. She began fishing around her magical pocket for her string-staff then remembered it had an ax head on it. "Ooops," she said. "I must have forgotten my harmonica at home."

"Zhat is a lie," insisted Frenchy, "you're too chicken to join Wolfberry."

"Who would want to be in Banana Company anyway?" asked Holly Holly, fully decked out in Christmas red, "especially with all the crimson in Wolfberry."

"A coward would, that's who," said Frenchy. "After all, yellow is their favorite color."

The other climbers snickered, except for Holly Holly, who had a puzzled look on her face.

"Yellow?" she asked. "Is that because chickens are born yellow?"

"Yellow-bellied," said Dargen in his know-it-all sort of way, only making it worse. "It basically means Tiz has no guts," added the young warlock.

"Quiet!" insisted Frenchy. "No one's talking to you, *bore-lock* — you bore-locks should go to B Company too."

"Now, now," said the colonel, "that's enough." Frenchy huffed then joined her cronies as the old man trained his monocle on Tiz. "Hmm," he said considering. "Band aye?"

"They could use my help," pleaded Tiz as her heart thumped like a big bass drum. It was screaming, "*Add me to the drum corps — I won't even need an instrument*!"

The colonel looked at her. "You mentioned the harmonica," he said. "But I'm sorry the harmonica's already taken."

Tiz slumped in defeat.

The colonel didn't seem to notice. "A harpy plays it," he continued, "though with *her* claws she spends more time cutting the harmonicas in half than playing them, but anyway — you'd have to choose another instrument," he said finally, "the only ones left are kazoo, violin and accordion."

"I'll take the kazoo," said Sombra from behind them. Tiz whirled around, thrilled to be reunited with her friend. But the distraction might have cost her.

"The violin," said Dargen elegantly. "I'd love to play it."

The colonel lowered his monocle at Tiz. "Looks like it's the accordion for you," he said.

Tiz wasn't exactly thrilled. "Is it a magic accordion?" she asked.

"It is if you play it well enough — magic to my ears," he said with a smile that basically said "no way."

"Ugh," said Tiz, disappointed.

"Do you know what accord means?" asked the colonel.

"Well, it's sort of like...harmony," said Tiz.

"That's right, Red," he said, blowing Tiz away with her nickname. And what was even more shocking was that she didn't mind him saying it.

Tiz narrowed her eyes at the old man. She'd always wondered about her father, ever since she learned about the birds and the bees. And the way he said "Red" even made her feel...well, sort of safe. Suddenly, she didn't want to disappoint the old man. "That's fine," she said, trying to sound upbeat. "I'll make the *Pine Tree Polka* the school's fight song by the time I'm done."

"That's the spirit," said the colonel, "now come along."

A barrage of boo's and hisses from Wolfberry Company bombarded the new members of B Company's first platoon. Tiz swore she even heard a few curses and hexes shouted her way as they left.

But so what, she thought, *you can't curse someone that's already cursed.*

CHAPTER SEVENTEEN — SHE'LL HAVE TO PAY

TIZ EXPECTED EVERYONE IN THE BAND to laugh as the colonel handed her a banana yellow accordion, but instead, they clapped.

A tall young troll holding a harp looked down at her. "You," he said. "Very strong. Me, could barely move the bellows."

"Please don't tease me," said Tiz. "Just don't. I've been through a lot the past few days."

"Fineus Grug, me never joke," he said with a straight face.

Tiz flexed her muscles and the troll smiled back.

Fineus had the kindly face of a choirboy and a big mop of black hair that went with it. Though he didn't look any older than Tiz, he was twice as tall and his arms were as thick as trees.

He must eat a lot of truffles to get that big and strong, thought Tiz. Plus, there might have been other benefits too, because his green skin didn't have a single wart on it.

"Nice to meet you," said Tiz, extending her hand. "I'm Tiz — Tiz Phoenix."

He shook it with a big pearly smile, not one yellow tooth.

Tiz had never met a troll before. She had always imagined them spending most of their time under bridges or on video game message boards. She had no idea that they could be so talkative. Fineus introduced her to over twenty other kids. The first were two vampire girls, who Tiz bonded with immediately because they also had a skin cream to wear, and a lot of it, one that protected them from a million different types of suns outside their windows. Next she met a boy dragon, a mummy, a siren who did a great imitation of an ambulance and a harpy that wanted to play the harp but kept on cutting the strings with her talons, so she got stuck playing the harmonica.

But there was one boy in the back of first platoon that Fineus didn't introduce her to. Standing there alone, he had black feathery wings on his back that marked him as a fallen angel.

The grim-looking boy wore a gray hood over messy black hair. She could barely make out his pale face, but from what she saw, it wasn't nearly as scary as she would of thought. It was bony, but by no means ugly. His dark eyes were as narrow as two slits, ones that seemed bent on hiding something, shrouded in mystery. She looked at him like a storm cloud, curious if there was any blue sky beyond.

The fallen angel fidgeted with a dark guitar engraved with glowing runes — an impressive specimen. Out of the corner of his narrow eyes, ones that looked as menacing as two arrow slits, he caught her staring at him then strummed his guitar as his wings flashed with flames like a phoenix.

"Who's that?" asked Tiz gazing at the fallen angel as he extinguished his wings.

"Fire bad," said Fineus. And if anyone had a reason to fear it, a troll did — it was their kryptonite, preventing them from regenerating.

"Yeah, fire bad," said Tiz as if she'd fallen under an enchantment. "But what's his name?"

But before anyone could answer the boy started singing as sadly as the lament Tiz sang for Sombra, his words like a spell:

Madder than a burning bird,
She's lost her way,
She'll have to pay,
Death will make sure of it,
To where she goes,
She may never return from,

CHAPTER SEVENTEEN

For in the underworld,
Even a burning bird will burn,
but there's still time,
For even the looming dead can learn,
but if not,
They'll burn the burning bird.

His wings flared once again as he finished his song.

Listening intently, Tiz had soaked up every dark drop faster than a sponge at an oil spill.

"Someone get him a tissue," said Sombra in her weary way. "Whatever his name is."

"It's Char," grumbled Fineus.

"Ha, that's probably just short for Charlie," said Sombra with a nervous laugh.

But no one else laughed. Then something came out of Tiz's mouth that shocked them all, herself more than anyone. "He's my guardian angel," she said, sounding certain of it.

"What!" exclaimed Sombra. "Did his weird song give you brain damage?"

"Fire bad," repeated Fineus.

"Yeah," said Sombra. "Play with it and you know what happens. You'd be better off flying into the sun — think of it that way, he's like the sun — no forget that — a supernova."

"Well, if he's a supernova, then I'll be a solar panel for his radiant energy," replied Tiz as though still in a trance.

"Stay away," warned Dargen. "He's not a guardian angel, he's a fallen one."

Tiz looked at Dargen. "If I were falling, I'd want someone to catch me," she said, throwing the words he said to her in the Unburnable Forest right back at him like a dagger, more hurtful than she even knew.

"But I thought angels like him fall *all* the way down," said Sombra, pointing toward the ground and the underworld somewhere way below.

"The abyss," said Dargen. "He got kicked out of there too."

"What did he do?" asked Tiz.

"Who cares," said Sombra. "If you go talk to him, you're the one that's going to be needing the tissue."

"So what, I want to know," said Tiz.

"No one know," said Fineus. "It a mystery."

"Not for long," said Tiz as she started walking toward Char, wiping off the skunky lotion on her arms with a tissue then handing it to one of the vampire girls with a wink.

When she got to him she extended her hand through the straps of her banana-colored accordion. "Hi, I'm Tiz Phoenix."

Ignoring her hand, the fallen angel stood there, carefully tuning his guitar. "Tell me something," he said in calm and collected voice. "If you hear a storm coming, do you seek shelter or stand outside and grab onto a metal pole?"

"It depends," said Tiz, lowering her hand in disappointment.

"On what?" he asked.

"Are you outside or inside?" she asked.

Tiz saw the corner of his mouth rise for what could have almost passed for a smile. "If I'm outside," he replied. "Then you'd better be in a storm shelter — no, better yet, a bomb shelter."

Tiz scoffed. "So then I suppose that makes you *the bomb*. Or at least you think you're *the bomb*," she said with a playful scowl. But before he could retort she interrupted him on purpose for not shaking her hand. "But you're right, if you were outside, I would definitely be somewhere else."

With that she turned her back then walked away with a smirk. She could tell that he was watching her without even turning around. From behind, she heard his guitar *MEOW* like an angry kitty, teasing her. Several cadets laughed. But Tiz didn't care. Her own grin grew as wide as her accordion as she came back to her friends.

"What did he say?" asked Sombra as Tiz strapped her accordion on like a backpack.

But before Tiz could respond a man with a *deep* southern drawl and a voice like a drill sergeant yelled, "A-TEN-HUT!"

That really confused Tiz and Sombra. Especially when all the other kids stood tall with their hands at their sides, stiff as boards while the two tree nymphs didn't understand why.

"What the heck did that guy yell?" asked Sombra, peering around the foyer.

"Something about ten huts or a ten person hut," replied Tiz as she spotted a tall square chinned man with four stars on his shoulders and a hoard of medals pinned to his chest. "Maybe someone lost one and he's trying to get their attention."

"Shush," whispered Dargen. "Or you'll get us in trouble. Stand up straight with your hands at your sides and *be quiet*."

"Don't tell me what to do," said Sombra as she shoved her kazoo in Dargen's face. "Unless you want *this* as a breathing tube."

Tiz worried that she might have to separate the two. "Shush!" she said *way* too loudly, accidentally shushing the man with the square jaw. He turned his head and glared right at her.

"YOU, RED HAIR, YELLOW ACCORDION, DROP AND GIVE ME FIFTY!" he yelled at Tiz.

Tiz took off her accordion and dropped it on the ground by her pack. She opened the sack and started looking inside for fifty gold coins, believing it was time to pay some of the tuition fees.

"I DIDN'T TELL YOU TO TAKE OFF THE ACCORDION, RED!" yelled the square-jawed man. "FIFTY MORE! DROP AND GIVE ME A HUNDRED!"

"Pushups," whispered Dargen. "He means a hundred pushups, not gold coins."

"Why?" asked Tiz.

"You shushed when you should be shushing," said Fineus out of the corner of his mouth like a professional ventriloquist.

Tiz sighed as she strapped the accordion on her back again.

By that time, she could already hear several kids giggling around her. "She'll never get a hundred," whispered a scrawny goblin, "not even if they shut off the gravity."

Unfortunately, the little monster was right. Tiz only made it to thirty-three as each pushup ended with a jerky squeak from her accordion to the delight of the entire academy. For the clasps that held the accordion's bellows together had come undone just as badly as the muscles in her arms and chest.

That's when Tiz got introduced to something much worse than a pushup in front of the whole school. It was a form of punishment for those that couldn't finish all their pushups — an embarrassing body position dubbed "the dying cockroach."

With her accordion still on her back, Tiz had to roll onto it like a capsized turtle, wiggling her arms and legs in the air.

The laughter had gotten so loud that Tiz could no longer hear the accordion squeaking underneath her. A familiar feeling of dread rushed over her, just like when she'd turned her heart seed into ashes, she wanted to curl up like a roly-poly and hide. She felt the sting of tears in her eyes. The last thing she wanted to do was cry in front of the whole school.

Yet, it wasn't Tiz that ended up doing the wailing. It was a familiar guitar, *screeching* above the laughter.

Tiz looked to the side. Char was shredding the cords on his guitar to a piercing roar, taking the attention off her just like a real guardian angel would have done. Tiz nearly shed tears of joy. But within seconds, two boarder hoarders, each with an arm patch that bore the letters MP (Mili-Tree Police), hauled Char off like he was just another nut, dragging him to a set of dark stairs that led downward.

"GET UP!" yelled the square-chinned man in his southern drawl.

Tiz sprang to her feet.

"TEN DEMERITS FOR YOU, RED!" he yelled. "AND SEVENTY-SEVEN FOR EVERYONE IN B COMPANY FOR ALL THE PUSHUPS YOU FAILED TO DO!"

The rest of B Company *groaned.*

"NOW THAT'S SEVENTY-SEVEN PUSHUPS TOO!" he yelled as all of B Company groaned again, dropping into pushup position.

"What's a demerit?" whispered Tiz, watching Dargen do pushups next to her.

"A bonus point," he replied. "But the opposite."

"Greaaaat," sighed Tiz, worrying that those would be the first of thousands to come her way. Worse, her poor company mates would suffer for it as well, absorbing collateral damage from her mistakes as if the demerits were like a water balloon grenade thrown their way. From now on, Tiz was going to dive on top of her "mistake grenades" in order to shield everyone else against them. She would offer to take all their demerits going forward, drawing enemy fire away from her fellow cadets by keeping the attention on her, no matter what.

But in her heart, her deepest concern was about Char and the mounds of demerits he would be buried under — ones that made her feel a hundred times worse than any of her own.

CHAPTER EIGHTEEN — TO BE OR NOT TO BE A LATRINE MACHINE

TIZ LEARNED QUITE A BIT at military formation that day, most of it, what not to do. The worst no-no's were called the *latrine machine laws*, because if you were caught breaking them you had the scrub the toilets until you were a lean, mean porcelain cleaning machine. And if you kept breaking them, the toilets would become the closest thing you had to a friend.

Potty mouth usually got you latrine duty for a month. Even expletives such as *shucks, drat, what the heck* and *oh fudge* earned you a week. "Be Obscene and Become a Latrine Machine!" was the slogan that hung over every single toilet. And if you said a bad word while chewing gum, well then, you'd better inform your friends you'd write them whenever you could.

In his deep southern drawl, Mr. Square Jaw gave a speech introducing the latrine machine laws. He started off by announcing that he was in charge of the academy and that his name was General Maximus Payne.

Tiz had no intention of repeating what another cadet had called him behind his back, but a part of her knew that General Payne had somehow heard him. The muscles on one side of his perfectly shaved face started twitching. The general then reminded everyone of latrine machine law number seventeen. No one was allowed to call him General Payne, or Max, or even Max Payne. You had to call him "sir."

According to General Payne, all male officers were to be addressed in the same way and female officers were to be called "Ma'am" (which was short for Madam). And if you were stopping to speak to an officer, then you needed to snap to attention and salute then wait patiently for the salute to be returned, otherwise, it could lead to more pushups. Tiz didn't bother to ask why, because her head was already starting to spin from trying to remember all the things she was being told.

Standing there, she listened to the general say that the best students eventually could become officers too, though not with the same authority of teachers and counselors. Student officers were more like powerful hall monitors and resident advisers (RA's for short), ones that could hand out demerits and make you do pushups until your lunch did the same thing. But they had to rise through the ranks (levels of authority) first.

Tiz had previously thought that the word rank only referred to *a bad smell*. And that the higher your rank became then the worse off you were. But here it was the opposite. It was just one more thing she had to learn.

The lowest rank was private, followed by corporal then various types of sergeants. If you became the highest level of sergeant (at the academy), called a master sergeant, you could potentially be promoted to the lowest rank of officer, called a second lieutenant. All of it was pretty confusing but Tiz listened intently. Having rank would be great and once she rose to the very top, she'd make all pushups outside of gym class illegal and never let anyone else boss her around. Plus, the prospect of combining her new found powers in her voice with giving commands would not only be exciting, but also, particularly effective, especially when it came to a certain French cadet.

It all sounded great until Mr. Square Jaw dropped a bomb on her plans in his speech. All new students started off as plebes instead of privates. If the school was a pond and all the students were various sizes of fishes, then plebes were the pond scum at the bottom. Until they proved themselves, they had to walk on the far right side of all hallways and salute every commemorative plaque that they passed in Iggy City, all six hundred and eighty-two.

Consequently, she paid extra attention to the different types of military commands she had to follow in order to avoid prolonged status as a plebe. Those misguided souls that stayed perpetual plebes had so much latrine duty they were called *ploops* instead of *latrine machines* because at least the latter could clean a toilet properly. And in the rare case that someone graduated as a ploop, they earned a lifetime achievement award coupled with a rusty medal in the shape of a toilet bowl; one that Tiz had no intention of getting.

Listening carefully, she learned that "A-ten-hut" was the general's way of saying, "stand at attention." So she practiced standing tall with her arms down at her sides and her hands neatly cupped, eyes facing front, chin level, no moving.

A position called parade rest was next and wasn't nearly as relaxing as it sounded, though better than standing at attention. It required her to stand with her hands together at the small of her back, thumbs interlocked, and her feet spread shoulder width apart.

"At ease," was her favorite stance. You could basically just stand there, but it still meant no talking.

After General Payne was done, Tiz was introduced to several upperclassmen that were in charge of her. The first she already knew, Fineus the troll was what they called her squad leader. A squad was a row of kids, and the squad leader was in charge of them. Tiz was happy that Fineus was hers.

Four squads, or rows, of cadets made up a platoon. And staying true to one of the school's oldest mottos, "Children Can *Never* Have Enough Supervision," each platoon also had a platoon sergeant and an officer called a platoon leader, both of them upperclassmen.

Tiz's platoon leader was a clean-shaven dwarf named Simon Sinz (who they called Simon Says) that looked a bit like a blond garden gnome without a beard. He was hard to see at times when Tiz was standing behind the other kids. However, his booming voice often made up for what he lacked in stature.

Fineus said that Simon had a bit of something called a Napoleon complex, whatever that was. Tiz asked if that had something to do with obsessively eating bowl after bowl of ice cream that was part strawberry, vanilla and chocolate, but was promptly informed by Dargen that those flavors together were called Neapolitan ice cream, not Napoleon. From that point on Tiz wrote stuff down.

Afterwards, they learned to march around the foyer while in step with their platoon. When they were done, one of the vampire girls, Molly Von Butterburg, who had long blond hair, perfect cheek bones and deep blue eyes that would hypnotize you if you stared too long, led Tiz and Sombra to a small shop where they were fitted for their new uniforms.

Both Tiz and Sombra received several sets of the following — name tags, a yellow jacket and skirt, a white-colored shirt, a yellow neck tab for girls instead of a tie, and black pumps instead of traditional dress shoes.

Sombra had always dressed like a vampire herself so she wasn't too thrilled with the colors for Banana Company as she put on a long thin hat that made her look like a short order cook. But for Tiz, it was a big improvement over her leafy dress for the Planting, even if she looked a bit like Tweety Pup.

Best of all, even as plebes, they got some bling for the their uniforms that the cadets called *brass* because of the type of metal they were made from. There were five shiny brass pieces to put on their ensemble, four on the lapels of their jacket and one on the side of their hat, toward the front.

The one on the hat reflected their rank, or in their cases, a giant letter P for plebe. The two jacket pieces on top were the school insignia — a bonsai-shaped tree with nine orbs orbiting it. The two pieces on the bottom were for the environmentalist army — a polar bear with a military hat saluting over a broken harpoon.

To Tiz and Sombra, they were the coolest things in the world until they got handed a polishing kit for not only their brass, but also their shoes. Apparently, the tips of their shoes needed to be polished to the point where they could see their own reflections in it like a pool of water. Tiz didn't know why, but if it meant a higher rank and no more pushups she would gladly comply.

After they finished getting all their things — uniforms, nametags, a cage for Pup Pup, books and bedding — Molly led them to their barracks. They took the spiraling yellow staircase all the way up to a rather ordinary looking set of double doors with a huge padlock (unlocked for the time being).

Inside was a common room with only two sofas and glaringly devoid of a TV. The sofas were bright yellow and shaped like bananas with matching throw rugs all around them. But they might as well have stored the ugly couches in mothballs anyhow, because every single cadet was busy in another part of the barracks, arranging and polishing their things or doing chores that were assigned weekly called *details*.

Branching off of the common room, and quite literally too, were two separate barracks, one for the boys and one for the girls. Each barracks held a dormitory with bunk beds and a locker room, one locker for their personal belongings and a second for their military things. Tiz coaxed Pup Pup into his cage with a hotdog then slid him onto the top shelf of her personal locker. Even though he was a puppet and didn't need to be right next to the air holes, she put him there anyway. He might have been ninety percent polyester and felt, but to her, he was no different than a real pet.

Tiz and Sombra also stored the rest of their belongings in their personal lockers then exchanged the combinations to their padlocks so they could share their things. Afterwards, they went into the girl's dormitory and claimed a set of bunk beds. Tiz agreed to take the top bunk, which she regretted later after finding out their beds had to be made so neatly and tightly that a coin could be bounced off the sheets. In order to do that she had to stand on Sombra's bed while her best friend groaned and complained. Regardless, she'd rather hear Sombra cry than the wail of a banshee or a harpy.

Done with their beds, they found out they had an hour before bedtime, which Molly told them was called *Taps* after the name of the bugle song they played just before lights out.

Eager to keep her mind off the witch's tree and the climb ahead, Tiz decided to start a different sort of climb, one that involved military ranks, her climb to five-star general.

Selling the idea as easily as lemonade on a hot summer day, Tiz talked Sombra into going back into the locker room so they could polish their brass ahead of tomorrow's inspection at morning formation.

Tiz organized her military locker first, folding everything into thirds according to the instruction sheet that had been neatly taped to the inside of the locker door. Tiz caught Sombra peeking at her several times as though she was a complete stranger, at least to cleaning.

"Who are you really?" asked Sombra, staring at Tiz, "and what have you done with my best friend, the one that would rather run away from home than clean."

Tiz shrugged. "I just want to change things around here — and back home," she said. "And to do that, you need power, rank, life trees, whatever it may be, but it all seems to revolve around power."

"You're starting to scare me," said Sombra, pausing. "You're not thinking about claiming the witch's tree for yourself, are you?"

Tiz shrugged again as she pulled out her pieces of brass, some environmentally friendly polish for them, and last but not least, a brand new brush. She sat on the long bench in front of her locker and joined countless other kids of all kinds, shining their insignias.

Sombra sighed and brought hers next to Tiz. She pulled out a piece that was the symbol for the environmentalist army — a polar bear with a military hat saluting over a broken harpoon. Around the insignia were the words — duty, honor and discipline. Sombra showed it to Tiz. "How will shining a piece of brass save the icecaps, keep a polar bear from being harpooned or even help you climb the witch's tree?"

"I don't know," said Tiz. "But if I don't shine it, I'll never get a chance to find out."

"PHOENIX! TIZ!" boomed the voice of Simon Says the dwarf, making the girls jump. "The general wants to see you!"

"Great," sighed Tiz as she clipped the last piece of polished brass onto her lapel.

"He didn't say Simon Says," whispered Sombra, "maybe you don't have to go."

"Nice try," replied Tiz.

"Well then, it was nice knowing you," said Sombra.

"If I don't come back," said Tiz as she got up. "Find Pup Pup a good home."

CHAPTER NINETEEN — FIRING WORDS, LAUNCHING TORPEDOES AND DIVING IN HEADFIRST

TIZ FOLLOWED SIMON SAYS out of Banana Company's barracks and down the yellow spiraling staircase into the museum-like foyer. Before long, they were marching through a hallway with columns straight out of the Roman Colosseum. Each column had a hoard of commemorative plaques that Tiz had to salute. Worse still, each plaque had a tiny arm, waiting to salute back. She saluted so many times that the last arm handed her a sling and a tissue.

Stuffing them into her pocket, Tiz nearly knocked over Simon as he stopped abruptly before what looked like a bank vault door complete with a combination lock, wheel and handle.

Simon knocked a few times, paused, then knocked again. "Tap code," he said. "You'll get the hang of it soon enough. It's useful if you're captured by the enemy and taken prisoner."

Taken prisoner? thought Tiz. *By who*? *Enemies of the environmentalist army*? *Were there poachers in space*? *The general was her enemy — would she be his prisoner*? Tiz didn't want to get the hang of tap code if it meant being one. And by the way, shouldn't she be taught something like that immediately? Or would that just encourage new cadets to tap all day long, begging to be set free. She wondered what kids were already saying secretly, especially about her. On second thought, maybe she'd better learn it.

Before she could ask for an instructional booklet, the wheel on the vault door started glowing and spinning on its own. Tiz and Simon stepped back as the door unlocked with a click and slowly swung open.

Tiz hesitated.

"Good luck," said Simon as he executed an about face and double-timed it out of there, making Tiz even more nervous.

"Red, what are you waiting for!" yelled the general from beyond the darkness of the door. "A ticker-tape parade and some giant puppet balloons? Get in here, cadet!"

Tiz used her cuff to give the brass on her lapel one last polish then straightened her posture and marched into the dark corridor, hoping to impress him. Behind her she heard the vault door clang shut, taking her out of rhythm for a second. Recovering, she marched down a long black hall lit only by stardust.

Tiz entered a large room that opened up like the observatory on a spaceship, right in the middle of the tree, allowing every stargazer to see upwards and downwards. It was breathtaking. She could see the nine spheres orbiting the cosmic tree like small moons. All the barracks, with their antique looks and fruit-like shapes, glistened on the branches outside, making Iggy City look like a celestial bonsai tree decorated for Christmas.

The view was amazing, until Tiz spotted Frenchy and the six other climbers from Wolfberry Company in their disturbing blood-colored uniforms. They were all standing in a perfectly straight line right in front of the general. Together, the tree nymphs from Wolfberry comprised seven of the *Nine Climbers*. Rumor had it that they were now referring to themselves as the *Heavenly Seven* — saviors of the universe. It was ironic to say the least, considering that their devilish attitudes and their reddish uniforms seemed like they were both carefully crafted somewhere in the fiery depths of hell.

Tiz wanted to execute her own about face and march out, but instead, she tried to stay positive. At least she didn't have to compete against her best friend since she already had a tree.

Ahead of her, the square-jawed general was pinning something on the shoulder lapels of Frenchy Yew's uniform.

Tiz nearly tripped over her own feet when she saw what

they were. The general was promoting Frenchy to corporal, three whole ranks above Tiz, who wasn't even a private yet, just a plebe.

Tiz saw that five of the remaining climbers from Wolfberry had already been promoted to private and Holly S. Holly to private first class, one rank below Frenchy. All of them wore their heart seeds over their chests as if they'd just been awarded magical Medals of Honor. Their seeds pulsed from the excitement, seeming to taunt a particular girl from Banana Company who was utterly devoid of one.

Tiz sighed, her heart sank as she fell in line next to Frenchy. Out of the corner of her eye she spotted a shooting star deep in space. Instinctively, she started reaching for it with her hand but luckily caught herself before she got very far. Instead, she stood there and wished that the general would promote her above the rest of the girls, making her a sergeant.

"Red, stop standing so straight," barked the four-star general in his drawl, his hoard of medals clanking together as he walked the line. "You're starting to bend so far back you look like a giant banana in that yellow uniform."

The rest of the girls snickered.

"Quiet!" insisted General Payne. "There ain't nothing funny about poor posture — no more laughing, not a single giggle."

Silence. Not even a cricket the size of a space ship hidden in a dark corner of the universe would have dared to chirp.

The general marched down the line in front of them. He stopped at Tiz and inspected her brass as she held her breath. After what seemed like an eternity, he gave out a grunt that sounded as though he was a bit surprised to find them polished.

Though proud of herself, Tiz suppressed a smile, just in case.

The general frowned. "Red, why are you here?" he

insisted.

"Sir, to conquer the witch's tree, sir!" replied Tiz.

The general pulled out a toy dinosaur with a huge head and tiny arms, holding it in front of Tiz.

"Red, do you know what this is?" he asked.

"Sir, yes, sir!" she replied. "It's a T-Rex, sir!"

"Wrong, plebe!" he shouted. "It's a Jy-ganto-saurus and it picks its teeth with T-Rex bones!"

Tiz wasn't sure that its stubby arms could reach its teeth, even with a long femur bone but she wasn't about to argue.

The general flicked open the flip-top head on the dino-toy and pulled out a square piece of candy, showing it to her. "And what's this?"

"Sir, smells like peppermint, sir!" she replied.

"Peppermint," chuckled the general. "Peppermint?" He started laughing harder. It was a hideous, high-pitched laugh that seemed uncontrollable, like a hyena being tickled.

Frenchy and some of the other girls started laughing too, probably because it felt more awkward not to do so. Plus, it was another perfect opportunity for them to schmooze.

"Peppermint," he laughed, his face turning beet red. Laughter seemed to be his weakness.

Tiz started giggling — there seemed to be a human side to him after all.

"I SAID NO MORE LAUGHING!" yelled the general. "ARE YOU GIRLS EVEN LISTENING TO ME! DO YOU UNDERSTAND THE WORDS FIRING OUT OF MY WORD SHOOTER!"

Silence. The general stared at Tiz. He put the piece of candy in the dino-toy's mouth and crushed it with its teeth. "Do you wanna be a snack for a Jy-ganto-saurus?" he asked Tiz.

"No, sir!" she yelled.

"How about the rest of you!" he shouted.

"SIR, NO, SIR!" yelled the rest of the girls.

The general narrowed his eyes. "The Unwithering Tree is like a huge herd of fire-breathing Jy-ganto-sauruses turned into a tree. And if you don't want to be its next snack, then you better listen to me and listen to me good," he replied as though he knew it all.

But behind his back, through the glass of the observatory, the same two witches from Wolfberry Company that had tried to escape before were at it again, paddling their bunk beds with broomsticks. One of them put her finger to her lips, pleading for them to stay silent.

"Sacré bleu!" yelled Frenchy, pointing at the escapees from her own company in the window.

The general whirled around and spotted them. "Down periscope!" he yelled like the captain of a submarine as a tube with a lens shot down from the ceiling.

Looking into it, he took dead aim and pressed a red button. Five boarder hoarders shot out from different tubes like torpedoes, converging on their fleeing targets while screaming, "*Cuckoo*!" Before Tiz could blink, the hoarders were hauling the runaways back to their barracks.

Tattling earned Frenchy another promotion as the general pinned sergeant stripes on her. Finished, he roamed the line again. "Now where were we?" he asked.

"The witch's tree," blurted Holly as if it was her favorite thing in the world.

The general scowled at her. "Itching to climb it, are we?" he asked.

Holly nodded. "I wanna to be the B-E-S-T, sir," she cheered.

"Well you ain't gonna do it by cheering from the sidelines," he replied. "Training, training, training. That means two new classes — Tactical Diversions and Exploiting Your Enemies' Weaknesses."

All the girls groaned — he had clearly exposed theirs.

"No exceptions!" barked the general. "But most of all,

you're gonna learn to climb like your lives depend on it! When I'm through with you, you're gonna be teaching capuchin monkeys what to do! But right now, you're like a bunch of little kittens that just crawled out of their cozy little baskets. But guess what you girls don't have that a tiny little kitten does?"

Silence.

"You girls ain't got eight lives to spare!" he yelled finally, glaring at all eight of them. "You got one chance, that's it. You conquer the tree, or it conquers you. So what's it gonna be?"

"Sir, conquer the tree, sir!" yelled the girls in unison.

"There you go again, getting ahead of yourselves," he said. "You haven't even chosen a spotter yet. What's a spotter Frenchy?"

"Zeh spotter is for the training," she replied. "Zhey catch you if you fall."

"Frenchy, you make Albert Einstein look like a flunky," replied the general as he pulled out a new set of insignias for her lapel and promoted her to staff sergeant. Tiz was now almost positive that Frenchy would outrank the general by the time they were done.

"Choose your spotters by noon tomorrow," he ordered, walking the line again, "then report to the training room after lunch. Be there at thirteen hundred hours sharp. Red, what's thirteen hundred hours?"

"That's *a lot* of hours, sir!" she replied.

"Negative, cadet!" he barked. "I mean what time is that on Earth!"

"One o'clock in the afternoon, sir!" she replied.

"That's right, plebe," he said. "And you better not be late! Do you understand, ladies?"

"YES, SIR!"

"Good!" he said, coming to a halt. "Now that I've said my piece, are there any questions?"

CHAPTER NINETEEN

Silence. Worn out, Tiz felt like she had survived a battle.

"There's one more thing," said the general. "Until you prove otherwise, each of you are gonna be treated like witches. And that means one thing."

Tiz swallowed hard, fearing the worst — a transfer to Wolfberry and an eternity of pushups, courtesy of Frenchy.

"You all get a pet," said the general instead. "It's called a familiar — choose wisely now, 'cause you're gonna use 'em while you're climbing to gain an advantage. So make sure you bring 'em to every Tactical Diversions Class. Aw shucks, forget that, bring 'em to every class. Get to know 'em like you know the back of your favorite shoe polishing brush. Do you understand the words firing out of my word shooter!"

"Yes, sir!" they sounded off.

The general looked at them with a suspicious eye. "Dismissed!" he barked.

Tiz whirled on her heels and double-timed it out. She could hear the other girls behind her giggling. There was no doubt who it was about — Pup Pup and her, but mostly, Char and her.

Frenchy was even pretending to be Tiz while begging an imaginary Char to be her spotter. "Zeh tree is so tall and your wings are so pretty, you are the guardian angel of my heart," she laughed, following it up with several "Le pukes."

"Blah, blah, blah!" said Tiz loud enough so they could hear.

"Halt, plebe!" ordered Frenchy from behind, trying to sound large and in charge.

Tiz stopped and spun on a dime, glaring at her rival.

"Drop and give me fifty," ordered Frenchy, most of her cronies smirking behind her as their heart seeds began racing with excitement.

Shielding her eyes from the barrage of magical lights, Tiz recalled her mother saying that flashing lights in video games could cause seizures, and now, she had a real fear of that same possibility. Even so, she wasn't about to listen to her enemy tell her what to do.

"If you want to see fifty pushups," replied Tiz. "Do them your *fudging* self."

"Oooooooooo," said her cronies in unison like they couldn't believe their ears.

"Zhat was an order," repeated Frenchy.

"You can't *make* me do anything I don't want to," said Tiz.

"Watch me," said Frenchy as she nodded to her lap dogs.

Before Tiz could cry out for the general, Frenchy covered her mouth as all of her cronies, except for Holly Holly, picked her up. They carried her down the hallway with all the columns, Holly nervously in tow, and past all the commemorative plaques that were saluting Tiz even though it was clearly evident that she had no free arm to salute back.

Where they were taking her, she had no idea. Every time she tried to yell *put me down* it was so muffled that Frenchy would call her a *big baby* then say, "There, *I put you down*, so shut up now."

Before long, the Heavenly Seven that were carrying her shoved open a door to the girl's bathroom and brought her into a stall.

"*Oh fudge*," mumbled Tiz under the muffling hand of her nemesis.

Facing the toilet with her head over the bowl, Tiz smelled pine scented cleaner in the water below — her little sisters' favorite scent — they would have loved it in here, but not under these particular circumstances, that's for sure. Leaning her head back Tiz read the slogan over the toilet: Be Obscene and Become a Latrine Machine!

Frenchy must have been watching her read it because she said, "So, you want to be a latrine machine, eh?"

But Tiz didn't bother to try to reply with Frenchy's hand still over her mouth.

"She can't be a latrine machine," said Holly nervously,

looking uncomfortable about the whole situation. "She's only a plebe."

Frenchy tipped her hat forward like an outlaw from a Wild West Show. "Well gosh darn it, I reckon you're right, cowgirl," she said in a surprisingly good southern drawl, similar to the general. "Hop-a-long Holly, you make Albert Einstein look like a flunky."

All the climbers laughed except for Holly. But even Tiz thought it was kind of funny, despite her predicament.

"Hop-a-long Holly, what sound does a banana make when you drop it in the toilet?" continued Frenchy, mocking the general quite liberally.

"Um..." replied Holly, thinking. "Ploop?"

"Bull's eye," replied Frenchy, shoving Tiz's face into the center of the toilet bowl with a splash.

The water was colder than expected. Holding her breath, Tiz now realized why the twins hated wet-willies so much and thought that karma might be having a good laugh at her for previously ordering her little sisters to give each other one. That's when she remembered her mouth was now free of Frenchy's hand. If she could only get her head out, then she could scream like she did in the forest when she accidentally set the trees on fire. Only instead of blowing them out like candles she could push the bullies back.

Flush! The *swirlie* commenced — her head was caught in a violent whirlpool. Water rushed up her nose and into her ears. There was no stopping it.

Through a gurgling sound, Tiz heard several of the bullies laughing. Frenchy shouted, "So *this* is how an evil witch washes her hair..."

The bullies laughed again.

Tiz wanted to scream but Frenchy kept flushing and flushing. Every time she tried to yell, more water just rushed into her mouth instead. She quickly realized that she had no chance of using her voice to fight them off. In fact, it was getting so bad, even her chances of surviving were slipping down the drain faster than the surging water.

Tiz couldn't breathe anymore. Within moments, she was going to drown with her head in a toilet bowl.

"Cut it out!" yelled one of the climbers from Wolfberry. "Or I'll tell the general everything!"

It was the voice of Holly Holly. One of their own was trying to come to her rescue.

Tiz heard one last flush. Then, it stopped. The water drained to the point where she was able to cough some of it back up into the toilet. But she couldn't have uttered the word *help* let alone scream like a banshee. The climbers holding her let Tiz go as she knelt in front of the toilet, gasping for air.

Frenchy kneeled right next to Tiz. "When I'm through with you, witch," she hissed, "you're gonna be just like your heart seed — broken *and* forgotten."

Frenchy flicked the water off her hands into Tiz's face then stood.

Tiz heard the footsteps of the girls leaving.

She glanced over her shoulder and saw Holly Holly still standing there. The girl with the bright red hair and rosy cheeks always had a smile on her face until now. "Sorry," said Holly apologetically.

Breathing heavily, Tiz could only muster one word. "Thanks," she said.

Holly nodded. "I better go," she said. "They're probably talking about me already. And I don't want to end up in the stall next door."

Tiz nodded, watching Holly leave in a hurry.

Woozy, Tiz got up and stumbled to the paper towel dispenser. It was out. Frenchy had taken the rest of them. "It figures," she grumbled as she shuffled toward the door.

When Tiz got to the hall she spotted Simon Says, waiting to escort her back to their barracks. "Whoa, how'd it go?" he asked, concern in his eyes as he stared at her dripping hair.

"Well, besides nearly drowning, let's just say I could use a bunk bed and some paddles," she replied, stepping past the dwarf and heading toward their barracks, hoping that he wouldn't ask her any more questions — she'd had her fill of them for one day, not to mention, the general, the Heavenly Seven and last but not least, toilet water. *Especially* toilet water.

CHAPTER TWENTY — I'LL TAKE ANOTHER LUMP BUT NOT TWO, THANK YOU

AFTER TIZ WENT TO BED, she tossed and turned in her top bunk the entire night as her best friend slept below her. She was afraid to tell her anything about what happened in the girl's bathroom, especially if it led to Sombra getting into a fight.

Tiz now realized she should have let Frenchy tease her and not replied *blah, blah, blah* to make it worse — two wrongs don't make a right. And telling Sombra could make it even worse, especially if she tried to get Frenchy back on her own. So Tiz decided to fall on top of this tiny "mistake grenade" as she crossed her fingers and toes, hoping that it wouldn't eventually explode into something bigger.

She didn't mention the *spotter* to Sombra either because she wasn't sure that her best friend was right for the job. And Tiz was pretty sure a *familiar* had to be some sort of creature or animal, and not a best friend, even if you were more familiar with them than the back of your hand. Regardless, the role of familiar already fit Pup Pup like a glove, or a puppet to be exact.

So Tiz planned on asking someone totally different to spot for her. It was someone that Sombra would hate even more than her best friend not choosing her.

Unfortunately for Tiz, it would feel like handing Sombra the negative clamp of the magical jumper cables all over again. Except this time, it was about a boy, one as dark and dangerous as the device they used that day. To Tiz, Char was her guardian angel, and if he agreed, he'd also be her spotter — a perfect combo.

In the morning, Tiz's dreams were rudely interrupted by a bugle blaring a song called *Reveille*. *It just has to have a*

French name to it, doesn't it, she thought to herself.

Worse, she still needed a clever way to ask Char to help her. Though who would want to be a spotter for someone that couldn't even finish all of her pushups? With that thought, Tiz slid out of the top bunk and started knocking some out.

Sombra yawned as she watched Tiz do pushups. "You forgot your accordion," she wisecracked.

Tiz started giggling as she pushed with all her might to finish her last one.

"And I was wrong about this place," said Sombra, watching with a mischievous smirk. "Prison would be *a lot* better."

Tiz fell to her chest, laughing — her last pushup sabotaged.

Sombra got up then pulled her friend to her feet, making Tiz feel even more guilty about wanting to choose Char as her spotter. To chase the guilt away, Tiz helped Sombra make her bed before they changed and headed off to eat their morning meal.

At breakfast, Tiz stared at her glass of water with a bit of trepidation after she'd swallowed enough of it from the toilet to last her a lifetime. It made her stomach feel queasy just thinking about it. That is, until someone slid over a box of her favorite fudge brownies, *Cocoa Lumps*. Staring at the packaging with its mascot in a straightjacket being chased by a hungry-looking mob, she instantly wanted to join the ravenous horde. There was no stopping her urge to eat now, consumption of a tasty treat was imminent — it was a sure thing. As she dove into one of the fudge brownies she recalled her mother saying that there were no sure things in life. Well, she was wrong. *Everyone's Loco for Cocoa Lumps* — even the queasy.

Next to her, Sombra asked Tiz to pass the box of brownies and she did without a word, all the time, munching on her selection quietly while staring at her water like it had been laced with poison.

Molly Von Butterburg, the vampire girl, asked Sombra if it was unusual for tree nymphs to be afraid of water, since Molly had heard that tree nymphs loved it as much as sunshine. Apparently, Molly had as many problems with sunshine as she did with certain types of water that could be thrown at vampires, making Molly deathly afraid of water balloon fights and swirlies in and around certain holy establishments.

To Tiz's horror, Fineus the Troll changed the conversation to something even worse. When he heard the term *swirlies*, he began explaining how the Heavenly Seven had been bragging about giving someone a swirlie near the general's office.

Listening intently, Tiz kept eating her meal, wondering if the troll knew it was her. If he did, he didn't say a thing. Either way, Tiz wasn't about to complain, or tell anyone for that matter. After all, who brags about their own swirlie?

After they ate, everyone in B Company headed to the band room to pick up their instruments. Drumming, tuning and squeaking, they proceeded directly to morning military formation in the main museum-like foyer in order go through their daily roll call and military drills.

At the end of it, the band played while the rest of the platoons marched out of the foyer and off to classes. Even on the accordion, Tiz managed to pick up the marching song real fast, and doing so lifted her spirits. The song basically played the same tune over and over, though simple, it was lively, adding some pep to the steps of the marching cadets. It sounded a bit like:

Dah-duh, Dah-duh — Dut-dut, Dut-dut — Dut-dut, Dah-duh...

When General Payne marched out he was so intense that he reminded her of a movie villain called General Invader from one of her favorite films, *Galactic Warriors*. In the film,

General Invader even had his own evil marching song called *Invader's Tyrannical March.*

Dunt — Dunt — Dunt — Boom — Ba — Boom...

Tiz loved playing it whenever her mother stormed into her room uninvited, hoping Mums would get the hint and leave. Suppressing a grin, Tiz decided to teach the band how to play it in case they wanted to test their bravery by teasing General Payne with it. And if not, at least it would put a smile on their faces.

After they were done playing at formation, the entire band returned to the music room to put their instruments away. Tiz waited for everyone to finish and told Sombra to go ahead to their first class without her. The first warning bell for classes to start began chiming away but there was still no sign of Char and his magical guitar. Tiz sighed and started off, fumbling with her map as she headed toward the door.

Distracted, she had forgotten one important thing. The door to the music room swung in *and* out, similar to a kitchen door at a dinner. Thump! Someone planted the door right in her face, knocking her over. She got up so angry while rubbing a new lump that her face blew up like a hot air balloon.

"Whoa," said Char, studying her jaw, "you've got lumps swelling on the side of your face."

"Those are my cheeks," she growled, "the lumps are on top of my head, thanks to you."

"Wow, for a second there I thought you had the mumps," he replied, looking at her face. "But you have to admit, you *do* take your fair share of lumps around here."

"So?" she replied, turning red, fearing that he also knew about the *Swirlie Situation.*

"Well..." he said, studying her face.

"Well what?"

"I think I have the perfect nickname for you," he said, staring at her cheeks. "From now on, I'm calling you *Lumps*."

Someone behind Tiz laughed. It was the vampire girl, Molly, she had been inside the instrument closet the whole time. Her pale face blushed fire engine red as she passed Char and ran out the door.

"Great," sighed Tiz as she stood up. "Now the whole school's going to call me that — I have enough nicknames as it is."

"That's the thing about nicknames," he said, calmly popping a toothpick in his mouth, "you don't get to veto them. Only the President of Mischief gets to do that, and that's me."

"Who cares, I still don't have to like it," she said, rubbing her head.

He watched her rub her bump. "You know what?" he said. "You rubbing your skull sort of reminds me of one of my old, fragile Cactus Cuties — the one shaped like a skull. It was just like you, it needed constant looking after."

"Um, first of all, *never* say that again. Second, Cactus Cuties don't need constant looking after," she replied. "You water them like once a month."

"Really?" replied the fallen angel. "Then no wonder mine died."

Tiz suddenly recalled knocking her own Cactus Cutie shaped like a skull to the floor in her bedroom, destroying it while trying to escape her mother's tree. But her selective memory alarm went off and prevented her from saying it. Even worse, her brain still wasn't working properly and put her on standby, making her teeter on her feet and look like someone that had no business climbing a tree, let alone the witch's tree.

Char stepped closer to her and examined her head more carefully. "Lumps, you don't look so good," he said.

That hurt her feelings to the point that she started snapping out of her daze. "Listen to me," she said impatiently, her whole plan of being suave and cool now out the door while she never made it past the doorframe. "I'll make you a deal."

"What sort of deal?" asked Char.

"You can call me whatever you want," she replied. "But only if you do something for me."

"That depends what it is," he said.

"Have you ever heard of the witch's tree?" she asked.

He nodded that he did.

"Well, I plan on climbing to the top of it," she explained. "But first I have to get better at it. And I need a spotter to catch me if I fall. A spotter for my training."

He pulled the toothpick from his mouth and held it out. "This is you," he said as he snapped it in two.

"No it isn't," she insisted. "But if I fall and don't have someone to catch me, then it might be."

"Lumps," he replied. "I can't save you."

"Then forget I even mentioned it," she huffed, pushing past the fallen angel, heading toward the door. "My mistake, I just thought when it came to falling *you'd* be able to relate." Tiz opened the door. "But never mind, I don't want your help. Heck, you can't even keep a darn Cactus Cutie alive."

"Wait," he said.

Tiz froze — contemplating. She had just broken the latrine machine laws twice in one sentence by saying *heck* and *darn* to him. Silently, she wondered if he was more impressed by that than affected by her guilt trip. Then for some reason she asked herself what Frenchy would do, probably because the girl seemed half-crazy, half-brave. *C'est la vie*, thought Tiz, as she turned back toward the fallen angel.

Char stepped closer to her. "Despite what you think, I have a reputation to protect here," he said calmly, buttoning up his banana-colored uniform over his belly. "I can't have you going around telling people that I'm yellow-bellied."

"So you'll do it?" she asked.

"Well, I can't have you calling me chicken, can I?" replied

the fallen angel, flapping his dark and very un-chicken-like wings.

Tiz smiled. "Thanks," she said.

"Don't thank me yet," he replied. "If you stink at climbing, well, don't expect to see me at a second practice."

"And if you stink at catching me," she replied, "I won't make it to a second practice."

He stifled a smile. "Speaking of *stinking*," he added, "there's one more thing."

"What?"

"Find a new perfume," he said, fanning his nose. "You do realize that I'm going to be catching you, don't you?"

Tiz turned redder than her hair. "It's a skin cream," she said.

"Whatever," he said. "Then get some new skin cream."

"That's fine with me, I hate it anyhow, so I *will* get a new one," she replied. "But don't be late for practice, it's right after lunch," she added as she left through the swinging door then popped her head right back in. "*Today*, after lunch."

He shook his head in disbelief. "I know," he said.

Tiz gave him an awkward thumbs up then left the band room blushing, her first climbing practice looming. She felt more nervous about it now than ever before. *Why did it have to be right after lunch*?

CHAPTER TWENTY-ONE — UNEXPECTED COMPANY

MORNING CLASSES WERE A BLUR for Tiz. Climbing practice was just around the corner and she was getting more and more nervous. So much so, she didn't eat any lunch, fearing that her new spotter would be wearing it, and considering his delicate sense of smell, would never spot for her again.

When she arrived outside the training room there was a massive crowd funneling toward an exit. She'd never seen so many people and creatures standing in line just to view a practice for an event. It seemed like the entire school was there, getting ready to watch a rock concert instead.

All the Mili-Tree Companies from A through Z had their own floating stands surrounding Iggy City hauled out into the zero gravity of the bubble. Tiz looked out a window of the school as the kids were floating toward their seats like astronauts inside a giant space station. And for once, none of them were trying to escape, making the practice seem even more important.

Tiz never felt so much anxiety about climbing a tree in her entire life, but this was Iggy City, this was the major league of tree climbing.

Tiz pushed open the training room door — she was late — all the other climbers were already outside.

After a quick change into her yellow climbing suit, Tiz strapped on her emergency pack with Pup Pup inside and stepped over to the training room door, looking out its window. She stood there and stared at one of the starting lines for practice at the roots of Iggy City, imagining how fast she would be able to scale the cosmic tree if they didn't activate the gravity inside the bubble.

As Tiz opened the door, she saw that the bleachers for all the companies were packed with kids, some of them with their parents sitting beside them. As the door thumped shut behind her, a sudden hush fell over the huge crowd. It felt like everyone was staring at her, especially the bulbous-eyed bee people in B Company, who quickly donned giant sunglasses as if to say, "We definitely don't know *that* witch — so buzz off."

Tiz took a deep breath and floated away from the training room door, drifting through the bubble and past the front of the viewing stands near the base of the tree.

A cascade of *boo's* pelted her from Wolfberry Company.

Banana Company didn't come to her defense either, staying silent, even the band, not a single toot from first platoon, no one raised an instrument. Though their arms were probably still sore from all the pushups they had to do because of her.

Then suddenly, Tiz saw someone stand up from behind a big tuba in the band and begin cheering for her. It was Mums, clapping and hollering encouragement to her daughter. She was supporting Tiz in front of everyone, including the other tree nymph mothers, not caring what people thought this time. She had said she was sorry, now she was proving it, putting her own life in danger just to be there for her daughter.

It meant the world to Tiz. So much so, tears of joy filled her eyes as though they were trying to wash away her grudge — maybe it was time to forgive.

Tiz wiped her eyes as she spotted another surprise that was nearly as big as her mother being there. Sombra was standing on the far side of all the Wolfberry climbers, hidden behind them while wearing her own set of banana yellow climbing gear. All of the other climbers were already standing at attention in front of General Payne and Colonel Monocle.

Tiz landed near them then she fell in line next to Sombra. She was so happy to see her there that she wanted to give her a hug — but having to do a ton of pushups before a climb wasn't exactly a recipe for victory.

Tiz and Sombra were the only two wearing the banana yellow uniforms of B Company, making Tiz wonder if her best friend felt just as out of place. "Oh my gosh," whispered Tiz out of the corner of her mouth so only Sombra could hear. "I'm so happy to see you, but what are you doing here?"

"The general said I could climb," replied Sombra. "There's always nine climbers, he kept repeating. I get the idea that he likes things to be exactly the same — no changes."

"Shhh," shushed Char from behind as all the spotters stepped up behind their respective climber. Tiz glanced to her left and saw the Dargen was spotting for Sombra. Frenchy Yew had a huge werewolf behind her, twice the size of Char. He growled at Tiz, but right at that second she thought about what Mums would want her to do. *Two wrongs don't make a right*, she reminded herself. So Tiz just smiled back.

Besides, she wasn't about to look away; she was so curious about everyone else's familiars that she was willing to risk a werewolf attack. Frenchy had a worm the size of a snake wiggling around in her backpack. Its round mouth had suction cups, no teeth, making it look like something from prehistoric times that nobody in their right mind would want to touch. That is, except Frenchy, who was petting it as tenderly as a rescued animal while sneering at Tiz.

Meanwhile, Pup Pup stared at the worm like it was the biggest hotdog he'd ever seen. Wagging his tail, he was about to take a leap of faith and find out for sure but Tiz distracted him in the nick of time. She pulled out a squeaky toy in the shape of a wolfberry that she bought from the school store (just for such occasions).

"Listen up!" shouted the general as his keen eyes suddenly locked onto Sombra like two sniper scopes. "So you *are* going to climb. Well, where's your pet familiar, cadet?"

Sombra pulled out an enchanted oven mitten she turned

into a purple cat.

"Kitten Mitten," said Sombra. "She's a bag of devouring — eats everything in sight — gone for good. I mean everything, fellow cadets. So don't even think about stealing her for an oven mitt. You put your hand up there and it's gone for good — you use it, you lose it."

Tiz hoped that didn't include Pup Pup, who Kitten Mitten was staring at like Pup Pup stared at hotdogs.

Frenchy giggled on the other side of them, unimpressed by the specimens Tiz and Sombra had chosen as their familiars.

The general cleared his throat again as he turned to Colonel Monocle. Even though the frail old man that looked like a mad scientist was standing right next to him, the general yelled, "Activate the gravity!"

The colonel raised his arm that looked like a gadget knife, selected a vise grip then pulled a lever at the base of the tree.

Slowly, everyone, including the viewing stands, sank down to the bottom of the bubble near the roots of Iggy City.

Afterwards, all eyes turned to the general. From a hip pouch, he pulled out nine baseballs like an umpire as he addressed the *Nine Climbers*. "I'm gonna throw them up in the air all at once and I want each one of you to catch a ball with one hand," he said.

Tiz and Sombra looked at each other, confused.

"*Do you understand the words firing out of my word shooter*!" barked the general.

"Yes, sir!" shouted the climbers.

"Good!" he yelled and without a count down he tossed all the balls into the air. The girls each raised a hand to catch one as the general watched. Tiz caught hers with her right hand. Everyone else caught theirs except Sombra, who grabbed at it desperately with her left hand as it kept bouncing off the bottom of the bubble.

Tiz was about to grab it for Sombra with her free hand.

"Red, don't you dare!" warned the general.

Pup Pup dropped his new chew toy with a squeak and almost leapt out of her pack after it, but Tiz pulled him back just in time then retrieved his toy for him. Watching Sombra bounce around on the bubble after the ball was like watching a monkey on a trampoline trying to catch a greased up banana. The stands started to cheer wildly as though it was the main event.

Tiz heard a squeal of happiness from Sombra. She finally succeeded in catching her ball, grabbing it with her left hand.

The general looked at Sombra who was smiling from ear to ear. "What did you learn, cadet!" he yelled.

"Sir, that I'm not good at catching things, sir," she replied.

"Negative, cadet! That you never give up!" he yelled. "Even if you are terrible! In this race, never give up on catching someone! If you fall, dust yourself off and get back up! Do you understand the words firing out of my word shooter!"

"Yes, sir!" yelled Sombra.

But it was Tiz who truly took that message to heart, hearing it like some kind of secret code — never give up on catching someone — especially if that someone is as mean as any witch and her name just happens to be Frenchy Yew.

"Now put those baseballs behind your back!" yelled the general.

Tiz and the other eight did so immediately.

"Tie 'em up," he ordered. Tiz felt Char tie her hand holding the baseball behind her back. Worse, it was her dominant hand, the most important one for climbing.

The general grinned. "Climbing the witch's tree is gonna be harder than climbing with one hand," he warned. "Now put the bags over their heads. That tree can spew a cloud of smoke into the air like an octopus sprays ink underwater. You won't be able to see a thing — so get used to it."

"Sir," interrupted the colonel. "The last time we started with the arm tied *and* the head bag, we lost half the climbers in the first practice — the true witch won with ease."

Tiz and Sombra looked at each other with widening eyes.

The colonel winked at them then looked at the general. "In hindsight, you said that we should have started with the arm tied first," he said. "It was an excellent suggestion, sir."

The general's face contorted. "Gosh darn it, you're right — I did say that. So today, we'll start with the arm."

All the climbers exhaled in relief, strangely comforted by the fact that only an arm would be tied.

"Don't get cozy, ladies," warned the general. "Have you ever been on a gigantic bucking bronco before? One that's twenty stories tall? With steam shooting out of its nostrils? No? Well Iggy City can imitate anything, even the witch's tree. So get your lassos ready and hold on tight, 'cause you're in for a wild ride!"

The crowd cheered!

The general signaled for the audience to be quiet.

The cheering subsided.

"Spotters," said the general. "Take the baseball from your climber — there's a number on it — lead your climber to the matching starting line at the roots. It's a shotgun start. If your spotter can fly, then they can only take you from side-to-side, not up. But if they fly around too much, they won't be there to catch you. That's the only rule. Everything else goes — an all out war. If you fall, you better yell for your spotter, especially if you're in a cloud of smoke."

In the stands, Tiz saw platoon leaders handing out things that looked like 3-D glasses and gas masks, knowing it would help the audience see through the smoke as well as breathe.

Tiz wanted to ask where her set was but was already being ushered by Char over to her starting line at tree root number nine.

When they arrived, Tiz looked back at her spotter. "Do you have an extra pair of those glasses and maybe a mask?" she asked.

"I don't even have a pair for myself," he said.

"*Great*," she sighed, pulling out a helmet from her emergency pack and strapping it on extra tight. Suddenly, she found herself longing for something to put over her face that would keep her from breathing in any smoke. Sadly enough, she was now on the verge of begging the general for one of his notorious head bags.

"On your marks!" yelled the stern man from afar, stretching his drawl out like a high note.

Tiz hurried to the starting line, scooting her toe right up to it. "Char, please keep an eye on Sombra too," she said, worried that Dargen might accidentally drop her best friend. "Think of us as one of those fancy jeweled eggs — beautiful to look at, but fragile."

Char laughed, but Tiz never meant it to be funny.

"Get set!" shouted the general.

Tiz leaned forward.

"GO!!!" yelled the general, firing a starting pistol into the air with a boom!

Tiz dashed up tree root number nine like a ramp, heading toward the first branch.

The crowd *ROARED*!

Tiz glanced to the side — Frenchy matched her stride for stride with Sombra not far behind.

Tiz heard Pup Pup growl and sped up. She grabbed the first branch with her only free hand, barely getting her fingers around it. While pulling herself up, a thought struck her head as if it was a coconut falling from above. Some tree limbs would be too thick for only one hand to work.

Tiz needed her best friend's help. The plan — get to Sombra — untie her hand — hope for the best. *Move, move, move*, she reminded herself. Tiz leapt to the next branch. She swung her legs around it, shimmying her way toward Sombra.

ROAR! A hydra head burst forth from the end of her branch!

"Pup Pup!" yelled Tiz. "Show him what you're made of!"

Pup Pup jumped out of her bag and scampered along the branch, hotdogs tumbling out of him like a lunch truck swerving to avoid an accident.

But it worked. Pup Pup lured the hydra head away.

Seizing the opportunity, Tiz began bounding from branch to branch like a gymnast. She tackled a maze of rising branches by flipping onto them as if they were balance beams, using her free arm to steady herself instead of climbing.

"Don't try that at home without a helmet on your dome!" yelled the general from below.

Tree nymphs were a different breed when it came to climbing trees. Especially when it came to balancing.

Tiz spotted a vine strung between two branches. She walked it like a high wire to get to the other side. But the vine started shaking. "Whoooooa!" yelled Tiz, as she desperately tried to balance herself but failed, tumbling over the side. Falling, she grabbed the vine as it started ripping from the tree — it was about to tear. Looking up, she saw a pair of banana yellow climbing shoes jutting out from a branch above, standing over her.

Kitten Mitten poked her head out from behind them.

The vine snapped! A hand grabbed her wrist! Tiz pulled herself up to the branch above with the help of her friend.

"Sombra!" blurted Tiz, as she started to untie her friend's hand. "You're a savior!"

"Well, I guess I sort of owed you one," said Sombra.

Wolfberry Company booed from below but the band in B Company started playing merrily, drowning them out.

"Squawk!" screeched Pup Pup on the branch above them.

But squawking and talking weren't the only after effects of the spell that had turned him into a parrot. Pup Pup started flapping all four of his paws as he flew over to a beehive sprouting magically from a branch and forming as rapidly as the ones Mums had created on top of her head.

CHAPTER TWENTY-ONE

"Squawk, make like a bee and buzz off," urged Pup Pup, "make like a bee and buzz off."

Tiz spotted the finished hive above them as Sombra started untying her hand. She was completely allergic. If a bee stung her it would be over. At that moment, Tiz wished she was a honey-loving bear with a thick coat of fur instead of a girl. But that image gave her an idea as Sombra freed her hand.

"We got to get out of here," said Tiz as she pulled a furry slipper from her pack that she used to make bear tracks. She shoved the paw into the opening of the large beehive like it was about to scoop out some honey. "Hurry up, lets go," she implored, not wanting to know what might come out of there. With their hands now untied, they both grabbed the branch above and started climbing.

A girl screamed!

Tiz and Sombra looked to the left. A hydra shook Jenna Oak in its mouth, growling as angrily as a dog that got a hold of its master's spray bottle. Luckily for Jenna, this hydra had no teeth. Tired of gumming her, it spit her out.

The crowd gasped!

Jenna fell toward the bubble, sending her spotter, a beefy centaur, into a full gallop, catching her just in time.

The crowd roared!!!

Sombra glanced down nervously. "Do you think the bubble is like a safety net?" she asked. "Because Dargen's not exactly half stallion."

"I wouldn't bet on it," said Tiz, unsure.

Sombra glanced down at Dargen as her spotter was in the process of putting a blindfold over his eyes in order to make catching his "delicate egg" more challenging. "Are you crazy!" yelled Sombra. "Take that thing off! Right now!"

"Don't worry," said Tiz. "Char's keeping an eye on you too."

Whoosh! A glowing banana whizzed by their heads. Then it looped back around like a boomerang. *Whoosh*!

They ducked under it again. Tiz looked up. The biggest monkey she'd ever seen was plucking another magic banana from a glowing bunch hanging above his head.

"We're on your side!" yelled Tiz, pointing to her banana yellow climbing suit.

"Banana-rang incoming!" yelled Sombra.

Tiz drew her slingshot out of her pack faster than a gunslinger and knocked the banana-rang out of the air with a truffle.

"Wow!" exclaimed Sombra. "They really are super foods!"

A third banana-rang whirled toward them.

But instead of ducking it, Tiz snatched it out of the air and flung it back at the monkey.

Whoosh! The monkey ducked the banana-rang but didn't see it cut the bunch above him. It fell, smacking him in the head. The furry primate tumbled from the tree and the general caught him right before he hit the bubble to a rousing applause from the audience.

Above, Tiz and Sombra climbed furiously, reaching the midpoint of the tree, ten stories up.

Below the two, Frenchy and her weird pet worm were gaining on them. With her hand no longer tied, she twirled the worm like a lasso, turning herself into the creepiest cowgirl in the universe.

Above all of them, the rest of the Heavenly Seven tried to get around a giant woodpecker protecting a huge nest of eggs. Looking desperate, the six climbers from Wolfberry formed a ladder with their bodies to reach a far away branch.

POOF! A huge cloud of smoke surrounded the six, pouring out of a hole in the tree trunk. They screamed for their mommies!

Below, mommies screamed for their kids!

Tiz heard the falling girls cry out for their spotters as they fell, down, down, down toward the bubble below.

CHAPTER TWENTY-ONE

The crowd gasped!

None of the spotters would get there in time!

Everyone covered their eyes!

The girls hit the bubble and bounced up like trampoline artists, somersaulting and twisting in the air before they landed on their feet.

The crowd cheered!

The magical smoke from above drifted down to Tiz and made her feel woozy, setting her endless imagination into motion. She saw herself the moment her heart seed was burning — throwing her necklace off and starting a tree on fire. The flames spread before the tree nymph's very eyes...

"*NOOOOO*!" screamed Tiz out of the blue, nearly blowing Sombra off the branch!

The blast from her mouth blew most of the dark cloud away.

"Holy smokes," said Sombra. "Are you okay?"

Still woozy, Tiz steadied herself on the branch. "I think so," she said, coming to her senses.

When the last of the smoke dissipated above them, they could see that even the giant woodpecker was gone.

But from below, Frenchy had climbed to within twenty feet of them.

Picking up Kitten Mitten, Sombra glanced down at their adversary. "What do Frenchy and a cheap lace doily have in common?" she asked Tiz.

"I don't know..."

"It's way past their time," answered Sombra, standing her ground like some sort of super heroine. "I'll stay behind and take out Le Pew. You go ahead."

But before Tiz could even protest, Frenchy struck first. She used her pet worm like a whip and snagged Sombra by the leg, yanking her from the tree before Tiz could grab her.

Sombra fell with her familiar toward the bubble below with a scream.

Char flew to catch her. But before he even got within fifty feet, Dargen calmly waved a glowing hand and Sombra began drifting down as gently as a feather. Holding onto her cat for dear life, she made it all the way down to the bubble below.

The sight of it gave Tiz another idea. If she was lighter she could climb faster. With Pup Pup hovering by her, Tiz slid her arms out of her emergency pack and let it fall, nearly knocking Frenchy off the tree.

"Sacré bleu!" yelled Frenchy from below.

"Take that, Le Pew!" yelled Tiz. "Le sack for you!"

Up and up climbed Tiz, now fifteen stories high, she only had five more stories to go to reach the top. She had always been the fastest climber in the Wailing Woods and was now confident in her lead, that is, until she glanced down...

Frenchy's heart seed pendant was glowing. Her climbing outfit was sprouting long spider legs. At first, Tiz thought she'd been bitten by something in the tree. But the smile on Frenchy's face said otherwise. Her adversary now had a full-blown spider suit, firing a web right at Tiz.

She dodged the first but the second one snagged the bottom of her shoe as she tumbled over the edge of the branch and dangled upside down by the webbing.

The crowd below gasped!

Frenchy crawled right up to Tiz, wearing her worm like a creepy scarf.

"Zeh Phoenix is caught in my web," said Frenchy to her pet. "Cut the web and let's see if *this* bird can fly."

Her pet dropped down to the branch and wormed its way toward the web.

Tiz tried to pull herself free.

Suddenly, a hailstorm of hotdogs rained down on the worm, knocking it from the tree.

"No!" yelled Frenchy. But Pup Pup was already landing on her head, licking her face — his jester's hat jingling merrily. "Stop that!"

CHAPTER TWENTY-ONE

Tiz used the diversion to pull herself up to the same branch as them and slip off the shoe snagged by the web.

The crowd below *ew'ed* and *aw'ed.*

Fighting Pup Pup, Frenchy the Spider ran out of branch, backing off the edge of it as the magical puppet leapt off her face, hovering in the air.

Tiz looked down, watching her nemesis fall.

The tree was hers to claim.

Tiz put her foot on the branch above as something sticky hit her ankle. She glanced and saw another spider web.

It was way too late to do anything about this one. Yanked from the tree, she too was now falling. Below, Frenchy was doing the same, but with a huge smile on her face as she held the web. Her spotter, the big werewolf, caught Frenchy.

Right after, Char caught Tiz next to them.

"You're cheating!" yelled Tiz. "Your spider suit's no fair."

The werewolf growled at Tiz. Pup Pup gave it right back as he landed nearby.

"Your pet gargoyle tried to blind me!" accused Frenchy. "You *are* the real witch!"

Half of the crowd started chanting, "*Witch, witch, witch...*"

"A-TEN-HUT!" yelled the general, silencing the audience.

The girls leapt from their spotter's arms and snapped to attention.

The general stared right at the two rivals. "A spider suit *and* a flying attack dog?" he yelled.

The girls held their breath.

"Amazing!" he shouted. "Great job, cadets!"

The audience cheered!

Tiz was in shock.

The general executed an about face flawlessly, turning toward the spectators. "It's a draw!" he yelled.

The crowd booed.

That's when Tiz noticed that Mums was gone. She glanced around desperately for her mother, searching amongst the students in B Company but could only find her empty seat.

Her mom leaving made Tiz even more upset as she looked back at the general. Tiz thought she had won the practice because she'd made it the closest to the top. But the general mumbled something about "close" only counting in horseshoes and hand grenades, and from the smile on his face, Tiz feared that he would be personally pelting her with them in the next practice if she didn't drop the subject.

So Tiz scooped up Pup Pup and her emergency pack then stormed off toward the training room with Char in tow as they walked under the glowing portals to the nine realms orbiting the school like moons.

From all the silence, Char must have realized how angry she was. "It's only practice," he said. "Let it go."

"Oh, I'll let it go all right," said Tiz, glancing up at the moon-like portals, "right after the realm of fire freezes over."

"I'm telling you, let it go," he said. "Besides, I have something that will not only cheer you up, but more importantly, make things easier for you, Lumps."

"What?"

"Meet me after lights out — in the common room."

"No way," she said. "If I get caught sneaking out after lights out, then it'll be 'lights out' for me. And when I'm out cold, they'll probably ship me off to Guristonia — wherever the heck that is."

"If you can't sneak out of the dorms without getting caught," he said. "Then you have no chance of beating the witch's tree."

Silence.

In a weird way — he was right.

"All right," she said finally. "But it better be worth it."

CHAPTER TWENTY-TWO — DEEPER THAN SKIN DEEP

WORRYING ABOUT MEETING CHAR after lights out that night, Tiz couldn't concentrate in any of her classes that afternoon. She accidentally started a fire in Elemental Chemistry. In Environmental Warfare, she couldn't hit a single fur coat with a paint bomb. And in Animal Search and Rescue she nearly got trampled by a baby rhinoceros named Little Nub Nub.

Even worse, by the end of the day, every time she made a boo-boo, another cadet would pinch one of her cheeks and call her by the pet name that Char had given her. "There goes Lumps," they would say, "piling up the bumps."

That night before bed Tiz decided not to fight the nickname anymore. Instead, she would embrace it. And if the fleshy lumps on the side of her face were part of the reason for the ridicule then she was going to make them stand out even more. Tiz took her make-up bag out and set it in front of a communal sink and mirror next to Sombra, who was washing her own face before bed.

Tiz opened a dark magical cream and began gently sponging it onto her cheeks. She needed a new skin cream anyway after Char insisted that she replace the smelly one that the colonel gave her. And she was more than happy to comply.

"Why are you putting make-up on?" asked Sombra. "It's time for bed."

"It's not make-up," replied Tiz as her skin started turning tanner and tanner.

"Well, it's not the stuff the colonel gave us," replied Sombra. "To drive away certain warlocks and fallen angels, right?"

"Heck no," whispered Tiz, wary of the potty mouth rules within the latrine machine laws, *especially* while near the latrine itself — she just wanted to visit, not live there. "It's a self-tanner."

"What?" said Sombra. "Why now?"

"Well, everyone's calling me Lumps, partly because of my big cheeks," said Tiz.

"So?" replied Sombra. "Why the tanner?"

"Duh — because *Everyone's Loco for Cocoa Lumps*," replied Tiz.

Sombra laughed. "Tiz, I like you," she replied, "but *you're* the one that's crazy." Sombra glanced around then whispered, "You're going to see *him* tonight, aren't you?"

Tiz shrugged. "Maybe," she replied, but the smile on her face grew too wide to hide the truth.

When they were done, Tiz unzipped the magic pocket Dargen had given her and dropped her stuff in. The zipper was an extremely handy thing, particularly its transferability. She could put it on all her clothes, even her pajamas.

With Sombra in tow, Tiz headed into the girl's dorm then climbed up into her top bunk, full of worry. She wanted to meet Char, but was afraid of getting caught. After the lights in the dorm went out, she tossed and turned like crazy. *Squeak, squeak, squeak*, squeaked her bed, sounding like her mattress was on top of chew toys instead of springs.

It had been a stressful day, but one good thing did come out of it. Tiz and Sombra learned a way to communicate without talking called *tap code*. Simon Says had mentioned it right before Tiz had to march into the general's office. The boisterous dwarf insisted that it was particularly useful if you were taken prisoner by the enemy. And since Sombra was now insisting that Mili-Tree Academy was *a lot* worse than prison as well as the whole institution being their sworn enemy, the two of them learned tap code right away.

It was also quite useful in the dorm after lights out, where whispering could get them both a hoard of pushups. By putting their ears up to the metal frame of their bunk bed and tapping on it lightly, Tiz and Sombra could signal different letters of the alphabet to each other, depending on the number of taps and pauses they made.

Tiz tapped out, "I need your spare pillow."

Sombra tapped, "Your cheeks are spare pillows."

Tiz tapped out, "Ha, ha, still need pillow."

Tiz looked down from her top bunk and Sombra hit her in the face with a pillow. "What was that for?" whispered Tiz.

"For getting self-tanner on my pillowcase," whispered Sombra, showing Tiz a dark spot from hitting her. "See."

"Gimme that," hissed Tiz, ripping it away.

"Shush," said Sombra, "use tap code."

"It takes too long," whispered Tiz, "I'll die of old age just yelling at you."

Sombra started tapping her reply back.

"Cut it out," whispered Tiz. "I'm not even sleeping on your silly pillow — I just need it to make it look like I'm still in bed."

Tiz stuffed Sombra's spare pillow under her covers, adding it to her own two. She molded them carefully to look like her body then quietly climbed down to the floor and slid under Sombra's bed.

"Bye," whispered Tiz.

Sombra poked the bed above her, pretending Tiz was still up there. "Stop talking in your sleep," she said.

Tiz got the message. With that, she started crawling under all the other beds toward the common room door as silently as a mole underground.

At the door, she waited for her platoon leader to go out then come back in before she snuck out into the common room.

But there was no one there. Her heart started to race. He lied to her.

"Hey," whispered a boy. "Up here."

Char clung to the cathedral ceiling, his back against it with his dark wings spread out like some sort of gothic painting in a church. He glided down and landed right next to Tiz, staring at her face.

"Your skin is darker," he said, looking at it closer. "Is that still mud on your face from when Little Nub Nub ran you over?"

"He didn't run me over," insisted Tiz. "And it's a new skin cream, not mud. I was paler than a vampire."

"Well, don't put anymore on, or else I'm going to start calling you Little Mud Mud," he said.

"If you call me that, I'll never speak to you again," she said, pinching him.

"Okay, okay," he said, retreating. "I'm on your side, remember?"

"So what did you want to show me?" she asked.

"It's not here," he said.

"Then where?"

He shook his head then held out his hand. "I don't have time to explain. Let's go."

"What? Where?" she asked, stepping back.

"You need to see for yourself," he replied.

"No," she refused. "The last time someone said that to me, I ended up in a burnt down forest — never mind, I don't even want to talk about it."

"If you don't trust me," he said, "should I really be your spotter?"

"Grrrr," growled Tiz. "If I go, you have to promise me one thing."

"What?" he asked.

"That you won't ditch me," she said. "No matter what."

He looked at her curiously as if trying to discern why through her eyes. Then slowly, his expression softened. "I won't," he replied.

Tiz thought he sounded sincere, but more importantly, was willing to give him the benefit of the doubt. "Okay," she said, taking his hand. "Let's go."

Char scooped her up in his arms.

"Whoa," she said. He was stronger than he looked.

Char flew them toward the ceiling.

Tiz's heart raced. They were going to crash. She shut her eyes, but they never hit. When Tiz peeked, both of them were as transparent as jellyfish. Char had phased them through the top of the barracks as ghosts. Now two specters, they were flying outside Iggy City, fleeing as quickly as the witches that paddled their bunk beds, heading toward the bubble surrounding the academy.

But instead of marveling at the stars an unexpected thing caught Tiz's eye. It was something she would have never seen if they hadn't taken the spectral form. Tiz could now see her heart beating and all her veins. And her heart didn't look like a normal heart. It looked like a giant red heart seed, pulsing fiercely. From it, sprouted veins that looked like vines, but not green ones, instead, bright red and orange, channeling flaming blood.

"What the heck! Why is that inside of me!" she blurted, freaking out, fearing now more than ever that she was the witch of legendary evil. "What the heck am I?"

"Try to calm down — that's what I want to find out," replied Char, flying with her in his arms. "That's where we're going."

With Tiz holding onto him, they passed through the huge bubble unseen, and as they did, a smaller one encased them, its magic protecting them as they picked up speed and rocketed away from Iggy City.

Tiz was so focused on the tiny flames surging through the veins in her hand that she barely heard the alarms from the academy. She didn't see the boarder hoarders flying around the bubble surrounding Iggy City like flakes in a snow globe, searching hopelessly for the two of them.

When they could no longer see the academy, Char changed them back to normal and Tiz was glad for it. Seeing her insides burning was unnerving at best and closer to terrifying. It was even scarier than streaking through space in a flimsy-looking bubble at break-neck speeds.

Ahead, in the distance, Tiz spotted something she first saw on the journey to the school. It was a bluish cloud of gas and cosmic dust that glowed from the light of a distant star of the same color. The cloud looked like the side of an evil witch's face, pointy hat and all.

"The Witch Head Nebula," said Char. "Its mind knows all things," he added mysteriously.

"Wait," blurted Tiz, "*stop, stop, stop.*"

The bubble eased to a halt.

Floating in space, Tiz stared at the eerie nebula. "It *will* know, won't it," muttered Tiz. "It'll know if I'm the witch."

Char nodded. "Do you even want to know?" he asked.

Tiz wasn't sure. There was such a finality to finding out. One so great it could crush her spirit if the news was bad and confirmed her greatest fear. "I don't know," she replied. "I just want to be Tiz Phoenix, nothing less, nothing more."

Silence. Watching the nebula, neither of them said anything for a while.

"Look at it," said Char, pointing to the Witch Head Nebula. "Isn't it weird that a cloud of space dust could clear everything up for you," he replied.

More silence. The witch-head cloud looked as creepy as could be. Tiz didn't want to talk about it, let alone go in it.

"It was probably an enchanted star at one time," added Char. "One that blew up. It changed. Just like everything does in the universe."

"Changed for the worse," said Tiz.

"Not necessarily," he said. "The cloud could form another star. Even though it looks like a witch right now, it could change."

Even while floating there she could see the cloud shifting. The whole universe was changing around her. And as powerful as the witch might be, even she was subject to the will of change. For the witch died and then returned. She *had* to change, but more importantly, *could* change.

Tiz reached her hand up toward the nebula, envisioning it bursting into a bright star. It gave her hope.

"Let's go," she said, staring at the witch-head. "I think I want to know."

Char nodded, and with a sudden jerk, their bubble resumed gliding toward the blue celestial cloud.

Tiz knew as much about the nebula as she knew about nuclear reactors — almost nothing. But after seeing the flames running through her body, she felt like she knew even less about herself.

Ahead lay the unknown, but there was something about the gloomy blue light illuminating the Witch Head Nebula that made Tiz feel a certain way. It made her feel sad and lonely.

As an accused witch, Tiz knew about those feelings more than she wanted to discuss. But if she gained the witch's power, she would change all of that. And if she had some power left over, she would come back and change the Witch Head Nebula too. She would make it into something better. She would transform it into the brightest star in the universe.

CHAPTER TWENTY-THREE — MINDING THE WITCH HEAD NEBULA

THE GASES INSIDE THE NEBULA reminded Tiz of the morning fog that clung to the Wailing Woods before the sun melted it away to reveal the forest's true identity. Ironically, she would be relying on an enchanted fog to clarify her own. Needless to say, she wasn't thrilled with the prospect.

Inside the bubble, Tiz hesitated to leave the safety of Char's arms. And who could blame her? The smothering fog outside their bubble was so thick she feared it would permeate their flimsy vessel and suffocate them. It was already bad enough that they were flying blind toward the Mind of the Witch Head Nebula.

"I don't like this place," said Tiz with a shiver. She had an eerie feeling that someone was watching them from afar, observing them right through the fog, wondering if they had the nerve to stay their course. "This darn fog," she complained. "I feel like we're in a flimsy little boat, floating toward a rocky shore — one without a lighthouse."

"There," said Char, pointing ahead. Floating in the distance, two glowing spheres the size of beach balls seemed to stare at them through the dissipating fog like a set of huge blue eyes. "There's your lighthouse."

"Oh my gosh — they're eyes," replied Tiz. "Giant eyes."

"The Mind's Eyes," said Char. "They're always open, even when the Mind is sleeping."

"If they start blinking I'm gonna freak out," warned Tiz.

Char didn't respond, making her even more nervous. Slowly, they flew between the eyes and the fog lessened. But the gases and the cosmic dust there swirled into curly shapes that reminded Tiz of a brain.

Char stopped the bubble at the edge of the Mind. "The

core of the universe," he whispered as though he was afraid of waking it, maybe even afraid that it might discern his own secrets. "And entering the Mind reveals your own core — it shows you what you really are."

"I *really* don't want to wake it up," said Tiz, biting one of her nails. "What if it's grumpy? Isn't one grumpy witch enough? Do you know I got blamed for waking the last one up?"

Char sighed — the kind of sigh a parent makes after they take you to the local swimming pool but then you don't want to go in the water. "So, you don't want to wake it up?" he said in a snarky tone. "Or you don't want to know the truth? Which one is it?"

"Hey," protested Tiz, crossing her arms. "Please don't talk to me like that, Mr. President of Mischief." She looked him right in the eyes. "Let's put the spotlight on you and see how you like it," she argued. "You're the fallen angel. Why were you expelled? And I'm not talking about school."

Silence. All the light seemed to leave his eyes.

Tiz felt guilty, still in his arms, she stared off to the side.

After a minute or two, she was unable to endure the awkward silence any longer. "Say something, please," she urged.

"I'll make you a deal," he replied. "If you can tell me who you really are, then I'll tell you more about myself."

Tiz looked away again.

"I know who I am," added Char. "Can you say the same?"

Tiz watched the gases and dust churn inside the Mind. "Maybe not," she said sadly. She was now ready as ready could be. "Go ahead, put me down."

Char gave her a nod of approval then set her down. "You'll have to go in alone," he instructed. But his serious manner only served to make Tiz even more nervous. "Our bubble ship will split — just use your own mind to tell it where to go."

Tiz nodded but didn't move, staring at the bubble. Walking into it would be like stepping off the edge of a cliff with only a flimsy net to catch you. If the bubble didn't split, then she'd die in the cold of space in an instant.

She closed her eyes then eased into it, feeling it stretch like plastic wrap. Daring a peek, she breathed a sigh of relief. Just as Char had said, it formed a separate bubble around her.

Commanding it with a thought, Tiz sent it gliding toward the churning cloud that comprised the Mind of the Witch Head Nebula — toward an answer she feared, yet desperately wanted to know.

Out of the blue, Tiz felt uncomfortably warm. Her bubble began flying through the cosmic cloud as though it was reentering Earth's atmosphere, flaming brightly. She felt like she was stuck in a sauna as she wiped sweat from her brow. Then the bubble started glowing even brighter, like it was a miniature sun. Tiz fell to her knees, light-headed and blinded by the light. White auras turned to black as she completely passed out from the heat, drifting and drifting into darkness...

As Tiz woke, she heard the shrill voice of a girl...

"*Welcome Tiz Phoenix, welcome to the fun house of your mind,*" screeched the voice.

Tiz peeked between her arms, but wish she hadn't, stunned by what she saw. She lay upon a bright surface lit with blue flames. But she didn't feel hot now. It was the opposite; she began shivering from the cold. All around her was a maze of mirrors like a weird fun house, one without a ceiling. Above, a frigid mist spouted up and arched over her as pale blue flames shot into the bleakness of space.

But bleaker still, a shadowy figure appeared in all the mirrors — a hooded girl bent over like an old woman — her hands hidden by her robe. Tiz squinted at the images but could not make out the shadowy figure's face within the darkness of her hood. If the grim reaper was a girl, it would have looked like her.

"W-Who are you?" asked Tiz, even though in her heart she already knew — she was gazing at *the witch*.

"*We are you*," said the hooded girls in the mirrors. "*We are reflections of our past, generations of us, why else would we dwell inside the mirror maze of your mind*?" Geysers of blue flames spewed into space! The fiery surface quaked!

Tiz wavered where she stood, but her initial thought did not. She was now sure that she gazed upon her greatest enemy. "Y-You're not me," she stammered, "y-you are *her*."

"*Tsk, Tsk, we better lose those nerves*," hissed all the witches in the mirrors in unison, sounding like one great big serpent. Then suddenly, the images started moving separately in their own mirrors — one twitching, one falling, one laughing, one crying. Just as quickly, they all froze in place. "*Lose those nerves, or we'll never get our tree back*," they said.

"Our tree?" questioned Tiz, dreading what she feared the most. "You mean *your* tree — and you can have it, what do you need me for?"

"*Like the bubble you came here in, you're the vessel*," said the witches, their eyes glowing red within the darkness of their hoods. "*A dark, cruel vessel...*"

"AAAAGH!" screamed Tiz, falling to her knees as she grabbed her head in pain. It felt like it was being squeezed by an invisible vise.

In her mind, the witches said, "*Oh yes, we can see the blue jay and WE know the wicked outcome of your slingshot, the one YOU are oblivious to...*"

Tiz had no idea what the witches were talking about, but before she could ask, the invisible vise atop her head tighten painfully as they dug even deeper into her mind...

"*That's just the tip of the iceberg, isn't it*?" they hissed. "*We can see all your delicious drawings — the Fog of Fear, the electrified fence — now that's our favorite. Oh how many creatures we shall destroy with it, such a delightful thing.*"

"It's not for killing!" shouted Tiz, shutting her eyes. "It's to prevent it, so that woodcutters don't hurt our trees!"

"*It's not for killing*," mocked the images. "*It's to prevent it, so that woodcutters don't hurt our trees*," they laughed, chanting it over and over until it became deafening. "*That's what they all say, until the first one dies*."

"STOP!" screamed Tiz so loudly that the next thing she heard was a CRASH. Her voice shattered all the mirrors.

Tiz covered her head as pieces clinked all around her, but when she opened her eyes, they were shards of ice and not broken bits of mirrors. No longer surrounded by the maze she was now kneeling on the frigid surface of a blue sun. Brilliant blue flames spewed up all around her, licking at the space above, cold and dark, as though it gave them sustenance to burn. Before her now stood the shadowy girl in the hooded robe, no longer multiplied by her mirrors, but just as horrible.

"You *are* evil," spat Tiz at the shadowy figure.

"Correction," hissed the witch. "*We* are evil — our own conscience — the little voice inside our head, the one that told us to hide our broken heart seed from our very own mother, so what does that say about us?" The witch raised her hands and the blue sun erupted in an explosion of light.

Tiz shielded her eyes, still on her knees.

When the light lessened, the witch held out her hand and in it beat a single red heart seed amongst an endless sea of blue.

A warmth rushed through Tiz — an overwhelming sense of joy. It looked just like her own heart seed...it had to be...it had to...

The witch stood over Tiz, offering her the seed. "Take it, it's a gift from *we* to *us*," she said.

Tiz trembled as her hand slowly rose toward it. The nearer it drew to the seed the more it began shaking, worse and worse. Then she noticed something about the seed that she had overlooked, blinded by her joy — it wasn't beating in rhythm with her own heart.

"Take it!" hissed the witch.

Tiz slapped it from the witch's hand.

The seed hit the flaming surface and shattered into ice.

"You're a liar!" growled Tiz.

The hooded girl stared at Tiz, then slowly began laughing. "Clever girl," she said. "Maybe there's hope for us yet."

"A dark seed of worry," said Tiz. "That's what you're planting. But I don't believe you. I know I'm not you. I'm know I'm not an evil witch."

But before the witch could reply Tiz lunged for her hood.

The shadowy girl disappeared in a burst of blue flames, leaving Tiz standing in a raging sea of blue fire.

Wicked laughter filled the ears of Tiz as the surface of the blue sun erupted even more violently than before.

"I'll find you!" shouted Tiz in the middle of the fire, falling to her knees again and pounding the surface with her fist. Suddenly, she went from feeling freezing cold to burning hot as all of the blue flames turned orange and red.

"I'll find out who you are!" screamed Tiz. "Then I'll beat you to the top of your own tree!" Explosions of pain began bombarding her head as she succumbed to the heat once again, passing out, deeper and deeper into darkness...

A soft blue light. Tiz awoke from her nightmare, wiping sweat from her brow. She was back in her little bubble ship near the edge of the swirling gases and cosmic dust that comprised the Mind of the enchanted nebula, but she felt different, very different, like going from the chill of winter to the warmth of summer.

Tiz could still feel radiant heat, but this time it was pleasant. It felt warm and comfortable, like sitting next to a cozy fire. That's when she felt them — wings completely made of flames — her very own fiery wings, like a phoenix, enveloping her. They were part of her own body, not unlike

Char's wings. She wondered if Dargen's spell that had turned her into an orange parrot had something to do with it, and like with Pup Pup, had changed her.

Out of the corner of her eye, she saw the fallen angel gliding toward her in his own bubble. His eyes were transfixed on her wings. "You're not the witch," he said.

"That's not what she told me," replied Tiz. "She even called us 'we'."

"She's a liar," said Char, though he wore a worried expression on his face like a grim mask. "She doesn't want you to look for her. But if you could see yourself, your wings, there's no doubt you're a phoenix through and through — the bird, tree and girl, all blended into one."

But to Tiz, he didn't seem to be the least bit happy about it. "Then why are you looking at me like I'm a ghost?" she asked.

"I'm just afraid it might also mean something else," he replied.

"What? That I'm a fallen angel too?" she asked, getting more and more worked up. "Am I dead? I'm dead aren't I?"

"Calm down," he said. "You're not dead."

Tiz wiped more sweat from her brow. "Then what is it?" she pleaded.

"Well, it's gonna sound — well, sort of weird," he said.

"Look around us," she said, glancing at the nebula and the bubble that held them. "Weird is what we're all about."

"Are you sure? Absolutely sure?" he replied slowly, seeming to give her one last chance to stop him. "Because you're not gonna like what I have to say."

"Try me," said Tiz bravely, her wings flaring brighter.

"Then brace yourself..." he said, reluctantly. "A phoenix is a highly sought after component for a certain spell — both a phoenix tree and the flaming bird. If used in just the right way, the components can bring someone back from the dead."

Looking at the fallen angel, Tiz shuttered, wondering if he wanted the components for his own personal spell.

"And *no*, they're not for me," he said, reading her face like a book. "As you can see, I'm already back from the dead. I wouldn't exactly need them, would I?"

"I knew that," said Tiz, but inside, she was glad to know for sure.

"Unfortunately, you're in more danger than you think," said Char somberly. "But at least you're not the witch."

"Then why do you still sound like someone just died?" asked Tiz.

Char looked away.

Tiz merged her bubble with his as her fiery wings faded away. He said nothing. Tiz took his hand. "Please," she begged, "tell me what's wrong. I need to know."

Char sighed. "I'm sorry," he said softly. "But you're dying...your life will burn bright like a bonfire, but not for long."

"What?" she blurted. "How do you know?"

"I can see your life force — your spectral form at *all* times," he said. "The fire in your veins, it's fading. It won't last for long — maybe a few weeks. It will leave you with each breath, then eventually, your last one will extinguish it."

Tiz turned away and he left her alone with her thoughts. She didn't want to believe him, though nonetheless, she did. In her mind, she heard him sing his stupid song about the *burning bird* with its dark lines, two of which at least held some hope...

...but there's still time, for even the looming dead can learn...

Now she understood why he had sung it. He saw that she was dying. "*I can't save you*," he had told her in the band room.

She turned back toward him. "What if I can win the witch's tree and claim the living key," she asked finally, realizing that the living key may not only be a physical tool, but also one that would help her live — a *key* to living. "What if I can beat her?"

"How?" he replied. "You don't even know who she is."

"I know how to flush her out," said Tiz. "When I mess with my mom's tree, like tickling it, she comes running. I could do the same to the witch's tree, but I have no idea how to find it."

Silence. Char seemed to be reflecting on something gloomy.

"What is it?" she asked, "what's bothering you?"

"What if I knew how to find it?" he said finally.

Tiz squeezed his hand. "Then I'd want you to take us there," she said, "right now."

Char's expression saddened even more. Slowly, he nodded.

The bubble eased forward then they sped away at the speed of light, back toward the way they came.

Char didn't say what path they would be taking and Tiz wasn't anxious to know. She had something else on her mind. "What if I tickle the tree," she said, "and it's me that starts giggling."

"Well..." said Char, "at least you'll be able to laugh about it."

Tiz elbowed him. "Sometimes I think you're being funny just to hide what you really want to say, to hide the truth. And don't bother asking me what I mean, you still haven't told me why you got kicked out of certain places." She pointed up to the heavens above. "*And* from down there," she said, pointing toward a darkness as black as the abyss.

"Well..." he stalled. "Someone had to come back here and keep you out of trouble," he added, changing the subject.

She poked him in the ribs. "You haven't even told me yet if you'll keep on spotting for me."

"That's because you don't *need* a spotter anymore," he said. "You can just summon your new wings and glide down."

"Glide between branches? With wings of fire?" she said,

looking up at him with her emerald eyes. "You obviously haven't climbed a tree before."

"Once," he said, "and it flicked me off like a fly."

Tiz looked at him curiously. But she certainly didn't need to ask which tree. She knew she would be seeing it for herself soon.

As they neared the school Tiz felt her skin go cold. Char transformed them into their ghostly bodies once again. Tiz tried not to look at the flames flowing through her veins. She already had enough to worry about as she gazed at Iggy City. "So, are we sneaking back in?" she asked. "I thought we were going to see the witch's tree?"

"We are," he said as he steered them toward the bottom sphere orbiting the school like a dark moon. It was the most foreboding one, bleak as an empty eye socket. As they approached it, a white mist in the black portal swirled into a grim-looking skull.

"The underworld," said Tiz knowingly after learning about the spheres. "What does a tree live off in the underworld?"

"You don't want to know," he replied. "Trust me."

Tiz looked up at him. "I do trust you," she said. "That's why I picked you to be my spotter."

"Maybe you shouldn't have," he replied.

"What? What do you mean?" she blurted. "That's not exactly something I want to hear, especially with where we're going."

He said nothing. As ghosts, they sped through the bubble protecting the academy and headed toward the dark sphere orbiting the lowest roots.

Tiz and Char both stared at the portal they were approaching, full of darkness and dread.

"You asked me why I was thrown out," he said finally, gazing at the abyss. "Well, I wasn't. I made a deal to get out."

"What kind of deal?" asked Tiz.

"One for a set of white wings," he said. "To get rid of my

charred ones. That's what I want."

"How?" she asked. "Tell me, I'll do everything I can to help."

He glanced down at her. "By destroying the witch," he said as they entered the dark portal. "If you touch her tree and *do* feel something, then get away from me, fly as fast as you can."

CHAPTER TWENTY-FOUR — THE LADY OF NIGHT AND LIGHT

BLACKNESS. One as dark as the last words Tiz heard from Char's mouth. "*If you touch her tree and do feel something, then get away from me, fly as fast as you can*," he warned. She was afraid of him now, knowing what he might do to her if her greatest fear indeed came true. The boy she once thought was her guardian angel was now anything but one. And if her worst fear came true, he'd be her angel of death.

As her eyes adjusted to the dark, she found herself standing near him in a small cave that led into a huge cavern about a dozen feet away. They were no longer ghosts, but Char's face looked as pale as one.

Tiz examined her own arms and her skin looked the same as his, pure white. "Well, so much for my self-tanner," she whispered, trying to ease the growing tension.

"Shhh," he shushed, pointing toward the mouth of their cave and the cavern beyond. "Look."

Auras of dim light gradually began to illuminate the cavern. Two lines of people, just as pale as them, shuffled along like zombies past the mouth of their cave and through the huge cavern along two parallel paths separated by a deep chasm.

The path on the left side of the cavern was as bleak and dark as a narrow ridge on the side of a dead volcano. Those walking on it wore black hooded robes and held lanterns lit with blue flames, ones that looked as chilling as the icy fires in the Witch Head Nebula.

The path on the right was much more inviting. To Tiz's surprise there was beauty there — flowers, shrubs and small trees. Those traveling it wore white hooded robes and carried lanterns of golden light that helped to keep the frosty auras of the blue flames at bay.

If she had to choose one side or the other, then it would have been an easy choice. Yet neither side looked truly happy so Tiz felt sorry for them all.

"They're dead, aren't they?" she whispered.

Char didn't respond.

"Where are they going?" she asked.

"To the gatekeeper, one we have to get past," he replied. "Down here, she's known as the Lady of Night and Light."

"The Lady of Night and Light?" asked Tiz.

"Don't look at her," replied Char. "That's all I'm going to say. Otherwise you'll get more curious than you already are. And down here, looking at the lady in charge will get you more than just pushups."

"Don't look at the Lady — I got it," she replied. "Even though she sounds *really* amazing, not a problem — I hope."

"Don't hope — know," he said as he reached behind a boulder and picked up two lanterns. As soon as he touched them, they both lit with blue flames. He handed one to Tiz.

She looked at it, disappointed.

"What's the matter?" he whispered.

"I was kind of hoping the flame would turn gold, you know, after you handed it to me," she replied.

"You haven't earned that," he said. "And neither have I." He reached behind the boulder again and pulled out two black hooded robes. Donning one, he hid his wings underneath the dark robe. With its hood up, he looked as grim as the witch from the eerie blue nebula while he handed the second robe to Tiz.

"Can't you just turn us into ghosts? So we can sneak by?" she asked as she donned it then put her hood up.

"It doesn't work that way here," he replied as he steered her shoulders toward the walking dead. "The rules are different here. And not everything's dead down here either — the witch's tree, the Lady, you and me — the smart survive. The dumb, well, they don't stay alive. So let's be little Einsteins — shall we?"

"Einstein's dead, genius," replied Tiz.

Char moved her forward, shuffling along right behind her. After about a dozen steps or so they both merged into the marching line of blue lanterns right behind a pale woman. They followed the procession toward a great hall in the distance that seemed to continue on forever, one side bright, one side night, like two halves of a split moon.

Tiz noticed that the pale woman walking in front of her discarded a crumpled photo. Tiz snatched it up on the fly in order to have something to look at instead of a certain *lady* up ahead; one who sounded like the most interesting individual in the universe to observe, and at the same time, someone she was absolutely positively not supposed to peek at no matter what.

Tiz flattened out the crumpled photo then wiped the dirt off of it. It was a picture of the pale woman with her arm around a beautiful little girl with blond hair and big blue eyes. The girl looked about the same age as the twins (roughly eight) and just as neatly dressed. Based on the photo, if Tiz had to guess, she would say it was the pale woman's daughter.

Wondering where the little girl was now, Tiz saw a rock skip across her path, coming from the direction of the golden trail across the chasm. Tiz looked to her right and had her question answered about the girl. Blond-haired and blue-eyed, the little girl raised a golden lantern above her head as she held out the same photo toward Tiz and walked stride for stride with her. The girl might have looked more like the twins, but after throwing the rock and holding her golden lantern above her head as though she was reaching for the stars, she reminded Tiz of herself.

The little girl yelled the word *mom* but no sound reached the path of the blue lanterns. It was as if the words were swallowed up by the chasm between them. She was either unable to speak or a dark spell was at work here. But thankfully, because of the light from the girl's lantern, Tiz could still read her lips.

Watching the little blond girl, Tiz noticed her blue eyes welling up with tears. She had been throwing the rocks to get her mother's attention, but she might as well have been throwing them into the chasm instead — the woman was lost in thought as dark and deep as the gorge between them.

Tiz wanted to say something to the mother but she reminded herself that Char was right behind her as they drew closer and closer to the Lady. Even worse, Tiz couldn't look up to see how far away the Lady was because she wasn't supposed to be looking at her in the first place.

Frustrated, Tiz was neither prepared for what came next nor in a proper state of mind for it. Though more than likely, no one ever could be.

The pale woman in front of her raised a wicked looking whip with nine short strands straight into the air. Walking, the mother lashed her own back — *whip, whip, whip...*

It was one of the worst things Tiz had ever seen. It felt like the moment she knew her heart seed was utterly and completely broken. For the whipping she was witnessing broke her real heart just the same.

The back of the mother's robe began to tear. It was a dark and sad thing. Tiz looked back down at the photo in her hand, trying not to watch, but there was her daughter again. Worse, Tiz knew she was just across the chasm, probably watching her mother hurt herself.

Tiz peeked at the golden path. The little girl dropped a rock from a limp hand. She was giving up hope. Maybe it was the realization that she would never see her mother again, and even worse, her last image of her mom would be like this, beaten and broken. It reminded Tiz of how Mums looked as she left her own daughter crying in the Unburnable Forest. All the emotion from that day came rushing back like a tidal wave — there was still a chasm between Tiz and Mums as well.

Tiz glanced again at the golden path. The little girl cried in her hands as she peeked at her mother punishing herself for something that might have led to both of their downfalls. But by the way the daughter was behaving, that "something" might also be forgivable.

Tiz's own eyes welled as she turned back toward the mother and watched her whip herself. She wanted desperately to intervene, but Char was right behind her, in turn, watching everything she did that might make them stand out to the Lady.

The whipping reminded Tiz of the time she was yelling at herself in the mirror after putting on the hideous dress for the Planting and Mums came up behind her to calm her down. Her mother had been there for her before, especially when Tiz burned her seed and the ashes blew away in the wind. Mums wrapped her arm around Tiz like a warm shawl, comforting her without a word.

A drop of blood landed on the photo of the woman and her daughter, staining it worse than any dirt and grime. How could Tiz just look away? Doing so, she felt her own heart was going to crack just like her seed. Tiz wiped the picture off on her own clothes. She could no longer bear to stand by and watch, no matter what the cost. This was no longer about her and her safety. It was about what was right.

As the whip came back, Tiz grabbed the pale woman by the wrist. The mother didn't fight it, holding the whip over her shoulder as they walk forward together.

Tiz slid her hand down to the woman's fingers and gently pried the whip from them. In its place, she slid the crumpled photo. Doing her best to send the mother a message, she pointed the woman's finger toward the other path then laid a comforting hand on her shoulder.

Tiz could feel her body shiver as the woman looked at the

photo.

"If you say you're sorry, then she might forgive you," whispered Tiz, knowing the sound of the woman's voice might not reach the girl, but that mouthing the words *I'm sorry* or any other gesture of contrition should work.

"Shhh," insisted Char nervously from behind.

Shaken by what she had been witnessing, Tiz wasn't in the mood to be told what to do, especially by someone that might turn on her before long. It was hard enough that she had to be near him, but now he was walking behind her. So she turned around and stuck her tongue out at him, letting him know exactly how she felt. Then, for added emphasis, she tossed the whip into the chasm as if to say, "Don't even think about hurting me either."

When she turned back, the pale woman was looking across the dark span at her blond little daughter holding a lantern as bright as her hair. Tears welled in the woman's eyes — it was now up to her. Tiz's message had gotten through.

But would they? In the distance, Tiz spotted the base of a tall throne made of gleaming ivory bones, fit for the Queen of the Underworld — the Lady of Night and Light.

The throne was still several hundred yards away, so Tiz decided to brave a look at her. She knew it was now or never. So she took a deep breath and glanced up, just for a second.

But she wished she hadn't.

The woman sitting on the throne of bones stared right at Tiz as coldly and expressionlessly as the statue of a goddess. The left side of her face matched the beauty of the right side of the path. Her skin there was fair and her hair so golden blond that it radiated light. But the right side of her face was black as night and her hair there was a ghostly white. It was as bleak as the left side of the path they were walking along. Tiz put her head down, afraid that staring at the dark side of her face would make the flames in her veins roar to life.

"Don't look at her again," whispered Char from behind,

"not even if we make it past her, not ever."

Tiz nodded. But it was like trying not to look at the TV when your mother told you there was a bad scene coming up that you weren't supposed to see. How would you ever truly know what was happening?

Tiz made herself watch her feet. The last time she looked up it seemed like they had at least five hundred steps to go. So she started the count down. Four hundred and ninety-nine, four hundred and ninety-eight, four hundred and ninety-seven...

With only twenty steps left, she stopped counting, confident that they would make it past.

"HALT!" yelled the stern voice of a goddess, powerful and dreadful, shaking the entire cavern.

Everyone stopped.

"I see that someone wishes desperately to gaze upon me..."

Despite her best try, Tiz couldn't keep her eyes down. She felt her head turn as if an invisible set of hands moved it.

Looking up, Tiz got her first close look at the Lady of Night and Light and feared that it would be her last. The dark side of her face was lifeless decaying flesh. In her hand she held a scepter with a skull at the tip, pointing it toward Tiz.

"Your mistakes, you've come to pay for them, haven't you?" she said with a queenly confidence. "Tell me, would you do anything to undo your missteps, to make right the errors of your way — *to choose another path.*"

Fear shook Tiz as if she once again suffered the bitter cold of the Witch Head Nebula, terrified that she would remain there for all eternity. And for once, the fear worked in her favor, keeping her throat clenched like a fist, silent as a deer in headlights, even over the strength of the goddess's spell.

"What say you?" insisted the Lady.

Tiz bit her tongue. She felt the fire in her veins flow into her mouth, but still she would not speak.

After what seemed like an eternity, the pale woman in

front of her spoke. "Your grace," she said, "it is true, I've long wished to gaze upon you — so beautiful, the face of death — yet equally as frightening." The woman stared down at her feet in shame. "You see, my mother left me to fend for myself when I was still only a child. And I too have stumbled along that dark path, doing the same to my daughter."

The Lady stared at both the woman and Tiz. Slowly, the Queen of the Underworld shifted her scepter from her decaying hand to her fair one. The rod began glowing with a golden light.

Tiz shut her eyes, fearing a great power would issue forth, destroying them both...

But it never came.

"Old mother," said the Lady at last. "Your daughter can hear you now. Beg her for forgiveness. In this matter, she shall be the Lady of Night and Light."

The mother bowed then turned and faced her daughter who was standing on the other path. After a moment, the pale woman simply fell to her knees before her child, sobbing.

"I forgive you, mother!" screamed the golden-haired girl at the top of her lungs. "I forgive you, mom!"

Tiz cried, wiping her eyes.

The Queen of the Underworld raised her grim scepter and a glimmering golden bridge spanned the chasm.

The mother scrambled onto it with her lantern as its light gradually changed from blue to gold and her robe turned from black to white. The woman ran across the path recklessly to her daughter and they embraced.

Soon after, the golden bridge disappeared.

Tiz was happy for them, hoping that one day she could feel the same kind of joy with her own mother. But since it seemed unlikely to take place any time soon, there was a sadness consuming her thoughts as well. So much so, she didn't notice that the Lady gave her one long last look, a knowing look.

"Proceed!" commanded the Lady. And every one did, moving slowly forward like a funeral procession. Too slowly for Tiz's liking, for she would have run if she could have.

CHAPTER TWENTY-FIVE — MEETING THE MONSTER INSIDE AND OUT

WALKING DOWN THE BLEAKEST PATH in the underworld while holding a lantern with a flame that was as blue as her mood, Tiz felt a hand pat her back as if to say, "Good job, you didn't get us banished to this place forever." She needed that encouragement and the reassurance was extra special coming from Char. As they marched up a rocky pathway she made a promise to herself. That if he stayed on her side, remained true to her, then she would also help him overcome his own problems. In fact, she swore to herself that she would try.

Without any warning, Char yanked her into an alcove — her thoughts rudely interrupted by the fallen angel that she just swore to save. He peeked out, glancing around to make sure no one noticed.

"Did the Lady see us?" she asked, worried.

"No," he replied. "And be glad she didn't, or she'd personally march us up the rest of the path. And if she did, then let's just say that an eternity at the academy would seem like a vacation compared to where we would be going."

Char turned around and set his lantern down. Using the sleeve of his robe, he wiped clean the dark stone wall behind them.

Underneath the soot and grime, a symbol had been carved into the ancient rock, one of a burning tree with branches like a hydra and a twisting tower made of thorns growing out of the treetop. Holding her lantern up to it, Tiz recognized the symbol instantly. "The Unwithering One," she muttered.

"It's a door," he said, glancing down at her. "Only someone that has the power of the burning tree can open it."

"Me?" she replied unsure. "I thought you said I wasn't the

witch."

"You're both fire and tree," he replied. "Phoenix and heart seed. You can open this passage."

Char hovered his hands over the symbol. "Put your hands here and here. One for the fire, one for the tree."

"But what if you're wrong," she said. "I'm pretty attached to my hands. Besides, I'm told they come in quite handy when climbing a tree — especially the witch's tree."

From behind, the shrill voice of an old woman shrieked, "Then allow *me* to open it, *deary*."

Tiz jumped — she knew instantly that it was some prior version of the witch. Now deceased, she lurked in the underworld.

But little did Tiz know that elsewhere, far away, her friends suddenly felt afraid for her; Pup Pup was barking madly in his cage, Sombra was having a horrible nightmare, and Dargen was frantically searching a magical map for her.

"So, you're *here* to replace me, I see, I see," said the witch, veiled in her dark robe, "you're here to be the new guardian of the Unwithering Tree. But be careful what you wish for, *lil' missy*."

"I didn't wish for any of this," said Tiz. "You did."

"My tree did," said the witch, her eyes glowing green within the dark depths of her hood, "and it wants to meet you. *For the tree is hungry*."

The witch summoned a wind as strong as a hurricane, smashing their lanterns into bits and pieces. The stone door behind them slid open — the wind trying to force them inside.

A gust lifted Tiz and Char off their feet, blowing them through the stone doorway and sending them tumbling into complete darkness. Tiz tried to scramble to her feet but the wind was too strong. She watched helplessly as the stone rose again and slammed shut, locking them into a pitch-black cavern, one from which she could see no escape.

"Can you see anything?" whispered Tiz to Char in the dark

cavern. Even with her eyes accustomed to penetrating the night in the Wailing Woods, Tiz had problems seeing in the pitch-black of the cavern they were blown into as if every bit of light had fled from the evil in this place. She would have even preferred the chilling aura of the blue lantern over this and was upset that both of theirs were shattered by the wind.

"I can see a little bit," replied Char as he took off his robe then flapped his wings. "Can you summon your phoenix wings, so we can get some light? I can't make mine burn without playing the runes on my guitar."

"I can lend you my string-staff," replied Tiz, taking off her own hooded robe. She was glad to be rid of it. In truth, wearing it made her feel like the witch.

"We don't need your staff," encouraged Char. "I've seen you do it — all on your own."

Tiz hesitated. "I'll try," she said finally then started humming softly like she was meditating.

"What are you doing?" he asked, alarmed.

"Shhh," replied Tiz. "I'm warming up my voice." And that she did. Though Tiz couldn't see it right away, her throat started glowing red, followed by her heart.

"Wow," said Char, listening and watching her. "It's beautiful."

Tiz felt her cheeks flush red. The warmth she felt from him at that very moment seemed to amplify her powers, just as her mother had said.

Fiery wings sprouted from her back, giving them some light.

Tiz gasped at what she saw — not more than a few feet away from her lay the bones of all sorts of beings, some still wearing their armor and cloaks while their axes, staves and daggers were strewn about, signifying a terrible defeat.

In the darkness beyond they could hear slow, heavy breathing, like a horde of monsters was sleeping.

"We're not gonna make it out of here..." muttered Tiz.

CHAPTER TWENTY-FIVE

"Are we..."

Char didn't answer. He didn't need to.

Fear filled Tiz's heart, fueling her wings, making them burn even brighter. With the added light, they could see the base of the sleeping giant that was the Unwithering One; a gargantuan carnivorous plant that looked part creature and part tree. A thing that neither seemed to fear fire nor was bothered by its brightness. It merely kept on sleeping, glowing an eerie green from the slime it secreted from its pores, making itself slippery and that much harder to climb.

The slimy green tree was the living version of the witch's symbol. It was by far the biggest carnivorous plant she'd ever seen. Heck, it was the biggest monster she'd ever laid eyes upon. Half of its branches were scaled like a snake and ended in the shape of a hydra head with thick bark for skin and poisonous sap dripping from its fangs. Though sleeping, they were no less imposing, billowing thick streams of smoke from their nostrils. Tiz counted twenty of them and stopped. Her eyes fell upon something even more disturbing. There were a few purple flowers growing in the canopy, wilting, but still clinging to life, ones she recognized immediately.

Whatever this witch's tree was now, it had once been a phoenix tree. Dark thoughts started racing through her mind. Was she herself the witch in a previous life? And if so, how did she conquer the tree and become her? But more importantly, was this her eternal fate? One to be repeated over and over? There were so many questions, but so far, very few answers.

Tiz tried to see higher up in the tree but she could only make out shadowy shapes at the edge of the light. Even still, through the maze of branches and hydra necks, she could see the outline of the Tower of Thorns at the top, rising up between a large gap in the cavern's ceiling.

At the very top of the tower, through a miniature window the size of fist, Tiz spotted a tiny pulsing red light, not unlike the one that once lit her old heart seed. Her real heart started racing with excitement, and to her elation, so did the pulsing light at the top. To Tiz, it was the strongest homing beacon she'd ever seen. There was no doubt it would belong to her if she got there first; the living key her mother's book mentioned, but more importantly, a new heart seed for whoever turned out to be the fastest and proved to be the worthiest. *My living key*, she thought as she stretched her hand toward it like a twinkling star in the night sky — her very own star, one that gave her hope. *My key to living...*

But a dreadful thought occurred to her as she stared at it. Not only could the other climbers claim it, but everyone would have to make a choice — to claim the seed or the tree. It would have to be one or the other — not both. And there was a part of Tiz that dreaded the witch claiming the tree, almost as much as she feared losing another chance at a heart seed. It was a choice that she would rather not think about, but yet, was now emblazoned in her mind as vividly as the Unburnable Forest as she stared up at the pulsating seed.

"Could that be yours?" asked Char, looking up. "Another heart seed?"

Tiz nodded, entranced. From above, she heard a girl singing softly. At first she thought she was imagining it. It was the lament she learned for the Planting. Tiz didn't know what to make of it. "Can you hear that?" she asked Char.

"Hear what?" he replied. "The hydras breathing?"

"No," said Tiz, lowering her arm. "Never mind." She didn't want him to think that she was losing her mind, even if she might truly be going crazy. But then Tiz saw a purple flower floating down from the direction of the tower like the handkerchief of an imprisoned maiden. Someone was trapped up there with the seed. Tiz was confident of that now and in her heart, she believed she could not only gain a new seed, but also help the previous nymph who claimed the tree. Maybe it was even a past version of herself, one she couldn't remember.

Whoever it was had relinquished her heart seed to claim the tree. And now, it was "up for grabs" so to speak. Personally, Tiz would be more than happy to claim it instead of the witch's tree. No contest.

Despite the witch's tree being a million times more frightening than she had ever imagined, she wanted to climb it even more now. No, she needed to do it, like a tree needs sunlight, and her light was beating in the top room of that tower.

Tiz turned her eyes back to the descending purple flower. It landed near the thick roots of the tree, ones that looked like the toes of a huge lizard. As the flower settled, Tiz noticed something strange about the root it landed upon. It wasn't just green and slimy like the others. In her light, it was also glimmering like stardust. It shimmered like another tree, the great celestial one whose branches reached to every part of the universe and that worried Tiz greatly. It was as though the Unwithering One was trying to escape the cave by merging with the most powerful tree in the cosmos.

If it succeeded, then not only would all her friends be in danger at the academy, but also everyone she loved back home. It would be a catastrophe of cataclysmic proportions, affecting every living being in every corner of the universe. Life as they new it would no longer exist. It would be some twisted and charred thing, like the forest her mother took her to, where Mums thought she was abandoning a witch.

"Everything will burn," muttered Tiz, repeating Marie Yew's warning while feeling an encroaching sense of defeat that seemed to be lurking just around the corner. "Everything will burn," she repeated, "except for *her*."

"You're starting to worry me more than the tree," whispered Char.

"Look at its roots," said Tiz. "It's trying to become Yggdrasil. It's trying to branch out to every part of the universe, including Iggy City. It's gonna spread like an illness

— a slimy green disease."

Char tiptoed over to the root and Tiz followed.

"*Great...*" he whispered, looking at the glimmering root, "this is *not* good, not good at all."

"It's because the new witch lives at the academy, isn't it," she said.

"I think so," agreed Char. "We have to find out who she is," he said, glancing at her. "We have to find out as soon as possible."

But Tiz was still hesitant to touch the tree. Especially with Char watching her every move. If she felt what the tree did, then she would be the one responsible for the cataclysm. "Everything will burn, except for *her*," she worried, now seeing her fiery wings in a different light. "Except for me."

"What did you say?" asked Char.

"Nothing," replied Tiz as though waking from a trance.

"Do you want me to gently tap the tree?" he asked.

"No," she said, mustering her courage. "It should be me."

"Careful," he said. "You can't wake it or we're done for. Be gentle. Treat it like your own skin."

"Don't say that," said Tiz. "I'm nervous enough as it is."

Char put a hand on her shoulder. "Remember what I told you," he said. "If you feel anything you have to —"

"Fly as fast as I can," interrupted Tiz, irritated and afraid. "I remember. How exactly could I forget? And quit hovering over me — give me some breathing room." But in her mind, she truly wanted space for a head start, just in case.

Char receded into the shadows behind her.

Tiz turned toward the Unwithering One and took a step toward the tree, tiptoeing past the bones of those that failed to conquer it. Nearing the trunk, as wide as several redwoods, she gradually extended her hand. It was shaking like a leaf. Her flaming wings were beginning to flicker like a candle being battered by a strong wind. Doubt nearly consumed her.

Her forehead sweating, she kept inching her hand toward

the tree. As her fingertips neared the ghastly green bark she feared she would feel the hairs on her arm begin to tingle. Closing her eyes, she kept easing her hand forward, finally touching the slimy bark. She recoiled like someone pulling their hand away from a spider's web.

"What?" whispered Char urgently. "What did you feel?"

Tiz sat there silently for a second. Slowly, her fingers slid onto the bark again. She felt nothing but the tree itself. A wide smile stretched across her face as she looked at Char.

Tiz curled her fingers and tickled the tree but didn't giggle. She scratched the slimy bark and still felt nothing...

But something else did.

Tiz heard a snort from above, her hand still on the tree.

"Your wings," whispered Char desperately while also in their light, "get rid of them, hurry."

Tiz extinguished her wings as quickly as smothering a candle. As the light faded, she could see a hydra head stirring above them, its steady breathing growing into an angry growl.

In the darkness, Tiz and Char snuck around to the other side of the tree trunk. Tiz felt her foot catch on a root. Before she could stop, she tripped, hitting the ground with a thud.

Tiz heard another snort from above. The hydra was sniffing for her. Char pulled her up and wrapped them both in his black wings, cloaking them in their darkness.

Tiz heard sniffing right over them. The breath of the hydra smelled like a garbage dumpster and its mouth was just as big, filled with razor sharp teeth.

One false move and it would strike at them like an enormous rattlesnake.

"Turn us into ghosts," whispered Tiz. "I'm afraid."

"I told you, it doesn't work that —"

"Try anyway," interrupted Tiz desperately, "please."

Slowly, Tiz and Char faded away, visible only to each other.

The hydra sniffed right in front of them, flames shooting

out of its nostrils. Tiz knew that ghosts fared poorly versus fire. So she held her breath, hoping that the dragon-like beast would do the same.

The hydra sniffed again, trying to gain their scent. It grunted angrily. After one last glance in their direction, it lifted its head up high, sticking it into a dark tunnel that Tiz hadn't noticed before and illuminating it with its fiery breath. Tiz pointed to it as if it were another star, a second one that gave her just as much hope. The fire faded as she lowered her hand. "Did you see it?" she whispered.

"I did," he replied softly.

They watched anxiously as the hydra head gradually returned to its place within the canopy of the tree and closed its eyes. In a few moments it resumed its slow and steady breathing, looking fast asleep.

Char changed them back to normal, his own eyes half-closed.

"You look as tired as the hydras," whispered Tiz.

"Yeah, it's the ghost thing," he replied wearily. "If I do it too many times, it drains me."

"How badly?" asked Tiz, worried. "Can you fly to the tunnel up there?"

"We're not leaving, not until we find out who the real witch is," he said. "Otherwise, she'll destroy the academy."

"How?" asked Tiz, not sure she wanted to know.

"You'll need your wings," he said.

"You're that tired?" she asked, growing more worried. "I'm not sure I can carry you."

"No," he said. "It's not that, but if I get caught doing what I'm about to do, you'll need to get out of here." He picked up a dagger lying on the floor. It started glowing faintly in his hand.

"You're going to stab the tree?" she asked. "Are you crazy?"

"Only its foot," he said, showing her the glowing knife.

"And *this* will make it real hard to heal. That way, when we get back to the academy, we can look for the girl with the same injury."

"No way," said Tiz, trying to grab the dagger from him.

Char held her off. "Go," he said. "I'll catch up to you. If you can, try to create a diversion, just for a few seconds."

"I'm not leaving without you," she replied. "And you're breaking your promise to me, you said you wouldn't abandon me, remember?"

Char answered by hovering the tip of the dagger over a slimy green root, right next to the one that glimmered like Iggy City. "Go," he said sternly, "I'm not gonna warn you again."

Tiz stood there, angry and defiant.

He shook his head in disappointment. Then he did what Tiz could have never done herself — he stabbed the dagger into the slimy green root.

Hydras ROARED above them, flailing in the darkness!

Fear spread through Tiz like a wildfire, spurring her burning wings back to life. For a second, the hydra heads seemed blinded by the light.

"Go!" yelled Tiz, refusing to leave until Char did. Anxious to flee, she watched as he yanked the dagger from the tree's toe and flew into the air, heading for the tunnel. Hydra heads lunged at him like cobras, snapping their jaws in vain as he flew circles around them.

He was stalling. Tiz knew he wouldn't leave until she did. So she leapt into the air and flew toward the tunnel. A hydra head lowered itself in front, blocking it. Tiz was going too fast. She was flying toward its giant mouth with no way to stop!

From the side, Char kicked the hydra head away and Tiz flew into the tunnel, hitting the back wall hard.

Char pulled her to her feet. "C'mon!" he urged. "Run, Tiz! Run for your life!"

With Tiz's wings lighting the way, they bolted down a tunnel as fast as their legs could take them. All around them, the stone walls started shaking while large rocks fell from the ceiling, threatening to crush them. As Tiz ran she began hearing a multitude of serpentine voices echoing in her mind, whispering, "*Come back...come back...to the top of the Tower we shall take you.*" Over and over as she ran with Char the bewitching voices kept repeating their offer to bring her to her new heart seed — a most tempting offer indeed. "*Come back...come back,*" they kept whispering. "*To the top of the Tower we shall take you...*"

Glancing back, Tiz spotted one of the hydra heads chasing them as it stretched its neck down the tunnel, its jaws wide open, gaining on them. As tempting as their offer was, she knew they were lying.

From behind, Tiz felt its warm breath on her wings. "Go, go, go!" she yelled. But it was too late. The hydra struck like a snake.

Tiz tackled Char to the ground as the hydra missed eating them by inches, slamming its head into the wall, stunning itself.

"Keep going!" yelled Tiz as she shoved Char. "Its neck can only stretch so far!"

"Are you sure!" shouted Char, readying his dagger.

"Just go!" yelled Tiz, shoving him again.

They scrambled to their feet and started running. They turned a corner and saw an eerie white light at the end of the tunnel. Tiz heard people talk about similar ones right before they died. Char got there first. It was coming from a narrow gap between stone walls. He tried to squeeze through with his wings, but he was too big. He couldn't fit.

Tiz reached into her magical pocket, searching for something — anything. That's when her hand felt two slimy things — Pup Pup's hotdogs.

"I'm sorry!" said Char from behind her as the hydra head

rounded the corner, slithering on its neck like a snake. He looked exhausted. "I'm too weak to phase us through."

But there wasn't enough time to answer him. She took his hand instead. Tiz tossed the hotdogs away from them and started counting. "One..."

The hydra stopped on a dime, gobbling the food. It was *indeed* hungry, just like the witch had said, feeding greedily.

That gave Tiz the time she needed. She reached out and touched its neck. "Two," she counted.

"What are you doing!" yelled Char, raising his dagger.

Tiz completed her counting by shouting, "TREE!" For the hydra was a part of the witch's tree. And because of it, a tree door opened in its mouth. Tiz pulled Char along by the arm. She never thought she'd feel so happy to be running into the jaws of a monster. They leapt over its teeth, tumbling into the portal as the massive mouth of the beast snapped shut.

Tiz and Char glided through the glowing tunnel of the tree portal without even flapping their wings. Tiz could tell it was Char's first time from the way his hand was shaking.

"Do you know where you're going!" he shouted, discarding his dagger.

"The witch's tree is linked to the academy!" she yelled. "Look for the stardust path!"

"There!" shouted Char, pointing to a glimmering path branching off to the left.

Tiz yanked his arm, steering them that way just in time as they barreled toward a white light at the end of the tunnel.

"Are you sure this is right!" he yelled.

"Right as rain!" replied Tiz.

"What does that mean!" he shouted.

"I don't know!" she screamed as they burst through the blinding light.

CHAPTER TWENTY-SIX — EVERYTHING THAT MATTERED

TIZ AND CHAR TUMBLED OUT OF THE PORTAL and into the museum-like foyer of the academy where she first met the fallen angel. It was quieter than a mortuary. And if they got caught, any hope of a bright future would be laid to rest by the general.

"I think everyone's still asleep," whispered Tiz as she looked at Char, who was well on his way to joining them.

"Can you ghost us through our barracks door?" she asked, helping him to his feet.

"I hope so," he replied, teetering.

Tiz extinguished her wings then slid her shoulders underneath his arm to support him. "C'mon," she said. "I'll be your spotter for now."

Tiz helped him toward the spiraling yellow stairs that led to B Company's barracks. She was absolutely buzzing with joy on the inside. She wanted to scream, "I'm not the new witch! Do you hear me! I'm not the new witch! We lived! We made it!"

As they neared the first step of the yellow staircase, she heard a familiar clicking sound echoing through the foyer.

"Boarder hoarder," warned Char right away as though it was the millionth time he had to avoid one.

"What do we do?" she asked, listening to its paws click closer and closer on the marble floor.

"Nothing," said Char, "we're back at the academy. As long as we're here, the hoarders don't care."

"Phew," said Tiz, overjoyed, so much so, she nearly planted a kiss on the boarder hoarder's nose — until she remembered its cuckoo clock.

Tiz smiled at the thought. She wished all her problems

could be so simple as they started climbing the stairs. Watching their feet go from step to step suddenly gave Tiz an idea. In order to find out if any of the other climbers' feet had been hurt, she'd invent a pair of spiked shoes that would work against the slime of the witch's tree and would offer them to the other climbers as a good will gesture. When they came to be fitted, Tiz could inspect their toes for any injuries. And since the whole situation had them in a bit of a jam, she dubbed her new covert mission *Operation Toe-Jam*.

Char liked the name of it more than the idea. To him, it sounded way too easy. He believed that they weren't the first to try and flush out the true witch by hurting her tree. Therefore, she might catch on to Tiz's plan, and in the end, put herself in even more danger. "It's too risky," he said. "We have to be more casual about it. Or we'll be casualties."

Reluctantly, Tiz agreed and decided to shelve *Operation Toe-Jam* for the time being. When they made it to B Company's barracks Char phased them through the door as he fell to the common room floor, nearly passing out.

Tiz felt just as tired as she helped him back up and said her good-bye. As they walked toward their separate dorms Tiz stopped and turned around. "Hey," she said in a hushed voice.

Char stopped but didn't face her.

From behind, Tiz looked at him curiously. "The dagger you used in the cavern, how did you know that one would glow when you picked it up?" she asked.

He looked up at the cathedral ceiling where he waited for her before. "It used to be mine," he said, "before the witch's tree flicked me off like a fly."

Silence.

"I'm sorry," said Tiz finally, not knowing what else to say.

"It took away everything that mattered to me," he said, looking down at his feet. "But I won't let it take you."

She felt her cheeks flush as his words warmed her heart too. As her spotter, he would be risking his own life for her as well. If one of them failed each other, both could die. She had to lean on him, and he on her, or else, she might never get the chance to have a life tree. "Two lives, one soul," she said, "if either dies, both must go."

Still facing away, he nodded somberly. "Get some sleep," he said, "you're gonna need it."

"You too," replied Tiz, wanting to give him a hug. With a sigh, she turned and headed for the girl's dormitory.

Tiz cracked opened the door and peeked in. It was pitch-black. She eased the door closed and slid across the smooth tiles on the floor, just like she did when she snuck out.

She counted the bunk beds as she crawled along and stopped under hers and Sombra's. The floor was cool and comfortable and her eyelids were so heavy she could have just stayed there and fallen asleep. But instead, she forced herself to her feet and grabbed the small ladder to her bed. Climbing it was taking the last of her energy. She couldn't wait to sleep.

Click! All the lights went on.

"A-ten-hut!" yelled the general.

Tiz froze at the top of the ladder as all the other girls started rubbing their sleepy eyes and looking around in surprise.

"Everyone! Get in front of your bed!" yelled the general. "A-ten-hut!"

Eyes around the room widened. Girls hopped out of bunk beds and scrambled to the front of them, standing at attention. On a top bunk, Molly the vampire girl popped out of a coffin and was so afraid, she stood there stiffer than a corpse.

"Molly, get down from there!" yelled the general. "Then drop and give me fifty! No, scratch that! You're a vampire, drop and give me two hundred and fifty!"

Although vampires were really strong, Tiz thought Molly was going to wet the plush cushions in her coffin standing there. But instead, a girl troll named Helen Grug, who turned out to be Fineus's cousin, picked Molly up and set her down right in push up position where she was supposed to be.

Tiz jumped down from her ladder and stood at attention at the foot of her bed next to Sombra, neither of the chatty friends saying a word, though Tiz was dying to talk.

General Payne paced down the center isle glaring at Tiz. "Can any of you tell me why you're all standing at attention?"

No one said a word.

"Red?" said the general, the veins pulsing on his thick neck as he stopped in front of her. "How about you?"

Tiz's voice deserted her faster than an AWOL soldier.

"I figured as much!" he shouted. "When one of you breaks rule number nine hundred and fifty-seven — no sneaking out after lights out — then guess what!"

More silence.

"Everyone else gets punished!" finished the general. "Do you understand the words firing out my word shooter?"

"YES, SIR!" shouted the girls.

"Do you know what you have to do, Red?" he asked.

Tiz nodded as she dropped down into push up position.

"Get up, Red!" he yelled. "And go to bed!"

Tiz was in shock. So much so, she flipped onto her back into the dying cockroach, thinking that's what he meant.

"No, no, no!" he yelled, pointing to her top bunk. "Don't you know what a bed is? Maybe you're too good for it! I guess you are, since you ain't been using it!"

Tiz hopped to her feet and scurried up the ladder as the other girls stood there. Lying on her bed, she felt guiltier than Goldilocks after being caught by Baby Bear.

"Comfy, Red?" he yelled.

Tiz nodded so he wouldn't yell again.

"Good!" he shouted. "Now everyone else drop and give me fifty!"

"What!" yelled Tiz, sitting up. "That's not fair!" she added, jumping down from her bed.

"Now it's a hundred pushups!" yelled the general. "And if

you don't get back up there it will be two hundred for every second you're down here!"

Tiz bit her tongue. If looks could kill, the glare she shot at the general would have turned him into a ghost. But instead of arguing, she listened and hurried back up.

She lay there watching as all the other girls were counting off their pushups, half of them didn't even finish twenty before the general ordered them into the dying cockroach, their hands and legs wiggling in the air.

Tiz saw that Sombra was one of them. What did she do to deserve it? Nothing. Tiz felt her heart sink as badly as the moment she saw Sombra trapped in her life tree. The thought brought back memories of the lament she sung. Hearing the kids groaning and the general yelling at them was starting to become too much for her ears to take.

So she did the first thing that came to mind. She expressed her frustration through her voice. She sang Char's irritating song:

Madder than a burning bird,
She's lost her way,
She'll have to pay,
Death will make sure of it,
To where she goes,
She may never return from,
For in the underworld,
Even a burning bird will burn,
but there's still time,
For even the looming dead can learn,
but if not,
They'll burn the burning bird.

Her wings ignited as she finished his song. The room gasped!

"Put those things out!" yelled the general. "And quit

singing that crazy song! You must be dying to be a latrine machine!"

But Tiz sang it again, doing her best to keep the attention on her as her wings brightened. The spellsong was so powerful that even the general couldn't turn away.

"I'm warning you, Red!" he yelled. "You'll be running banana-colored stairs all night if you don't stop!"

Hearing exactly what she wanted, she sung even louder.

"That's it!" yelled the general. "Get out of bed, Red! Double-time it! You're running *all* the stairs! Every single color!"

Tiz fluttered down from her bed and stuck her tongue out at him to keep the attention on her. She extinguished her wings then did cartwheels down the center aisle toward the door.

She could hear the general storming after her as he yelled, "Everyone else! Get to bed! Pronto!"

Tiz wanted to apologize to her friends. She wanted to yell that she was sorry, but to say that it wasn't exactly the best time to be doing so would have been a sizable understatement. It would have been like saying the witch's tree was as menacing as a bouquet of pansies. So she would have to wait. But when the opportunity *did* present itself (latrine duty permitting) she would go above and beyond the call of "doodie." She would say she was sorry to each and every cadet in B Company individually.

Running stairs all night, Tiz had plenty of time to think of what to say. During her punishment, she also told the general that the witch's tree was trying to take over the academy. But he didn't believe her, and after she suggested it, he made her run faster. Tiz ran until the morning bugle woke up the school, but she did it smiling from time to time, knowing she needed to be as fit as possible to have any chance of conquering the witch's tree, but more importantly, she was glad that it was her being punished and not her friends.

CHAPTER TWENTY-SEVEN — A DIFFERENT TUNE

AFTER THE MORNING BUGLE SOUNDED, General Payne ordered Tiz to get ready for school. Her legs felt like rubber as she limped into the girl's dormitory to make her bed. But to her surprise, it was Sombra that was limping even worse. Her best friend was making her own bed while favoring a foot.

Tiz hadn't noticed it when she returned from her late night adventure, though who could blame her, the general had been barking at her louder than a police dog at a puppy thief.

As Tiz watched her best friend limp around, the image of Char stabbing the foot of the witch's tree rushed through her mind. Could Sombra's foot hurt because of that? It couldn't, could it? After all, Sombra already had a life tree — but a life tree that had the witch's symbol emblazoned upon its bark. Worse, Frenchy's mom, Marie Yew, stressed that the witch was a notorious liar.

"Are you all right?" asked Tiz.

"Sort of," said Sombra. "I stubbed my toe on the bed last night when the general flipped on the lights and started yelling like crazy. I think I might've broken it." Grimacing, she sat on her bed then rubbed her toe through her sock.

"Let me see it," said Tiz.

"Huh?" replied Sombra. "Oh never mind, so that's where you went last night — druid school, to finish your medical degree."

"*Ha, ha*," said Tiz, plopping down next to her friend on the bed.

"Don't worry about me," said Sombra. "You were the one running stairs all night. How are your feet doing?"

"They're *real* sore," said Tiz, glancing at her best friend's foot. "I feel like I stubbed my entire body on those stairs."

"Forget the stairs," said Sombra. "Where did you go last night? I tried waiting up for you. Just so you know, I wanna hear every detail." Then Sombra picked up her pillow and started kissing it, pretending she was Tiz. "Oh Char, you're my guardian angel, I knew you'd be *Loco for Cocoa Lumps*," she teased.

Tiz smacked her friend playfully then told her almost everything, only leaving out the part where Char stabbed the witch's tree in the foot. She didn't like leaving her best friend in the dark, but Tiz wasn't sure if her friend was being completely honest about her own foot either.

The rest of the day went by quickly for Tiz. She didn't start a single fire in Elemental Chemistry and in Environmental Warfare, she hit four out of five fur coats with paint bombs. Best of all, in Animal Search and Rescue she managed to pull Little Nub Nub out of a mud pit all by herself, and even though he still charged after her, she just pretended it was his way of saying, "Thank you." Despite all her success, Sombra's sore foot was stuck in Tiz's mind like Char's depressing song, souring her mood.

Tiz felt like she no longer had a choice. Despite the danger, it was time to initiate *Operation Toe-Jam*. After school, Tiz crafted several beautiful pairs of climbing shoes, carving enchanted runes into the spikes at the bottom so they would dissolve any slime they touched. They were her greatest inventions yet. Best of all, they came in two breathtaking colors, banana yellow and wolfberry red.

Tiz set one of the wolfberry-colored shoes on the bottom post of the red stairs that led to W Company. Hiding, she saw several of the Heavenly Seven coming down, each with a new medal in the shape of a golden harp, signifying their membership. They stopped and began marveling at the shiny red climbing shoe. Frenchy even picked it up. When she put it next to her foot to see if it would fit, Tiz nearly squealed in excitement. The piranhas had taken the bait.

Smiling from ear to ear, Tiz headed to the band room to find her friends. But she figured it would be safer to sneak a peek at Sombra's foot when they were getting ready for bed.

Walking down a stardust hallway alone, Tiz felt the floor underneath her feet rumble. She dropped to her knees and put her ear to it. Iggy City rumbled once more. Tiz felt something oozing onto her palms. She lifted her hands and saw faint traces of green slime. Her worst fear was coming true — the witch's tree was taking over the academy.

Above her on the wall, a crystal ball that served as an academy loudspeaker started glowing and said, "*Due to solar winds moving through our location the academy is experiencing a little turbulence, therefore, today's climbing practice will be a closed one — climbers only. That is all, cadets. As you were.*"

"Solar winds?" scoffed Tiz. "What a bunch of poop."

Tiz pulled out a handkerchief and wiped off her hands as she resumed her walk to the band room — she had to tell Char.

Tiz pushed open the music room door and saw Sombra frowning while talking to Char and Dargen. Tiz had seen the very same look on her best friend's face the day she handed her the negative clamp to try to revive her heart seed. It was the look of betrayal.

Before Tiz could retreat Sombra spotted her.

"So, you think I'm the witch?" shouted Sombra, putting two and two together (her own toe and the toe of the witch's tree).

Everyone in the room stopped talking. It became so quiet that Tiz could hear a boy chewing gum down the hall. She could even hear him mutter a curse at the latrine machine laws and their fifty-six rules that all outlawed gum.

Tiz gave Sombra her best "I'm sorry" look. "Um, can we talk alone?" she asked, sensing everyone's stares, making her feel like she was wearing an uncomfortable uniform made out of eyeballs.

"You lied to me," said Sombra immediately, standing firm. "Char told me that you watched him stab the witch's tree in the toe. A tree's roots are its toes, right?"

There was a collective gasp in the room. Kids slid to the edge of their seats.

Tiz feared that if anyone from B Company blabbed about what they just heard and W Company found out, then her plan would be over. *Operation Toe-Jam* was now in jeopardy.

"Yeah so, a tree's roots are its toes," said Tiz cautiously.

"And this time, you weren't digging for truffles, were you?" asked Sombra.

"No, we were digging for something else," replied Tiz. "A clue."

"You need to get a clue all right," insisted Sombra, "a clue to who your friends really are. Ones that don't complain when they have to do pushups for you."

Silence. Tiz had no reply.

"You know what you are?" said Sombra, glaring at Tiz. "You're the blue jay we saw on the truffle hunt — the one that was up to no good. Unless you get caught Tiz, you just do whatever you want — all day, all night you're a blue jay — not Lumps, not Red. All Day, Blue Jay."

With that, Sombra stormed out of the band room. Slowly, most of B Company followed her, trying to chirp like blue jays but sounding more like parakeets. As Dargen left, he looked at Tiz and shook his head in disappointment at the Phoenix that he helped rise from the ashes of the Unburnable Forest, now sinking to a new low.

Tiz glared at Char, the only one left in the room. "What exactly did you tell her?" she asked, looking worried.

"The truth," he replied. "I'm guessing you left out a part or two."

"You shouldn't have said anything," grumbled Tiz. "If the

real witch finds out we're looking for a hurt foot, then she won't be the only one limping around, we'll be joining her, and we'll need more than just crutches, she'll make sure of that."

"So, you *do* think it's Sombra," said Char.

"I didn't say that," said Tiz, unable to mask her concern.

"You didn't need to," said Char. "The look on your face says it all."

"*Wrong*," said Tiz abruptly.

"Well, I hope we're both wrong," said Char. "But unfortunately, I think you're right."

"No way — Sombra has a new life tree," said Tiz. "Frenchy's mom said the witch couldn't do that, because she already has the Unwithering One."

"Did Sombra's tree have anything strange on it?" he asked, picking up his guitar and pointing to one of its magical runes. "Like one of these?"

Silence. Tiz didn't want to admit that her best friend's tree had the witch's symbol on it, especially after Char blabbed about everything. But she was now short on allies, and lying to him would only make it worse. *You can't make something right by doing something wrong*, thought Tiz, hearing her mother's voice inside her head. But in her own opinion, it wasn't a clear-cut call to make. Could she trust him after he blabbed?

Slowly, step-by-step she would try to rebuild that trust, carefully choosing what to tell him and what not to, giving him a chance to earn it back. "Sombra's tree had the witch's symbol on it," she said finally.

"Then her life tree might be a fake," said Char. "Just like the tree nymph that owns it."

"It can't be," muttered Tiz, remembering how Sombra came to her defense when she was accused of being the witch. "Maybe she's being framed by someone else."

Above them on the wall, an academy loudspeaker started glowing and said, "*Climbing practice will be starting in thirty minutes...all climbers please report to the training room.*"

"Crud," she groaned. "We got to go. Meet me at climbing practice. I need to get my things."

As she left, she didn't tell Char that those things included the new climbing shoes that went along with *Operation Toe-Jam*.

CHAPTER TWENTY-EIGHT — OPERATION TOE-JAM

TIZ DOUBLE-TIMED IT through the museum-like foyer on her way to get her things for practice — time was of the essence. She had to implement her plan before word of Char stabbing the witch's tree and his ensuing blabbing spread like a destructive wildfire. If the witch heard any blabbing about the stabbing, then she would be grabbing and nabbing Tiz, knowing that her foe was looking for an injured toe.

Hurrying up the yellow stairs to B Company's barracks, Tiz reminded herself to bring the new climbing shoes as well as a tape measure and a notebook to record the dimensions of their bare feet. And bare feet it had to be, she would insist upon it, telling them that her measurements would account for the thickness of the ideal climbing sock — polyester blend and sweat-wicking. She reminded herself to bring a pair so that the other climbers could change into them for their measurement, and thus, get them to remove their own.

Repeating her list, Tiz finished climbing the stairs. When she got to the common room it was bustling. No one was allowed to watch the practice that day because of all the shaking and rumbling Iggy City was doing — and it wasn't because of solar winds like they were saying — it was the witch's tree.

In a hurry, Tiz pushed her way through the locker room. "Sorry — excuse me, sorry about that..."

Her plan was waiting in the wings more anxiously than a boarder hoarder crammed into a torpedo tube watching witches that were trying to escape the academy. And she wasn't about to mention her operation to anyone, especially Char, who kept secrets as well as he cared for Cactus Cuties.

Tiz started on her combination lock when she noticed

something strange on her fingertip — a tiny green leaf. Thinking it might be from her eco-friendly gardening class, she tried to flick it off without any luck. Confused, she brought the little leaf up to her green eyes as they widened with realization — the leaf wasn't stuck at all, it was growing out of her fingertip as if it was the end of a branch.

Her eyes fixating on it, she watched as a tiny flower bud sprouted from its stem then blossomed into a little purple flower.

"Holy smokes," worried Tiz as she stared at her little finger-garden.

Why was it happening? Was it from touching the witch's tree? Did it have to do with the energy inside her? Or was it both?

Right there and then, she knew Char had been right. The Tiz everyone knew *was* dying. She was *leaving* in a different way, a literal way; she was leaving to become a tree.

Tiz flexed her finger with the leaf and flower. It felt stiffer than the others and harder to move. Her heart raced as she plucked the growth from her fingertip then stuffed it into her pocket. She wasn't exactly sure why she squirreled it away, but it had been a part of her a second ago, and if she'd lost a tooth, then she would have kept that for sure.

Tiz wiggled the same finger again and it felt a little better. But if it stiffened while climbing the witch's tree all the arthritis cream in the universe wasn't going to help her. With the way things had been going for her she felt unluckier than a lottery participant that had lost the only winning ticket.

Glancing at her fingertip where the growth used to be, she wondered if it was even possible for the transformation to be reversed regardless of why it was happening. In her mind, she envisioned sprouting more and more leaves until she looked like the leafy dress she put on for the Planting, minus the dress.

Tiz erased the thought from her mind as she found

everything she needed for *Operation Toe-Jam* and shoved the items into her pack.

After a quick change into her climbing gear, Tiz hurried out the main door of her barracks and down the yellow stairs. This time she was happy to have practice. Once it started, she could take her mind off things, at least for a little while.

As she arrived at the door to the training room a chew toy fell out of her pack and hit the ground with a squeak. In her rush, she had forgotten Pup Pup in her other locker, but there was no time to go back.

Tiz pushed open the training room door and her jaw nearly dropped to the tile floor. She saw Sombra there, laughing it up with the other climbers from Wolfberry while changing into her banana yellow climbing suit.

All the other climbers were there except Holly, who was probably still getting grief from the other tree nymphs in Wolfberry for coming to Tiz's aid in the *Swirlie Situation.* Holly had threatened to tattle on them to the general. Regardless, the other climbers probably still liked Holly better than Tiz. Heck, Tiz would even bet on it based on the evil looks she was getting from six of the Heavenly Seven.

Trying to avoid their glares, Tiz glanced at Sombra but didn't say anything to her, even though she wanted to just as much as she wanted to reach the top of the witch's tree.

Frenchy Yew sat down right next to Sombra and helped her new best friend put on a yellow climbing pack. Noticing that Tiz was glancing over, Frenchy took a blood-red Wolfberry medal and pinned it on Sombra's yellow pack.

It was like a cherry on top of a bitter banana sundae that Tiz wasn't about to swallow. Unable to bite her tongue any longer, Tiz looked at her best friend. "So we're still a team, right?" she asked.

Sombra scoffed.

Frenchy cozied up to her new best friend, putting her arm around her while pretending not to see Tiz. "Zeh blue jay," she said. "It will chirp all day if you pay attention to it. But if you ignore it, zhen '*vua-lah*' — it will simply fly away."

The other climbers from Wolfberry started chirping loudly.

"That's a parakeet," insisted Tiz, "*not* a blue jay."

They ignored her. So Tiz decided to bring out the heavy artillery. She pulled out the Wolfberry climbing shoes — the one constant in the universe was that girls loved brand new shoes.

All the climbers marveled at them, even Frenchy. "So, it was you zhat invented the shoes," she hissed jealously. "I can't believe it. They are nearly perfect."

"A peace offering," said Tiz, glancing at Sombra. "They come in banana yellow too." Tiz pulled out a back up pair she'd made for herself, offering them to her best friend. "Here, take 'em, we're the same shoe size," she added. "No need for me to look at your foot, no measuring, no nothing."

Sombra looked at the shoes warily.

"Please," said Tiz apologetically. No matter what, she cared about her friend way more than the success of *Operation Toe-Jam*. "Take them, I know you'll take good care of them. *I trust you.*"

Sombra took the shoes, and to Tiz's delight, began unlacing her own.

"I want a pair," insisted Frenchy quite rudely, taking off her own shoes.

"Me too," said the other climbers one by one, following Frenchy's lead.

"Okay," said Tiz nervously, pulling out her tape measure and notebook. "Take off your shoes for now, both of them — one foot can be bigger than the other. Oh yeah, and when I get to you, your socks will have to come off too, so I can get it exactly right." Tiz reached into her pack and pulled out the socks she brought. "I only have one pair. You can wear these or do the measurement barefoot — it's up to you."

"Ewww," said Frenchy. "I wouldn't share a clothes line

with your nasty socks. And if you try to put zhem on me, then KAPOW!" She kicked her foot past Tiz's face. "More bumps for *Lumps*."

Her cronies laughed but Tiz was too nervous to care. "Then bare feet it is," she said, kneeling in front of Cindy Elm to measure her feet first. Tiz watched anxiously as Cindy slowly peeled off her socks, wondering what the tree nymph sitting in front of her might have already heard about Char stabbing the foot of the witch's tree. *If she has a scar, I can't overreact*, she told herself.

But the only danger that came from Cindy's feet was in the form of a cheesy odor, otherwise, they were unscarred. Eyes watering, Tiz measured the girl's smelly pair of dogs as fast as she could then moved on to the next climber.

Already tense, the room grew strangely quiet, making Tiz sweat. Plus, there was Sombra, who knew exactly what Tiz was doing. If she spilled the beans, then it would be all over — the bitter end.

Tiz never thought she'd "go out" in such an odd way. She could see the headline already, "School Girl Dies and is Buried after a Tragic Foot Measuring Accident, Bringing New Meaning to the Terms Hammer Toe and Trench Foot."

"Hurry up," insisted Frenchy, "zeh practice will be starting soon."

One by one, Tiz held her breath as she worked her way down the line, her hand trembling more and more, and not just because some of their feet smelled like death, but because she feared that if she found a scar she'd get a first hand whiff of the real deal herself.

Tiz watched as socks were slid down one at a time, her heart nearly stopping each time they reached the bottom. Feeling both relief and disappointment, she made it through five of the Heavenly Seven without finding anything wrong.

Frenchy was the last one left in the room.

Tiz kneeled in front of her nemesis, forcing a smile.

"Admit it," said Frenchy. "You don't like French people, do you."

"That's not true," replied Tiz. "When I was three, my imaginary friend was French. I still love *her* to this day."

Frenchy narrowed her eyes at Tiz. "Peel my socks off then wash my feet," she insisted. "Zhat is a true peace offering."

Tiz bit her tongue. "Fine," she said as politely as she could.

Slowly, she began peeling the left sock off...inch by inch... her hands trembling...

Nothing.

Not even a callous. Each toe was perfectly painted with wolfberry red toenail polish.

Tiz breathed a sigh of relief, but in her heart she was more than a bit disappointed. She grabbed onto the right sock and gradually peeled it down. She closed her eyes, knowing a scar had to be there...

"What's zeh matter?" said Frenchy. "Afraid of a few toes?"

Tiz slipped off the sock — it smelled like roses.

She peeked...

Nothing.

Her other foot was as perfect as the first.

Tiz quickly took the measurements as Cindy Elm brought over a bowl of water for Tiz to wash them. For a second, she was sure they were going to shove her face into it.

"There's no need for the water," said Frenchy. "Swirlie Girly can lick them clean."

The other girls laughed as a bell rang.

"It's time to go," said Sombra, coming to Tiz's aid, though a scowl she threw at Tiz said otherwise.

"Saved by the bell, but this is only round one," said Frenchy, pointing outside and toward the starting lines for climbing practice. "You won't be so lucky out there, Swirlie Girly. Zeh universe is a giant toilet bowl, and *le ploop* —

you're the thing floating in it."

"*Wrong*, I don't float — not even like a butterfly — though they *are* awesome," said Tiz, standing up. "I just sting like a bee — you'll see." Tiz pointed at Frenchy. "You're the stinker floating in the cosmos, *Le Pew* — and I'm gonna flush you right out of the tree! Do you understand? Wee-wee?"

"Ha!" scoffed Frenchy, offering Sombra her hand. "Come on," she said. "Let her buzz like a little bee — she can't sting us, especially with her words and her endless strings of them."

"They're called sentences," said Tiz.

"See," said Frenchy, shrugging it off, "I feel nothing."

Tiz ignored her, watching Sombra closely. "Sombra, you're still my first mate," she said. "No matter what."

"Nope, not anymore," replied Sombra. "I'm the captain of my own ship again. And I'm back on board the *Suspicious*." Sombra took her new best friend's hand and turned away from Tiz.

Frenchy smirked as she led Sombra out of the training room and into the bubble surrounding Iggy City. The remaining climbers started buzzing loudly as they followed them out of the training room then slammed the door shut with a thud. Though it was little consolation, at least they were better at buzzing than chirping.

Tiz heard the training room door from the hallway creak open. "Are they gone?" asked Holly Holly, poking her head in the door in her cheerleading outfit, pompoms in hand.

"Yeah," said Tiz, "at least for now."

"Phew," said Holly as she limped into the training room.

Tiz gawked at Holly's foot — thoughts of Char stabbing the root of the witch's tree rushed through her head. Hoping it wasn't so, Tiz started telling herself that the other Wolfberry girls must have done it to her for stepping in and saving Tiz from more swirlies.

Holly plopped down on the bench near Tiz, not bothering to change into her climbing gear.

CHAPTER TWENTY-EIGHT

Cautiously, Tiz kneeled down in front of Holly while holding up a red climbing shoe — Holly's favorite color too. "I'm gonna make one of these for you," she said. "I just need a measurement is all, so please, take off your shoes and socks."

"Sorry Tiz, no shoe-zies for me today," said Holly in her usual exuberant way as she suddenly stood up and started limping toward the exit that led to the viewing stands.

"What happened?" asked Tiz, surprised and afraid at the same time.

Holly stopped at the door. "Oh nothing," she said merrily. "But I'm going to have to sit this session out I'm afraid. I had a bit of an oopsy at cheerleading practice yesterday."

"What kind of oopsy?" asked Tiz, growing more and more concerned.

"Well, let me put it this way, if you go out for the cheerleading team, don't partner up with a werewolf — they're all claws," replied Holly. "Especially one named Stanley, he was so clumsy the other day. I don't know how Frenchy does it — she has one for a spotter you know. Anyway, over night, my foot swelled up, and now the other girls are calling me Sasquatch — that's why I'm kind of avoiding them right now. You know how they can get."

"What about your foot?" said Tiz. "Shouldn't you see the school healer or something?"

"*Nah*," said Holly like it was the silliest idea ever. "It'll be okay, don't worry, I'll just cheer for you and the other girls today. It'll be F-U-N! Fun!"

"That's okay," said Tiz worried that her cheers might be something closer to hexes. "But I could still measure your good foot."

"No thankies," said Holly politely. "That won't be necessary."

"I insist," said Tiz, walking over to Holly and kneeling down next to her foot.

Holly stepped back, glancing around. "I *know* what you're doing," she whispered in a very Un-Holly like voice. "And you better cut it out, if you know what's good for you."

"Um..."

The whole tree rumbled as Tiz was still trying to process everything. All along, she had been worried that her best friend might be the new witch, hurting their friendship in the process, while in reality, it had been Holly the whole time.

"Um..."

But before Tiz could think of something clever to say, Holly's eyes began glowing red like some sort of evil Christmas doll come to life as she balled her hand up. A slimy green branch shot out of the wall with a knot on the end of it like a fist, knocking Tiz out cold as she gave out a loud groan that half-said, "Oh no, not again..."

CHAPTER TWENTY-NINE — PROBLEMS AND PROBLEMS AND EVEN SPORE PROBLEMS

WHEN TIZ AWOKE she found herself with a brand new lump on her head to add to her collection as she lay in a damp cell lit by a couple of torches on the other side of the bars. By the looks of it, she was in the academy's dungeon, somewhere near the roots of the tree. But she didn't know what was worse, her new dwelling or the thin branch that she just spotted growing out of her nostril. Dreading what she had to do next, Tiz closed her eyes as she grabbed the branch protruding from her button nose. Taking a deep breath, she counted to "tree", yanking it out like a gigantic nose hair.

"Aaagh!" she groaned as her eyes watered.

But at least counting to "tree" had given her an idea — she was going to try to open a tree door back to her barracks.

That's when she noticed the stardust walls were a different color. They should have been pitch-black. Instead, they looked as slimy and green as the witch's tree.

Tiz sneezed — something unusual was in the air and she saw it clinging to her clothes. Wiping her sleeve with her finger, she examined a thin layer of spores. "*Oh great*," she groaned.

The transformation of the academy was quickening along with her own mutation. And if the spores were playing a role, then what were they doing to the other cadets?

Now more than ever, Tiz had to reach the top of the Tower of Thorns. She needed to claim the glowing seed she saw dangling in a tiny window there as it pulsed in rhythm with her own heart. *The living key*, she thought, *my key to living.*

Tiz put her hand on the slimy wall and counted to "tree."

Nothing.

Suddenly, she heard tapping coming from the darkness

beyond the bars of her cell — someone was tapping on their own bars. No, scratch that, someone was using tap code to say, "You are not alone."

"Who's there?" called out Tiz. "Please, let me out!"

"I should make you respond in tap code," said Sombra from the shadows.

Tiz spotted her best friend's silhouette in the darkness, standing outside her cell — she was not a prisoner.

"I'm sorry," said Tiz earnestly. "I'm sorry for even thinking that you were the witch."

"Too late," said Sombra as she stepped into the torchlight.

Tiz couldn't believe her eyes...

Sombra was wearing the blood-red uniform of Wolfberry — she was on the other team.

"No..."

"Holly's in charge now," said Sombra. "And I'm not sure if you've noticed or not, but she's a bit obsessed with the color red. She even has a new school slogan — *If you don't go red, you're better off*...well, you know. So what's it going to be, Red?"

A violin began playing sadly from a cell in another part of the dungeon — Dargen was down there.

Sombra had been telling the truth. Tiz was not the only one imprisoned.

A guitar joined in, sounding just as melancholy. It was Char.

Soon, it sounded like everyone from the band was playing, all of them reflecting the dreary mood of Banana Company. They were down, but holding out. And that gave Tiz hope.

She stepped toward the bars in her yellow climbing gear. "As a Phoenix, you know that the color red is sort of in my blood," she said, putting her hands on the bars. "But I think I'm going to stick with the color that I have on now."

Sombra stepped right up to Tiz and put her hands on the bars next to hers. "You're making a mistake," she said as she discreetly slid something small and cold into Tiz's hand.

From the ridges on it, Tiz could tell it was a key without looking — Sombra was trying to help her — she was faking.

"Think long and hard about what you want to do," whispered Sombra as the music helped drown out her voice.

"Zhat is enough!" shouted Frenchy from a distance.

The instruments squealed to a halt.

Frenchy stormed in, follow by the rest of the Heavenly Seven minus Holly, all of them in their blood-red uniforms.

Frenchy marched right up to Sombra jingling a key ring right in her face while pointing at the door to Tiz's cell. "Zeh key for the Blue Jay's cage — where is it?"

Sombra shrugged. "Ask yourself," she replied. "I thought you were in charge of all the keys."

Frenchy looked long and hard at Tiz. "Zeh blue jay is a thief by nature," she said as she turned her gaze toward Sombra. "And so are you." Frenchy waved a hand and her cronies grabbed Sombra by the arms. "Take this skinny *Mop* to the witch. She can use her as a broomstick."

"Stop!" yelled Tiz.

"THIS IS NOT A JOKE!" screamed Frenchy. "Do you know what the witch will do to me if I don't find your key!"

"You're just lucky she didn't put you in here with me!" shouted Tiz, coming to her friend's aid. "Or I'd show you real fear!"

Frenchy turned toward Tiz. But instead of shouting back at her, she eased right up to her cell as her eyes began to well.

Frenchy looked terrified. "I beg zeh witch to put me in a cell, safe like you," she said. "Locked away here you have no idea of the terrible things she makes me do." She looked back at the climbers behind her. "Make no mistake — no one is coming to help us. We are all going *red* in one way or another. If not by Holly, then by climbing this wretched tree, so we can feed it as she makes her way to the top. How could she do this to us? How could she do this to *me*?"

Frenchy fell to her knees and began doing something Tiz didn't think the huffy girl was capable of — tears began streaming down her cheeks. It was as unnatural as watching an ogre cry. If this was what the witch did to her allies, then what did she do to her enemies?

Watching her nemesis reduced to tears, Tiz realized that Frenchy was not only afraid for her own life, but also scared of losing her best friend, Holly Holly, for good. A feeling that Tiz could relate to, fearing that she had lost her own.

Frenchy wiped her eyes. "Holly is losing her mind — it's like she's possessed, and even worse, she's losing control of the witch's tree."

"Then let me help," said Tiz.

Frenchy scoffed. "You help me?" she said. "You can't even help yourself — why would you help me?"

Tiz paused. Not because she was searching for a reply. She knew the appropriate answer. But it wasn't an easy thing to say. She had to make a choice, the most difficult one of her short life...

At the top of the Tower of Thorns, there was more than just another heart seed waiting for her. If she made it there, a key decision loomed as well. She could either claim a new seed or claim the witch's tree — preventing the real witch from doing so. But it would have to be one or the other.

"Frenchy, you already have a heart seed — *a real one*," said Tiz finally. "But not Holly. Her heart seed is a fake. And I think she needs a new one to ditch the spirit of witch inside of her, the one possessing her. Because I've seen that wicked spirit outside of Holly, so I know it's possible to separate the two of them. If we work together, my voice and its powers combined with the new heart seed might be able to help her with that. I might be able to drive her out for good, like an exorcism, or something close to that."

"Go on..."

"Listen to me, Frenchy," implored Tiz. "If you decide to

claim the witch's tree, then you'll become just like the witch." Deep down inside, Tiz feared that Frenchy would be a lot worse but she wasn't about to open that grisly can of worms. "And even worse, you'll waste your real heart seed. Don't let that happen. It's the worst thing you can ever do. I know, *trust* me. Keep your seed, and if someone has to prevent the witch from reclaiming her tree, then let it — then let it be..."

Silence.

Tiz didn't want to promise that she would do it. And she was glad that Frenchy didn't make her.

Instead, the usually bold and brash French girl just shook her head dismay. "We cannot defeat her," she despaired, "it is impossible."

"Not if we keep fighting each other," said Sombra, struggling to break free of Frenchy's cronies.

"Why should I believe you, *Mop*?" said Frenchy. "Why should I trust either of you?"

Slowly, Tiz revealed the key that Sombra had given her. "Here, so you don't get in trouble," said Tiz. "But you have to promise to help us — we're all in this together."

Frenchy stood up, staring at the key.

Tiz eased it toward her.

Frenchy snatched it away. "You almost had me. You should have joined us long ago — now it's too late," she said. "Holly will be *very* disappointed in both of you."

"Not as disappointed as I am with you," said Tiz.

"I'll show you *true* disappointment," said Frenchy with contempt as she unlocked the cell door. "You're coming with me."

"What? Where are we going?" asked Tiz, suddenly finding the damp cell more inviting.

But Frenchy ignored her question as she gave her key ring to one of her cronies. "Go unlock the others," she ordered as the academy rumbled and quaked. "Bring them all here."

Before long, most of the band stood in a single file line,

clutching their instruments like life vests on a huge ship heading for an iceberg. Char and Dargen were the last two to arrive — the latter looking noticeably different. The sleeves and pant legs on Dargen's yellow uniform were both at least three inches too long — he was now the same height as Tiz.

"You're shrinking," said Tiz, alarmed.

"Merlin's disease," he replied. "Not quite shrinking, but more like aging backwards. It's a wizard and warlock thing."

He *did* look younger. "The spores," said Tiz knowingly.

"Quiet," ordered Frenchy. "It's time for B Company's band members to start their new classes."

"New classes?" asked Tiz. "Who's teaching them?"

Frenchy scoffed. "Zhey are not teachers," she said, "you will not be so lucky. They're creatures — so they don't teach, they *creatch*."

"Creatch?" questioned Tiz. "That's not even a word."

"Zhat's because you haven't learned it yet," said Frenchy. "But the creatures will *creatch* you. Oh yes, they will *creatch* you. But don't worry, you might not have to meet all of them, because you probably won't survive the first one."

CHAPTER THIRTY — CREATURES DON'T TEACH, THEY "CREATCH"

WHEN FRENCHY TOLD THEM THE NAME of the first class she was taking them to, Tiz thought the huffy girl might actually be right for once — no one would survive. The class was called Zombie General. That was the full name of it, nothing more to explain it. When Tiz suggested that it sounded more like the monster from her worst nightmares rather than a subject Frenchy reminded her that zombies loved brains, especially from students that were too smart for their own good, and the more brainy she acted, the sooner she wouldn't have to worry about her lessons anymore.

"Does Zombie General like apples?" asked Molly Von Butterburg, holding up a shiny red one.

"Does it have a brain inside of it?" asked Frenchy, glaring at the vampire girl.

Molly fell silent, sagging back a few paces.

"Then it better *at least* have some worms in it," huffed Frenchy.

Molly sagged back even further, defeated.

Panic began to set in and some of the straight A students, like Dargen, began pressing Frenchy for what the subject truly was called, even though there probably was no official name, and in all likelihood, she just made one up to fill the void.

But even so, they just kept pressing and pressing until Frenchy gave in. "Digging, it's called Digging!" she yelled. "So save your energy for it! You'll need it!"

"That's not a class," insisted Molly, who was a darn good student. "That's just something you do."

"Don't you worry Molly, you'll be digging for answers while you're down there," said Frenchy. "Holly wants something found that's buried in the marshes. And you're going to find it, otherwise the hole you end up digging will be for you."

"No thanks," said Molly nervously, "I already have a coffin. It's *really* cozy."

"I don't care," replied Frenchy. "If you slept in the dirt, at least your pathetic apple would have some worms."

Tiz cleared her throat. "There's marshes down here?" she asked, trying to change the subject to something *slightly* less grim.

"There are now," said Frenchy. "The Underground Marshes are in the roots of the celestial witch's tree. And if you don't follow orders, you'll be visiting permanently."

"How does a marsh just spring up?" asked Tiz.

"Like I said, things are changing — nothing for the better," insisted Frenchy.

"My Merlin's disease," said Dargen as he continued to age backwards, now looking only ten-years-old. "The spores from the witch's tree are accelerating it." The sleeves on his uniform seemed to agree — they were even longer on him now. In a matter of hours, Tiz would be carrying him around like a baby.

Dargen turned toward Sombra and lifted up a strand of willow leaves that was growing in the middle of her dark locks. "No immunity," he said. "I think tree nymphs are a bit more resistant to the spores of the witch's tree, but even you can only hold out for so long."

Sombra tucked the leafy strand underneath her thick hair like someone in denial then looked right at Frenchy. "What are we digging for?" she asked urgently. "I wanna know. No playing around this time."

"Zeh witch didn't say what it was," said Frenchy, "only that you'll know when you find it."

"But —"

"Stop asking me questions! I don't know!" barked Frenchy as she opened a door to a dark tunnel that led down into the very roots of the tree and into the Underground Marshes.

"How are we supposed to see down there?" asked Helen Grug, squinting her big troll eyes. "Not all of us can see in the dark."

But before Frenchy could yell at her, they saw flashing lights at the bottom of the tunnel. A swarm of the largest fireflies Tiz had ever seen was flying up the tunnel toward them.

"I'm sorry," said Frenchy behind them nervously, fear filling her eyes. Along with her five cronies from Wolfberry, she pushed the door shut on them, slamming it loudly.

Sombra turned to Char with a terrified look on her face. "Can you phase us through the door, please?" she begged as the rest of the band desperately tried to force it open.

"There are too many of us," he replied.

"We shouldn't go anywhere," said Tiz stepping forward toward the approaching fireflies. "We have to find out what the witch is looking for if we're going to have any chance of beating her."

Though far from the voice of a hero, her confident tone seemed to embolden them, as Tiz hoped it would. She'd used her loud voice for a million things before — complaining, yelling and screaming — but rarely for its ability to lead. And when she did lead at times in the past, it was usually for some silly quest and not anything serious. Standing there, looking at the fear in the eyes of her friends, she realized that leading was more than just about giving orders, it was about instilling courage.

"Do what you're told," she said, barely believing that she was the one saying those words. "And don't argue. If we listen until I figure out something, we'll make it out of this. I promise."

The buzzing from the wings of the giant fireflies in the tunnel grew deafening as the huge insects grabbed all the members of the band, instruments squeaking all over the place. The bugs flew them back down the tunnel toward a smell much worse than the skunky lotion that Tiz had to put on her skin in order to keep the druids in D Company from following her around like a pack of love-sick puppies.

Flying through the tunnel as she held her nose shut, Tiz watched in awe as the root widened into a vast three hundred and sixty degree marsh. Marsh on the ceiling, marsh on the walls and marsh almost everywhere. The few spots that weren't marsh dripped green slime shimmering with stardust.

"Eww!" shouted Sombra over the drone of the flapping firefly wings as she slapped her arm to kill a mosquito. "I knew it was going to be gross, but not this gross!" The firefly transporting Sombra in its arms gave her a nasty shake that seemed to say, "You just crushed my best friend — maybe I'll do the same to you!"

Living in the wild, tree nymphs were no strangers to bugs, but this was a marsh on steroids. Tiz was too afraid to crush the blood-sucking mosquitoes on her own arms because the big bugs were watching her with hundreds of eyes apiece. And who knows what the fireflies were signaling to each other as their bulbous tail lights blinked back and forth, but from the frantic pace of it, it couldn't be good.

Suddenly, several of the mosquitoes siphoning her fiery blood burst into flames.

The giant firefly carrying Tiz through the air glared down at her.

She gave it an apologetic smile along with an innocent shrug — what else could she do?

Just when she thought it couldn't get any worse, Tiz saw that the bugs were the least of their worries. During their descent, Tiz spotted a group of about forty zombies from Z Company standing around the entrance to a cave in their zucchini-colored combat fatigues. They were never a fun-loving group to begin with and were always closely monitored by the teachers at the academy. But now, the spores of the tree seemed to have a much more sinister effect on them compared to everyone else. They looked more rotten than ever and in every single way. Sprouting from their skin, there were polyps, boils and pustules galore — each one looked like it was on the verge of going *boom.* Even the bugs didn't want to go near the explosive-looking, hardcore military zombies.

So the fireflies dropped the band members into the dark, soggy marsh with a symphony of loud *squishes* that must have seemed like a military cargo plane doing a supply drop of juicy brains to the zombies because they all started groaning and staggering toward the new arrivals through the tall grass.

Suddenly, a guttural groan boomed from the cave that sounded like a harpooned polar bear. The zombies halted on the spot, giving new meaning to the phrase "stopping dead in your tracks." None of them dared to move — not even a moan.

Tiz heard shuffling feet along with the clanking of metal as if some powerful monster had been chained but broke free. Out of the cave and into the marsh shuffled what remained of General Maximus Payne. And what remained was a one-eyed zombie who hadn't polished a medal, shined his shoes, shaved his square jaw or even combed what remained of his hair in at least a day. He embodied everything the old general hated. And Tiz could see that hate in his only eye as he glared at her.

Frenchy was right. They would be digging their graves down here. And after they were six feet under, they'd come back looking like the general — no forget that — there'd be nothing left of them after the zombies were done.

Molly offered Zombie General her apple and he smacked it out of her hand, sending it tumbling into some tall weeds. Within seconds, some creature hidden inside was crunching it greedily. Tiz's stomach started to growl as Zombie General stared at her like he hadn't eaten in a thousand years.

"Uhhh," he groaned in a myriad of different pitches and tones. And the weirdest thing about it was that Tiz understood what he meant. She spoke Zombie and she didn't even know it. Like the lament she sung to help Sombra, she understood what he wanted merely through the tones. It had been the same with the fireflies. Even though she didn't realize it at the time, she had even understood their fast-paced flashing lights as anger — just like angrily flashing heart seeds.

"Zombie General wants us to dig like our lives depend on it," she said.

"What?" blurted Sombra. "When did you learn to speak Zombie?"

"I didn't," replied Tiz. "I just understood is all. I guess I'm more in tune with things than I thought."

The other zombies started groaning louder, staring at her like she was indeed a little Einstein.

Dargen elbowed Tiz and spelled, "B-R-A-I-N." "Stop acting like you have one," he warned.

The zombies groaned even louder as they turned their attention toward him. They knew how to spell — damn the academy.

Zombie General growled at his drooling underlings.

"That's a good growl," said Tiz. "If there is such a thing."

Zombie General turned Tiz away from the cave and ushered her toward the marsh with a shove. The whole band started marching behind her through the soggy grass under the watchful eye of Zombie General and his undead platoon.

"I guess it's almost time to dig," said Tiz.

"We could use some shovels," suggested Sombra.

Drooling zombies *groaned* at her.

"Sombra, hush up," urged Tiz while marching through some tall grass. "No more good ideas," she whispered. "Not until we find a way to ditch them or this march will be our funeral procession."

"Maybe we should use tap code," suggested Sombra. "We could snap our fingers instead of tapping."

"No," said Tiz adamantly. "I'd rather be a zombie."

Before long, Tiz led her band mates and their new shuffling chaperons all the way to the edge of a dark swamp whose trees and bubbling water glowed an eerie green. It looked like a giant witch's cauldron stuffed with too many ingredients as a layer of ghostly fog hovered over its surface.

"*Aaaaaaaaamp*," moaned Zombie General, pointing toward the darkness deep inside the swamp and beyond the glow.

The old general had always loved to yell, "Do you understand the words firing out of my word shooter!" Now, very few cadets actually could and found themselves in the conundrum of getting closer to a hungry zombie to hear him better or staying farther away and risk being asked to repeat what he said without hurting his feelings.

Suddenly, Tiz heard splashing. Another group was emerging from the shadows of the swamp. It was Apple Company, their granny-apple green uniforms glowing eerily in the light as they were being closely guarded by another platoon of zombies.

Out came abominable snow boys and girls, their white fur completely covered in mud, marching out while hunched over, looking exhausted. Several plucked leeches out of their fur as most of the band had to look away, except for Molly who eyed them like a hungry dog would a treat.

"Go back," grunted the biggest abominable snow boy as he struggled to trudge out of the slop.

"Did you find anything?" asked Tiz desperately, hoping that they wouldn't have to go in after all.

The huge mud-covered ape boy fell face first into the muck — out cold. Two zombies pick him up and hauled him off.

"I guess that's a 'no'," said Sombra.

"*Knooooow*," groaned the zombies.

"Oops..."

"Sombra, *please* be quiet," pleaded Tiz as they watched the giant ant-people from A Company crawl by at a frenzied pace.

It was as though they had been driven mad by something in the swamp. The giant ant-people were crushing the bugs buzzing around them, not giving it a second thought. Some of them were desperately cleaning green slime off their antennae as though it was toxic waste.

Tiz sneezed and a purple flower flew out of her nose — her symptoms were getting worse. The spores from the witch's tree were a hundred times more potent near the swamp. She didn't want to think about how bad they would be inside.

The swamp bubbling before her was so creepy-looking she didn't even want to shut her eyes to blink. So if the myth about sneezing with your eyes open was true, then she was sure to sneeze her eyeballs out if she entered the green soupy wasteland. Though Zombie General would probably love for that to happen anyway. He would more than likely just scoop one up and pop it in his own empty socket then eat the other one like an olive.

After a few minutes, all of A Company finished trudging out of the swamp, or more accurately, what used to resemble A Company.

"*Aaaamp*," ordered Zombie General pointing into the swamp.

It was their turn.

Tiz turned around, looking at her band mates. Everyone was staring at her. "We'll be okay," she said with as much courage as she could muster.

"Really?" said Helen Grug, pointing to another thin branch that had sprouted out of Tiz's nose.

Tiz plucked it out. "There, it's as good as new," she said, eyes watering. "See?"

Zombie General pushed her into the swamp and the other zombies followed his lead, shoving the band in with a symphony of squeaks and groans, ones that weren't just coming from their instruments this time.

CHAPTER THIRTY-ONE — THE NAMELESS SWAMP

HOME IS WHERE THE HEART IS. But what if that heart was filled with evil and appeared to suffer from leprosy? What would its home look like then? The answer is the Nameless Swamp.

The zombies blended perfectly with the ghastly surroundings — creepy spore-covered trees, insects with missing eyes and gurgling ponds that spewed a putrid mist into the air — they were so at home that Molly started calling them swombies.

Hearing whispering, Tiz glanced back at her friends, concerned. She had a growing feeling that they really were inside a giant bubbling cauldron, with all of them serving as its ingredients, the witless swombies too. So the sooner they found what the witch wanted and got the heck out of there, the better.

Ahead, it grew even darker and more menacing. The marsh they trudged through to get to the Nameless Swamp had been dismal enough with only a little bit of light from the giant fireflies and the stardust from the green slime of the witch's tree. But the fireflies wouldn't go into the swamp for some reason so it was just the eerie green glow of the water and the trees.

Worse, there was no path. Tiz led them through the best she could, weaving them past huge bog-like pools of water, deeper and deeper in, all the while, trying to figure out a way to ditch the zombies. Meanwhile, more squeaks and groans began bellowing from the instruments behind her as the band slapped and smacked the bugs on them. They were getting more and more desperate. So much so, a few cadets even allowed Molly to peel the leeches off them, but promptly gasped when she popped them into her mouth afterwards like liquid-filled candy.

On her tippy-toes, Tiz led them past a pond frothing up at them like the mouth of a rabid sea monster. She peeked at the murky water as though a giant tongue might burst out for a taste at any moment.

Something grabbed her shoulder — she jumped.

It was Char.

"Don't do that," she said, staring nervously at the water.

The fallen angel glanced at the zombies. "I wonder what they're looking for," he whispered from behind.

"I bet it's the witch's body," suggested Sombra. "She dies and comes back, right? What could possibly sniff out a dead body better than a small, ugly horde of its own kind."

"Possibly," said Dargen, looking alarmingly younger. "But it doesn't seem likely. Why would the witch want to be a zombie?"

"Yeah," said Tiz, fighting off a sneeze. "I bet it has something to do with climbing the you-know-what."

The zombies must have thought she was right because one of the shorter ones reached for her head like a starving kid would a lunch box.

As she ducked out of the way, Zombie General slapped the grabby zombie's hands aside.

"*Ine*," groaned Zombie General as he stared at Tiz's head.

Everyone grew silent, knowing that the word that he had fired out of his word shooter was "mine."

Double-timing it, Tiz led them into a soggy grove full of twisted, strange-looking trees without a single leaf. In fact, the trees looked more like the giant roots of the witch's tree, ones that had curled back into the academy and poked up into the swamp.

"*Alt*," ordered Zombie General and everyone halted, having gotten somewhat used to his new stunted language. Out of the blue, he pushed Tiz down to the soggy grass. "*Ig*," he groaned, pointing at the ground.

Soon, the rest of the band found themselves in the same position with at least one zombie watching over each of them. Apparently, zombies hated to dig. And who could blame them, assuming that one day they had simply woken up from a cozy lil' dirt nap to find themselves alive and six feet under.

Having her own hole to dig herself out of, Tiz reached into her emergency pack and pulled out her mole mittens to begin excavating the surrounding area for the mysterious prize.

Zombie General stared at the claws on her mittens as he growled.

Quick as a cat, they went right back into her pack.

Digging up mud and slime with her bare hands, Tiz glanced around for a hint of something that the zombies themselves might have overlooked, something that might swing the balance of power over to the band.

She peeked over the edge of some nearby grass and into a pond. The thing she was looking for was down there, staring right back at her — not a secret weapon, not an underwater ally, not even a hidden escape tunnel. Instead, Tiz was gazing at her own reflection — it was up to her to help her friends. No one was coming to save them, just like Frenchy had said.

In the reflection, she saw Zombie General leaning over her, staring at the back of her head like a menu.

But this was no time to panic. Tiz mustered all the courage she could, not only for herself, but also for her friends. Glancing around, she began staring at one of the root-trees covered in stardust as she remembered something about the cosmic tree itself. It was an ash tree, but for Iggy City, it was pruned like a bonsai tree. Regardless, it was *still* an ash tree. And something special could grow near the roots of one.

Tiz started sniffing the air like a hungry bloodhound. And for once, she actually smelled something that didn't reek like sweaty zombie socks. "I smell the buried treasure," she proclaimed. "And it smells delicious." She stood and sniffed the air a few more times. "It's on the other side of this pond."

But there was no way to walk around it. Two wide streams fed it from both sides.

Zombie General growled in disapproval.

Tiz ignited her wings to the *ew's* and *ah's* of her fellow band mates as Zombie General staggered back from her.

Tiz felt her nose itch. She sneezed and flames shot out of her mouth and nostrils, making her feel like a baby dragon with hay fever. Luckily, her flaming gift to the swamp missed everybody, landing in a pool of water with a steamy hiss.

"Holy smokes," gawked Sombra.

With her wings blazing brightly, Tiz could have escaped if she wanted to. And she saw that fear in Sombra's widening eyes. But even the threat of the witch and her tree couldn't make Tiz ditch her friends. No way. She wouldn't abandon them. She was going to try to ditch the zombies instead.

Tiz flew toward the other side of the pond as Zombie General grunted words at her that broke ten latrine machine laws in one sentence — understanding Zombie now felt like a curse.

Landing with a squish on the other side, Tiz pulled out her mole mittens to the howling displeasure of Zombie General and dug frantically at the base of one of the gnarled root-like trees. She scooped mud aside as fast as she could, fearing the swombies would take their anger out on her band mates; ones she loved and whose help she would desperately need.

Digging at the base of the tree on her knees, Tiz thought back to when Sombra was stuck in her tree. Just like this, it was a desperate and grim situation. One Tiz tried to solve on her own, but in the end, it was the collective voices of all the other tree nymphs in the Wailing Woods that helped to free her best friend. There was strength in numbers. And when those numbers worked together in harmony, forming a powerful collective voice, the sky was the limit. Together, they could reach the stars while a lone wolf could only howl at the moon (not unlike Zombie General was doing at her).

Coming back to "Earth", or mud more like it, Tiz took off her mole mittens and stuffed them back into her pack — they were caked in sludge and had become too heavy. Now off, she immediately noticed that a new leaf had sprouted from her fingertip.

Just as she was about to pluck it off, she caught a strong whiff of the buried treasure she was searching for — the apple of the witch's eye, the zombie prize, the thing that might save them all. To her, it smelled as strong as a smelling salt but without the bad part. For its aroma was just as pleasing as her mother's majestic truffle mousse. And there was a reason for that...

Even through a layer of mud, the buried treasure began glowing near her knees like a miniature sun, right by a root of the root-tree. The prize was oval-shaped, just like a football. It was the most divine and potent smelling truffle she'd ever seen — a celestial truffle from the great cosmic tree. And when she touched it, something amazing happened. The leaf on her fingertip simply disappeared. Best of all, the aches and pains in her fingers went with it. They no longer felt like they belonged to a ninety-year-old woman that had played professional handball all her life. Harvesting the football-like truffle with both of her hands, Tiz hoisted it above her head — she had scored an agricultural touchdown.

And now it all started making sense to her. She very well could be holding the *true* living key. An object that grew at the bottom of the witch's tree that could be carried by a climber all the way to the top in order to prove that they made the journey. Although, she did remember Dargen saying that the tree would know if you climbed it. If so, then it could feel every single different climber on its bark as if they were big insects crawling on someone's skin. And therefore, the tree could track the honesty and fairness in their chosen path, penalizing anyone that flew up instead of only side-to-side.

So maybe this living key would help open the door to the Tower of Thorns instead, or if not, unlock the secret at the top of it.

Tiz's mind was racing as fast as her heart while considering all the possibilities. "I was right — it was here all along!" she yelled from across the pond, unable to contain her excitement anymore. "And it's amazing!"

The zombies weren't the least bit happy for her, growling angrily that they couldn't snatch it away from their brainy little adversary. To them, the truffle itself must have looked like a golden brain, lighting up their eyes with intense desire.

"I think I'm gonna keep it for myself!" shouted Tiz, sniffing it as though she was getting ready to devour it. "It smells so darn good, I think I'm going to eat it! Sorry!"

"AAAAAARRRRRGH!"

Ten zombies marched into the pond after her.

Tiz watched them anxiously.

Halfway through, the ten began slowing and slowing. Soon they couldn't move at all. They were stuck in quicksand up to their knees — just as she planned. She was ditching them, literally. And the more they struggled the deeper they sank.

Tiz stifled a smile as the swombies growled at her.

The thirty remaining moved toward the water to help the other ten.

Go, go, go, thought Tiz, urging them on in her mind.

But they didn't. Zombie General stopped them with a guttural command.

It was time for plan B — and that B stood for Battle-ax.

Tiz balanced the celestial truffle perfectly on top of her head. To the zombies, it was like a gob of heavenly whip cream on their favorite dessert.

While they howled, Tiz unzipped her magic pocket and pulled out her string-staff — the one that now looked like a heavy metal rock star's guitar, bottomed-off with a real ax head.

Without a word to her band mates, she started marching in place while playing the marching song they played every day at morning formation. She strummed a simple but powerful beat from her magical strings that urged anyone hearing it to lift their feet and walk in place:

Dah-duh, Dah-duh — Dut-dut, Dut-dut — Dut-dut, Dah-duh...

The band members stood up and started lifting their feet. Sombra was first to join in with her kazoo. Dargen rolled up his sleeves so they wouldn't get in the way then added his violin. Char lit up his guitar with the same beat. One by one, the whole band joined their instruments to her song.

DAH-DUH, DAH-DUH — DUT-DUT, DUT-DUT — DUT-DUT, DAH-DUH...

They were no longer the gloomy band playing sadly in their cells. They were inspired, and so was Tiz. So much so, she started warming up her voice by singing the sounds of the beat.

DAH-DUH, DAH-DUH — DUT-DUT, DUT-DUT — DUT-DUT, DAH-DUH...

The instruments of the other cadets suddenly started glowing.

Zombie legs began to quiver. One even lifted a foot. They were resisting, but with the combined magic of her strings and her voice, the collective bellowing of the band imploring them to march and their lust for the celestial truffle on top of her head — resistance was futile.

Several zombies started marching in place with the band as

Zombie General growled at them. Then two more joined in. Zombie General grabbed one of their legs but ten more joined the stomping. Within moments, all of them were marching in place except for their illustrious leader. Zombie General was now face down in the muck, reduced to restraining the smelly foot of one of his minions.

In years to come, the following strange and terrifying moment would be referred to by several names: *The Swamp Swan Song, The March of the Swombies* and last but not least, *Tiz's Last Stand.*

With her own heart glowing red so brightly from the magic of her lost heart seed that it lit up her throat, Tiz bellowed a command to the beat of the music that the simple-minded undead struggled to withstand.

"ZOMBIES!" she yelled, lifting her knees as high as she could, "FORWARD, MARCH!"

And march they did! Ignoring the cries of their master, the thirty remaining zombie minions shuffled forward into the marshy waters in far less than perfect rhythm — but no one was about to complain, except for a certain undead general.

DAH-DUH, DAH-DUH — DUT-DUT, DUT-DUT — DUT-DUT, DAH-DUH...

The music grew so loud it drowned out the screams of their leader.

Zombies were getting stuck left and right in quicksand, unable to free themselves.

With her wings blazing, Tiz flew into the air and hovered above Zombie General, playing her song.

He watched her as his only eye seemed to fall into a trance.

"ZOMBIE GENERAL!" she yelled confidently, her heart glowing within her chest like a magical medal of bravery. "YOUR EYE, FRONT!"

His eye glowed orange as he snapped his head toward the

water.

"FORWARD, MARCH!"

But he didn't budge. The band played in a frenzy — but it was going to take more — the perfect marching song for someone as evil as him — a song she taught her band mates, one worthy of her favorite movie villain, *General Invader*.

"BAND!" yelled Tiz. "*INVADER'S TYRANNICAL MARCH*!"

DUNT — DUNT — DUNT — BOOM — BA — BOOM...

The band played flawlessly. It was as though General Invader was judging the performance personally, just begging to crush the first instrument that played off-key.

Zombie General's only eye flared brightly as if it was about to go supernova. He finally had a song worthy of him. He marched toward the pond as though he was invading a miniature nation.

Tiz saluted him.

He gave her a small nod then saluted back. He looked as happy as she'd seen him as a zombie. That is, until he got stuck even sooner than the other ones. But by then, all their menacing growls had less teeth than the zombies themselves.

Tiz landed by her friends as they played, watching Zombie General moan amongst his comrades. She made a chopping motion with her hand and the band cut the music.

Sombra ran up to the edge of the pond and yelled, "Now drop and give me fifty!"

Several zombies did, getting their hands stuck as well.

"That means *you*, Zombie General! Drop and give me —"

"Sombra, that's enough," said Tiz extinguishing her wings as she put a calming hand on her friend's shoulder.

"But what do we do now?" asked Molly over the zombie groans. It was the million-dollar question. In a way, they were just as stuck as the zombies in the Nameless Swamp.

CHAPTER THIRTY-TWO — THE WITCH, THE TOADY AND THE HUNGRY TREE

TIZ HELD OUT THE CELESTIAL TRUFFLE as it illuminated the faces of her band mates as well as the slimy root-trees around them with a golden light. "Everyone touch the truffle," she said. "As soon as I did, the tree growing out of me, well, it stopped. I'm pretty sure this thing is called the living key — our key to living."

Everyone thrust their finger onto the glowing truffle so fast that Tiz was surprised it wasn't skewered into a hundred different pieces. And the second Sombra did, her vine-like strand of hair lost its leaves then change back to normal. Right after Dargen touched it he regained five inches and his uniform finally fit again. Soon, every weird symptom affecting the group had simply faded away like an allergic reaction after a shot of adrenaline.

"Phew," said Dargen in relief as he watched Tiz turn toward the pond to study Zombie General.

"Do you think he's good at catching things?" asked Tiz, briefly cocking her arm back with the truffle like it indeed was a football. "He did make us catch those baseballs at the first climbing practice, after all."

"Um, Tiz?" questioned Sombra. "Are you thinking about doing what *I think* you're thinking about to doing?"

"I'm going to try to help him," replied Tiz bluntly.

"*Don't*," pleaded Sombra, latching onto her arm.

"But if we leave him like that, we're no better than the swombies," she said. "Two wrongs —"

"*Don't* make a right," stressed Sombra. "Do you really want to trust Zombie General with the living key?"

"I think it'll be okay," said Tiz. *I hope*, she thought to herself.

Sombra let go of her arm and Tiz ignited her wings, taking to the air. She hovered over Zombie General as he growled up at her. "I'm going to toss this up and I want you to catch it with both hands, not just one," she said, holding it up. "So catch." She lofted the magical truffle toward him, and thankfully, he caught it.

But nothing happened.

Zombie General just looked at it greedily, opening his jaws to devour it.

As it approached his lips, his entire body began glowing as he halted the truffle right before his teeth. Without a single bite, he began transforming. His missing eye regenerated. Old, decaying flesh became new. Patchy hair became full and combed neatly. A tattered uniform turned beautifully pressed, all its medals gleaming.

Tiz sighed in relief, echoing everyone's sentiments.

"Help me!" called out the general from below. "Please!"

Tiz swooped down and did exactly that, grabbing him by the wrists as the other zombies groaned at her. She couldn't yank him out though, that is, until Char flew over and helped. Slowly, they pulled the general from the muck to a smatter of applause from the band, most still looking at him warily.

Tiz and Char set him down at the edge of the pond, far away from their uneasy classmates, though several *still* took a step back — just in case.

Tiz eye-balled the general not unlike he would have done to her if she didn't polish the brass on her uniform. "What about the other zombies," she asked. "Can we help them?"

"That's a negative, they're from Z Company — zombies for life," he replied just like his old self as he raised the glowing truffle in his hands. "This living key right here, well, it would fry them faster than a binary star system fries vampires."

Molly, who was already in the back, receded even further.

"Welcome back," said Tiz, saluting the general.

She was pretty sure she detected a smile as he snapped to

attention then returned her salute. "Thanks, Red," he said, more fatherly than she would have ever expected.

Overjoyed, Tiz felt the hairs on her arms stand at attention. At that moment, she sensed that he might actually be proud of her. That maybe he had even liked her all along. That he had been hard on her in the past because he cared, not because he disliked her, and *that* particular hunch reinforced that she had done the right thing. Standing there, Tiz studied the general's eyes, ones just as bright and green as her own. Could he also be the father that abandoned her family long ago? And if so, did he still care about them?

The general tossed the truffle back to her and she caught it with her dominant hand, not unlike the first climbing practice.

He nodded. "So it begins," he said, stepping onto a fallen tree like a stage. Looking right at Tiz he proclaimed, "You have found the living key! Now the door to the competition has been thrown open! Nothing, and no one, can stop you!"

BOOM! A root-tree nearby exploded into flames. Everyone dove to the ground, covering their heads! BOOM! BOOM! BOOM! Three more burst apart.

Then it stopped.

An eerie silence.

Everyone eased to their feet, listening intently.

Cackling laughter in the distance filled the air...

She was coming...

"*Hahahaha*!" shrieked Holly the Witch, flying madly in on a broom, one decorated like an evil Christmas tree. From it dangled red lights with devilish ornaments — pitchforks, pointy horns and Santa Clauses in flames (even Mrs. Claus). Even more horrifying, Holly's face had changed for the worse, turning unnaturally red, wolfberry red, one half of it frozen in a permanent grin, the other half frowning. Her bright red face now resembled a cursed opera mask with split personalities. "*Nothing* will stop you?" she shrieked, landing in front of Tiz and sticking her long hooked nose, red as blood, right in her face. "Don't be a fool! *I* will stop you!"

Tiz glared at her enemy. "I'm allergic to evil," she said. "And trust me, you don't want me sneezing in your face."

"You don't," said Sombra, backing her friend. "Her sneezes are a hot mess. Then again, it might be an improvement."

Holly the Witch silenced Sombra with her own glare then turned her attention back to Tiz. "Give me the living key, *lil' missy*," she hissed, reaching her hand toward it.

Tiz pulled it back.

"Foolish girl!" shrieked the witch so loudly that everyone had to cover their ears. "Let's settle this right here — you and me, *deary*. One of us gets the tree."

Tiz flared her wings. She was going to yell at the witch like a banshee.

The witch raised her red hands to cast a curse.

"*CEASE YOUR BICKERING*!" gargled a deep voice from the depths of the pond, stopping them both in mid-spell. "*TO CLAIM THE UNWITHERING TREE — YOU MUST DO SO FAIRLY, OR ELSE, YOU SHALL NOT BE WORTHY...*"

Out from the water leapt a gargantuan toad the size of an elephant, high into the air, its bulbous eyes glowing green as if it was under a spell. All the band members scattered to make room for its landing. Molly tripped over a rock so Tiz pulled her across the mud and out of the way before the creature landed in the swamp with a squish, splashing everyone in the vicinity with muck.

The enormous toad had a huge mouth that looked like a giant Venus flytrap with rows and rows of sharp yellow teeth that would have put a great white shark to shame. Worse still, those teeth were surrounded by a set of bright red lips that made its grin resemble a joker from an evil deck of playing cards.

To Molly's horror, he puckered those red lips right at her. "*Croak*, I await your kiss my princess, *croak,* turn me into your handsome prince," he said.

"Um..." stalled Molly, fishing around in her pack frantically. "Do you like apples?" she asked, producing a shiny red one.

The giant toad *CROAKED* at Molly so loudly, that for a second, Tiz thought the vampire girl had indeed croaked for good as she shut her eyes and fell, fainting from the putrid smell surging from the beast's ghastly mouth.

Luckily, Tiz caught Molly then shot a glare at the monstrous toad in response. But as much as Tiz disliked it, the red-faced witch seemed to hate it even more.

Steam hissed from the witch's nose as she wiped off the mud the toad had splattered on it. "Croaker the Joker, you insolent toady!" she shrieked, pointing a long red fingernail at him. "How dare you get your filth on me! I am the mistress of this tree! I am your master! You are under the spell of the tree! I command you to break free of it, immediately!"

"SILENCE!" boomed the toad, his big round eyes glowing green. Without any warning, he shot his tongue up into one of the root-like trees and snatched a large fly stuck in an enormous web, dragging the whole thing down along with the huge spider that had spun it. The owner of the web tried to scurry away but Croaker sucked them all into his giant flytrap of a mouth, chewing them obnoxiously so everyone could hear the crunchy bug parts and see them gushing out.

"Tiz," whispered Sombra, tugging on her friend's sleeve. "Make him chew with his mouth closed. Charm him."

"*You* charm him," said Tiz. "He likes kisses, so pucker up."

"*Not* what I had in mind for my first kiss," replied Sombra.

Croaker must have heard, because he puckered his lips at her then laughed when she winced. He then resumed his chewing, smacking his bright red lips even louder.

All the cadets cringed as they watched the grotesque toad finish off his meal with a loud disgusting *BURP*!

"Heed my bright — red — lips!" he boomed in a deep, guttural voice (and what a set of lips they were). "For I am the Lips and the Tongue of the Unwithering Tree! Through me speaks the tree, *croak*. We are one being, and the tree is hungry, *croak*."

Tiz hid the celestial truffle behind her back. She didn't like the fact that he always seemed to glance at her when he said, "*Croak*." In a way, Croaker the Joker was like a daft and reclusive wizard she once read about that shot fireballs recklessly in random directions. But instead, Croaker used something even more deadly, his tongue. Watching him snatch every big bug in sight while under the control of the tree, she now realized that the Unwithering One would be her ultimate enemy, one even greater than the witch herself.

"Answer me this!" boomed Croaker out of the blue. "*Croak*, what do you *all* have in common with a toad?"

Silence. Not even a cricket was stupid enough to chirp.

"*Croak*, well, it's *NOT* a quick tongue, that's for sure," he grumbled impatiently.

"I think I know," said Tiz, stepping forward, but not wanting to say it. She was just trying to be brave for everyone else.

"Oh goody, *croak*, goody," said Croaker merrily, his bulbous eyes glowing brighter and brighter green. "Tell the tree what you know."

"Well, except for maybe Molly, someday, we're all going to *croak*," she said joylessly.

Croaker grinned and said, "Maybe even *sooner* than you know, *croak*." Suddenly, his tongue shot toward Tiz.

She ducked.

His tongue snatched a second huge spider that was dangling right over her and would have more than likely bitten her.

The witch didn't like that at all. "You stupid, fat toad!" she yelled. "That spider would have eaten the Phoenix girl! If you're not going to eat her, stop eating the things that will!"

"SILENCE!" boomed Croaker. "Or the Lips and the Tongue of the Unwithering Tree will smile upon thee..."

"How *dare* you!" hissed the witch as she advanced toward the gargantuan toad, pointing her broom at him while the tip of it lit up like a flamethrower ready to spout.

It was now clear — the witch had lost all her ties to the tree. Easing toward him, she didn't even limp anymore. Losing her bond seemed to allow her to heal her foot. Halting fearlessly right in front of the gluttonous monster, she raised the fiery tip of her broom menacingly, threatening to incinerate one of his glowing green eyes.

But when Croaker grinned at her with his rows and rows of sharp teeth, the witch thought twice about what she was doing. Slowly, she lowered her weapon of choice then eased back several steps.

Tiz wished that the witch hadn't changed her mind, because Croaker turned his glowing eyes toward her. Fearing his gaze, let alone his kiss, Tiz fidgeted nervously with the celestial truffle behind her back.

"Show me the living key!" insisted Croaker the Joker, "show it to the tree, *croak*!"

"Promise me that you won't snatch it away," said Tiz sternly.

"Unless you'd rather have a kiss, *croak*," he said, inching his cavernous mouth closer to her. "*SHOW IT TO THE TREE*!"

Tiz would have rather kissed the bottom of another toilet. And she knew Croaker couldn't be trusted with a cocoa lump let alone the most important and mouth-watering truffle in the universe. So she slowly revealed it to him as she conjured the power of her voice. Her throat began glowing red as she said, "You don't want the celestial truffle, Croaker. It will make you sick." She waved it past his bulbous eyes like a hypnotist. "You don't want the truffle — it doesn't exist."

Like a red lightning bolt, his tongue shot out and snatched it out of her hand.

A tuba played *Invader's Tyrannical March* again to the delight of Croaker.

Sombra shook her head. "Well, he *definitely* didn't want it," she said.

"You're *definitely* not helping," replied Tiz as she shot a glare at the goblin playing the tuba. "And neither are you!"

The tuba squeaked to a halt as Croaker laughed, his belly jiggling and rumbling, anxious to welcome the truffle into its new permanent home.

But instead of devouring the living key, Croaker set it on top of his head, just like Tiz had done, making the swombies still stuck in the pond groan loudly. Croaker snared another giant fly and started munching. His tongue was so precise he could have probably snatched the eyelash off a flea at a thousand paces, if fleas had eyelashes. Smug as smug could be, Croaker grinned devilishly under his new glowing hat.

The witch saw an opportunity to snatch it from the snatcher, mounting her broom, quick as a cat. But Croaker was faster, snatching her broom and devouring it as it exploded in his stomach, causing his belly to ripple.

Cadets backed away, and luckily they did, because his belch was a flamethrower.

"*Croak*, your *broom, broom, broom*, go *boom, boom, boom*!" laughed Croaker at the witch. "But you won't be needing it. No, no, no. No flying to the top, little flies, *croak*. Only climbing. Or the door to the Tower of Thorns won't open. So let the Ascension begin! To the starting line, *croak*!"

"Excellent," hissed the witch, "because I'm tired of your croaking."

"*Croak* or don't *croak*!" grinned Croaker. "I care not, *croak*, but in the end only one can claim the tree, and the tree-me wants the very best, and the rest, well, *croak, croak,*

croak!"

The academy began rumbling louder than Croaker's stomach. Vines resembling the tentacles of a giant squid shot out from every direction in the swamp and grabbed each and everyone of them, even the witch, though instead of screaming like all the normal cadets did, she started cackling wildly.

The real Holly Holly would have been terrified, and more than likely, was trapped somewhere deep inside the witch — a captive witness to it all — a prisoner in her own body like Tiz had been inside her grim cell.

"*Woooo-weeeee*!" screamed the witch madly while in the grasp of a tentacle. She was laughing as though she was enjoying a carnival ride instead of being whisked toward the outside of Iggy City by one of the horrifying arms of the gargantuan carnivorous tree. One that was *very, very,* hungry.

CHAPTER THIRTY-THREE — THE ASCENSION

MASS HYSTERIA REIGNED outside the academy. At the bottom of the protective bubble, teachers turned into creatures were chasing cadets, even though some of the students were more fearsome-looking monsters than the mutated teachers themselves. And Little Nub Nub, the baby rhino with the Napoleon complex, seemed to be chasing the whole lot. It looked like an evil circus where all the mistreated animals got loose.

Above all the chaos, Tiz and the rest of the band were in the grasp of the tentacles that were whirling around and around what used to be the academy in an amusement ride from hell. They were orbiting the witch's tree like some of the portals to the nine realms above them, ones that were wavering up and down precariously on the thin celestial vines tying them to the tree.

Tiz watched helplessly as more tentacles seized the boarder hoarders battling the witch's tree, crushing the giant clockwork squirrels like they were merely wind-up toys. The guardians of the school fell past her in bits and pieces, raining down onto the chaos below — they were now truly on their own.

Struggling to free herself, Tiz looked up and spotted something she had gazed upon in the darkest cave of the underworld, high atop the witch's tree. There, under the starlight, the Tower of Thorns was forming. The door to the tower stood closed at its base, at least twenty stories up. Above that, the sharp tip of the tower poked into the huge bubble full of breathable air around them perilously, stretching it as though it didn't care, for the tree just seemed to keep growing in every direction.

Tiz was terrified. Her hands started trembling. This was

much more than she bargained for. They never trained for something like this. Before long, more than one bubble was sure to burst — everyone was in danger.

And just as she was about to give up hope, she saw a red light pulsing in the tiny window at the top of the tower. She reached her hand toward the heart seed dangling there like a star. It gave her the hope she desperately needed. So much so, she unzipped her pocket and pulled out the ruby necklace and phoenix pendant that her mother had given her, putting it on.

In the distance below, near the starting lines at the roots of the witch's tree, Tiz saw that the tentacles had been busy in other parts of the academy, gathering cadets and their things. There, the witch was pacing in an open area by herself. And no one dared to stand near her. The other climbers from Wolfberry were huddled as far away as possible from her with their pets and spotters.

Suddenly, Tiz heard familiar dog barks — one of the tentacles must have brought her own pet outside.

"Pup Pup!" she yelled as the tentacle carrying her dropped her by her familiar near the starting lines. Tiz scooped him up and whirled him around, his tail a blur, wagging happily.

Outside the academy there was no more floating, the gravity of the situation now matched the real gravity that was pulling them downward as they walked on the roots of the tree. Tiz felt like she was back on Earth, her emergency pack was as heavy as ever, even before she put Pup Pup inside.

Ahead, she saw Colonel Monocle bound and gagged, tied to one of the slimy roots. The elderly man that reminded her of a mad scientist looked to be in horrible shape. His monocle was cracked and his gadget-knife arm was missing half of its tools. But even still, Tiz was glad to see he wasn't a Zombie Colonel — at least not yet. Though in truth, he was a mindless servant anyway. His eyes were glowing the same eerie green as Croaker's — he was under the spell of the tree.

The red-faced witch ran over to him and tore off the disheveled man's gag. The colonel's voice sounded like a megaphone as he yelled, "*Climbers, to your starting lines*!"

Tiz and Char scrambled toward theirs but Croaker leapt in front of them, the celestial truffle glowing atop his head. Her spotter put himself bravely between Tiz and the grotesque giant toad as Croaker licked his bright red lips. But instead of using his tongue to snatch one of them up, he used it to pluck the living key off his slimy head. Stranger still, he didn't eat the savory treat. Instead, he tossed it over to Tiz.

"Thanks," she said, inspecting the glowing truffle. "I think." As if climbing the tree wouldn't be hard enough, she would now have a bull's-eye on her back once she put the truffle in her emergency pack. The shining football-shaped fungus was the only living key, the one thing Mums's book said could unlock the secret at the top of the Tower of Thorns. And everyone wanted it. No, they *needed* it to complete the Ascension.

"*Croak*, don't fall," warned Croaker, "because if your spotter doesn't catch you, well..."

His tongue shot out and snatched a giant fly that had escaped the swamp. Croaker laughed, his body jiggling as he hopped away, diving right into the middle of the chaotic fray at the bottom of the bubble.

Her hands trembling once more, Tiz grabbed one of Char's to steady her own then ran with him to the tree root that was her starting mark. Once there, she sized up their competition that was already waiting nearby. There were nine climbers and eight of them had their own spotter and familiar — twenty-five participants in all. On Tiz's right, Sombra held Kitten Mitten in front of Dargen. To Tiz's left, Frenchy the Spider wore her weird pet worm like a scarf next to her werewolf spotter. With *no* spotter and *no* familiar, the red-faced witch was on the far side of the tree trunk — exactly where Tiz hoped she would stay. But there were also five more climbers along with their helpers to deal with, waiting at their tree roots to start.

Farther down, on Tiz's right, stood Gomorrah Blackthorn in a dark suit adorned with small white flowers called the "Spike." Ebony liquid dripped from long, dark spines making her look a bit like a poisonous sea urchin. Her familiar was in a jar, its slimy body dripping out of the sides as Gomorrah tightened the lid. Her spotter was a boy that looked like a giant clump of dirt, called a mound man.

Past them, Cindy Elm crouched down on all fours, looking more like a leopard than a girl. She wore a spotted outfit with long climbing spikes on her fingers. Her familiar was a black cat the size of a small panther with long claws as well. Their spotter was a harpy, one who'd never heard of a nail clipper either.

Next, Alice Alder wore a climbing suit made of crow feathers and a black mask with a long beak that made her look just like the bird. Tiz wondered how she could see through its narrow eyeholes, believing there must be some magic involved that enhanced her senses. When she saw a glowing hawk perched on her shoulder instead of the bird she resembled it confirmed her suspicion. The keen-sighted hawk must have served as the eyes of the magical mask, allowing Alice to peek ahead and around every corner. Her spotter was a half-boy, half-raptor called a mantor whose stubby little arms looked too short to be catching anyone.

Further down, Bethany Rowan wore a green-scaled suit called the "Scaler." One that made her look like an emerald-colored dragon. Her scales were covered in protective runes that looked like half moons and gave her outfit an eerie green glow. She held a small salamander in her hand whose skin bubbled like a vat of toxic acid. Its breath didn't look any better from the tiny green cloud surrounding its head. It seemed as perfect of a match for the slimy witch's tree as the big green troll standing behind them, serving as their spotter.

Finally, there was Jenna Oak, who stood in stark contrast to the other tree nymphs. She had a white climbing outfit with wings that made her look like Pegasus — the winged horse. Her familiar was a young griffin and her spotter was a well-groomed teenage centaur. Tiz smiled at Jenna Oak but the angelic-looking girl sneered back at her as though Tiz had been responsible for how Holly had turned out.

Right then and there, Tiz knew she would have to count on her friends and her familiar as much as they were counting on her. *No pressure*, she thought as she stuffed the celestial truffle in her pack to free her hand. She was a good climber, but climbing with one hand on a tree covered in slime would quickly earn her a one-way ticket to Croaker's mouth.

That image reminded her of something important — Pup Pup was in the pack with her truffle. "Pup Pup," she said. "The truffle's not for you, play with your wolfberry toy for now." She heard a couple of squeaks and knew it would be okay.

Looking up, she couldn't believe her eyes. Six of the nine realm portals, the ones orbiting above her, had now become giant obstacles, expanding and contracting as they sucked in the few remaining boarder hoarders battling the tree. Seconds later, a hoarder fell out of the frosty portal in a block of ice, shattering on a branch. Another flew from the portal of fire in flames, crashing into the tree trunk with a huge explosion.

Below the starting lines, the dark portal to the underworld opened like the mouth of a great beast and out poured an endless stream of skeletons, brandishing axes and swords carved from bones.

Tiz heard the red-faced witch cackle with glee. "Kill the other climbers!" she screamed. "Leave none of them alive!"

Little Nub Nub shattered the knees of the first fifty skeletons, but they just kept coming. As the little rhino skidded by the witch's tree, he inhaled a cloud of pollen spores and sprouted a dozen extra-long horns which he gladly put to good use.

Nearby, from the two portals flanking the grim one to the underworld, evil looking dwarves and elves with red hair began pouring out with their own cruel axes and swords, all of them joining the skeletons and following the witch's orders — right toward the other climbers!

"LET THE ASCENSION BEGIN!" yelled the colonel in his megaphonic voice. He raised his bound arms as a starter's pistol emerged from the one resembling a large gadget knife.

"ON YOUR MARKS!"

"GET SET!"

BANG!

All the climbers took off. The race for their lives began!

From below, Croaker watched them anxiously, licking his bright red lips amidst the chaos of the bubble as the horde of evil denizens from the three dark realms chased the climbers.

Tiz sprinted up her tree root with the celestial truffle in her pack. Even though she tried to hide it, the bull's-eye was indeed on her back as she grabbed the first branch and swung her legs up to the next one, one after the other.

Climbing and climbing, a pulsing red light caught Tiz's eyes. As she kept going, she looked at the top window of the tower. A small red beacon in the form of a seed was beating excitedly, right in rhythm with her heart. And as much as she wanted to stop the witch, she wanted to claim the heart seed in the top window even more. That way, she could have a life tree that wasn't so mean. Then she could go back home. She could get back everything that mattered to her.

If the gods of climbing smiled upon her and she made it that far, then would she claim the witch's tree or the heart seed?

She didn't know for sure.

Above her, the slimy green tree that took over the academy was shifting and flailing. It looked like she was climbing a gargantuan monster with dozens of snapping heads and swinging tentacles, not a tree. And the door to the Tower of Thorns was at the top of that mess, at least twenty stories high. Worse, Tiz had no idea how she and Pup Pup were going to climb past six of the remaining haywire portals that would suck them into other realms like magical versions of Croaker's mouth.

And what would be waiting for them on the other side?

She didn't even want to guess, let alone, find out.

Besides, she had more pressing problems. Right above her, the thick canopy of the tree reminded her of a hedge maze, one climbing upwards instead of spreading across the sprawling garden of some wealthy manor. Tiz had to choose between several branches going upwards but couldn't see which one came out on top.

Suddenly, the thick canopy shook.

Tiz dodged to her left, and lucky she did. Gomorrah Blackthorn dropped down from her hiding spot in her spiked black costume, poison dripping from its spines. Her dark heart seed was beating with excitement, ready for a fight.

"Give me the living key!" barked Gomorrah. "Give it to me! Or I'll poke you full of holes!"

Tiz pulled out the glowing football-shaped fungus.

But behind Gomorrah, on a lower branch, Sombra yelled, "Over here! Throw it to me!"

Tiz lofted the glowing truffle toward her friend in the most important game of *keep away* in their entire lives.

The golden truffle spiraled through the air as Gomorrah turned around to watch it, in utter disbelief.

Seizing the moment, Tiz raced up behind her distracted adversary, reaching carefully between her poisonous spines then ripping her heart seed necklace right off.

Gomorrah *shrieked* as her magic outfit deflated like a balloon.

To Tiz's delight, her own yellow climbing outfit sprouted spikes from the magic of Gomorrah's seed. "Did you say something about holes?" she said. "Because there seems to be one in your plan."

"Shut up! Give me my heart seed back!" hissed Gomorrah.

"Flame up," said Tiz as her new spikes lit up like torches. Stalking toward her adversary as if to push her from the tree, Tiz resembled an ancient spiny dragon from the realm of fire.

Gomorrah retreated. "*No*," she begged. "Please don't, Croaker will eat me without my spikes!"

Tiz held up Gomorrah's rapidly beating heart seed, swinging it like a hypnotist. "We're gonna do something we both don't want to. We're going to help each other," she said in a very charming voice. "It's called *Operation About Face*."

Gomorrah's eyes began glowing orange as she nodded. She was thoroughly entranced and would have danced off the end of the branch if Tiz told her to do so. It was tempting. But the more Tiz thought about it the more her stomach sank. It didn't feel right and the little voice inside her head agreed.

"You can have your spikes back," said Tiz instead as she touched Gomorrah's dark outfit, causing the spines to regrow.

Tiz clipped Gomorrah's pendant onto her own ruby necklace. As much as she wanted her own heart seed, she didn't plan on keeping Gomorrah's, instead, she would keep it safe.

"Help!" screamed Sombra from the other branch. She was in a tug of war over the cosmic truffle with a long strand of spider webbing, stretching down from above.

Higher up in the witch's tree, Frenchy, in her black eight-legged costume, had shot a web down from a branch twenty feet above and was now trying to pull the truffle to her.

Tiz plucked a flaming spike from her new and improved outfit and armed her slingshot with it. *Thwang*! It flew at the web.

Frenchy tugged on her end and the web yanked the truffle out of Sombra's hands.

The shot missed!

CHAPTER THIIRTY-THREE

"Dang it!" yelled Tiz.

Frenchy blanketed Sombra with a web, pinning her to the branch. The spider-girl then turned and scurried up the tree.

"Gomorrah, go after her!" ordered Tiz. "Get that living key back, and if you can, grab her heart seed too! Go!"

Gomorrah hurried up the tree after Frenchy.

Luckily, Sombra was pinned to a branch that was below Tiz and wouldn't get her in trouble for flying. So she summoned her fiery wings and glided down toward her best friend. Mid-flight, Tiz saw a cloud of spores burst from a hole in the tree, engulfing Sombra. In order to help her friend, Tiz pulled up and flapped her wings, blowing the spores away.

As she landed, Sombra had a drowsy look in her eyes from inhaling half the cloud.

Tiz arched her wings and began burning away the web pinning her friend to the branch.

Sombra looked up at the huge tree above her wearily. "There's no way we'll make it to the top without resting," she yawned. "We should build a nest. Can Pup Pup fetch twigs and leaves? You're a Phoenix, build us a warm and cozy one, just like the snug tree hollows back home."

"Get a hold of yourself!" shouted Tiz, shaking her best friend free of the web. The power of Tiz's voice was the only thing keeping Sombra awake. "We're not doing any nesting! Right now, on a scale of one to ten, your energy level is at a one! I need you to dial it up to a TEN!"

Sombra began using Tiz as a pillow. "You're so soft, how did you get this soft?" she asked as her pet familiar, Kitten Mitten, curled up at her feet.

"Oh no you don't — no naps," said Tiz, pulling out smelling salts from her emergency pack and sticking them under her friend's nose.

"*Whoa*," said Sombra, snapping out of it.

"You're a soldier!" barked Tiz. "And we're in a war!"

"Yes, Ma'am!" replied Sombra, all fired up. "Less snoring,

more warring!"

"AAAAAGH!" screamed Gomorrah, falling past them with her spikes.

Below, even Croaker hopped out of the way. Gomorrah was going to pierce the bubble and blow everything up.

Suddenly, her spotter, the mound man slid under her in a puddle of sludge then rebuilt himself. With a squish, she stuck into him harmlessly.

"Phew," said Sombra. "She *really* stuck that landing."

Tiz glanced at the top of the Tower of Thorns. It would pierce the bubble before long. "We got to get to Frenchy," said Tiz. "If the tower pops the bubble, everyone's a goner."

"Go!" yelled Char from below, "what are you waiting for!"

Right underneath them, he was kicking skeletons and dwarves from the tree. Dargen was pushing nimble elves off with spells. But there were too many. They were closing in.

Tiz and Sombra started climbing faster than monkeys in zero gravity.

Above, hydra heads were snapping at the other climbers like a basket full of angry cobras. That is, until Frenchy started webbing their mouths shut while clutching the living key in one hand.

"I want her necklace," said Sombra, climbing side by side.

"You got it," said Tiz. "Leave the truffle to me."

"Wee-wee," replied Sombra, as they neared the half-way point of the tree, ten stories up.

"There's the witch," said Tiz, pointing up to the base of the Tower of Thorns at the top of the tree. The red-faced girl, half frowning, half grinning, was waiting to ambush Frenchy.

"*Incoming*!" yelled Char.

But it was too late. The orbiting portal that led to the realm of ice was barreling toward Tiz and Sombra from the side.

"B-but we're not allowed to go in there!" yelled Sombra as if the magical doorway might actually care.

CHAPTER THIIRTY-THREE

The frosty portal hit them with a loud clink that reminded Tiz of crystal glasses colliding. But instead of sliding through a snowy tunnel into another realm, the realm came to them.

The bubble surrounding the mutating academy transformed into a snow globe, but instead of gently floating flakes, a freezing cold blizzard raged inside.

A gust of frigid wind blasted Sombra. "I'm definitely awake now! Level ten, Ma'am!" she yelled, her teeth chattering.

All the climbers were now clinging to a bluish witch's tree covered in ice in the midst of a blizzard. The green slime on the previous tree had been bad enough, but the icy blue bark of this gnarled and wicked tree gave new meaning to the word slippery, especially in the frigid gusts of wind. Above them, all the fruit-shaped barracks now looked like festive ornaments on a frosted evil Christmas tree.

But at least the hydra heads and tree's tentacles had frozen in place. However, they didn't look any less menacing. The serpentine eyes of the frozen hydras followed the tree nymphs, daring them to climb past. They looked like they were just "playing opossum", waiting to break free of the ice at the very last second.

From the middle of the tree, ten stories up, Tiz and Sombra slowly began climbing again through the blustery storm.

"Nice weather for a nest!" yelled Sombra.

"We're not building a nest!" yelled Tiz, though in truth, she would have loved to crawl into a nice and warm one herself.

Above, pointy icicles dangled precariously over them like crystal spearheads. Beyond, they could see the portal to the realm of fire orbiting the icy tree and melting the snow from its blue branches.

Suddenly, the icicles above them started shaking. Something else was climbing the tree below them. Something massive.

The icicles started falling.

Tiz used her fiery wings like an umbrella, shielding herself and Sombra. The icicles that hit the flames melted into a mist with a hiss.

Below, the remaining ones fell past them through the snowstorm, shattering against the body of a frost giantess climbing up toward them. Her skin was as icy blue as the tree and her long hair, white as snow, blew in the wind. She was knocking off skeletons, dwarves and elves by the dozen with a swipe of her arm. A huge double-bladed ax shimmered on her back. Its cruel steel looked like it could cut a branch in half with one swing.

"She's not a tree nymph!" yelled Sombra.

"You tell her that!" shouted Tiz.

Assisting each other, Tiz and Sombra climbed as fast as they could, for the arms and legs of the giantess below them were so long she scaled two branches for every one of theirs.

Sombra glanced down. "She's gaining!" she blurted.

Croaker must have been starving by now, because a long red tongue snatched the giantess by the ankle and yanked her from the frozen tree like she was a big blueberry *Popsicle* being snagged out of the freezer.

"I hope he doesn't eat her!" worried Tiz.

But the *BURP* from below said otherwise.

"Dargen! If I fall, you better catch me!" shouted Sombra as she noticed him casually putting on his favorite blindfold. "What is wrong with you! Put that away, you —"

"Let it go!" yelled Tiz, pulling Sombra up toward the next branch.

Croaker shot his tongue at them, but luckily it missed and stuck to the icy tree trunk like it was a frozen metal pole.

Up and up the two friends climbed, confronting several of the Wolfberry nymphs in their path. They had to choose between tossing their competition off the Christmas-like witch's tree or trying to make them their "little helpers."

First, they plucked the Pegasus wings off Jenna Oak's

costume then sort of borrowed her favorite necklace. After Tiz said a few persuasive words that made Jenna's eyes glow orange, she was absolutely delighted to join *Operation About Face*.

Sombra put on Jenna's pendant and gave herself a pair of white wings then she promptly stuck her tongue out at Dargen, who couldn't see her do it through his blindfold anyway. After they gave a more "charming" version of Jenna a new set of wings, the three went hunting for more necklaces.

Before long, Sombra and Tiz were flashing like Christmas trees themselves, Tiz with three and Sombra with two. Jenna Oak, Cindy Elm, Bethany Rowan and Alice Alder were all part of their small army. Even Gomorrah Blackthorn caught back up to them, bringing their total to seven — the new Heavenly Seven. Things were looking up for *Operation About Face*.

Too bad they couldn't say the same for Frenchy, who was missing several spider legs from her costume after trying to battle the red-faced witch single-handedly near the top of the tree.

Even worse, the witch had taken the living key from Frenchy and was now hoisting it triumphantly over her head.

Frenchy was retreating backward down the tree, not paying attention as the portal to the realm of fire closed in. Sombra used the opportunity to sneak up behind Frenchy and grab her pendant, yanking it from her neck.

"Watch out!" yelled Tiz.

Too late.

When the flaming portal hit Frenchy and Sombra it turned the tree from icy cold to steaming hot. All the snow melted on the spot, gushing down like a hundred waterfalls.

Fifteen stories high, Tiz clung to her branch desperately as water rushed by her, barely able to hold on. Five stories higher, the witch cackled wildly at the base of the tower. But the other climbers hadn't been so lucky. Sombra washed down to a tree limb ten feet below, and the rest were even farther down, clinging to their own branches precariously.

At the bottom of the bubble, all the cadets that were battling skeletons, evil dwarves, dark elves and teachers turned creatures were now splashing around in a massive pool. Croaker, his tongue freed by the heat, floated on a fallen branch, sitting on its dense cluster of leaves like a lily pad. Licking his bright red lips, he stared at the pool with all the cadets from A through Z Company floating in it like an enormous bowl of alphabet soup.

Watching Croaker from fifteen stories above, Tiz clung to her branch. She looked up toward the door to the Tower of Thorns that was still five stories above her. Near it, a row of hydra heads that had been frozen now began stirring. The red-faced witch saw it too, dashing for the door with the living key glowing brightly in her devilish hands.

"Go after her, Tiz!" yelled Sombra from below, handing Tiz the pendants she'd claimed from the other climbers. "You're our only hope! I can't claim the tree!"

Tiz added the pendants to the ones she had seized, quickly clipping them onto her own ruby necklace. Done, she climbed as fast as she could while she watched the witch duck into the Tower of Thorns. Above, a row of hydra heads guarding the pathway to the door began opening their eyes.

Pulling herself onto that path, Tiz bolted for the tower, running between them.

The hydras roared, snapping down at her one by one.

Three more, two more, one more — the last one bit down on her spiked climbing suit, but it was the hydra that felt the pain, hissing angrily as it pinned her to the pathway.

Tiz ignited her wings, scorching its eyes. With a piercing cry, the hydra let her go.

She rolled into the Tower of Thorns as the door slammed shut behind her — total darkness, full of mystery. So dark that even all the light from the captured hearts seeds and her fiery wings couldn't pierce it. Only one thing did.

The witch's laughter, coming from somewhere up above.

CHAPTER THIRTY-FOUR — A PRICKLY SITUATION

PITCH-BLACK. The witch's laughter faded, but the damage was done, its shrill cry invoked a fear that weakened and chilled like a sudden illness. Tiz was afraid. Very afraid. She hadn't felt like this since Char threatened to hurt her in the underworld. Like then, she felt alone. All alone.

For the heart seeds that she and Sombra had taken from the other tree nymphs were now mysteriously gone. In the darkness, she couldn't feel them with her hands. Her wings were gone too. In fact, nearly everything was gone, including her emergency pack and Pup Pup. She just had the clothes on her back, but even they felt different.

"Wings, ignite," she said.

Nothing.

But then slowly, a brightening lantern illuminated her surroundings. Though eerie, it was a welcome sight.

In its light, she saw that she was now wearing her pajamas from back home instead of her climbing suit. Easing to her feet, she stood in a narrow archway at the bottom of a spiraling staircase and a very familiar one at that. For it looked just like the one that led up to her bedroom within her mother's tree home.

But how?

Tiz heard high-pitched crying coming from upstairs as though someone had suffered a great loss.

"Holly?" she called out, hoping that the girl might have somehow freed herself from the grasp of the witch's lingering spirit and removed the red face of the witch that both grinned and frowned like an evil mask. For even the witch couldn't conceal the conflict inside Holly, and more importantly, the battle being waged therein. It showed in the clashing expressions on her blood-red face. "Holly, are you up there?"

Yet there was no response from above, only more wailing.

Tiz began climbing the stairs as cautiously as a cat that knew a rival was lurking around the corner, waiting to pounce. *This can't be real*, she kept telling herself. Yet even the smells from the kitchen below were familiar: the smell of phoenix bark, majestic truffle mousse, and most distinctively, freshly picked chrysanthemums, Mums's favorite.

To Tiz, the spiraling stairwell felt as warm and cozy as it usually did when she climbed it at home. It was familiar to the point that even the top stair creaked as Tiz stepped on it. There she paused. She saw that her name was still on her bedroom door and not the name of one of her little sisters.

"Hush up," said the familiar voice of a young girl on the other side of the door as a second one sniffled.

No, thought Tiz. *It can't be*. She put her hand on the doorknob, listening carefully. But she didn't hear them say anything more — only crying.

Slowly, she turned the knob as the door *creeeaked* open, and strangely enough, she saw something she expected after hearing the sniffling — two things actually, her little sisters, Verruca and Vervain, all snug and cozy in her bed.

Beyond them, night loomed ominously outside her bedroom window, seeming darker than usual somehow. Tiz had an eerie feeling that if she tried to escape through that window then she would fall straight into the abyss. All around them, the shadowy room was dimly lit by ten pairs of candles.

A gust of wind blew in through the window, shutting the door. Tiz tried the knob but it wouldn't turn. She was trapped.

With the twins relaxing in her bed, the last thing Tiz expected was to hear them crying like they'd lost their favorite dolls.

Yet this was all too familiar. And gradually, Tiz began to

remember this particular night. For it had been the worst night of her life. It was the night that the twins dropped her heart seed necklace, the night of the bedtime story, the night of the frozen tree on the edge of the snowy cliff. It was the night Tiz's world started shattering and exploding like the snowy globe the twins had pulled from the story bucket. The night she began losing everything that mattered to her.

Tiz patted her pajama shirt for the pendant her mother had given her — it was now suddenly underneath it. Grasping her ruby necklace, she pulled out her heart seed pendant. It was beating faster and faster, right in rhythm with her heart.

It was perfect.

Tiz heard the twins crying even louder and suddenly remembered what it was about. Some of the things Mums had said about the Great Seed Planting at dinner that night had the twins shaking like leaves, knowing that one day they'd have to go through it themselves. Even though the chance was small, if something went wrong with the actual planting or something happened to the heart seed, a young tree nymph could die. And maybe cruelest of all, any planter that perished might not even know it. Oblivious, she would be imprisoned within her tree, dreaming inside of it for the rest of her days.

In her mind, through some dark magic, Tiz saw herself trapped inside a tree, just like Sombra had been. But the image didn't fade right away, freezing in her mind as it sent a shiver down her spine. A dreadful thought occurred to her. *No...*

Did I die the day my heart seed was cracked? *Am I merely dreaming all of this*?

She pinched her arm, but to her horror, didn't feel anything.

Please, let it be a lie, thought Tiz, *it can't be true. I didn't die. Did I*? *Is that why the twins keep crying*?

More dark thoughts invaded her mind. Her vision became clouded.

CHAPTER THIRTY-FOUR

Did Mums try to plant my heart seed for me after she saw that it was cracked? she wondered. *Did she do so desperately*?

Did I dream of her abandoning me?

The underworld. Char. All of her brushes with death suddenly flickered through her mind and ended in bright white light.

What if I *am* dead?

Her ears began ringing.

Then she heard a single voice in her head. Her spotter's voice. Char kept repeating something he said to her once. It was after Tiz emerged from the Mind of the Witch Head Nebula. She heard him say, "*Calm down, you're not dead.*" Then, she heard, "*Keep going, you're not there yet, keep climbing, keep fighting...*"

Her spirits rose. And the sinking feeling that reminded her of the underworld in every single way began lifting. But it also stirred up a memory of something she'd learned as a child as well as at the academy. She had been taught that the roots of the great cosmic tree reached far down into the underworld. Whether or not it was the witch's tree now didn't matter. The roots would still be there. And even if she was trapped within that dark realm below, as a tree nymph, she could use those roots to climb out. She could fight for a second chance.

Tiz heard the twins sniffling again, this time even louder.

The magic of the tower was at work here. An evil magic.

They need you, said a little voice inside her head. *Help your little sisters*.

Suddenly, the haze began lifting from her eyes and she could see more clearly again. She found herself leaning against the wall of her bedroom. She steadied herself the best she could as the twins sobbed to the point of exhaustion. If it was possible to perish from crying, then she was looking at two children that would soon be its victims. Her very own kin, the little sisters she loved.

It was now clear to Tiz that the rules of reality within the tower were not the same as those outside of it, just like Char had said about the underworld. Here, reality was as twisted as the tower itself. It was a strange, frightening, and above all, dangerous thing. The tower's black magic was making her relive the worst day of her life. It had planted a dark seed of worry in her mind and was now nurturing it, trying to convince her that she wasn't alive. But what it was doing to her little sisters was even worse. Crying endlessly, they were now far past the point of exhaustion and at the very brink of succumbing to it.

Tiz mustered all the courage she could, channeling it through her voice. "Don't cry," she urged, just like she had done on that very same night. "If I don't survive the Planting, you can have all my things," she said. But instead of going around and snuffing out the candles like she had done that night, Tiz kept them lit, hoping they'd hold back the eerie and unnatural darkness that was creeping in through the window.

"We don't want your things," sniffled Verruca next to Vervain. Above their heads the name "TIZ PHOENIX" was engraved on the headboard. The twins looked as snug as kittens in a basket in the middle of their older sister's bed.

"You're sure? You don't want anything?" asked Tiz, trying to hide her concern under a smile.

"Well..." hesitated Vervain.

"Can I hold your heart seed?" asked Verruca. "Just for a second?"

"Um..."

"Pleeeeease," begged Verruca. "It'll make me feel better."

"Sharing *is* caring," sniffled Vervain.

Tiz hesitated as painful images of what happened the first time raced through her mind, causing her heart seed to do the same. Even now, Mums's warnings echoed in her head...

"Swear that you won't let your little sisters touch it," she said. "Otherwise you'll never get it back *and* your dreams will turn into nightmares."

"Pleeeeease," begged Verruca once again.

"What if I make you a deal instead?" asked Tiz. It had been a deal she made with her little sisters to clean her room that had gotten her into the whole mess to begin with. Now she was hoping that one might be her way out. One that would both stop the twins from crying and get her out of this room.

"What kind of deal?" asked Verruca, tears streaming.

"Well, I can let you hold my necklace for a little bit, or..."

"Or what?" asked Vervain.

"Better if I show you, wait right there," replied Tiz as she began hurrying around her room. She went to her dresser first, pulling two things out discreetly and covering them with her hands so the twins couldn't see. Then, she went to her toy chest and found the second components she needed. Combining the items from the dresser and the chest out of the view of the twins, she now had an identical item for each sister. Tiz put one in each hand and hid them within her fists.

"What are you doing over there?" whined Verruca while Vervain began bawling even louder.

Time was running out as Tiz approached the twins with the secret items that she concealed within her balled up hands.

The twins' eyes lit up, though their sobbing continued.

"What are you hiding?" asked Verruca.

"Nuh-uh," said Tiz. "You have to choose between holding my necklace for a little bit, or keeping what's inside my fists."

"But we don't know what's inside," cried Vervain. "How can we know if it's any good?"

"You don't," said Tiz. "But if you don't pick them, you'll never find out."

The twins looked at each other. Their curiosity seemed to slowly overwhelm their desire to hold Tiz's heart seed. For they preferred to keep all the things that they touched, not merely borrow them. And Tiz knew that better than anyone.

Plus, the twins coveted their older sister's things more than anything. And having the chance to keep one of her belongings was a rare opportunity.

Right at the same time, each twin reached out and touched one of Tiz's fists, indicating that they wanted what was inside.

"Not yet," said Tiz. "Before I can give them to you, I need to be sure you have a safe place to keep them in your room, upstairs. Can you show me a good hiding spot?" Tiz stepped over to the door and stood right by it. "Can you open the door for me, please?"

"What if you don't like what you see upstairs?" asked Vervain.

"Promise you won't get mad," said Verruca.

"I promise," said Tiz. "I won't get mad."

"You swear?" asked Verruca. "Cross your heart?"

Tiz crossed hers. "I swear on my heart seed," she said.

Sniffling, the twins staggered from her bed, barely able to walk. But when Verruca turned the knob, it clicked and the door opened.

"C'mon," said Tiz, rushing out the door then waiting at the first of the spiraling steps that led up. "Let's go to the top and I'll show you my surprise."

Slowly, they made their way up. Tiz waited for them at every step, afraid that if she lost sight of them, they'd be gone for good, or fall, or even worse, succumb to the exhaustion.

She waited for them at the very top, right at the twins' bedroom door.

Vervain put her hand on the knob and looked up at her older sister. "You promise you won't get mad?" she sniffled.

"I swear," reassured Tiz, holding out her fists that were concealing the two goodies. "Look at my hands, I can't even cross my fingers like this while I promise. Even if I wanted to."

"What about your toes?" asked Vervain.

"Really?"

The twins crossed their arms, defiant.

Tiz rolled her eyes as she slid off her slippers and peeled her socks off with her feet. "I swear," she said with her toes uncrossed. "I won't get mad, no matter what."

Vervain looked at Verruca and her twin nodded. Together, they put a hand on the doorknob and turned it. Tiz breathed a sigh of relief when it clicked. She would have never gotten into the top room without their help.

When Tiz stepped inside, old feelings of enmity rushed back when she saw all the cheap imitations of her mole mittens and bear-track slippers lining the walls. Though it was little consolation, at least there weren't Poodle Pupp Pupps yipping at her like a pack of angry Chihuahuas yet.

"Nice room," said Tiz as calmly as she could. "I see you've been busy."

"You promised you wouldn't get mad," said Verruca.

"I did, didn't I?" said Tiz as though she was going to change her mind. But instead of chastising the twins, which would have surely made them cry their last and final tears, she smiled at them and held out her hands concealing the gifts. "Do you still want them?"

The twins looked at each other then nodded, staring at their older sister's hands.

Slowly, Tiz opened her palms.

And by the look in the twins' widening eyes when she did, they weren't disappointed.

Before them, Tiz held out two beautiful toy heart seeds, blinking as rapidly as her very own. In the recent past, she had planned on using them to fool her mother after her little sisters had broken her real heart seed. But in end, the batteries were as dead as her plan. Though now she had replaced those batteries out of the view of the twins. Concentrating, Tiz recalled the scary things that Mums had said to them about the Great Seed Planting at dinner that particular night. Specifically, the grim possible outcomes that made the twins cry in the first place. With that in mind, Tiz chose her words carefully when speaking to her little sisters.

"You two can practice taking care of these hearts seeds first," she said. "So by the time you get your real ones from Mums, you'll be experts. That way, the tiny seeds of worry she planted about you getting hurt won't grow. You'll be okay."

"Hmm," considered Vervain. "You really think so?"

Tiz nodded. "Think of these two hearts seeds as the opposite of seeds of worry," she said, "think of them as seeds of hope."

Tiz raised them up high like two shining stars as the twins reached their hands toward them, just like their older sister would have done.

"Will they beat in rhythm with our hearts too?" asked Verruca.

Tiz nodded that they would. "When I made these, long ago, I carved magical runes into them. They'll beat in rhythm with the heart of whoever holds them or wears them around their neck." Tiz lowered the toy seeds. "Here, take them."

The twins wiped their eyes as Tiz handed them the seeds. Immediately, they began pulsing rapidly, right in rhythm with the excited heartbeats of her little sisters. Gradually, their crying ended, replaced by two big smiles.

Suddenly, Tiz heard a *croak* inside her mind that made her jump. The Lips and the Tongue of the Unwithering Tree began speaking to her telepathically. "*Very good, croak, very good indeed — sharing is caring*," it said with a hint of disdain.

A warm gust of wind blew in from the darkness outside as a growing weariness began taking hold of Tiz. She grew sleepier and sleepier, feeling drained from her climbing and all her deeds thus far as she heard the croaking voice of the witch's tree...

"*But now you must wake up, croak*," it said.

"But I *am* awake" said Tiz sleepily.

She couldn't fight the growing weariness.

Tiz slumped down to the wooden floor, drifting into a deep slumber to the echoing voice of the witch's tree, one that seemed infinitely more powerful than her own...

"*Wake up, little Phoenix, croak, and rise up from the ashes...*"

CHAPTER THIRTY-FIVE — RISING AND FALLING

TIZ SMELLED SOUR MILK so pungent that it curled her upper lip as she woke. She found herself buried in a garbage heap so big that it rose and fell over the entire floor of a small circular room, covering every last inch. There were mildewy plastic bottles half-filled with beverages, aluminum soda cans and rotten empty food containers galore just to name a few.

Something also smelled burnt as she spotted garbage that was singed. She wasn't rising from ash, she was rising from trash. It looked like she had been tossed into a garbage compactor and left for dead. Sadly, her mother had been right. "One day you just might wake up buried in a pile of trash, you'll see," said Mums about cleaning her bedroom. And today was that *oh so* lucky day.

Glancing up, Tiz saw that the roof of the room was cone-shaped and covered in thorns — she was at the top of the witch's tower, but how she'd gotten there, she wasn't quite sure.

Even more surprising, it didn't look anything like the pinnacle of a witch's laboratory. There were no bubbling cauldrons, no shelves full of weird-looking spell ingredients soaking in formaldehyde or even a pack of feral black cats that would have done Tiz a favor by aggravating her allergies, making her nose so stuffy she wouldn't have to smell all the garbage.

Out of the corner of her left eye, Tiz glimpsed a pulsing red light, hanging in a tiny window the size of a fist. As she took notice of it, it began beating faster, perfectly in rhythm with her heart.

Easing to her knees on the garbage mound, it felt like someone had tied a weight to her back — her emergency pack was back where it was supposed to be and as heavy as ever. Her pajamas were gone and her yellow climbing suit was back too. More pulsing lights bombarded her eyes, this time they were hanging from her own ruby necklace. Looking down, she saw the hearts seeds from the Wolfberry climbers that she and Sombra had defeated clipped onto it, beating rapidly.

Thankfully, they were all still alive. And just as mercifully, so was she, though the dark magic of the witch's tree had tried to convince her otherwise.

But what was the purpose of this strange and disgusting place?

Tiz spotted something jutting out of the garbage in the center of the room. It was a pedestal made out of a tree branch, one that was shaped like an arm, its twisted and gnarled hand reaching up to clutch something — but the object was missing.

Tiz suspected that it was meant for the living key that the witch now possessed, but nothing she expected was actually coming true, so who really knew?

Looking back toward the red pulsing light, she saw that it was a heart seed beating inside a pendant, hanging from the top of a windowsill by its necklace. It was her sun, pulling her hand toward it. But suddenly, a shadow fell over it.

Rising out of the garbage, Holly the Red-Faced Witch, stood in front of it, one side of her lips frowning, the other half grinning as she held the celestial truffle in her hand.

Kneeling in the trash on the other side of the room, Tiz was too far away from the pedestal to stop her.

"This isn't what you expected," said the witch, "is it, *deary*?"

But before Tiz could answer, she watched the witch set the living key down on a mound of garbage as if it was just another piece of trash and then walk up a pile to a lever on the thorny wall. The witch pulled the lever and even more trash started pouring into the room through holes in the ceiling.

A half-full soda can hit Tiz in the head with a thump, adding one more lump to many. She picked it up as a green carbonated liquid poured out of it. She read the brand name: *Witch's Brew.* Underneath the name, the slogan said, "Recycle this and all the money goes to you — cheaper brew!"

The witch picked up her own can of it. "You know, I tried to make things better," she said despondently. "But even though I brewed the soda with a magic potion in it, they still wouldn't recycle it. Me, and my tree, we tried everything to the point that it made us sick. But now I know there is no cure." The witch tilted her can of the *Witch's Brew*, pouring out the rest of its bubbling green liquid. "There's no solution to the disease called pollution. There's only death."

"So you're just giving up?" said Tiz, "is that it?"

"Oh, *I* never give up," hissed the red-faced witch as she pulled the lever again, burying Tiz in another landslide of garbage.

"Stop!" yelled Tiz, trying desperately to dig herself out. Gasping for air, she was afraid she'd suffocate if any more trash filled the room. "You're going to kill us both! No more garbage! Please!"

"What? Don't you like to recycle?" asked the witch. "Because I do, I even recycle myself from time to time, haven't you noticed?"

"Not like this!" shouted Tiz. "Please, no more!"

"You'll have no choice if you claim the tree," said the grinning and frowning witch. "If you think the tree looks slimy and evil, you should see what the pollution eventually does to you, lil' missy. You'll need a new body. Are you prepared to do that?"

"A new body? That's crazy," said Tiz. "Heck, I never even wanted your tree. I just want the heart seed in the window."

"Then give me the *real* living key," said the witch. "I

know the one I took from Frenchy is a fake. A duplicate, one that you had your little puppet make."

"No, it's not," said Tiz adamantly. "I told Pup Pup not to touch it. You buried the real one under the garbage."

"Liar! I'll bury both of you if you don't give it to me!" screamed the witch, pulling the lever again. An avalanche of garbage poured into the room, filling it halfway to the top. The arm-like pedestal in the middle was now nearly buried, only its fingertips were still poking out.

Rapidly, more and more garbage fell on top of Tiz, smothering her. "STOP!" she yelled, trying to unbury her face. "I CAN'T BREATHE!" She wanted to use her wings to free herself, but it would have set all the garbage on fire.

Tiz heard a bark from her pack as she shoved trash away from her head. Pup Pup was trying to get out. He was just as stuck as she was — most of her body under the garbage.

"Show me the puppet!" hissed the witch, her hand bursting into flames on the lever. "Or I'll rain fire down upon you! I'll turn this room into an incinerator! One so hot, even you won't survive the heat, Tiz Phoenix!"

"*Don't*! He doesn't have the truffle! I swear!" insisted Tiz.

"SHOW ME!" screamed the witch, pulling the lever halfway down as her red hands raged with even more flames.

"Okay, okay!" yelled Tiz, freeing one arm and reaching back. "But I know he doesn't have it!"

Tiz undid the clasp and pulled out Pup Pup.

Her familiar's stomach was glowing a vibrant gold as bright as the original living key.

He had eaten it.

"Never mind," said Tiz.

"Cough it up, fur ball!" screamed the witch.

"Run Pup Pup, run!" yelled Tiz, propelling her pet forward.

Fear filled Pup Pup's widening eyes as the witch gave chase. He scampered through the garbage as fast as he could.

The magical puppet was so afraid of the red-faced witch that more fake truffles started "pouring" out of his back end.

Tiz had to do something, and quick. The witch was gaining on her pet with every single step.

Pulling herself out of the garbage and onto the top of the heap, Tiz ran through the undulating trash, stumbling over and over until she reached the tiny window with the dangling heart seed. And to her surprise, the miniature window enlarged, spiraling open to a size big enough for her to fly through. She could escape with the prize that she coveted desperately. Realizing that possibility made her heart and the seed race even faster.

Beating brightly, the new heart seed was just hanging there for the taking. She could claim it by putting on the necklace and then go. The witch could have the witch's tree and Tiz could have what she truly wanted, her very own life tree. All she had to do was put it on. All she had to do was leave Pup Pup to the witch — to abandon him, to let her friends down, to turn her back on everyone that needed her help — everyone she loved.

From the bubble below, Tiz heard the desperate screams of her classmates and friends. She watched Helen Grug drowning, until Dargen levitated her out of the water.

Clutching the dangling pendant in her hand, Tiz pressed it against her forehead. She wanted it badly as she recalled something Dargen had said to her in the Unburnable Forest, his voice echoing in her mind. "*Mountains*," he said. "*Why do people climb them*?"

Looking out the top window, Tiz heard herself responding, "*I don't know — to see if they can get to the top*?"

"*Maybe*," he replied in her mind. "*But I think it's to see farther. To see what they couldn't see before, about the world, but more importantly, about themselves*."

Tiz heard the helpless cries of her friends from below even move vividly now as it brought her back to reality. Many of them were battling for their lives and the lives of their friends. Watching, she was inspired by their heroic deeds. The black magic of the tower had been at work again, planting another seed of doubt and worry in her mind, and once more, trying to make it grow.

Would she just abandon her friends to their fate? Would she still flee with the new heart seed?

No way...

Tiz lifted its necklace off its hook and began chasing the witch, who in turn, was still pursuing Pup Pup over the undulating mounds of garbage. Somewhere deep inside that wicked-looking, red-faced girl was Holly, the classmate that had defended Tiz against the bathroom bullies. She was the friend that had tried to help her revive her old heart seed.

Now, Tiz meant to return those favors a hundred fold as she unclasped the new ruby necklace on the run. Gaining on the witch, Tiz realized that running all those stupid stairs for the general was now paying off. Tackling the witch from behind, Tiz slung the necklace around the stunned girl's neck.

At first, the red-faced witch gasp for air as if Tiz was choking her. But soon, she found out that Tiz had done something much worse to her. Tiz had given Holly her first *real* heart seed. For the one she had been born with was a fake.

"*I don't want thissss*," hissed the witch, grasping at the necklace as if it was still choking her. "Take it off me!"

"*Free my friend*!" shouted Tiz, her throat glowing red, adding her magic to that of Holly's new heart seed. "Let her go!"

The witch didn't answer, gasping for breath.

But slowly, Tiz could see for herself that it was working. For Holly's new seed began beating in rhythm with Holly's heart, not Tiz's.

"Release her!" demanded Tiz. "She has her own, real heart seed now, not the fake one she was born with. Go away! *Set her free*!"

The witch *SCREAMED* as Holly's face began to turn from red to normal then halted, reversing back to red again.

"You won't banish me!" hissed the witch in an Un-Holly like voice, struggling to stay inside. Holly's whole body trembled, but she was unable to shake free of the witch.

It would take more.

One by one, Tiz unclipped the beating heart seeds of Holly's friends off her own necklace and attached them to Holly's. Holly's friends weren't there to support her, but the collective magic of their heart seeds was. "Like my little sisters always say," added Tiz, clipping the last one on, "sharing *is* caring."

"AAAAAAGH!"

In a flash of white ghostly light, the spirit of the witch drifted out of Holly's mouth within a foul-smelling mist, leaving the rosy-cheeked girl unconscious on the trash heap. Holly was alive, but her new heart seed beat more slowly than the rapidly beating ones of her friends from Wolfberry.

Tiz looked up and recognized the witch's ghost. It was the old crone with the hooked nose she had the misfortune of seeing in the ashes of her ruined heart seed when they were blowing away in a cold wind. But that wasn't the only time. The spirit also showed itself within a pile of swirling leaves near Sombra's life tree when her best friend was trapped. And as a ghost, the witch looked even more sinister than before.

"Don't *even* think about trying to possess me," warned Tiz. "The spirit of my heart seed burns inside of me like a fire, as a ghost, you cannot survive it," she added as the power of her voice slowly brought the specter of the witch to her knees. "You can't hurt us anymore. So leave us alone!"

"*Mercy*," shrieked the ghost of the witch in the hair-curling voice of an old, whiny woman. "Please, hear me."

"Go," said Tiz, pointing to the window. "Before I change my mind. Leave, before I rain *my own* fire down upon you."

CHAPTER THIRTY-FIVE

"Wait," begged the ghost. "Hear my plea, I beg yee."

Tiz crossed her arms defiantly. "Don't make me regret my decision to spare you," she said, igniting her wings. She knew that one good swat from them could destroy the ghost. "This is just another trick of yours, I know it."

"Ain't no trickery, deary, I swear it," shrieked the ghost of the witch, recoiling from the fiery light of Tiz's wings. "I just want you to free me from the tree." The ghost pointed a long ghastly finger toward the slimy wall, coated in thorns. "Look right over there, see for yourself, child. Save me, please. Don't just leave me there, *all alone*."

Looking closer, Tiz saw the outline of an old woman with a hooked nose trapped underneath the bark of the slimy and thorny tower wall. It was a silhouette that looked just like the ghost, its face full of fear. The witch had been afraid when she'd sacrificed what remained of herself for her final spell to be reborn. She was frozen in terror — no different than anyone else would have been. Seeing how scared she looked reminded Tiz of Sombra's petrified expression when she was imprisoned within her new life tree. Seeing how alone the witch looked reminded Tiz of how she herself felt after her own mother abandoned her. Somehow, as strange as it was, it made her feel sorry for the old hag.

"How?" asked Tiz cautiously. "How do I free you?"

"How else?" said the ghost, her voice growing bolder and bolder. "You must claim the tree."

Tiz shook her head "no" and extinguished her wings. "I don't want anything to do with this polluted and evil tree," she insisted.

"But you *could* free me," whined the ghost. "And if you do, I'll go away, *forever*. My old body is better than nothing. You'll see..."

"What do you mean?" said Tiz. "I'll see."

Pity filled the old ghost's eyes, surprising Tiz. "You poor, naive child," said the spirit with a surprising amount of tenderness. "You're dying, lil' missy," she said, similar to what Char had once told her, "as a ghost, I can see the flames inside you fading. And soon, it'll be too late for you to do anything. So what other choice do you have? You *have* to claim the tree. And when you do, you can get rid of me too. Set me free, just like *I* did in the end for your dear old Holly. You did it once before, I know. You set Sombra free..."

A crackling sound emanated from the garbage around them near the buried pedestal in the center of the room.

It frightened Pup Pup so much, he barked at it. Tiz picked up her familiar and pet him to calm him down. Together, they watched the crackling garbage anxiously, half-expecting Croaker to leap out. Slowly, blinking in and out while materializing on top of the trash heap before their eyes were the bodies of the seven remaining climbers, all sleeping, including Sombra and Frenchy.

"If you don't claim the tree," warned the ghost of the witch, "one of them will. And since you don't have their charms, you won't seem quite as *charming* to them, now will you, deary? Not at all. No, the Wolfberry climbers will fight you for the living key. Are you prepared to hurl all of them out the window? Because you'll have to. You can't control them anymore, not a single one."

The ghost of the witch grinned wickedly. "But I can, without their charms, I'll possess one of them. I'll make a *new* friend."

The other climbers were still asleep, fading in and out. But soon they would fully materialize.

If Tiz took the pendants off an unconscious Holly to charm them, then the helpless girl might not have enough strength to keep the witch out.

And if she left the pendants on Holly, then the witch would claim one of the climbers, maybe even Sombra.

"Hmm," contemplated the ghost, floating over to the materializing climbers, all of them still sleeping. "I'll think I'll try Frenchy on for size," she said. "What a *wonderful* world we'd create together. One in our own, perfect image."

Tiz heard screams again from outside, far below, and rushed to the enlarged circular window. All of her classmates were fighting for their lives, swimming desperately in the bubble below.

"The first thing Frenchy and I would do," said the ghost, "would be to get rid of all that annoying screaming. And I know exactly how, lil' missy. We'll make Croaker the size of a dragon, that should help increase his appetite a bit. Don't you think?"

Tiz looked back toward the buried pedestal. The witch's ghost was now floating right over Sombra.

"Or I could possess your best friend," said the ghost. "Here's a question for you. Would that make us best friends too? We could share her you know. After all, sharing *is* caring."

If steam could have shot out of Tiz's ears it would have. She marched to the pedestal with the intention of doing the last thing she ever wanted to or expected to, bolstered by a little voice inside her head that kept saying, "*Help your friends*."

Tiz set Pup Pup down and said, "Start digging boy, unbury the pedestal. And hurry. Just think of it as a giant bone."

Pup Pup whimpered as if he didn't want her to claim the tree, and to him, the thought of the pedestal being a bone only seemed to worsen his grim and sad look.

"*Please*," said Tiz. "Please, help me. So I can try to help all of us."

Loyal as could be, Pup Pup reluctantly began digging for his master, his torso still glowing from swallowing the living key.

Tiz pulled out her muddy mole mittens with their long garden-shear like claws as well as her bear-track slippers with their own sharp nails used for climbing. She knew she was in for a fight with what she was about to do. She put them on and quickly helped Pup Pup dig out the area around the pedestal.

"You better hurry, *deary*," warned the witch's ghost, "I'm getting more and more antsy for a new body. Soon, I won't want my old one anymore."

"Shut up," said Tiz, having had her fill of the whiny ghost as the spirit cackled gleefully in response.

With the Hand and the Arm of the pedestal freed from all the surrounding garbage, Tiz took off one of her mole mittens and put her hand near Pup Pup's mouth then said, "Be a good boy and give me the living key. Pup Pup, spit it out, please."

He looked up at her with his big sad eyes and whimpered again. He didn't want her to put it on the pedestal. He didn't want her to get hurt. Right there, she realized that's why he ate it, not because he was hungry. The tears in his eyes told her so. To Pup Pup, she was more than his owner. She had brought him to life. And giving her the truffle would mean taking away hers. "*Don't go*," groaned Pup Pup, "*don't go*."

Tiz felt her eyes well as those sad words nearly broke her own heart. Right then and there, suffering, she realized that her mother must have felt just as rotten when she had to leave her daughter in that grim and charred forest — a sorrowful moment that Pup Pup had helped her through. Gently, she pet her puppy's brow. "It'll be okay, boy," she said, even though she sensed deep down in her heart that it would be far from okay. "It'll be okay..."

Reluctant as a dog regurgitating a mysterious treat that he found in the backyard, Pup Pup begrudgingly allowed Tiz to open his mouth and reach in for the living key. But even as she tried to pull it out he bit down on the truffle and played what might be his last game of tug of war with her.

"Please, Pup Pup. Don't make this any harder than it already is," pleaded Tiz, tears stinging the corners of her eyes as she tried to soothe him with several more pets.

With a final whimper, Pup Pup relented.

Tiz eased her muddy mole mitten back on. Resigned to her grim fate, one that would eventually have her looking like the ghost hovering before her, she took one last deep breath as the tree nymph she knew for thirteen years — Red, Lumps, the Blue Jay. Thinking of her family and friends, with her left hand, she slammed the living key into the Hand of the Unwithering Tree. Instantly, the truffle disappeared as the pedestal grabbed her fingers on her left hand, interlocking hers with its own, squeezing tightly.

But what Tiz didn't know is that the Unwithering One had never experienced anything like this — a winner that didn't want its power. One that didn't want to claim the tree. One that only did it to help the friends that she loved. A red-headed tree nymph that saw an actual tree as her enemy. One tree and only one tree, this tree, wanting to destroy it instead.

The slimy and evil tree feared her. So it did the only thing it could, it tried to claim her as she tried to claim it.

Tiz felt something oozing out of the pores of her skin. Slime was turning it green, also trying to smother the flames inside her. She was beginning the claiming of the tree with a fight, her powers merging with its own. She used her newfound energy to fuel the inferno inside her, to ignite her emotions. She had one angry thought as she screamed at the top of her lungs like a banshee. "*I'm going to break this tree*!"

Blinding light filled the tower as she tried to bend the evil tree to her will, using her whole body to wrestle with the pedestal as though it was the arm of a giant. She now firmly believed that she needed to pin it to the floor to win its obedience. Clutching the Hand, Tiz felt the power of the tree surging through her in a rush of adrenaline. Her abilities grew much stronger, reaching out into the cosmos through the endless stardust branches of the celestial tree...

Like the day she flew through one of those branches to the academy, she heard the haunting music of a symphony in her mind and the angelic voice of a woman singing one word over and over — *weeping*. Though it was in a language foreign to her, Tiz now understood the word even more than the first time Dargen explained it to her. For in her mind, she saw more and more of the endless universe through the tree, and at the same time, became attuned to all things. And while doing so, its indescribable beauty made her cry.

In the distant blackness of deep outer space she bore witness to her free arm made entirely of stardust, reaching toward the Witch Head Nebula. And when her fingertips touched it, the gaseous cloud exploded into a giant blue star that she held in her palm. For a moment, it even began pulsing like her old heart seed.

On Earth, deep within the Wailing Woods, she saw Mums listening to her daughter's ceaseless scream, falling to her knees in tears inside her tree home, covering her ears.

Nearby, she watched Farmer Everly weeping inside his house as every bottle of liquor in his bar shattered into a million pieces while his windows remained oddly untouched.

The fate of the universe balanced on the edge of a knife...

The blade was the pedestal of the Hand...and Tiz Phoenix was trying to tip things in her favor by pinning it to the floor. Slowly, she began bending its grip to her will, trying to help her friends.

Turning her eyes toward the ghost of the witch, Tiz discerned something through the translucence of the specter. She realized her violent scream had another effect; the vibrations had cracked the tree-bark prison like glass.

It was by way of one of those fissures that the ghost of the witch slipped through like smoke to her imprisoned body.

Tiz saw that it began moving, struggling to break free. Wrestling with the arm, she said three words..."*Let her go.*"

The whole tree began shaking violently.

The walls started cracking even more. Wizards, warriors and all manner of creatures began hatching from it like eggs.

CHAPTER THIRTY-FIVE

Thanks to Tiz, the witch was the first to free herself completely, emerging in a tattered black dress while green slime dripped from her hooked nose. Her long gray hair was thin and stringy, missing in patches as though she bathed in toxic waste. The old hag clutched a rotting broom in her hands, and with a cackling laughter that filled the room, she mounted it and flew right through the only window, fleeing from the tree that had been her prison.

But at least she had kept her promise.

All around Tiz, Sombra and the other candidates materialized, waking up like those that had been trapped behind the bark.

Tiz kept grappling with the Hand, trying with all her might to exert her control, hoping desperately to pin the entire pedestal to the ground. Even Pup Pup was now pulling on her pant leg with all his might, trying to help her. The sight of it gave her courage, it filled her heart with much needed hope.

And no matter what anyone else believed about her, Tiz knew that she was no witch — she had always been a tree nymph. And even in this far corner of the universe, she possessed great influence over all things growing and green. "*Obey me*!" she screamed at the tree. "*I've proven myself*! *I claim the Unwithering Tree*!"

The tree shook violently, knocking everyone else to the floor.

Energy coruscated through Tiz like lightning. Her eyes started glowing a haunting green.

But the Unwithering Tree resisted with all its might. Even though she claimed the tree, the Unwithering One had another plan to get rid of her. Throughout time, the tree never withered and died, but the witch that claimed her did...

Tiz suddenly gasped for air, struggling to breathe. She felt like her lungs had collapsed within her chest. Her skin started wrinkling into that of an old woman before her own worsening eyesight. The tree was aging itself, and thus, aging her. But what was a few millennia to an immortal tree?

Nothing.

Yet to Tiz, it would soon spell her doom.

The Hand and the Arm of the Witch's Tree slowly began turning the tide of their wrestling match, inch by painful inch, as Tiz saw her own arms grow older and more frail.

With tears welling in her green eyes, Tiz saw that Sombra was awake. Her best friend was staring right back at her, her own eyes equally full of terror.

Sombra rushed over and began trying to help Tiz pull the pedestal in the other direction.

But by now, Tiz had white hair to the floor as she collapsed to her knees. Soon it would be over.

"Don't give up!" yelled Sombra. "Promise me, you won't give up!"

Frail and exhausted, Tiz nodded only once.

"I need you to keep fighting!" screamed Sombra as she spotted the other climbers waking up. "Help me!" she yelled to them. "Help me pin this thing!"

Holly, who had somehow been able to rise to her feet, mustered the little strength that she had remaining and rushed to their aid as quickly as she could.

Frenchy and the rest of Holly's friends rose to their feet, hesitating, watching with bewildered amazement.

"Get over here!" yelled Holly.

Heeding the cries of her best friend, Frenchy was the first to rush over followed closely by the rest of the Heavenly Seven.

Together, they all tried to help a frail, old Tiz push the pedestal toward the ground.

But they could not budge it any further.

Only Tiz could move it and she knew that grim reality while kneeling on the ground in despair. There, her chin buried in her chest, she prayed for the one thing that would make her feel like her old self again and not merely old, the one thing that could turn the tide and that which she desired above all else — her original heart seed.

At that precise moment, her friends battling for her, Tiz saw a pulsing red light where her heart stood beating in her chest. Right then, she knew that her old seed wasn't truly gone for good. It was merely in a different form.

As if agreeing, its power started glowing brighter in her chest for everyone else to see, including the tree. Her original heart seed was still inside of her, and now she was going to bring it back...she was going to remake the heart seed herself. Nothing could change the fact that she wanted it back, and now she had the power to do something about it as she glanced down at her ruby necklace and the phoenix pendant dangling from it.

With that very thought, her long gray hair began turning red.

There was hope again.

But as quickly as it blazed to life, it was now being smothered by the tree. Before her eyes, she saw that her greatest wish wasn't turning out at all like she had hoped. The spirit of her heart seed wasn't being channeled into her pendant — it wasn't forming a new seed directly inside of it.

Instead, she was aging backwards toward the day she was born, the day her heart seed once pulsed within her belly button.

The sinister tree was using her desire against her, fulfilling her wish, but in a dark and twisted way.

Before long, Tiz would be too young and too weak to fight anymore.

She was running out of time. The window on her new powers was closing and she still wanted to help her friends. After all, it was the reason she risked all of this. And if she failed to save them. It would all go to waste.

Tiz stared at the long claws of her digging gloves on her free hand and imagined them growing to the size of swords.

The blades instantly elongated and sharpened.

The tree countered again, turning her skin to rigid bark and her hair to leaves. Her arms felt stiff. The tree was trying to imprison her, contain her like it did to the witch.

Tiz *SCREAMED* louder than a thousand battling valkyries...

But nothing happened this time. She was shrinking like Dargen had been because of his Merlin's disease, only much faster. And as an infant she'd be defenseless against the tree.

Though first, she had to get her friends clear of her deadly enemy.

"Get by the window, all of you!" screamed Tiz, now the same age she was before — thirteen. "I can lower you down!"

"What about you!" shouted Sombra.

Tiz paused, turning younger and younger, her yellow climbing outfit growing longer on her. She felt her eyes well as she looked at her best friend. She sensed that she was saying good-bye to her for the final time. "I can't go," she said, her hand held tightly in the vise that was the grip of the witch's tree. "Someone has to lower you down. You can't climb out. The thorns on the tower would poison you. I know it for sure..."

Tiz flexed the fingers on her free hand and with a mere thought, tentacles burst forth from the walls. Tiz used one to grab Sombra first as her best friend cried out for her to stop, to let her stand by her. "I'm your first mate!" she screamed bravely.

But Tiz couldn't allow it — only a captain should go down with her ship. So Tiz lowered her best friend out the tower window despite her pleas to stay.

Next, Tiz went after the seven other climbers.

Frenchy screamed as she tried to escape Tiz's tentacle. She didn't make it. Tiz corralled them one by one, even the pet familiars, especially Pup Pup, who fought valiantly to remain at the side of his creator and master to the bitter end.

Gently, Tiz lowered the group of them out the tower window, all the way to the water at the base of the tree, setting Holly right in the general's arms and Pup Pup in Sombra's. Tiz didn't even drop Frenchy into the water to get back at her for the swirlie, though she was tempted to, instead, guiding her into the arms of her spotter, the big werewolf.

Inside the tower, there were now many other beings — warriors and creatures that were still breaking free of the tree bark as though they'd been swallowed by the hydra heads and trapped there for centuries. Tiz even began looking for Char, the boy before he died, but didn't see him there. Even still, as the mistress of the tree, she could now do something the Unwithering One didn't allow her to do before.

Tiz opened dozens of tree doors. "Go!" she ordered to the newly freed beings. "I can't hold the doors open for long!"

The prisoners listened, piling through the glowing portals as fast as they could.

"Be as you once were!" she screamed. "Everyone, be free!"

At the base of the witch's tree, teachers turned creatures transformed back to normal. The evil skeletons, dwarves and elves poured back into their dark portals. Every single cadet watched anxiously as the tree shook more violently.

Croaker the Joker's eyes stopped glowing green. No longer under the control of the witch's tree, he leapt into the bubble surrounding the academy. It formed a smaller one around him as he escaped into the darkness of space.

Back in the tower, there was no escape for Tiz. The Hand squeezed her fingers as tightly as a vise.

"*CEASE*!" groaned the Unwithering Tree inside her head, its desperate voice creaking and moaning as it pleaded to her directly. "*YOU'LL DESTROY BOTH OF US*!"

Tiz felt her red hair grow shorter. Her body, younger and younger. "GET BACK!" she yelled toward the window at the very top of the tower.

Below, everyone swam away from the base of the shaking tree.

Clutching the pedestal with both hands, Tiz ignited her body along with her wings, forming the image of a burning phoenix. A blaze engulfed the room, bathing the pedestal in fire and setting the garbage ablaze. Tiz couldn't pin the pedestal, so she began hacking at it with the fiery blades on her gloves while desperately digging at the wood with her bear-claw feet, trying to sever the pedestal in two.

Every time she struck its side she felt a pain in her own ribs so great it buckled her knees, bringing her down to the ground again. Blood stained the side of her yellow climbing suit above her hip. Still, she kept striking, only taking comfort in the knowledge of one thing — that if she had pinned the pedestal, each blow would have felt infinitely more painful. Then, she might have given up, or even worse, just like Croaker, been enthralled by the tree for millennia after millennia.

Shrinking as she grew younger and younger, Tiz saw a pulsing light right at her belly button. It was beating in rhythm with her heart, holding her gaze...

She heard the voice of the angel, singing *weeping* over and over again...

In her mind, Tiz was being transported somewhere else...

Gradually, she saw a blurry golden light illuminate a sea of darkness. As if it was a star, she reached her hand toward it and it gave her hope. As the image sharpened, she saw her grandmother, her red hair streaked with gray, robed in white, holding two golden lanterns on the beautiful path of light in the underworld, one for her, one for her granddaughter.

Along each side of the path stood a singing chorus of weeping women also robed in white. There too, were the pale woman and her blond little daughter, singing with the chorus, all their voices rising.

Tiz no longer felt any pain even though her hand was

being crushed by the witch's tree, only relief and happiness as she smiled at her grandmother, tears of joy in both of their eyes.

"I'm coming, grandma," she said. "Wait for me, please..."

With her last bit of energy, inside the top room of the Tower of Thorns, Tiz Phoenix rose up from her knees and flung off her glove that held her flaming blades. For finally, it was now time for the true plan B. Reaching deep down into her magical pocket she pulled out her battle-ax and reared back with it.

With one final blow from its blade, she severed the pedestal of the Hand with a deafening boom.

Her mind somewhere else, she didn't hear the Tower of Thorns explode nor feel any pain from the blast as it destroyed the head of the beast.

Tiz didn't see the students below watching the tower fly apart and the tree flash with flames, purging its evil features — hydras, buzz saws and tentacles crumbling into ashes.

She didn't witness all the students diving under the water in the bubble to avoid the fiery falling debris.

She didn't know the academy slowly changed back to a bruised and battered version of its former self, though nonetheless, freed of the disease that was the witch's tree.

As the water drained from the bubble below, Sombra, Dargen and Char rose to their feet. The three friends watched anxiously as something small drifted down from where the Tower of Thorns used to be, gliding lower and lower on a pair of little fiery wings, it pulsed steadily, emitting a red light not unlike a homing beacon.

Sombra caught it in her palm like one would a falling feather as its little burning wings folded back. Yet despite the flames, the small red thing wasn't hot at all as it began beating more rapidly in her palm. Raising her arm as high as she could, Sombra held aloft a newly formed heart seed for everyone else to see.

CHAPTER THIRTY-SIX — THE GUARDIANS

A SMALL PILE OF DIRT in the Wailing Woods. The sun shined its last rays of the day on it as it set in the background.

Sombra had planted the winged seed near her own life tree, a huge weeping willow, the very next day. She wasn't about to give the seed to Tiz's mother — no way. Not after Mums had abandoned her own daughter, throwing her out of her home and all. Sombra wasn't about to trust her with it or anyone else for that matter.

And neither was Pup Pup, who guarded it day and night.

Sitting there, Sombra watched the puppy march back and forth past the dirt pile like a little soldier on guard duty as she stifled a smile. With his jester's hat tilted forward in a very serious manner, the little wiener-dog puppet even did his best to execute a proper *about face*. But since he had four legs instead of two, pivoting his tail end looked like an eighteen wheeler that went into a icy skid. Pup Pup would pivot his front paws then scoot his little behind around afterwards in a swooping arc. It was pretty adorable and brought much needed joy to an otherwise nerve-racking situation.

For it had now been two months, twenty-eight days, ten hours, six minutes and thirty-seven seconds since Sombra had planted the winged seed and not a single thing had happened. It hadn't grown into a life tree like she had hoped. And it certainly didn't bring her best friend back.

Soon, all the repairs at the academy would be complete. Sombra would have to go back to school again without her. Who was going to help Pup Pup guard the heart seed then?

In the forest, all around them, day was slowly darkening into night as Sombra sat under her own life tree, staring at the patch of dirt where she had buried the seed. In the shade on the other side of her tree sat Molly Von Butterburg, slathering on more mystical sunscreen while looking equally as tense about the whole thing.

Sombra gazed up at a split moon rising as it reminded her of the evening she dug for truffles with her best friend. *What am I doing wrong*, she thought to herself, going over a list of things in her head. *I watered it with toe root extract, herbal tea, lemonade, everything she likes or would need.*

Turning her gaze back to Pup Pup and his patrolling, Sombra pulled out her kazoo and decided to give the steadfast guard a peppy marching beat to help pass the time. She hummed:

Dah-duh, Dah-duh — Dut-dut, Dut-dut — Dut-dut, Dah-duh...

Sombra heard Molly join her flute to the upbeat cadence. Together, they played flawlessly in hopes that somehow their friend might hear them. Sombra even imagined Tiz marching right out of the underworld, using the dark tunnels she had heard about from her best friend.

About a stone's throw away, Dargen joined in on his violin, playing a lively song that blended perfectly with the beat.

Sombra spotted him in the shade of a tree, staring right at the orange setting sun as though a certain Phoenix might be hiding there.

Next, Sombra heard guitar strings join their instrumental chorus. Not far away sat Char, strumming his guitar. His black wings blazed with fire from the runes on his instrument.

Their music served as their voices, ones full of hope, calling out to their friend.

Pup Pup suddenly began barking at the mound of dirt.

Sombra saw that it was glowing red. It even pulsed a few times then faded completely away. Worried, she began digging up Tiz's heart seed.

Pulling it from the hole, Sombra was relieved to see it was

still beating. "Phew," she said to the seed, brushing the dirt off of it. "Tiz, don't scare me like that."

Watching it, she realized that the heart seed wasn't beating like a normal heart. Nor was it pulsing in rhythm with the music. Tiz's seed was beating in a completely different manner.

"What's it doing?" asked Molly over her shoulder.

"Keep playing," said Sombra, "she's listening."

Molly quickly resumed as Sombra studied the pulsing.

"It's tap code," said Sombra, "she's trying to tell me something — she's spelling out a word."

Tiz's heart seed beat in pulses as Sombra said the letters out loud...

"H,"

"O,"

"M,"

"E,"

"Home," said Sombra, her eyes widening with realization "That's it! Her home! Her happy place!"

Sombra raced toward the Phoenix family grove despite what Tiz's mother had done.

Her friends ran after her.

"Keep playing!" shouted Sombra.

They did, their lively song reflecting their hope, playing more and more frantically as they ran after Sombra. Molly held a huge umbrella over herself as she did, keeping the setting sun at bay as well as anyone could while playing the flute. Suddenly, the shadow from the umbrella got larger, shaped like wings. Molly looked up and saw Char shielding her from the sun. Smiling up at him, she gave him a thank you wave.

Soon everyone was pouring out of the woods. More band mates joined the song — Fineus the troll on his harp, a harpy on a harmonica, and a dragon on an oboe.

They all ran after Sombra, running toward the Phoenix

Family Grove.

It seemed like half the forest was now following the parade. Animals, birds and reptiles, joined in, scampering, bounding and prancing. All manner of beasts and creatures from the academy tailed them — centaurs, unicorns and chimeras — no one pouncing on each other either, everyone in harmony.

Out from the treetop homes poured entire tree nymph families.

"What's going on down there!" yelled Frenchy Yew from atop the porch of her mother's tree home.

"C'mon!" yelled Sombra, inviting her to see. "And bring your French horn!"

Running into the Phoenix grove at dusk, everyone met there, forming a large circle around it. In the center, Sombra spotted her own mother, Gertrude, running in.

"Mom!" yelled Sombra as she ran toward her mother, holding out Tiz's heart seed. "Mom! I think I got it! I think I know why! She needs to come home!"

"What!" exclaimed Gertrude. "Have you gone crazy?"

"Let her speak," said Mums Phoenix, dropping down from her tree, the twins in tow.

"They're not like us," blurted Sombra to her mother. "They're Phoenixes, they can come back. They can come back home. I was being selfish, planting her tree next to mine. But that's not where it's supposed to be. Tiz needs to be here. Here, with her family."

"Look!" said the twins in unison, their eyes widening.

Tiz's heart seed was beating stronger. And like a homing beacon that found the heart of its signal, it was fluttering faster than a humming bird's wings.

"Now, now, don't go getting their hopes up," said Gertrude Willow.

"Hope is all we have," said Mums, watching the seed anxiously.

Pup Pup's tail started wagging. He dug a hole in the center of the Phoenix grove faster than a groundhog.

"Good boy," said Sombra, petting him, "what a good little helper you are."

Gertrude Willow crossed her arms with a huff. "Well, out of all the crazy things I've ever heard, this may take the cake."

"We need to do it right now," insisted Sombra even though the last of the sunlight had faded away minutes before and left the Wailing Woods in nearly total darkness. Besides the half moon above whose face eerily resembled that of the Lady of Night and Light, the only other light came from the orange glow of candles in the oval windows of Mums's tree home and Tiz's bright red heart seed.

"A Great Seed Planting at night?" questioned Gertrude as the whole gathering encircling them listened anxiously.

"Zhat is preposterous," hissed Marie Yew. "You can't be —"

"Quiet, mother," said Frenchy Yew to the surprise of all, shooing her mother back with her French horn. "Zeh Phoenix girl helped us all. Even Holly, who was *really* mean to her."

"*Hey*," protested Holly.

Frenchy elbowed Holly playfully, giving her a smile that said she was glad to have her own best friend back.

"Really?" questioned Sombra. "That's all you've got to say?"

"Stop asking questions," barked Frenchy, playfully. "Get your best friend back, just like I did. Zhat is an order."

Sombra shook her head as she turned to Mums and the twins. "Phoenixes, are you ready?" she asked.

They nodded.

"Then let the first ever Great Seed Planting at Night begin," said Sombra to the cheers and roars of all the magical beings, creatures and tree nymphs gathered there.

"A Planting at night?" huffed Marie Yew. "Now *that's* an ill omen."

"Shush, mother," said Frenchy. "You and your omens have been wrong before."

"Agreed," said Mums, giving Marie a look that said, "don't even think about saying another discouraging word."

Meanwhile, Sombra offered the twins the seed then suddenly pulled it back. "Be very, very careful this time," she said to them. "One of you, hold it with two hands. Then the other one needs to cup their hands under it, like a safety net."

They did exactly what she said as Sombra eased it over to them, making extra sure that they didn't drop it this time.

The twins kneeled down and gently placed the beating seed at the bottom of the hole Pup Pup dug.

"A second chance," said Verruca.

"For all of us," added Vervain.

"For all of us," agreed Mums, her eyes welling.

With that, the three carefully covered the seed with dirt.

After a few moments, the only thing growing was an uneasy murmur from the gathered crowd. Nothing had happened.

"Did you feel that?" asked Sombra, sure that the ground had rumbled.

"Feel what?" asked Molly.

"I did," said Mums.

"So did I," said the twins in unison.

The ground started to shake. Tree nymphs grabbed onto each other.

"You see!" yelled Marie Yew, "I warned you — nothing good can come from waking the dead!"

"Speak for yourself," said Molly the vampire girl, her cat-like reflexes counter-acting the quaking ground beautifully.

"A true phoenix," said Dargen, using Char to steady himself. "It may die, but it *always* rises from the ashes."

Before their eyes, a tree began growing. One more beautiful than any of them had ever seen. Born under the moonlight, it shimmered like quicksilver. Purple flowers adorned its bright red leaves that unfolded like fiery wings. Visible within its trunk stood a familiar silhouette, reaching for the stars in the night sky with a single outstretched branch-like arm.

Mums eased closer to it, and gradually, she raised her own arm, touching her hand to that of her eldest daughter who was like a statue within the silvery tree.

Instantly, the bark on the trunk began cracking.

Tiz was trying desperately to come back...

Mums put her foot on the trunk of the silvery life tree. And with tears of joy in her eyes, she pulled her daughter out to the cheers and cries of the gathering.

Steadying each other, mother and daughter stood face to face as the cheering died out. It had been a while since they had last parted in such an ill manner. There, in front of the open wound on the tree, festered an even greater one between them, an open wound that needed tending to immediately. And the look on their faces showed that they both knew...

"Two lives," began Mums, tears streaming, "one soul..." she said to her daughter.

Tiz began crying. "If either dies, both must go..."

"I'm so, so sorry," said Mums, crying, "for everything."

"I forgive you," said Tiz, tears welling in her own eyes. "I'm just glad I can say it to you, that means everything to me."

"I love you, Red," said Mums, "I always have and I always will."

"I love you too, mom," said Tiz as they embraced.

There, mother and daughter stood as the twins approached.

"What about us?" asked Vervain.

"Yeah, we don't love you any less," said Verruca.

Tiz embraced the twins, tears in her eyes. "I have a message," she said, kneeling by her little sisters. "Grandma says 'hi.' And she told me to tell you that she's sorry, but she couldn't come back with me — her time here was done."

"Awww," said the twins in unison, eyes welling.

"We're sorry about everything too," said Verruca.

"Yeah," said Vervain. "We missed you."

"Me too," said Tiz, stroking their hair.

Sombra stepped forward with Dargen and Char at her sides.

Tiz rose to greet them.

But Sombra and the two boys stopped abruptly and stood at attention like soldiers preparing to greet one of their own that they now held in highest esteem — like a captain that went down with her ship.

Sombra was the first to salute Tiz, holding her hand there, waiting for it to be returned.

Dargen followed her lead, doing the same.

Then Char, who preferred detention over saluting, but for her, did it anyhow.

One by one, the rest of the gathering began saluting. Molly then Helen and Fineus, the troll cousins, were the first few. Then the Wolfberry climbers were next in a row. Holly elbowed Frenchy then Frenchy elbowed her own mother so they all saluted, holding it there. Colonel Monocle saluted with his gadget arm, all its tools repaired and glimmering brightly in the moonlight. But there was one salute that made Tiz's eyes well — the general stepped out of the crowd, his hoard of polished medals clanking. Snapping to attention, he paid his own tribute with one heck of a flawless salute.

The respect they showed her made the hairs on her arms stand at attention. After a few seconds of choking back more tears, Tiz saluted back, trying to live up to what they thought of her. She cared about all of them. Even the feisty general.

But it was Sombra, Dargen and Char that had gotten her through the final battle. So Tiz broke off her salute and threw her arms around her three closest friends all at once.

Sombra didn't know it, but over her shoulder, Tiz was staring at Farmer Everly in his eye patch as he stepped out from behind a gnarled and ancient oak tree in the distance and tipped his cap to the red-haired girl.

But in Tiz's eyes, he didn't look like a farmer at all. His cap was a glimmering golden crown resting upon a prominent brow. His mane of gray hair bore patches of red locks as bright as her own hair that surged down past his ears into a kingly beard. Of his round, kindly face, only his eye patch looked the same. His rake was a tall shimmering spear that he held upright as one raven landed on each of his shoulders — his little watchers. Tiz gazed upon the All Father of the Norse gods. Her real father. The One-Eyed King, Odin.

She had found her ax blade in his barn, Farmer Everly's barn, and now knew it wasn't merely by chance.

He'd been watching out for her all along. Especially, in the underworld. But that was their secret for now. Though that knowledge brought a huge smile to her face as she watched him do something that she was puzzled by at first. He held up a cracked robin's egg. It began glowing, and within moments the egg healed, hatching into a fledgling that quickly grew into a beautiful young bird and flew away, chirping happily.

Right at that moment, Tiz realized that she had accidentally knocked that robin's egg from the tree with her slingshot — a horrible misdeed in the eyes of any tree nymph, let alone the one that inflicted it. Even still, her father had given her a chance to redeem herself. He would always be there for her, and for that matter, all living creatures, every single being, not only all things good and green, but also the broken and the forgotten.

Seeing him care for the egg — something that seemed so small and insignificant — warmed all the chambers of her heart at once. More tears trickled down her cheeks as she broke off her embrace with her friends.

The twins stepped over to Tiz with Mums in tow.

Verruca looked up at her big sister. "Don't cry, if you want, you can even have your old room back too," she said.

Tiz tried to suppress a smile, but failed badly.

"What?" said Vervain innocently. "We *even* cleaned it."

"You mean cleaned it out?" teased Tiz.

The twins playfully stuck their tongues out at her as she gave it right back.

"Tiz doesn't need her old room back," insisted Sombra, a mischievous smile spreading across her face as she pointed toward Tiz's new life tree. "Just like a young phoenix, one reborn, she needs to improve her nest building skills. We all know when she's not trying to save the universe, she *can* be a bit of a slacker."

Laughter rang out from the gathering.

Tiz smiled at her best friend as she wiped the tears from her own cheeks. "This time, you're right as rain," she said. "A nest — no forget that, not *just* a nest — a feasting hall. A *real* warm one too, big enough to feed all of our families and friends — every last one of them."

Tiz turned toward the gathering. "And best of all, I'm going to make my mom's majestic truffle mousse for everyone!"

The whole gathering cheered! Eventually, they would all be boarding the *S. S. Delicious.*

Tiz leaned down over Pup Pup, petting him. "I hope you're hungry, boy," she said to the magic puppet of replenishment as he licked her face, "because I can't cook very well, and we'll need to make at least two pieces for everyone."

Pup Pup barked happily — eating truffles was sort of his thing now.

Laughter and more cheers filled the air. The band began playing merrily and everyone started celebrating, many of them dancing.

Sombra hugged Tiz once more.

Together, they stood there like two halves of the split moon above them, two best friends, now closer than ever before.

Made in the USA
San Bernardino, CA
07 November 2015